# *Ancient Tales*
# *in*
# Modern Japan

Copublished with *Asian Folklore Studies*

# *Ancient Tales in* Modern Japan

## An Anthology of Japanese Folk Tales

Selected and Translated
by FANNY HAGIN MAYER

INDIANA UNIVERSITY PRESS
*Bloomington, Indiana*

*This book has been produced from camera-ready copy provided by ASIAN FOLKLORE STUDIES.*



Manufactured in the United States of America

Library of Congress Cataloging in Publication Data
Main entry under title:

Ancient tales in modern Japan.

Bibliography: p.
Includes index.
1. Tales—Japan. I. Mayer, Fanny Hagin, 1899–
GR340.A5 1984 398.2'0952 84-47746
ISBN 0-253-30710-4
1 2 3 4 5 89 88 87 86 85

# Contents

# Introduction

# *Ancient Tales in* Modern Japan

This volume is the first overall sampling of Japanese folk tales to be prepared for Westerners. More than half of the selections have never been translated. In nooks and corners of the Japanese islands, folk tales are still being recited for young and old alike, and collectors are still searching for them to present to readers.

It would be difficult to ascertain exactly how ancient the legends and tales that can still be heard in Japan really are. The present anthology contains themes that will already be familiar to students of Japanese literature. For those who are not familiar with the old writings of Japan, I will name a few in their chronological order and show their points of contact with some of the tales in this collection. Others are mentioned in *The Yanagita Guide to the Japanese Folk Tale* (hereafter referred to as the *Guide*).[1]

The earliest written work in Japan is *Kojiki*,[2] a compilation of tales concerning events of "ancient times." Since it was completed in 712, we can speculate that tales were present in the land long before that. The *Kojiki* is full of references to birds, animals, plants and a variety of landscapes which show the interest people had in those times in settings like those found in the folk tale. There are transformations of men into birds, of deities into animals, and the like, which also remind one of folk tales. The story of the White Rabbit of Inaba[3] has not continued in oral tradition, but it is a popular tale in children's books to this day. The sympathetic rat and his children who guided Ōkuninushi no Mikoto in his flight[4] reminds one of the friendly rats in "Rat Jōdo" (No. 133). The tragedy of the crocodile wife, who had been transformed into a woman,[5] recalls "The Snake Wife" (No. 28).

The *Kojiki* was said to have been set down the way it was recited by one Hida no Are, a kataribe, or "reciter." Those who recite folk tales are still called kataribe today. If the kataribe passes away without leaving a disciple in his family or village, the stories become extinct in that place.

Yanagita wrote in his introduction to the *Guide* that it was likely that themes from folk tales had been picked up by chance and embellished in literary works, but the earliest to be recorded were by order of the Imperial Court. In 713 a decree called for *fudoki* (gazetteers) to be compiled in the various provinces. Legends and tales by village elders were among the items to be recorded. The *fudoki* exist today primarily in fragments, but there are references to other no longer extant texts. One such reference is the story of Urashimatarō in

*Tango fudoki.* He was a fisherman who was invited to the Dragon Palace in the sea. Although this particular tale has been lost to folk tales, several tales tell of trips to the Dragon Palace. "The wife from the Dragon Palace" (No. 27) is one such tale.

Tucked into the ninth century *Nihon ryōiki,*[6] a collection of Buddhist tales, we find the folk tale about a fox-wife who, transformed into a woman, bore a child to a man. "The Fox Wife" (No. 24) is an elaborate version of that theme, still preserved in Northeastern Japan. The early twelfth century *Konjaku monogatari shū*[7] adds an embellishment to it by having the husband confronted by both his fox-wife and his true wife.

Many themes from folk tales can be recognized in *Ujishūi monogatari*[8] of the thirteenth century, but two complete versions recall those in this collection, "The Sparrow with a Broken Back" (No. 127) and "The Old Man who Got a Tumor" (No. 140). *Kaidoki,*[9] a travelog written in the same century, elaborates the story of Kaguyahime, which belongs to the "Takenoko Dōji" (No. 5) type. Yanagita points to several references concerning it in his *Guide.* Although he says it has been lost to oral tradition, I believe it may yet turn up in collections made later than his notes.

Tales were popular in the literature of the Heian and Kamakura periods (794-1185; 1185-1333). Their literary form has little in common with folk tales, but one finds frequent mention of them. Such mention becomes more and more scarce in the periods that follow to early Edo, a period beginning in 1615. During those periods (Muromachi, Momoyama and early Edo), however, tales known as *otogizōshi* were popular. These were retold upon various occasions, such as night watches, or as diversions at other times. Most of them are now lost.[10] We find them in "Issun Bōshi" (No. 8) with the same title and "Shutendōji" under the title "The Origin of Fleas and Mosquitoes" (No. 298) in this anthology. Themes from several other *otogizōshi* can be recognized among the tales collected here.

It can be seen from these few examples that oral tales contributed to the body of Japanese literature until early modern times, or the Edo period. The circumstance which buried them from wider notice was probably the development of printing. Publishing houses sprang up in urban centers, and the country was flooded with cheap, illustrated booklets which caught the fancy of busy city folk. Such printed works have received the attention of Westerners, but the folk tale, which continued to be handed down orally in rural and mountainous regions, has escaped their notice. It is this body of folk tales to which I referred in my opening statement.

We are still awaiting a proper perspective on the role of oral tales in the history of Japanese literature. I have read through Edward Putzar's recent translation of a Japanese study in the history of Japanese literature.[11] He writes in his Introduction:

> . . . . even though Chinese graphs or characters were known to Japan during the late fourth century, a general knowledge of Chinese writing among the aristocracy does not seem to have prevailed until after the reign of Empress Suiko (r. 592-628). The literature before that date was orally transmitted (p. 5).

In several other passages he refers to oral literature, to orally transmitted literature, and even to "narrative folk literature" (p. 14).

Abe Akio discusses aristocratic literature in his chapter of Putzar's book, about the Heian period, then adds:

> . . . . this does not mean that there was no literature of the common people . . . we find only the slightest interaction between popular (oral tradition) and aristocratic literature (pp. 40-41).

The *setsuwa* (tale) genre, which Putzar mentions as story literature in his Introduction, had three distinct strains in it by the medieval period (1185-1600). These were stories about life among courtiers and aristocrats, those about popular interest, and Buddhist tales which were intended to provide simplified explanations for Buddhist doctrines. The *otogizōshi* also appeared in this period.

We find no mention of oral tales in the chapters in Putzar's volume on the Modern Period (1600-1868), covered by Nakamura Yukihiko, or in the Contemporary Period (1868-1945), treated by Saegusa Tatsukata. These scholars have overlooked the oral transmission of tales. It is hoped that the broad scope of oral tales in the present anthology will attest not only to their survival in modern times, but to their vigor as well. All the source material here was available before 1945, and there is a great upsurge of interest in folk tales today in Japan.

In 1889 W.G. Aston opined:

> To the fiction of the seventeenth century belong a number of children's tales, which retain their popularity even at the present day, unless they have been swept away of late years by the advancing tide of European civilisation.[12]

In a footnote on the same page he adds, "Most of these have been translated by Mr. Mitford in his Tales of Old Japan." (Mitford furnished only nine tales.)

This brings us to the attention of nineteenth century arrivals trying to find oral tales in Japan. In 1858 treaties were signed with the United States, Great Britian, France and Russia. Considering that by then the movement to collect folk tales was well underway in Europe and was including parts of Africa and Asia, it was not surprising that Westerners hoped to learn about folk tales in Japan. Those inquiring were an assortment of diplomats, missionaries, teachers, and businessmen. The searchers were not very articulate about what, exactly, they were looking for. British Minister Sir Rutherford Alcock, for example, referred to "Hanasaki Jiji" (No. 136) and "Shitakiri Suzume" (No. 126) as legends, and called another story a fable. A British businessman, C. Pfoundes, entitled his article in *The Folk-Lore Society* "Some Japanese Folk-tales."[13] His choice of the term was an early one, perhaps the earliest in print in English.

A.B. (Lord Redesdale) Mitford, Second Secretary of the British Legation in Japan, labeled a section of his *Tales of Old Japan* "Fairy Tales," but in his Introduction he called them "Baby Stories."[14] He gave as sources for eight of his nine tales little separate pamphlets with illustrations. These were probably *akabon*, mainly woodblock prints, which appeared after the Genroku Period (1688-1700). He said that he selected "Elves and the Envious Neighbor" (No. 140 in the present volume) from a book on etymology and proverbial lore, which I have not been able to identify.

W.E. Griffis seems to have been the one of his times to have actually heard tales in Japan in a family circle. He had such experiences during his sojourn in Fukui as a teacher. He referred to several authentic folk tale themes and gave a complete example of one about an excitable man (No. 239 in this book) in his *The Mikado's Empire.*[15] But the earthy themes of the folk tales offended his Victorian sensibilities, and he turned to creating stories about Japan for children. He admitted that most of them were suggested to him by what he saw rather than heard in Japan.[16] He was even more candid in his introduction to *Japanese Fairy Tales.* He wrote:

> The stories in this little volume are the direct result of what I saw and studied through these doors [in art and literature]. Some were suggested by native custom and artist's pictures, while others were spun from my own brain. . . . Several of the others have been adapted from native legends and operas.[17]

Due to restrictions in travel, a limited knowledge of the language, and other circumstances, Westerners' contacts with the Japanese were limited, for the most part, to men in official and educational circles and city folk. It was beyond the imagining of such Japanese that foreigners attached any importance to their humble, homespun folk tales. They introduced in their place the classics of their land, old myths, hero legends, and traditional customs. It must be said that in spite of these obstacles the Westerners met the challenge admirably, and the results of their labors are still highly esteemed.

The publishing house Kōbunsha began to put out stories in separate booklets illustrated by various artists and written in English by foreign residents in 1885. Hasegawa Takejirō bought the firm and continued the series, eventually printing it in little crepe paper volumes, one story to each. These are being reproduced even today. German versions by A. Groth and French versions by J. Dautremer were included in the series at about the same time. Some of the tales were based on mythology, some were hero tales and legends, and fifteen of them can be identified as folk tales. The books were made with color illustrations and the style was intended for juvenile readers.

Iwaya Sazanami was interested in the appearance of literature for children in Europe, particularly the tales by Hans Christain Andersen. After a trip to Europe he took up the job of retelling Japanese myths, legends and folk tales for children. He published one elaborately illustrated booklet each month for two years during the period 1894-1896, through Hakubunkan.[18] Twelve of these were translated by Hannah Riddell and Tsuda Ume.[19] Eleven of his original stories can be identified as folk tales, and nine of these were translated.

The tales of Mitford, Griffis, the Hasegawa series, and Iwaya's little books formed the nucleus of children's stories which have more or less defined the scope of Japanese tales known abroad, even into the present century. Unfortunately, these were all embroidered to suit the tastes of little blue-eyed folk in the West, and bore little resemblance in style and content to the simple oral tales of Japan. For this reason, the stories in the present anthology will often seem crude and harsh to those whose ideas of Japanese folk tales are based on the nineteenth century versions.

I have made a careful study of the Japanese children's tales introduced to the West in the Meiji era. I found considerable duplication, but by stretching the list I was able to get to a total of forty recognizable tales. Only twenty of these can be considered to be based on folk tales.[20] I have taken time to review the efforts of early Westerners in Japan to find and report tales because even among present day scholars there is little curiosity about the Japanese folk tales. If Western scholars give these stories any thought, it seems to be to look on them as the sugary children's stories which are to this day retold and re-illustrated *ad nauseam*.

At present, Western scholars have attempted to isolate motifs in the Japanese folk tales and incorporate them in an international motif index. It is highly doubtful that those who consult this index have ever read or could read complete versions of tales in Japanese from which the motifs have been lifted. The folk tale is a literary entity and should be examined as such. A few Japanese folk tales have been translated, but the present anthology presents for the first time the whole range of tales which are enjoyed in Japan.

The folk tale brings us to people in Japan who through the centuries have known little of the religious and literary innovations instituted by the elite of their land, but despite this isolation some of its aspects seem native to all Japanese. One is their pleasure in expessing sentiment in brief poems or songs. The *Man'yōshū* is an anthology of poetry compiled in the early to middle eighth century. It contains many poems by unnamed common people, particularly in its fourteenth book. Even today folk from all walks of life participate in the annual New Year poetry contest sponsored by the Imperial family. Brief poems are scattered through the tales presented here, such as the one by the lovelorn swain (No. 16), the ribald ditty of the fox-officials (No. 190), and the song accompanying the jig of the ghost of the little toothpick (No. 187).

The Japanese take great pleasure in the sound and the feel of words. This is evident in their invention of names, especially those in pairs which closely resemble each other. One can imagine the skill required for the narrator to keep from confusing them. There is humor in the choice of names in the tales which may escape foreigners, but it is quite evident in the story of the child with a long name (No. 234). The abundance of homonyms in Japanese furnishes humor, also, as with the names of the two doctors in No. 219. Homonyms are difficult to render in translation, but the ruckus between the tea peddler and the sieve peddler arbitrated by the buyer of old metal (No. 244) is one of the examples which I attempted. Japanese inventiveness with onomatopoeia also defies translation. I have retained a few of the originals. They are an important device accompanying the narrator's gestures and facial expressions.

Love of humor might be called a characteristic of the Japanese. I found that nearly one-third of the 122 tales recited by 90-year-old Nagashima Tsuru for Mizusawa Ken'ichi were humorous.[21] She lived in her 250-year-old house ten miles from the end of the nearest bus line in the backhills of Niigata. She surely is an example of the plain folk in Japan.

The importance of the family is another concept shared by most Japanese, but the family in the folk tale does not reflect Confucian teachings. Women, particularly old women, share work and dangers with their men. The wife frequently dominates her husband. A woman will arrive at a man's door and ask to be taken in. She stays on as his wife. This is contrary to the carefully arranged marriages in society at the samurai level and above. A younger brother may succeed in life when his older brother fails. Family life is enjoyed by animals, birds and even trees. And a demon, not to be excluded, carries off a maid and sires a child by her.

Men get ahead in life by the work of their hands. The man who breaks sod for his garden patch in the hills is often rewarded by the unexpected discovery of treasure. The result is that he becomes a chōja. This character belongs to the folk tale. He is not, as the lexicons would have it, a millionaire. There is virtue in the treasure that brings prosperity. And prosperity does not make him a "big shot." He and his wife will live without worry about food and clothes, but frequently their blessing is a lovely bride for an unpromising son. The Japanese still look upon the continuance of their family through the virtue of a good bride as the greatest blessing of all. There is something refreshing about the ending of a story in which the old man or his family becomes a chōja.

The world of the Japanese folk tale is its land, its mountains, waterways, plants, animals, and the changes of its seasons. It is a world in which man is not dominant. It is shared by all life, visible and invisible. Deities are close at hand to hear petitions. Demons with their power to transform themselves furnish thrills—the she-demon being the most terrifying! Spirits of the dead remain close by in the mountains to watch over the needs of their families. Mountains are not just a backdrop. Trees in them furnish firewood and nuts, and other plants in them provide food to be gathered. Paths through the mountains are fraught with danger. Water in the tales is found in mountain springs or pools and in streams in little valleys.

Guardian spirits in the water may be either benevolent or malevolent. The seashore or the sea also opens adventure to characters. I analyzed another one-narrator collection of tales made by Mizusawa, this one a total of 105 tales furnished by Takahashi Nao, eighty-four years old.[22] The setting of thirty-one of her tales was the mountains, and twenty of them had rivers or streams as part of their setting.

To be sure, it takes more than setting to provide a tale. If one tries to board public transportation in Tokyo he is likely to conclude that everyone either works or goes to school in Japan. But men and women work in folk tales, too. Grandma Nao's tales picture men or women at sixty-five different occupations. There are a few shadowy officials and priests who hardly count and a couple of men who are too lazy to work. Very few seem to be studying. This is in marked contrast to themes in Korean and Chinese folk tales, where heroes are often studying for the civil service examinations or on their way to take them.

Some misinformation about Japanese legends and their relationship to folk tales must be corrected. Japanese never confuse the terms. Legends are brief statements of an incident said to have occurred at a specific place. The folk tale is set in a "certain place" which is not named, and a complete story takes place there. Some narrators may incorporate local names into their tales (Nos. 2 and 326), but other versions of the tale will not have them. Some folk tales come to be told as legends, such as those of Kōbō Daishi in No. 77, and a legend may become a folk tale (No. 305), but that does not mean that a legend tells a story. And while I am making corrections, I will say that it is a mistake to call a Japanese folk tale a "fairy tale." There are no fairies in the world of the Japanese folk tale.

Some stories in this volume show remnants of older forms. These may be difficult to detect at first. "Momotarō" (Peach Boy, No. 1) is a sample of Sasaki Kizen's early reporting and certainly has little appeal in its style. By comparing it to his rendition of "Man-eating Mushroom" (No. 116), one can see great progress during the five-year interval between the two recordings in his ability to set down what he heard. Or, it may be a difference in the two narrators. But this version of "Momotarō" is particularly interesting because it has so little resemblance to the standard version found in children's books. We see no river and no animal helpers in it. The fact is, there is a version where Momotarō was born from a chestnut. Perhaps there were no peaches where that one was told.

The version of the tale in this collection says the peach rolled to the old woman's seat. "Momo" can mean thigh as well as peach. There may be a trace here of old tales in which a child is born from various parts of the body. There are Yubitarō (Finger Boy), Suneko (Shin Child) or Mamesuke (Callous Boy). The little chap they call Peach Boy may well have been a Thigh Boy. Another version of this tale is still transmitted on an island in the Inland Sea. In this version the woman gets a peach that was floating downstream and takes it home. She and her husband eat it. Their subsequent rejuvenation makes it possible for them to have a son the natural way.[23]

It will be noted that opening formulas and closing formulas are present in some tales. I have retained them where they have been passed on, for they are a part of the tale, but I have not tried to translate them. They are usually in dialect, and any wording in English would lose the rhythm and flavor of the original. For that matter, some have very little meaning beyond calling the attention of the listener to a story about something that happened a long time ago. The English equivalent is "once" or "once upon a time." At the end of the tale the narrator says that this is what is said to have happened. Neither the opening nor the closing formula vouches for the story being true. It is simply the way the narrator heard it, an attitude which is not apparent in the telling of a legend.

I have not attempted to unify the style of the tales Yanagita chose as examples and those I selected. Some of the tales are well told and heard in a family circle (No. 90), and others have been elaborated by professionals into a form called "katarimono" (No. 50). Such narrators were frequently itinerate entertainers. Rhythmical passages in some tales could only be present if heard from a zatō (blind minstrel). They would be emphasized by his shamisen or biwa, as in No. 146. Other tales have been reported more or less in outline form as something heard at second hand, as is the case with No. 148.

The General Index shows that several contributors are greatly responsible for complete collections of tales. Sasaki Kizen and Iwakura Ichirō were key men in this field. But there were no Grimm Brothers in Japan, nor were the two rolled up into one. The ninety collectors whose work contributes to this anthology lived all over Japan—in thirty-seven prefectures and Osaka, to be exact. When Yanagita published his *Guide*, Iwate Prefecture furnished the greatest number of tales, but present day collecting has shifted its center to Niigata Prefecture. This may change as more and more collectors work elsewhere. We can say that the folk tale is being collected all over Japan at present. It is also widely enjoyed. A popular program on commercial television, for example, weekly presents tasteful versions of legitimate folk tales, prepared by legitimate scholars, to large numbers of viewers.

This anthology gives the reader an opportunity to sample tales shared by many collectors. If the reader will multiply their number by those who reported or recited tales and add to them the number of listeners who enjoyed them, and picture that throng reaching far back into the past generations, he will feel that he is penetrating deep into the hills and forests of Japanese culture found on all the islands that make up the land.

After 95-year-old Onozuka Kita had recited many tales for me in Niigata, she said she would go to the Next World before me. She would await my coming and look forward to enjoying stories with me there. It is her spirit that assures us that folk tales have a future as well as a past in Japan.

Fanny Hagin Mayer

## Footnotes

1. *The Yanagita Kunio Guide to the Japanese Folk Tale*, a translation with editing by Fanny Hagin Mayer of *Nihon mukashibanashi meii*, Yanagita Kunio, supervision, Nihon Hōsō Kyōkai, ed. Nihon Hōsō Shuppan Kyōkai, 1948.
2. *Kojiki*, completed in A.D. 712. The *Nihon Shoki*, completed in 720, recorded similar events with multiple lines of transmission and commentary, but this study will utilize only *Kojiki*. For an English translation see Donald Philippi, transl., *Kojiki*, Princeton University Press 1968.
3. Ibid., pp. 93-95.
4. Ibid., pp. 99-100.
5. Ibid., pp. 156-157.
6. *Nihon ryōiki*. Vol. 1, No. 2.

7. *Konjaku monogatari shū*, Bk. 27, No. 39.
8. *Ujishūi monogatari*, D.E. Mills, transl., Cambridge University Press, 1970, Nos. 3 and 48.
9. *Kaidōki*, an account of a journey taken under Imperial command from Kyoto to Kamakura in 1224.
10. *Otogizōshi*. Several full texts with annotations can be found in the Iwanami *Koten Bungaku Taikei* series of classical Japanese literature (vol. 38, *Otogizōshi*, Ichiko Teiji, ed., Iwanami Shoten, 1958).
11. Edward Putzar, *Japanese Literature, A Historical Outline*. University of Arizona Press, 1973.
12. W.G. Aston, *A History of Japanese Literature* (1899). Charles E. Tuttle, 1972.
13. C. Pfoundes, "Some Japanese Folk-Tales," The Folk-Lore Society. Vol. I, Preface, xiii (1876).
14. A.B. (Lord Redesdale) Mitford, *Tales of Old Japan*, Macmillan and Co., 1871, 134.
15. W.E. Griffis, *The Mikado's Empire*. Harper & Brothers, 1876, 491 ff.
16. W.E. Griffis, *Japanese Fairy World*. James H. Barhyte, 1880, viii.
17. W.E. Griffis, *Japanese Fairy Tales*. George G. Harrap & Co. (no date, but probably after 1908), vii-viii.
18. Iwaya Sazanami, *Nippon mukashibanashi nijūyon hen*.
19. Hanna Riddell and Tsuda Ume, transl., *Japanese Fairy Tales*. Hakuseido, 1914.
20. Fanny Hagin Mayer, "The Discovery of the Japanese Folk Tale," *K.B.S. Bulletin* 81 (Dec.-Jan., 1967). Kokusai Bunka Shinkokai, 5-15. Now available in *Introducing the Japanese Folk Tales, Asian Folklore and Social Life Monographs*. Vol. 50. The Orient Cultural Service, Taipei, 5-24.
21. Mizusawa Ken'ichi, *Tonto mugashi atta ge do, Dai-isshū*. Miraisha, 1957.
22. Mizusawa Ken'ichi, *Yukiguni no o-baba no mukashi*. Kodansha, 1974.
23. Takeda Akira, *Sorae baku-baku*. Miraisha, 1965, 14.

# Notes by the Translator

Several matters concerning the selection and translation of the tales in this anthology, and its appended material, should be explained to those who may read it. Some of the cross-references in the Cross Reference Table (pp. 339-346) contain the notation "Ex." This refers to the version of a tale which was considered normative by Yanagita Kunio, and which he printed in summary form in *The Yanagita Kunio Guide to the Japanese Folk Tale*. (See below for publication information on works cited in this preface.) At the time Yanagita supervised the compilation of the *Guide*, he anticipated that more suitable or complete versions of other tales would be available in the future. These stories are not marked as "Ex.," and for them I have selected a sample to translate.

An asterisk * **before** a number in the column of the table devoted to Seki Keigo's *Nihon mukashibanashi shūsei* means that the version which I have translated in this book is one that Seki considered to be representative. Both Yanagita's and Seki's works are used in cross-reference today in Japan to identify a tale in a new collection to indicate that it is considered to be a genuine folk tale. Items belonging to traditional legends or memorabillia or fiction are bound to appear among newly gathered tales.

Another item in the cross reference table that needs some comment here is "Jiten." This refers to *Nihon mukashibanashi jiten*, or "A dictionary of the Japanese folk tale," edited by Inada Kōji et al. The *Jiten* is the work of many persons, with varying approaches to the items they have written about. Some entries give specific comments on a tale type with a specific title, but with several readings for the tale. Other titles are buried within a long discussion or background including early literary or *maki e* (picture scroll) versions. If the tale in question has been afforded this latter type of treatment, I have marked it with the symbol "†." One of the greatest values of the *Jiten* is that it often gives up to date information on the distribution or collection history of tales, though this of course will become less timely as the years pass.

The geographical area represented in the tale and the name of the collector, when this information is known, follow each tale in the body of this work. In the "Notes to the Stories" (pp. 319-332) I have given the published source of each tale. I have also included the name of the narrator or informant and other facts that were available. This is a practice of Japanese collectors which has been observed for many years. A tale has its roots in a particular place in Japan, and the present rendition has the individuality and charm of a specific narrator, the one who recited it.

Yanagita placed a line to the right of important tales in the Table of Contents of his *Guide*. These have been set in **bold face** in the alphabetical list of titles at the end of this book. Some tales may seem very close in content to their neighbors, but usually there is some difference. I have tried to remain faithful to the Japanese story titles in my renditions, but I have made some modifications to facilitate alphabetizing the tales. Yanagita's grouping of tales and their main divisions have also been retained, although some readers may not be satisfied with them. One exception is the last chapter of this book, "The Fascination of Folk Tales," which is an entire "Part" in Yanagita's work but which has been treated as a "chapter" here.

Numbers to the two German and three English translations in the cross reference table are the numbers of the tales in their collections. They account for about 200 of the tales in the present anthology. The numbers for Seki's *Shūsei* are those of the tale-types in its text. They are the numbers employed in cross-reference by Japanese collectors. Cross-reference to Yanagita's *Guide* is done by tale-type name, because Yanagita did not number his tales. The numbers for Hiroko Ikeda ("H.I." in the table) are those in *A Type and Motif Index of Japanese Folk-Literature*, her modification of numbers in Antti Aarne-Stith Thompson, *The Types of the Folktale*, Second Revised Edition.

A few words of evaluation should be made for the items selected for cross-reference. Fritz Rumpf (whose work is designated "F.R." in the table) was sent to Japan in the mid-1930's to make a translation of Japanese folk tales. Eugen Diederichs was to include them in his famous series, *Die Märchen der Weltliteratur*. Rumpf's *Japanische Folksmärchen* was published in 1938. Although it was among the first Western works in the field, it received little recognition in the United States. Rumpf's source material was limited, but he recorded faithfully the geographical area represented, the published source, and even the narrator for most of his selections. Horst Hammitzsch was commisioned by Diederichs to update the work of Rumpf. His translation under the same title appeared in 1964, and is designated "H.H." in the cross reference table. He retained many of Rumpf's selections and notes, but he broadened the scope of the work by using Seki's three-volume popular selection of tales. Seki rewrote tales from many collections, but he gave only geographical designations for the tales. Fewer than half of the tales in these three volumes are the normative versions he used in his *Shūsei*. But Hammitzsch frequently refers to Seki's *Shūsei*, by which the collected source can be identified. Both German scholars include selections which Japanese do not consider as belonging to oral tradition, but they give scholarly notes to identify them. They note themes in the tales that have been reported elsewhere in Asia, particularly in Korea and in China.

The English translations are one by Robert J. Adams and two by me. Adams ("R.A." in the table) made selections from Seki's popular volumes. For that reason, his translation gives little information beyond the geographical designation for his selections. It happens that none of those he selected was collected by Seki. One of my translations was of Yanagita's *Nihon no mukashibanashi, jō* ("M-1" in the table). Yanagita touched up these selections considerably, and gave little information about the sources of his selections, but for many years it was considered by Japanese to be the representative collection of folk tales. Rumpf translated thirty-six of them for his volume. Yanagita's later work, *Kaitei ban Nihon no mukashibanashi*, which I also translated ("M-2"), named the collector, the published source (a total of fifty-one), and the geographical area for most of his choices.

The "kata numbers" Adams used in his notes and in his Index of Kata Numbers (pp 209 ff) and which Ikeda listed in her Cross-Reference Table, (pp 366 ff) refer to numbers Seki offered in his "Types of Japanese Folktales," an English work that has never appeared in Japanese. They do not lead to the numbering in the text of Seki's *Shūsei*. Both Hammitzsch and Ikeda refer to the *Shūsei* by page, not the tale-type number. The 12-volume work by Seki, *Nihon mukashibanashi taisei*, obviously has different pagination, but it retains the numbers in the text of the *Shūsei*.

I had to rely upon the generous assistance of a number of libraries to obtain copies of some of the tales in this anthology. I am indebted to the Library of Congress and to the Japanese collections in East Asian Library of University of California, Berkeley; University Research Library, University of California, Los Angeles; and Hoover Institution of Leland Stanford University in my own land. I have received material from Japan from National Diet Library, the prefectural libraries of Miyagi and Ōita, and the library of Narita San, and many items from Yanagita Bunko at Seijo University. I hereby express my gratitude to all these libraries for their assistance.

After I decided to translate and to publish this anthology, the question arose in my mind as to rights to the tales. Although it might not be a problem, I could hardly use stories gathered by many collectors whom I had met and who were my friends without contacting them. If I bypassed other living collectors or their heirs, that would hardly be acceptable. The result was that although eventually word came to me from the Ministry of Education through the Foreign Ministry clearing rights to me, I had received a generous response from all those whom I had contacted and from heirs of the deceased collectors whom I could reach. I can offer no more than my thanks to them. I have given a complete list of collectors represented in this anthology in the General Index at the end of the book. This index, incidentally, includes a large number of motifs as well as names, and makes extensive use of multiple listings in order to present relevant material in the same place. Animals and plants have been listed only when they appear in an active role in the stories. All Japanese names, both in the index and throughout the work, have been rendered in the Japanese fashion, with family name followed by given name. The only exception is Hiroko Ikeda, who signs her name in the Western way.

I am also indebted to Maruyama Hisako and Ishiwara Yasuyo for their advice in making selections for this volume and to Ōshima Tatehiko for helping me contact collectors or their heirs.

Additionally, I would like to express my gratitude to the staff of *Asian Folklore Studies* at Nanzan University in Nagoya, Japan, where this book was prepared for publication. The editor of the journal, Peter Knecht, undertook the negotiations that ultimately made publication of both this volume and its "sister," my translation of Yanagita's *Guide*, possible, and special thanks go to Akazawa Yasuko for her heroic battles with a not-always-friendly computer and word processing program that resulted in the typing of the entire manuscript used in the production of the camera ready copy for the book. I would also like to acknowledge the support of the Japan Foundation, whose grant aided in the publication of this book.

The illustrations used in this book are photographs of Edo period printed and illustrated versions of folk tales. The originals are the property of the Hibiya Library in Tokyo, and I am grateful to Mr. Mori Mutsuhiko of the library for his permission to make the photographs. I am also grateful to Mr. Nagao Nobuyuki, who graciously took the photos and declined any fee. The photos on the cover and at the beginning of Part I are from a version of Momotarō, and those on the frontispiece and at the beginning of Part II are from "Bumbuku Chagama."

I wish to repeat my thanks to the collectors, their heirs, and to others whom I could not reach but whose work is included in this anthology. Their contributions, whether full-blown tales, outlines, or brief reports, were made with sincerity. In spite of the lack of unity of style in their writing, their work offers a great contribution to the understanding of the folk tale in Japan. I pass it on in the belief that readers in the West will welcome and enjoy their efforts.

Fanny Hagin Mayer
Whittier, California

## References Cited

Adams, Robert, transl.
*Folktales of Japan* (edited by Seki Keigo). Chicago: University of Chicago Press, 1963.

Hammitzsch, Horst, transl.
*Japanische Volksmärchen*. West Berlin: Diederichs, 1964.

Ikeda, Hiroko
*A Type and Motif Index of Japanese Folk-Literature*. Folklore Fellows Communication No. 209. Helsinki, 1971.

Mayer, Fanny Hagin, transl.
*Japanese Folk Tales*. Tokyo: Tokyo News Service, Ltd., 1954. First appeared in *Folklore Studies* (now *Asian Folklore Studies*) XI/1, 1952. Translation of Yanagita Kunio, ed., *Nihon no mukashibanashi, Jō*, 1930.

———
*Japanese Folk Tales, A Revised Selection*. Tokyo: Tokyo News Service, Ltd., 1966. Also available in *Asian Folklore and Social*

*Life Monographs*, Vol. 37, Taipei: The Orient Cultural Service. Translation of Yanagita Kunio, ed., *Kaitei ban Nihon no mukashibanashi*, 1960.

Rumpf, Fritz
*Japanishche Volksmärchen*. Jena: Diederichs, 1938.

Seki Keigo
*Nihon mukashibanashi shūsei*. Three Parts (6 volumes). Tokyo: Kadokawa Shoten, 1950-1958.

Yanagita Kunio, supervision
*Nihon mukashibanashi meii* [The Yanagita Kunio guide to the Japanese folk tale]. Tokyo: Nihon Hōsō Kyōkai, 1948.

# PART ONE

# *Folk Tales in Complete Form*

# *1. Propitious Births*

## 1. Momotarō

Once upon a time an old man and an old woman went to view cherry blossoms. While they were sitting on the ground to rest and eat their lunch, a peach came rolling to the old woman's seat. She picked it up and tucked it into her bosom and went home with it. After she had wrapped it in cotton and put it into bed, it split open and a little baby boy was born from it. The old couple wondered what to name him, and decided, "Let's call him Momonoko Tarō [Peach Boy], because he was born from a peach."

Momonoko Tarō looked after the house alone and studied when his mother and father were working in their garden patch. While he was studying one day a crow came flying up and lighted on a persimmon tree by the back door. The crow called, "I brought you a letter from Hell." In this letter the demons of Hell demanded that the best millet dango in Japan be brought to them. Momonoko Tarō asked his mother and father to make the dango, and he set out with them to Hell.

When Momonoko Tarō arrived at Hell and knocked at the gate, the demons came out and said, "We'll try the best dango in Japan." Momonoko Tarō gave a dango to each of them. The demons got drunk on them and rolled over asleep.

Momonoko Tarō hurriedly put the Princess of Hell onto a cart and pulled it away. The demons woke up later and started to chase them on their fire-cart, but by then the couple were far out at sea and the fire-cart could not reach them.

Momonoko Tarō reached home at last with the Princess of Hell. The Emperor heard about his feat, and Momonoko Tarō then received a great sum of money. His family became chōja and they prospered without difficulties.

Sasaki Kizen
Shiwa-gun, Iwate

## 2. Rikitarō

To begin with, there was a shiftless man and woman once upon a time. All year long they were covered with filth. They said, "Here we are, childless, and at this age there is little reason to think that we can have one. Let's scrape the dirt off our bodies and make a doll of it."

They rubbed all the sweat and grime into a pile that grew as big as a mushroom and made a baby of it. They called him Konbitarō ["The boy from bodily filth"] and took good care of him. But the child was a great eater. If his parents gave him one shō of rice, he would clean it up; if they gave him one *to* of rice, he would clean that up; and he grew until he could eat five *to* and three shō at a meal.

The lazy man and woman complained when their boy began to eat five *to* and three shō at one meal. No matter how hard they tried, they could not keep up the supply. Konbitarō said, "Don't worry, Grandpa, I'm going to set out on a journey to practice feats of strength. Make me a metal rod that weighs 100 kan."

His father was surprised and asked, "What are you going to do with a metal rod that weighs 100 kan?" Konbitarō declared, "I want to use it for a walking stick." His father had to agree. He emptied his purse to get the blacksmith to make the 100 kan rod.

Konbitarō took the rod and set out twirling it gaily in one hand. He walked along thumping and clanging his rod until he came to a cross-roads on the highway called Kamaishi. There he saw a huge man walking toward him with a red portable Fukayama Daigongen shrine on his back. Konbitarō reached out with his metal rod and barely tapped the shrine with its tip, but the red shrine splintered like tree leaves falling to the road.

The strong man carrying the shrine flew into a rage at that and shouted, "Do you know who I am? I am the strongest man in the world. My name is Midōkotarō." As he said that, he reached out and took the metal rod from Konbitarō. When he started to hit him with it, Konbitarō thought he had met a good match. He caught hold of the rod and swung the man up into the air. He waited for him to fall, but he did not come down. Instead, Midōkotarō cried out overhead, "Help, save me!"

Konbitarō looked up and saw Midōkotarō caught on the top of a pine tree by the side of the road. "How about it? Have I put some fright into you?" asked Konbitarō as he tipped the pine over and uprooted it to rescue Midōkotarō. He said to Midōkotarō, "There's no reason to be enemies. How about coming along with me as my follower?" Midōkotarō joined him.

They went along and came to a place like the quarry at Sedonagane Pass. A huge man was splitting stones with the palm of his hand. A chip of rock came flying toward Konbitarō, but he blew it back, and it struck the man on his forehead. The man grew red with anger. He shouted, "Who are you? I'm Ishikotarō, the greatest in the world, and still you hit me with a rock!"

Konbitarō thought there must be many who are the best in the world.

He turned to Midōkotarō and said, "Step up and try wrestling with him." Midōkotarō obeyed and grappled with Ishikotarō. He struggled with all his might for a long time, but he could not win. Then Konbitarō said, "I'll try!" After Midōkotarō withdrew, Konbitarō gripped Ishikotarō's neck and thrust him up to his head into the pile of splintered rock. Thus Ishikotarō became the second follower of Konbitarō.

The three went off together until they came to a town like Tsuchizawa by a castle. Although it was still daylight, all the doors to the houses were strangely closed and there was no sign of anyone around. They found a beautiful girl sobbing and crying at the house of what looked like the home of the biggest chōja in town. They asked, "Why are you crying?"

She replied, "A frightful monster comes here on the first day of each month to carry off a girl from this town. It is my turn today, and that is why I am crying."

"There, there," said Konbitarō, "If that's the trouble, the three of us will destroy the monster for you." He followed her into the house and told the people there to put the girl into their Chinese chest. He placed Midōkotarō in the yard, Ishikotarō at the door, and he went into the house and crouched in front of the chest to wait, wondering how soon the monster would come.

The monster arrived when it was growing dark. He shouted, "Is my bride there? If she has run away, I'll catch her and skin her and roast her and eat her up!" His voice sounded like a broken bell, and he seemed big enough to knock the house down.

First, the monster met Midōkotarō in the yard and swallowed him in a gulp. Then he confronted Ishikotarō at the door, picked him up with the tip of his fingers, and swallowed him in a gulp.

Konbitarō was angry to see his first and second followers swallowed. He swung his 100 kan rod around and went toward the monster, shouting, "Fine. Now I will meet you!" The monster threatened him for a while. Then he reached for the metal rod and folded it over in the middle like a cake. "This is a match to the finish," shouted Konbitarō as he threw his metal rod aside.

The struggle continued for a long time and matters looked bad for Konbitarō. He did not seem to be getting anywhere, but then he kicked the monster in a vital spot, which caused it to blow Midōkotarō from its right nostril and Ishikotarō from the left and then die.

The people at the house, who had been watching, came flocking out, rubbing their hands in delight. They exclaimed, "With your help, our daughter and all of us have been saved. How can we repay you?"

The men did not want any reward. They only asked for rice cooked in the big five *to* kettle used for boiling linen. The rice was cooked and the three ate their fill of it. "What unselfish men you are," declared the family. "We admire your lack of greed. Our daughters are not much to offer you, but please stay as our sons-in-law."

So Konbitarō was married to the oldest daughter, the one he had saved, and his two followers were married to the second and third daughters. Konbitarō sent for his mother and father from the village, and they all lived in comfort after that.

*Dondo hare.*

Hirano Tadashi
Waga-gun, Iwate

## 3. Urikohimeko

One day an old man went to the hills to cut firewood and his old woman went to the river to do the washing. The old woman picked up a melon that came floating downstream. When the old man and old woman cut it open to see, a beautiful little girl came out. The little girl grew bigger and wove at the loom every day.

The old man and old woman went to town to buy a sedan chair so they could take their little girl to visit the Chinju Shrine, that of their local deity. While they were gone, an amanjaku came and asked the girl to open the door a little for her.

When the girl opened it a little, the amanjaku pushed it wide open. She said, "Let me pick persimmons in back for you." She led the girl behind the house, stripped off her clothes, and tied her to the persimmon tree. Then she put on the girl's clothes and sat weaving at the loom.

The old man and the old woman came home with the sedan chair and said, "Now get into the chair, little maid." They put the amanjaku into it and started to the Chinju Shrine. The girl cried out, "Oh, you put the amanjaku into the sedan chair!" The old man swung his sickle up and cut off the head of the amanjaku. He tossed it into the millet patch behind the house. The millet was stained with blood and has been red since that time.

Takagi Toshio
Matsue, Shimane

## 4. Nishiki Chōja

*Mukashi attaji o na.*

Once upon a time there was a girl called Uruhimeko. While everyone at her house was working in the garden, Uruhimeko would weave at the loom, *kiikarari batayara.*

One day a yamauba came slowly down from the mountain and looked in at the window. She asked, "Uruhimeko, what are you doing?"

Uruhimeko answered, "I am weaving." The yamauba said, "Give me cooked rice to eat." She knew that the rice chest at Uruhimeko's house was full of rice, that the big kettle was in its place, and that firewood was in the woodshed. She told Uruhimeko to cook the rice, to make riceballs, and put them in a row on the unfastened wooden door for her to eat.

Uruhimeko listened meekly and did as she was told. The yamauba sat in front of the board, took down her hair that was as coarse as a bundle of wisteria vines, and there on the top of her head was a big mouth. She tossed a riceball, *pon*, into that mouth on her head and chewed it up, *pakuri*. After she had eaten all of the riceballs, *pon-pakuri pon-pakuri*, she went back up the mountain.

The next day while Uruhimeko was weaving, *kiikarari batayara, kiikarari batayara*, the yamauba came slowly down the mountain again and looked in at the window. She asked, "Uruhimeko, what are you doing?" Uruhimeko answered, "I am weaving."

The yamauba said, "Give me plums to eat that are growing on the big tree over the kitchen." A big plum tree grew by the kitchen with so many red plums on it that the branches were nearly breaking. When Uruhimeko said, "Eat all you want," the yamauba climbed right up the tree and ate all the plums. She did not leave a single one.

The next day when Uruhimeko was threading the shuttles for the pattern in her loom, the yamauba came slowly down the mountain again and looked in at the window. She asked, "Uruhimeko, what are you doing?" She answered, "I am threading my shuttles."

The yamauba exclaimed, "What beautiful thread that is! It makes me feel like eating it, so hand it all over to me." Uruhimeko got out all her white, black, red, blue, and gold pattern thread and gave it to her meekly. The yamauba opened that big mouth on her head and ate all the thread, sucking it in and smacking her lips.

When she had finished, she said, "Come and look below the window tomorrow morning, Uruhimeko. There will be something special there, so take good care of it. Mind you do!" Then she went back up the mountain.

Uruhimeko cried because she had nothing to weave the next day after the yamauba ate all her pattern thread. When the family came home from the garden in the evening, they asked, "Uruhimeko, why are you crying?"

She answered, "The yamauba ate all my pattern thread up and I have nothing to weave." They tried to comfort her and said, "Even if she ate all the thread, you can spin more and dye it. Then you can weave it, so stop crying. Hurry and eat your supper and go to bed."

When Uruhimeko went to look out the window the next morning, there were things that looked like a yamauba's turds heaped high on a straw matting. When people saw them, they said, "Anything as dirty as that should be thrown into the dung vault."

But Uruhimeko said, "No, no, the yamauba said to take good care of it, so it would be bad to throw them into the dung vault. We must wash them and set them aside." She got everybody to help. They held their noses as they carried them on their backs to the stream behind the house and dumped them into the river. The turds melted and became five-tinted Chinese red brocade. The brocade unfolded and floated in the current, reaching the first bridge, then the second bridge, and as far as the third, too beautiful for words. The family was called Nishiki Chōja [brocade Chōja] from that time, and they were respected everywhere.

Fujiwara Sōnosuke
Senhoku-gun, Akita

## 5. Takenoko Dōji

Once upon a time there was a cooper's apprentice called Sankichi. He went to the bamboo thicket on the hill behind the shop to cut bamboo to make hoops for casks. While he was cutting, he heard a voice from somewhere calling him. "Who are you?" he asked.

It answered, "Here I am, Sanchan." "Where are you?" he asked. "I'm in the bamboo," it answered. The young man went to the center of the bamboo grove, but nobody was there.

While he stood there thinking it strange, the voice came, "Sanchan, let me out of the bamboo!" He hurriedly sawed a bamboo and toppled it. Out came a little man. Sanchan nearly fell over with surprise.

As he looked closely, the little man who had come out of the bamboo said, "At last, Sanchan!" His voice was big compared to his body. "What are you?" asked Sanchan as he put the little man onto the palm of his hand.

"I got caught by a bad bamboo sprout and put into bamboo, so I could not go back to the Sky World. Then you came along, Sanchan, and I asked you to rescue me. Nothing could make me happier than to be saved by you."

Sanchan asked, "How do you know my name?" The little man declared, "I know everything in the world."

Then Sanchan asked, "What is your name?" He answered, "I am called Takenoko Dōji."

"How old are you?"

"I am 1234 years old."

"Are you going right back to the Sky World?"

"If I do not repay you for your kindness before I go back, the princess will scold me after I go back, so I will go after I repay you."

"How are you going to repay me?"

"I will grant whatever you wish."

"Do you mean it?" asked Sankichi. "You are not lying, are you?"

Takenoko Dōji declared, "People from the Sky World never lie." Then he taught Sankichi a magic formula Sankichi repeated it three times: "Takenoko Dōji, make me a samurai. Takenoko Dōji, make me a samurai. Takenoko Dōji, make me a samurai." He turned into a real samurai immediately, and set out upon a journey to practice military arts.

*Shotte shimai.*

Maruyama Manabu
Tama-gun, Kumamoto

## 6. The Ghost That Cared For Her Child

Once upon a time a woman died in childbirth. The family pitied her and buried her instead of cremating her. They put a one mon coin in her coffin, according to the custom at her village, and carried her out to the edge of the moor.

From that time, somebody came every evening at about the same hour to buy ame. A hand would be thrust between the same doors and the same coin was always used to pay. The storekeeper thought this strange, and he sent his clerk to follow the customer.

She went as far as the garden patch, but there she turned into a flame and leaped off. The flame went out at the grave. The clerk was sure it was a specter and ran home astonished.

The next day two or three people went to the grave where the flame had gone out to investigate. They found a hole in the new grave. This seemed strange to everyone. When they dug to see, they found a wide-eyed baby boy sitting there. He had been born after the woman had died, and he was being nourished by the ame.

It seems that this child became a famous Buddhist priest later.

Seki Keigo
Shimabara, Nagasaki

## 7. The Eagle's Foundling

Once upon a time there was a widow living with her baby and a wet nurse. When they all went to the hills one day to gather mulberry leaves, the little one was left wrapped in a kimono by the edge of the mulberry patch while the two women picked mulberry leaves.

An eagle carried the child off while they were working. A charm was fastened onto the child, and the mother had a similar one, and that was all she had left. She seemed to lose her mind with grief.

After the women went home, the mother asked the wet-nurse to look after things while she set out with only her charm, saying she would depend upon it. She was a beautiful lady, but after five years and then ten had passed, her clothing became tattered and her face so soiled that she looked like a crazy woman. She was still searching after thirty years.

In the meantime, the unusual voice of an eagle and the voice of a crying child were heard in the top of a maidenhair tree in the grounds of a temple. A novice tried to climb the tree to see, but the eagle attacked him and would not let him climb.

When the priest tried, he could not get as far as the nest. He put on a wide brimmed hat and finally reached the nest. There was a human child being given good care but without a single toy. The priest carried the child down and took him to the temple to care for him until he grew up.

Thirty years later, the mother came to the bank of a river, still looking for her child. Only one priest was on the ferry that was waiting for passengers. The woman, looking like a beggar, went up and asked to get on the ferry, but she was so filthy that the ferryman refused. The priest spoke up and told him to let her on. With that, she was allowed to ride.

The priest and the boatman were talking about the big celebration that would be held at the temple that day. A man who had been carried away by an eagle as a baby would be made a superior. The woman who looked like a beggar was very happy as she listened.

When they reached the other side of the river, she went immediately to the manager of the temple, but he drove her away with, "What are you here for!" She insisted she had come to see his master. He declared she was not the right sort of person and scolded her each time she came back to him.

The head of the temple finally heard this and rebuked his manager. He said, "Do you think you can send anyone away without letting him in when he has come to see me!" The head, himself, came out and listened to the woman's story.

She seemed to be the mother of the man who was to become superior that day. He asked for some sign, and she brought her charm and the garment that had been around the child. He hurriedly had a bath heated for her to get into.

The woman who had been so filthy then became so beautiful that it was hard to recognize her. The head of the temple loaned her some of his wife's clothes and in them she looked even more lovely. Then the manager arranged for her to see the high banner as it passed. While she was looking toward the place where the procession would end, the new superior noticed her. He asked that she remain where she was until he returned.

When he came back and met her, he found that she was his mother from whom he had been parted thirty years before. The mother then went home free from anxiety.

Seki Keigo
Shimabara, Nagasaki

## 8. Issun Bōshi

*Mukashi atta gena.*

Once upon a time there was an old man and an old woman who never had had any children in all their years. They wanted one somehow or other, so they decided to go every day to Kannon to make their petition.

Presently, the old woman's thumb began to swell. They thought at first that she might have been stung by a poisonous insect, but as it continued to grow bigger, they realized that it must be the child they were to receive from Kannon, and they were very happy. Then one day the thumb tore open with a loud bang and out came a little child no bigger than a bean. They called him Mamesuke [Bean Boy] and took good care of him.

Years passed until Mamesuke was seventeen years old, but he still was no bigger than a bean. One day he asked his parents for permission to leave, declaring he would come back a rich man. He insisted upon going and finally set out. His parents worried for fear he would be hungry on his way, so they fixed some parched flour and put it into a box for him to take.

Mamesuke walked along carrying it until he came to a big house. It was a wine maker's place where many men were employed. He went in to get work, but he was so small that nobody noticed him. He hid under a wooden clog at the entrance and called, "How do you do? Please let me fire up the kettle."

When the people lifted the wooden clog, the little man came out. Mamesuke said, "I'm willing to tend the fire under the kettle. Please hire me." They decided to let him stay in a corner of the workroom and tend the fire. He was very good at that, and everyone petted him.

There were three daughters in that family, but the middle one seemed the nicest. Mamesuke wanted her very much. He went secretly into the room where the three girls slept one night and smeared parched flour that his mother had given him all over the mouth of the middle girl. Then he threw what was left into the stream behind the house. The next morning, he was crying in front of the kettle when his master, the first one up, found him. He asked, "What are you crying about? Are you homesick?"

"No," answered Mamesuke, "I'm crying because all the parched flour my mother gave me when I left home is gone."

"We'll fix some more for you, so don't cry," said his master. Mamesuke was not satisfied. He said, "If it isn't what my mother made, I don't want it. Please find out who ate it."

One after another the men were wakened and questioned, but each one said he didn't know anything about it. Finally, the three daughters were left. The oldest was called first. She was angry when she was questioned and declared she didn't remember eating such a thing. When the second girl got up, a lot of flour was around her mouth. She began to scream, "I can't remember eating it!"

Her father said, "Now we know who ate it, so let's grind you some more."

But Mamesuke insisted that it would be no good unless his mother made it. He demanded that the middle daughter be given him to make up for it. His master could not settle it any other way, so he decided to give Mamesuke the girl.

Mamesuke set out in delight with the girl to take her home. It did not help matters to just be angry, so the girl thought that she would find some way to kill him. He walked ahead briskly, and she could not catch up with him. When she would drop behind on purpose and wait, he would say, "Hurry up, Lady, hurry up!" If she tried to chase him to step on the hateful little chap, he would still be ahead of her.

They reached Mamesuke's home at last. His parents were happy to see him home safe and with his master's daughter as his bride. They prepared a bath for them and said, "You must be tired. Please enjoy the bath."

Mamesuke was the first to get in. He said, "Lady, come and scrub the dirt off me." She thought that at last her chance had come to kill him. She picked up the bamboo broom and stirred and beat the water with it.

There was a big noise as Mamesuke's body tore open, and out stepped a handsome youth. His parents were surprised at the noise and came running.

He said, "I am Mamesuke and I have been deeply obliged to you for a long time. Now I have turned into this form. This girl and I will take good care of you together, so please don't worry any more." So his parents and the girl rejoiced and they all lived happy together.

*Medetashi, medetashi.*

Suzuki Tōzō
Sado, Niigata

## 9. The Gift Child of the Gods

Once there was a childless couple. They wanted a child, but no matter how much they wished for one, they did not receive one. Since there seemed nothing else to do, they decided to put their faith in the kami. They received a revelation because they believed earnestly and were devoutly united in their faith. They were told, "If you sleep with a hatchet by your pillow, you will have a child."

They had their child, such as it was, according to the word of the kami. Although one of its hands was normal, the other was a hatchet. The parents could not help worrying even though their child was one especially granted to them, for as he grew bigger and they put him out in the yard to play, he would only fight with his friends and injure them with his ax hand. The parents could not let matters stand even though their child had been given them by the kami because of their faith. They talked it over and decided to take him to the hills and abandon him.

One day the father took his child with him to the hills. The mulberry trees were loaded with ripe red berries. The man said to his son,

"Climb a mulberry tree and eat berries while I go over there to piss." The child was happy as he climbed the tree, but his father took that time to leave him and go home.

After that a demon came to eat the boy, but the boy killed him.

The rest of the story is forgotten.

Iwakura Ichirō
Kikaijima, Kagoshima

# *2. The Lives of Unusual Children*

## 10. The Snake Son

Once upon a time there was an old man and an old woman who were very lonely because they had no child. One day the old man picked up a snake and brought it home from the mountains. He gathered straw and bird feathers to make a bed for it and took good care of it. The old couple gave the snake the name Shidoko and petted him. When they went near and called him, "Shidoko, Shidoko," the snake soon began to come crawling out right away.

In the meantime, Shidoko grew gradually until it was about six feet long and as big as a bamboo. It would eat a wild boar or a small bird every day. That was all it did and otherwise it was very gentle. The old man and woman were happy with it.

Then one day the villagers came to them and said, "Shidoko has grown too big, and he might harm children in our village. Please drive him away soon." The old couple said, "We can't possibly drive this snake out."

But the villagers made such a clamor that there was nothing else to do but to agree. The old couple called Shidoko, weeping, and explained that he had to go away. Shidoko grieved and shed tears of blood, but it could not be helped. He left his home and went right up the hill behind the house.

The old man and old woman wondered where Shidoko would go and they followed him. He crossed the back hill and went to a big rice field where he began to dig up the dirt. They thought it strange and went the next day to see, but in place of the rice field, a lake had suddenly appeared there. Then grass grew all around it and in the spring so many lovely flowers bloomed there that the villagers heard about it. They went with their lunches to see it.

One day the daughter of the chōja in the village lost her footing by the lake and fell into it. The sightseers from the village milled around in excitement, trying to save her, but the lake was too deep for them. They could not rescue her. Then Shidoko appeared suddenly and crawled into the water. He brought the girl up to the surface in his mouth, much to the delight and astonishment of the villagers. The girl started to breathe immediately. Her maid who had accompanied her was sent to tell her master the good news.

The chōja gave Shidoko many treasures and thanks for saving his daughter, and, beyond that, he took charge of the old man and old woman so they could live comfortably wherever they wished. Shidoko went away somewhere happy. The old couple went to live with the chōja and lived happy for the rest of their lives.

Maruyama Manabu
Kamoto-gun, Kumamoto

## 11. The Mudsnail Chōja

Once there was an old man and an old woman. While they were weeding in their rice paddy, a voice from somewhere said, "Grandpa and Grandma, please rest."

They wondered who it was and looked around, but nobody was there. They started to weed once more, but somebody said again, "Grandpa and Grandma, please rest." The old couple decided to rest a bit even if nobody was around. As they sat on the border of their rice paddy, a mudsnail came rolling along and crawled onto the old man's knee. It said, "Please take me as your son, Grandpa." Since the old man had no child, he took the mudsnail home to be his son.

The next day the mudsnail said, "Please saddle the horse for me, Grandpa." The old man asked, "What are you going to do if I saddle it?" The mudsnail said, "I am going to get a bride."

"Is there anybody who will give a bride to a mudsnail like you?" exclaimed the old man.

But the mudsnail insisted on having the horse saddled. There was nothing else to do, so the old man put the saddle on the horse. The mudsnail grasped the lead rope and rolled along leading it. In that way he arrived at a big house in the village and crawled up onto the rim of its open hearth. He said, "Please give me a bride." The people at the house said, "That's funny! Who would ever give a bride to anyone like you?"

The mudsnail said, "Then I'll scatter boiling water around!" And that is what he did.

The people cried, "Stop that! We'll give you one, we'll give you one!" But when the mudsnail stopped scattering the boiling water, they said again, "Who would ever give a bride to anyone like you?"

"Then I'll scatter hot ashes," declared the mudsnail, and that is what he did. The people cried again, "Stop that, we'll give you one, we'll give you one!" Since there was no other way, they gave him the daughter of the family as his bride.

The mudsnail put his bride onto the horse, grasped the lead rope, and went rolling along, leading the horse home. The old man and the old woman were delighted.

The bride, however, hated the mudsnail and glared at it every day. Finally, he said, "If you hate me that much, take me to the stone where we pound straw and smash me!" The bride was glad to have the chance and took him to the rock. There she crushed him. But when she did that, he turned into a fine youth. She was happy over that and they lived together pleasantly.

*Dotto harai.*

Noda Tayoko
Sannohe-gun, Aomori

## 12. The Frog Son-in-Law

Once there was an old man and an old woman who did not have a child, not even a deformed one. They petitioned Kannon for a child, even if it were not like an ordinary one, even one like a frog, if only they had a child they could give their name. Soon the woman's stomach grew big, and when the time came, she gave birth to a child like a frog. Since he had been granted to them by Kannon, they cared for him lovingly despite the way he looked.

A number of years passed and the child grew up to the age when he should be getting a wife. His parents felt sorry for him and said, "You are old enough to marry now, but we cannot find a girl to marry you although we have looked everywhere."

He spoke up and said, "I am going to look for a bride so beautiful that she will surprise you. Don't give up hope." The next morning he said, "I am going to set out to hunt for a bride now, so please give me a bag of wheat flour."

His parents thought that strange and asked what he wanted the flour for. He said it was something important in looking for a bride, but he would not tell why. He only asked them to wait and see. He went hopping into the house of the wealthiest man in a certain village. There were two beautiful daughters in that family. The frog said at the entrance to the house, "I am a traveler, but there is no inn nearby. Please let me spend the night here."

The gentleman of the house said good-naturedly. "It's not much of a place, but please come in." When it came time to go to bed, the little frog watched where the sisters slept, making sure they would sleep side by side in the same room. The older girl seemed especially pretty and good-natured to him.

The frog pretended to go to sleep, but in the night he went to where the girls were sleeping. He put wheat flour onto the lips of the older girl to make it look as though she had been eating it and left bag of flour by her pillow.

The next morning the frog got up early and pretended to be surprised as he declared, "My wheat flour is missing!" The people at the house asked anxiously, "Where did you put it?" He seemed worried and said, "I put it by my pillow when I went to bed last night, but it is gone. Something strange is going on. Somebody here has taken it. Maybe it was one of your daughters, for that one who is at the marriageable age is a big eater. One of your girls must have taken it."

"Our daughter would never do such a thing," answered the parents.

The frog held to his plan and said, "There is no telling what anyone might do. If she has eaten it, what will you do?"

They answered, "We do not think our daughter ate it, but if she has, we will let you do as you please with her!"

"Then I will make her my wife," the frog announced.

They said, "If she has done such a thing, we would be ashamed of her and would not let her stay. You could take her wherever you want!" Then the frog pretended not to know as he asked, "Where do your daughters sleep? Let's go together to see."

They went to the room where the girls slept and saw the bag of flour by the older girl's pillow and the flour around her mouth. "Look there! See, your girl has been eating it. I'll take her according to your word," declared the frog firmly.

The shocked parents woke their daughter up and accused her. She insisted she knew nothing about it, but there was the bag of flour and some of it around her mouth which she could not explain. Her parents said that she would have to go away with the frog even if his looks were not good. The girl cried and protested that she could not remember doing such a thing, but there was no help for her. Her parents had made up their minds. She had to go with the frog, her eyes swollen with tears.

The frog said, "You are my bride, so come along with me." When they reached his house, he said, "This is my house. Make yourself comfortable. You are my bride from today." Although the girl hated him, she gave up because there was no help for her.

Presently the frog brought the bamboo stick used to stir the fire. He sprawled on his stomach on the matting and said, "I'm tired. Thump my back with this bamboo. You can thump me hard enough to kill me, I don't care how hard. Hit me hard enough to split the stick!"

The girl thought, "I'm ashamed to go through life with this sort of man. I'll beat him to death!" She hit him with all her might. Instead of the frog's dying at the sound of the whack, the frog-like man turned into a more splendid youth than could be imagined anywhere in Japan. He said, "I have had a face like a frog until now, but I am a child granted by the kami and this is how I really am."

The girl, who had been crying, suddenly changed when she heard that. She was happy she had come to such a family.

Seki Keigo
Minamitakaku-gun, Nagasaki

## 13. The Snail Son-in-Law

Once upon a time there was an old man and an old woman. Since they had no child, they petted a slug as though it were their child. One day the slug said, "Please give me three grains of cooked rice." After the old man gave them to it, it took them secretly to the home of the wealthiest man in town. There he put the rice at the edge of the mouth of the only daughter.

He went to the door of the house and sobbed and cried. The master of the house came to the door to ask why he was crying. The slug said, "Your daughter took my precious rice and ate it."

"That could hardly be," protested the master. "It could happen, it could happen," complained the slug. The master said, "Then please forgive her."

"No," it said, "No, I'll not forgive her unless you give her to me!" The master thought there was no help for it and gave his daughter to the slug. The slug got a needle from the girl, and the two of them went off toward his house.

Along their way they saw some demons wrestling. The slug made fun of them. "That's funny. Somebody said something," said a demon. When he looked, he saw a slug on an oak leaf. He declared, "What an impudent fellow," and put the slug into his nose.

The slug began to prick the demon's nose with the needle. The demon could not endure the pain and cried for it to stop, but it wouldn't. "I'll give you treasure if you will stop," cried the demon.

So the slug stopped pricking the demon and received a little magic mallet. He said to the girl, "Hit me with this and say for me to become a man six feet tall." When the girl hit the slug, he became a handsome man. Then he shook the little mallet and said, "I want a house and a storehouse." At that, a splendid house and storehouse were made. They lived comfortably together after that.

Moriwaki Taichi
Mino-gun, Shimane

# 3. *Unpromising Marriages That Became Happy*

## 14. Netarō, the Lazy Man Next Door

Jinshirō was a single man, and he lived on nothing but baked turnips.

The young men in his village talked things over and decided on a plan to get a wife for Jinshirō. Several of them hung straw sacks between them and walked along in front of Asahi Chōja's house. The chōja thought this unusual and asked, "Who are you fellows?"

The young men kept on walking as they answered, "We are Kabuyaki Jinshirō's men going for green leaves." The leaves would be used for fertilizer. A crowd went by another time, everyone carrying hoes across their shoulders. When Asahi Chōja came out and asked who they were, they said, "We are the men who dig the rice fields for Kabuyaki Chōja."

The chōja was thinking that this Kabuyaki Chōja must be a very wealthy man indeed when someone came from Jinshirō to ask for the chōja's daughter to be Jinshirō's bride. Asahi Chōja consented immediately.

The girl went to Jinshirō's house and found that it was no more than a shed, and when she wanted to cook rice, she discovered there was none to cook. She had three bolts of silk, and so she sent her husband to town with one to buy rice. But he came back empty-handed twice because someone took the silk from him. He finally got some money for the last bolt and started home, but along the way he saw some children tormenting a crippled hawk.

Jinshirō gave the children his money for the hawk, and set it free. He stayed there watching the hawk and enjoying it, instead of going home. The crippled hawk flew down to the moat and caught a kappa. The kappa said it would give treasures to Jinshirō if he freed it. He gave Jinshirō a Life Mallet and a Life Bag. Jinshirō thought the bag would be handy for carrying turnips, so he kept it, but he could not think of any use for the mallet, and threw it away. Being the daughter of a chōja, his wife knew that if they did not have both the mallet and the bag, they would not be any good. She went herself to get the mallet.

First she shook the mallet and out came a big house. Jinshirō thought that was fun. He tried shaking it and saying "Komekura, come out!" but only a lot of little blind men came jumping out. [A play on words: "ko-mekura" means little blind men, and "kome-kura" rice storehouse.] His bride was astonished, and shook the mallet correctly. Then rice and rice storehouses came out for some time. The young couple invited the father-in-law, the chōja, to a big banquet. When it was over they threw all the dishes into the river. To light the road for their guest's return trip, they burned their house.

Then it was the chōja's turn to invite them. When the feast was over he would have liked to throw the dishes into the river, but he couldn't, because that would mean he would have no more. Then he said he would light the way for his son-in-law to return home, and burned his house down.

Since he could not rebuild it, Asahi Chōja went to Jinshirō's little shed to live. Then Jinshirō shook out a new house for him with his Life Mallet.

Yanagita Kunio
Hachinohe, Aomori

## 15. The Cow Bride

Once upon a time there was a beautiful girl who petitioned the kami to give her a good husband. A young man who knew what she was going to do went to the shrine and pretended to be the kami.

The young man asked, "Woman, what brings you here?" Thinking he was the real kami, the girl answered, "Kami Sama, please grant me a good husband."

He said, "So that's it. Then it would be well if you go to a certain village to the home of a certain young man and have it settled on what day you should be prepared to go to the young man's home to be his bride."

The young man told her about his own home.

When the day came, the girl prepared food, dressed herself correctly, and climbed into a sedan chair to go as the bride to the young man's home. As she went along, a feudal lord came toward them, riding his horse at the head of a line of men. When the men carrying the sedan chair saw the feudal lord, they were frightened and ran off.

The feudal lord saw the abandoned sedan chair in the middle of the road. He had his men open it and he saw the lovely girl in it. He ordered her to be taken out immediately and put onto his horse. He told his men to put a suckling calf into her chair in her place. With that done, he gave his horse the whip and took the girl home with him.

The sedan carriers who had run away came back presently. "Now, let's go," they said, lifting the chair to their shoulders and carrying it to the young man's house.

The food was ready there, relatives from nearby had been invited, and everyone was waiting, expecting the bride's arrival any minute. When the sedan chair arrived, the young man would not let it be set down outside. He had the sliding doors to his house removed, and the chair brought right inside. The little black calf jumped out as soon as the chair was opened. It went frisking around, trampling on dishes and food, causing great confusion. The young man declared, "It's enough for you to like me, isn't it? There's no reason for you to turn into a calf and trample things in the house, is there?"

Thus it turned out that the girl received a splendid feudal lord as her husband, just as she had petitioned.

Iwakura Ichirō
Kikaijima, Kagoshima

## 16. Shirataki of Yamada

Once there was a wealthy man who had twelve daughters. One of the young men working for him loved the daughter called Shirataki [White Falls]. He asked his friends to help him win her in some way. His master heard about it and called the young man to him one day. He said, "I hear that you want Shirataki. If you can compose a poem with some meaning about this, I will let you have her." The young man said promptly:

"Rice shoots wither in the drought;
Refresh them with water that falls from Shirataki."

The father said that this had meaning and gave him Shirataki. Thus the young man realized his long cherished dream of receiving Shirataki as his wife.

Fumino Shirakoma [Iwakura Ichirō]
Minamikanbara-gun, Niigata

## 17. The Tasks of the Son-in-Law

Once upon a time the only daughter of a chōja went to Settsu to enjoy Arima hot springs. A young man happened to go to enjoy the hot springs, too, and he stayed in the room next to hers at the inn. The girl was beautiful and the young man handsome. Meeting as they did every morning and evening, they became friends and fell in love. The time came presently when the girl had to go home.

Although the two young people had fallen in love, they had not told each other their names nor where they lived. Now that the girl had to go home, she wanted to leave her name and the name of where she lived for the young man. She wrote the following poem for him:

> If you long for me, ask the insect that sings in the summer for botamochi
> At the bridge that never decays in the Land of Seventeen.

She was sure that if the young man were really sincere, he would solve any riddle in order to find her. If he were the kind that would not solve the riddle and come, he would not be worthwhile. She handed the young man her note and said, "This is what I am called and this is where I live, so please come." Then she left him and went home.

Soon the young man decided to leave Arima and go to find where the girl lived, but he could not understand the poem. As he walked around on the streets, he met a blind masseur at the edge of town. He knew that blind masseurs had sharp wits and thought that this one might understand the poem if he asked him. He told the riddle to the blind man and asked for help. "Well, let's see," remarked the blind man and stood with his arms folded for a while. Then he clapped his hands and said, "I understand it. Land of Seventeen would be a young land or Wakasa. The bridge that never decays is a stone bridge. The insect that sings in the summer is a **semi** [cicada], so the family must be Semiya. Botamochi is another name for **ohagi** [both mean rice cake], so the girl's name is Ohagi. If you ask for Ohagi at the Semiya family, I am sure you will be understood."

The young man was delighted. He thanked the blind masseur and promptly set out for Wakasa-no-kuni to look for the girl. He asked his way many times until he came to a surprisingly great chōja's place. It had a marvelously built gate and a long plastered wall around the house, and was surrounded by storehouses. The young man was astonished. He was sure that no unknown man would be admitted to such a place. He spent the night at an inn, thinking about what to do.

The young man went to the gate of the Semiya mansion and swept the ground in front of it neatly the next morning when it was just beginning to be light. The guard drew back the gate at the regular hour and found the approach swept spic and span. He was surprised and wondered how it happened when he had not ordered it swept. He thought it might have been done to humiliate him.

But the next morning it was swept clean again and on the next, too—three days in a row. The guard concluded that there must be a reason back of it and got up early the next morning to catch whoever it was that was doing the sweeping. While he was waiting, presently he heard the sound of a broom. He opened the gate hurriedly and caught the young man.

"Just who are you?" he asked the young man. "What do you mean by coming to somebody's gate every morning? What are you up to?"

The young man answered, "I'm not a dangerous man. Many people seem to be employed here and I would like to get work. Please ask your master to hire me. The only reason I have been sweeping in front of the gate every morning is because I wanted to ask this. Please do it for me."

The gateman agreed to propose this to his master. He went directly to him and said, "I have come to ask you to hire a man for odd jobs. He has been coming every morning and sweeping in front of the gate and asks to be hired."

His master agreed good-naturedly to hire the young man. From that time the young man who had managed to become a servant of Semiya started with the lowest work, that of bath heater and yard sweeper. He wore soiled clothes and was blackened from work. Although he lived in the mansion day and night, he had no chance to see the girl he loved.

It happened that the girl had been betrothed to a certain man since she was a child. That man had been as great a chōja as Semiya formerly, but his fortunes had declined until he had become poor. There was all the difference in the world between him and the Semiya family. Besides, the girl never had liked him, but because the arrangement had been made by her parents, there was no way for her to say she did not want to marry the man.

And the young man the girl had liked at Arima hot springs had not solved the riddle she wrote for him and did not seem to be looking for her. Days and months passed quickly until the time when the promised wedding ceremony would have to be performed. She consented to it because her parents had settled the matter.

A good day and a good direction were selected presently, but two more men were needed to carry the sedan chair for the girl. The bath heater was selected to hold the pole at the front and another man at the rear position. The day for the ceremony came at last. The girl, dressed in her long-sleeved dress with a padded gown over it, got into the sedan chair in bright, clear weather. The bath heater at the forward position and the other at the rear lifted the poles of the sedan chair briskly to their shoulders and the accompanying people formed a brilliant procession as they left the chōja's house.

When the family had gone about half of their way, someone said, "The sedan bearers look very tired. Let's rest a little." So they paused. As the men set the sedan chair down, the man at the front shouted, "Hoikita!" and looked back. At that moment the girl in the sedan chair looked out and they saw each other. The girl suddenly clasped her hands over her bosom in severe pain. Since they could not have the wedding with the bride suddenly taken ill, they sent a messenger ahead to the house to announce that the wedding would have to be put off.

The sedan chair was returned immediately to the Semiya home, but the girl became so ill that she could not lift her head. The family was astonished. Everyone milled around, calling for a doctor and calling for medicine, but when the doctor came running and examined the girl, he could not find anything wrong with her organs. If there was nothing wrong with her body, it might be love sickness, they thought, and the girl's parents and her nurse took turns going to her as she lay in bed to ask what was in her heart. But the girl was too shy to say a word.

Then a famous fortune teller was hired to see what was the matter. He said it was really love sickness. His divination showed that she loved somebody at the mansion. When he was asked how to discover who it was, he told them that if he showed their daughter his handwriting, they would know.

The parents called out all seventy of their clerks, errand boys, and men servants, not omitting a single one, and had each write something to show their daughter. The servants were happy, for one of them would be chosen to marry the girl. One after another wrote his best, but after the girl read what was written, she would not even look up to see who wrote it. Every servant they could call a servant showed his writing, but the girl did not like any of them. The family thought it over, but then recalled the bath tender they had hired recently. He was a man, too, so they decided to let him try. What he wrote was:

> If you long for me, ask the insect that sings in the summer for botamochi
> At the bridge that never decays in the Land of Seventeen.

The other men laughed and made fun of it. They said, "A silly thing like that will hardly catch the daughter's fancy! How foolish you are!"

When the young man took his poem to the girl's room and showed her what he had just written, the girl lifted her face for the first time and broke into a smile. Then the family heard about everything that had happened from what had gone on at Arima hot springs. The Semiya family decided to marry the young man to their daughter. They celebrated a wedding and the young people became a happy couple.

That is why this story is like the saying, "A strong purpose can go through a rock barrier."

Dobashi Riki
Nishiyatsushiro-gun, Yamanashi

## 18. The Wife from the Sky World

*Mukashi sō na.*

Once upon a time a peddler who sold clay parching pans went into the foothills to sell his wares. This was in the afternoon of the 6th Day of the Seventh Month. He saw a group of beautiful girls who had come for a dip in the water and had stripped off their clothes. He had a sudden impulse to steal one of their beautiful robes. He took one and hid it in his basket.

The man passed the place on the hill on his way home in the evening. One girl was there crying alone and looking toward the sea. He was sorry for stealing her robe, but there was no reason to give it back to her then. But he thought he should help her in some way. He could not think of what to say, so he tried spitting, but she did not turn around. When he walked toward her, the sound of his footsteps did not make her turn around. He tried scaring her by taking out one of his parching pans and breaking it with a big noise, but she would not turn around.

The man began to break his parching pans from his load, one after another, and he went up to her and hit her bottom with the last one. When she finally turned around to face him, he asked, "Why are you crying?"

She sobbed as she answered, "My robe disappeared while I was bathing and I can't go home. My friends had theirs and went back." The peddler felt sorry for her and took her home to care for her.

It happened that the peddler was not married and he persuaded the girl to become his wife. Then they had a child. The peddler continued to go out to sell parching pans. While his wife was nursing her three-year-old son one day, she happened to look up at the rafters. She saw something black hanging from a shelf. Looking closer, she saw it was something wrapped in oiled paper. She wondered what it could be. She got a ladder and took the package down. It proved to be her robe.

She thought, "That man must have taken it and hidden it. What a good place! Spiteful, strange things have gone on."

The woman hurried to get ready to go back to the Sky World. She put on the robe, picked up her little son, and was climbing onto a cloud at the front entrance to the house when her husband came home. He was surprised.

"You're up to something," the man said. "Where are you going?" The wife was in too much of a hurry to talk back.

The wife only said, "I love you, too, but please give me up. I am Tanabata of the Sky World. If you want to see me, make a stack of 1000 pairs of straw sandals and climb up to me." By the time it had dawned upon the man what she was saying, she mounted the cloud and disappeared.

The parching pan peddler was so grieved that he could hardly bear it, but it takes time to make a thousand pairs of sandals. He kept on thinking how he wanted to go soon, but it took even more time to count the sandals. When at last he had made 999 pairs, he thought, "Only one more pair! After this pair, I start to climb!"

The man looked out of the front entrance and saw that a white cloud had come to meet him. He got onto it and started up toward the Sky World, but when he was high enough to touch it with his hands, he could go no further. His wife, who was weaving upstairs, happened to look down and see her former husband, the parching pan peddler, struggling because he was one pair short of the 1000 pairs of sandals. She thought he had forgotten to count them because he had been in too much of a hurry. He looked so pitiful that she reached down to him with the rod she used to send her shuttle back and forth and managed to pull him up.

The peddler's wife had a father and mother and she told them the parching peddler was the father of her child. Her parents had wanted to get a good son-in-law for their daughter from somewhere, but here she was with that kind of man from the Lower World. Well, they let the parching pan peddler stay and put him to work, but they hated him and gave him difficult tasks.

One day the mother-in-law told the peddler to dip up water with a basket. He wondered how he could manage, but his wife showed him how to put oiled paper into it. Then he could dip up the water. His mother-in-law thought, "That did not bother him. Men from the Lower World are clever."

The mother-in-law then said, "Go out to the field and sow this millet." After the man had finished sowing it, she said, "I did not tell you to sow it there. Go and pick it up."

The poor man thought he could never do such a task and he concluded that his mother-in-law was trying to make him go back to the Lower World. His wife went to him and told him to send pigeons to gather the millet. They brought enough back to fill the straw sack.

His wife told her husband that when a melon was cut and eaten in the Sky World, there was danger that water would flow out of it and she warned him never to eat a melon for any reason. Her parents told their son-in-law to cut a melon in rings and eat it. At first he decided not to eat one, but he wanted to eat one so much that he finally cut one to eat one day. Water immediately gushed out of the melon and swept him off his feet.

The man's wife, who was weaving upstairs, thought it was a strange stream. She concluded that her husband had cut a melon ring in spite of her warning. She called and called to him, but he was hard of hearing and could not hear her. She lifted her hands to show him as she called, "Even if you are carried away on the stream, we can meet once a month!" Her husband could not hear and called back, "Did you say once a year?" Then he was carried away.

That is why Tanabata comes only once a year.

*Sō ja sō na, sōrae bakubaku.*

Takeda Akira
Shishijima, Mitoyo-gun, Kagawa

## 19. The Wife's Picture

*Tonto mukashi attate no.*

Once there was a slightly stupid man called Gonbei. Even after he reached the age of thirty and then forty, nobody came to him to be his bride, so he lived alone in his little hut. One evening a prettier girl than could be seen anywhere around came to his hut and said, "Please let me stay tonight." Gonbei was astonished, but he let her stay.

Then the woman said, "Since you seem to be a single man, please take me as your bride." Gonbei was happy to take her as his bride.

The trouble was that Gonbei was so completely devoted to his bride that when he would be making straw sandals, he kept watching her until sometimes he would make them five or six feet long before he noticed, or when he was making a straw raincoat, it would get to be ten or twenty feet around, and nobody could wear it. Then it came time to dig in the garden patch. After he would dig a row, he would think of his wife and run home to ask, "Are you there?"

Once Gonbei had seen her, he could go back to his garden patch, but after he dug a little more, he would run back to his hut once more and ask, "Are you there?" In this way he never could get any work done.

Then his wife went to town to get an artist to draw her picture. She gave it to Gonbei and said, "This is the same as I, so take it to your garden patch and hang it on a mulberry branch. You can look at it all the time you work." She sent him with it to his garden. After that Gonbei looked at the picture as he worked. One day a big wind blew the picture up and away. Gonbei went home and told his wife what had happened. She comforted him by saying, "I'll get another one made."

The picture was carried up to the sky and went fluttering down into the yard of a feudal lord. When he saw the picture, he wanted the woman as his bride. He gave an order to his men, saying, "There must be a woman as beautiful as this picture, so go and search for her." They took the picture with them and asked everywhere around, "Do you know a woman who looks like this picture?"

At last the men came to Gonbei's village. They asked, "Do you know a woman like this?"

Somebody said, "The girl at Gonbei's place looks like that woman." The men went directly to Gonbei's humble hut and found the girl who was really as beautiful as the picture. They said, "It is the order of the feudal lord. We will take you with us."

Even when Gonbei begged them to set her free, the men forced her to go with them anyway. Gonbei cried until his tears mingled with the drippings from his nose ran in a stream five or six feet long.

As his wife was dragged away, she cried, "There is no help for me, but come on New Year's Eve to the castle to sell New Year pines. If you do, I am sure there will be a way."

Presently New Year came, and Gonbei carried the pines cheerfully on his back to the front of the castle. He shouted. "New Year pines! New Year pines!" Then the woman who had not smiled even once broke into a happy laugh. The feudal lord was happy, too.

He said, "Call in the man who is selling pines." The lady laughed again. The pleased feudal lord said, "If you like a man selling New Year pines that much, I wonder how happy you will be if I try selling them."

He dressed Gonbei in his fine clothes and put on Gonbei's dirty ones. He swung the pines up to his shoulder and called, "New Year pines! New Year pines!" That seemed to amuse the lady even more. The happy feudal lord went outside his gate and walked around, calling, "New Year pines! New Year pines!"

Then the lady ordered the servants to fasten the gate securely. When the feudal lord came back to his iron gate after a while, he was astonished to see it closed. He shouted, "The feudal lord is outside! The feudal lord is outside!"

But nobody came to open the gate for him. Gonbei and his wife employed the many servants in the castle and lived there happy for the rest of their lives.

*Ichigo buran to sagatta.*

Honma Kite
Nakakanbara-gun, Niigata

## 20. The Stork Wife

Once upon a time there was an honest man of good character. He saw a stork in the grass one day when he was cutting grass in the hills. It did not try to get up or to fly as his work brought him near to it. When he went up to see he found an arrow in its back. He felt sorry for the stork and took out the arrow. The bird flew away somewhere with a happy look on its face.

In the autumn of that year, a young woman who was a stranger came to the man's house one evening and said, "Please let me stay here tonight." The man felt sorry for her and let her stay. The next day she did not seem to be going, but stayed on and washed and mended the man's old clothes.

After two or three days had passed like this the woman said, "I have no special place to go, so please let me stay here." The man considered how things were, how kind she was, how well she worked, and how unpleasant it was to live alone, and said, "Please stay."

Thus they became man and wife.

New Year was near, but the man was poor and they could not make any preparations for it. His bride did her best to weave a length of cloth and she told her husband to take it to the feudal lord to sell. He took it promptly to the feudal lord, who paid him a lot of money for it. The feudal lord said, "This is beautiful weaving. Bring me another length of it."

When the man went home and told his wife she thought it over for a while. Then she said, "I am not sure if I can weave another length, but I will try. Please do not look in where I am weaving." She went into her room, and presently the husband heard her start to weave.

The husband thought it was strange that she could weave such beautiful cloth and wondered why she forbade him to look until she was finished weaving. He looked at her secretly through a knothole. He was astonished to see a naked stork plucking her few remaining feathers one by one with her beak and weaving them carefully. Then the stork said sadly, "Even though I asked you so earnestly not to look, why have you done it? I can stay no longer since I have been seen in this form. I am really the stork you rescued and I wanted to repay your kindness in some way. Now there is nothing I can do. I hoped this weaving would repay you, but now that you have seen my form, I must go."

Her husband could not stop her from flying away sadly, naked as she was.

This cloth is called shokukō brocade.

Kitaazumi-gun, Nagano

## 21. The Wild Duck Wife

A rag buyer named Zen'emon spent 150 of the 300 mon he had to save a wild duck. He had earned an unusual amount of money that day. In the evening a girl came to his house and asked him to take her as a bride. She started a mochi shop and they became very prosperous.

Since the couple had saved a lot of money the wife asked permission to visit her family. Her husband refused that, so she gave up the mochi shop and became a weaver. She asked her husband not to look in on her while she wove. He disregarded her wish and looked in, but pretended he knew nothing.

His wife came out of her room on the seventh day. As she handed her weaving to her husband she said, "There is a flaw in one place in this because you looked in on me. Even so, it is far better weaving than anything else. Sell it and live on the money in comfort for the rest of your life."

When Zen'emon went to sell the cloth, his wife left her tail feathers with a note in the wooden measuring box and went away. The note said only, "I will be in this place." Since there was a tail [o] in the measure [masu], her husband concluded that his wife would be at Masuo in Osaka. Zen'emon went to Masuo Pond and saw many wild ducks there, but one of them had no tail feathers. It came over to him and caught onto the hem of his garment with its beak. Zen'emon gave the pond the name Kōnosu so the wild duck would never be forgotten.

Sugiwara Takeo
Sakai-gun, Fukui

## 22. The Copper Pheasant Wife

This tale is about Yasuke, who used the tail feather of a copper pheasant at Sakagami on the order of Tamura Shōgun.

There was a man named Yazaemon at Furuimaya who made a living by gathering medicinal herbs in the hills. When he went into Mt. Ariake as he always did one day, he was carried off by the demon Gishiki. His wife mourned for him and put all her hopes on her lovely three-year-old son Yasuke. They lived in great poverty. She always told him, "Never kill a living thing. Living things have mates and have young."

Yasuke grew to be 21 years old, a brave young man and loyal to his mother. His mother told him to go to the year's end market at Hodaka on the twenty-eighth day of the last month of the year. He saw a large copper pheasant struggling in a snare under a small pine tree along his way. He could not help feeling sorry for the bird, and set it free. He took the 500 cash from his pocket and tied the coins to the snare. The bird flew far away, looking very happy. Yasuke's pocket was empty, so he went home and told his mother what he had done. She was delighted.

On New Year's Eve Yasuke was away from home and his mother was busy preparing food when a graceful, beautiful girl of about 17 or 18 knocked at the door. She said, "I missed the way to Ikeda and I am in trouble. Please let me stay here tonight."

Yasuke's mother was a sympathetic person and it was already dusk, so she welcomed the girl. When Yasuke came home, he and his mother asked the girl to become his wife. She consented, and after a simple ceremony, they were married. The new bride tried her best to serve her husband and his mother.

The spirit of Tamura Shōgun appeared to Yasuke in a dream about two years later. He said, "I am looking for a man born in the year of Elder Brother Wood and Rat in the month of Elder Brother Wood and Rat who will feather an arrow with a tail plume with thirteen bands from a copper pheasant, and who will serve me."

Tamura Shōgun knew that Yasuke was born at that time, and that command was especially for him.

Yasuke's wife said, "I will go to my former home and bring you a tail plume with thirteen bands from a copper pheasant."

Yasuke and his mother were delighted. When he examined the tail plume his wife brought back, there were certainly thirteen bands on it, and he danced for joy. He used it to feather his arrow shaft. He knew that he would be rewarded generously for his feat and that his home would be secure after that.

Yasuke saw his wife write him a note and go away the next morning. She wrote, "I am the copper pheasant you rescued below the little pine tree three years ago. I came to repay you for your kindness. Your household is at peace now and you do not need me. The plume with thirteen bands is from my tail."

The mother and her son wailed in grief, but they did not try to seek the girl.

Legend says that Yasuke was born in the famous Yamura and that his name was Yasuke.

Ota Hakuichirō
Minamiazumi-gun, Nagano

## 23. The Bird Wife

A certain poor man took care of a wounded wild goose. The bird came to him in the form of a young girl and they married. Then they had a child. The wife wove at her loom every day. One day while the husband was away, his wife left his child and disappeared. She left only a needle on a dish on a shelf with no hint as to its meaning.

A fortune teller said that it meant that the woman was in Harima [**hari** means "needle"], near Sarasawa [**sara** means "dish"]. When the young man went to Sarasawa Pond, there were many wild geese there. Among them was one that had a bare place on its breast where the down had been plucked. It came obediently to the man and told him she was the mother of his child. She had gone to him to repay his kindness and had woven down from her breast. She asked the man to sell the weaving at a good price and to care for their child with the money. She parted from him sadly.

According to tales of the old men and old women in this region [Akita], the man, who had been poor, then began to prosper and became the wealthy ancestor of Kōnosu Monzaemon of Osaka. It is well known that this tale is confused with the romantic legend of Shin Hasedera. It is said that the name Kakunodate was formerly Kōnodate, "kō" meaning wild goose, because there were many wild goose nests there.

There is a written record of the Sashiki family of Kakunodate that the feudal lord went with his eldest son to look in the forest for young birds in wild goose nests on the ninth day of the first month of the second year of Enpō [1675].

Muto Tetsujō
Senhoku-gun, Akita

## 24. The Fox Wife

Long ago the wife of Abe no Yasuna returned to her parents' home for three years because she was ill. Her husband was troubled because he could no longer look after the house and things at home.

One day when he was fishing at the stream a wrapping of reeds came floating downstream. "Another abandoned child," he thought as he opened it, but he found a white fox. He took her home and built up a good fire to warm her. She said, "I will surely repay your kindness" as she went off into the hills and disappeared.

Some days later a woman came to Yasuna's door and asked to stay as his servant. He let her stay and presently a little boy was born to them. They called him Dōjimaru.

One day Dōjimaru said, "Look, Father, my mother is sweeping the yard with her tail." He looked but could not see it. Only the child saw it. Then Yasuna climbed up into the rafters to look, and, sure enough, he was astonished to see that the woman had a tail. He drove her away saying, "Your disguise has been discovered." Then the woman who had been away because she was ill came back.

When the fox left, she wrote a poem:

If you long for me, come to Shinoda Forest in Izumi
And inquire for regretful Kuzunoha.

Then she went into the hills and was seen no more.

* * * *

It happened that a certain feudal lord (some say he was a chōja) became very ill. He would groan with pain every night at a certain time. A number of strong samurai and attendants were set at watch around him, but the feudal lord continued to suffer.

Now Dōjimaru had a magic rod into which his fox mother had entered. He could understand what any animal was saying if he put the rod to his ear. One day he put the rod to his ear and heard three crows, one from Izumi, one from Yamato and one from Kumano, meet and begin talking.

The crow from Kumano said, "Times are good in Kumano, and there is a good crop of the five grains." The crow from Izumi said, "In Izumi the kamo melons are doing well. They are so big that they can divide one of them into the southern melon and the northern melon." The crow from Yamato was the last to speak. He said, "At my place the Shōgun lies in bed and is about to die. The reason is that a snake, a frog, a slug, and a fly are under the floor. If they would take them out, the Shōgun would get well."

When Dōjimaru heard that, he disguised himself as a fortune teller and walked by the feudal lord's house. He called, "There is going to be a great calamity. I pity those who do not know it." Someone finally paid some attention to him and he was able to cure the feudal lord.

[Translator's note: The first part of this story, through the note left by the fox wife, was told by a different narrator than was the second half.]

Oto Kenzō
Izumi-gun, Osaka

## 25. The Clam Wife

Once upon a time there was an unmarried man. A lovely bride came to his place from somewhere. He set out for work every morning and returned in the evening. After his bride came, the taste of his food greatly improved—the bean soup he had made before had never once tasted good, but now it was fine. He was mystified by how she was able to make such good soup.

One day he pretended to go to work, but he hid behind his house to see. His bride got out her earthenware bowl and put lumps of bean paste into it and started to crush them. When the paste was smooth, she spread her legs apart and urinated onto it.

The man was furious and drove her right away. His bride tried to apologize, but he would not forgive her. Then she turned into a big clam and started to move slowly away. The bean soup was good because it had clam juice in it.

Mukaiyama Masashige
Kamiina-gun, Nagano

## 26. The Fish Wife

Once there was an honest fisherman in a certain place. He cast his net or used a net to catch little fish every day, but because he had no spirit of greed, if he caught more fish than he needed, he would set them free in the stream. He would only earn enough for the day and was very poor. For that reason he had no wife.

One day a beautiful young girl came to the fisherman's house and asked him to let her stay. He said, "I am very poor so I can't keep you. Try asking somewhere else." But she insisted, "I have come because I love your generosity. Please take me as your wife."

The fisherman said, "I can't take such a beautiful bride as you, for I am just a poor man. You can see that I could not take care of you. Please go home." But still the girl insisted, saying, "I came here because I counted on you. Please let me stay, because I am all alone."

Since there was no use talking to the girl, the fisherman decided to keep her as his wife.

The husband went as usual every day to fish for a living. The bean soup every morning and evening suddenly became very good after his wife came. When he asked why it was so good, his wife only laughed and would not tell. It was the same bean paste, but when he tried to make the soup it did not taste good. But when his wife made it, it was good. He decided to watch her secretly sometime, but he never had a chance.

One day the husband said he would go to town the next day and made his preparations the night before. In the morning he went out the front door, but then went secretly around to the back and climbed into the rafters to hide.

When his wife thought it was about time for her husband to come home in the evening, she started to get supper ready and to make soup. Her husband wondered what she would do. She got the lumps of bean paste from the cupboard and began to crush them in her earthenware bowl. Then she bared her bottom and urinated into the bowl. She put the soup over the fire in the open hearth.

The man was surprised by the dirty thing he had seen her do. When she went outside to get water he climbed down from the rafters and put dust on his sandals. He pretended to have just returned from Morioka and that he did not know anything that had happened.

At supper the man did not touch the soup which he usually ate with such relish. His wife became suspicious and asked why he was not eating it. He answered, "I was not going to say anything, for I feel sorry for you, but please stop doing dirty things."

The wife suddenly realized what had happened. She turned pale and said, "I really wanted to live with you for the rest of my life to make you happy, but since you found out, I cannot do it. I really am not a human being. I will return to my former home and let you live alone. I can never forget your kindness. Please come tomorrow to the stone at the edge of the pond where you usually go. You can see my true form there. There is something I want to give you." His wife went away somewhere in the night.

The fisherman would have kept her and lived with her if she had not done that dirty thing, but he felt uneasy that she was not human. He decided, at any rate, to go to the edge of the pond the next day to find out everything.

When he climbed onto the rock as his wife had told him to do, the woman was already there and waiting for him. She was dressed even more beautifully than usual and seemed happy. The man went over to her cautiously. The woman smiled as she handed him a beautiful lacquered box. She said, "I will give you this. I am really a fish which you set free once." Then she suddenly disappeared into the water. The box was full of gold and silver treasure.

*Dotto harai.*

Sasaki Kizen
Iwate-gun, Iwate

## 27. The Wife from the Dragon Palace

A woman who had lost seven in her family lived with her youngest son, the only one who was left. Nowadays, if a man is healthy, he can earn enough to eat in this world, but long ago a man who had no property could not live. So this youngest son would go into the mountains to gather flowers and go around as a flower peddler, but he could not earn much. He passed a long beach one day when he could not sell any flowers. He decided to offer his flowers to the Dragon God, and he threw them into the sea.

A tortoise appeared and led the young man to the Dragon Palace. Along the way, the tortoise said, "If the Dragon God asks you if you want anything, tell him you want his daughter."

It seemed to the young man that he had been enjoying himself in the Dragon Palace for three days, but three years had really gone by when he decided he wanted to go home. The Dragon God asked him if there was anything he wanted, and the young man said he wanted the God's daughter. So the Dragon God gave him his daughter.

The young man went home after he received his bride at the Dragon Palace. He found that his mother had died because she had had nothing to eat. Her body was leaning against a big rock. His bride had brought something called a Life Whip from the Dragon Palace. She scattered some water over the mother's body and tapped her with the Life Whip. The mother began to breathe, and with the third stroke she was restored to her former self. It is said that a Life Whip must be used with three strokes.

The mother was restored, but there was no house for the three of them to live in. The young man started to cut trees to make one, but his wife took out the little magic mallet which she had brought from the Dragon Palace and shook out a fine house. It was so beautiful that it shone. Then the bride shook out rice and storehouses. They suddenly became very wealthy.

The bride was the most beautiful woman in the world. The feudal lord heard about her and decided that he wanted her for his own wife. One day he sent for the young husband and ordered him to bring 1000 koku of rice. He said that if he did not come with it, he would take the man's wife from him. The young man went home hanging his head in sorrow. When his wife asked him what the business at the feudal lord's was, he would not answer. Even though a man has his own way of thinking, his wife scolded him and asked what he had to do. He finally told her that if he could not deliver 1000 koku of rice to the feudal lord, she would be taken away.

The wife declared that there was nothing to that. She purified herself at night and went down to the seashore. After she looked out to sea and beckoned, several hundred horses came out of the water loaded with rice. They took it to her yard where it was stacked as high as a mountain. Her husband was delighted. He had his men deliver it quickly to the feudal lord. There he asked that the 1000 koku of rice which he had brought be accepted. The steward came out to see if it were true, and there it was, 1000 koku of rice stacked up neatly. He ordered several hundred horses to be brought out to carry the rice to the storehouse.

Presently, the feudal lord sent for the young man again. He demanded that 1000 fathoms of rope be delivered on the next day. If the young man failed, the feudal lord would take his wife as his own bride. When the young man went home, his wife asked again what the business of the day had been. He told her what had happened.

That night his wife again purified herself and went down to the sea shore. When she beckoned, 1000 fathoms of rope appeared. When this was presented to the feudal lord, he said, "I will bring 699 followers with me to see your wife on New Year's Day. Prepare 77 jars of foaming wine and feast us."

The feudal lord arrived on New Year's Day leading his 699 men. He disguised himself as the lowest in rank and the rest were all disguised in reverse order of their rank. The wife looked out through a corner of the window and took it all in at a glance, and memorized everything. She fastened back her sleeves and brought out the 699 trays of food immediately. She asked the men to wait a moment before they started to eat. Then she led the feudal lord, who had been seated at the lowest place, to the head seat. She had the 77 jars of foaming wine, each containing four *to*, brought out, and she served the company a lavish meal.

After a while, the feudal lord demanded some sort of entertainment. The young wife asked what kind of entertainment he would like. He said he wanted a rowdy workman's song. She agreed to give him rowdy entertainment. She opened a little box and several hundred men, all looking alike, came out of it. They put on an amusing dance and song. When they were finished the feudal lord demanded quiet entertainment. She opened another box, and this time several hundred men with towels tied around their heads and swords in their hands came out. They waved their swords and then cut off everybody's head, from the feudal lord's right on down. A great river appeared and carried off all the beheaded men to the sea.

Iwakura Ichirō
Kikaijima, Kagoshima

## 28. The Snake Wife

There was a very happy couple living in a certain mountain community. They had no special problems in their lives, but they had no child. Then the wife, who seemed quite healthy, suddenly died from a cold. Her weeping husband accompanied her body to its resting place in the meadow. He lost all spirit after that and passed his days only looking around vacantly.

One day a beautiful woman came from somewhere and asked to stay at his house that night. The man was lonely and invited her in to stay. She spent the night there, but instead of leaving in the morning she did all sorts of work around the house. The same thing happened the following day. Before they were aware of it they had become husband and wife.

The wife became pregnant after some time had passed. When the month approached for her delivery, she said to her husband, "Please build me a little hut where I can give birth to my baby. Do not look in for any reason until I have untied the cord and come out."

The husband agreed and built the shelter quickly. As he helped her into it, she said over and over, "Please do not look inside." The man obeyed his wife and at first did not look into the hut, but when one day went by and then another, he was worried about what was going on inside. He wondered if his wife had delivered her baby yet, or if she was ill and suffering. He went quietly to the hut so his wife would not notice and looked cautiously through a knothole in a board of the shelter.

The man saw a huge, frightful snake there coiled around a baby. The man was so terrified that he let out a cry. He tried to control himself, but he wondered what sort of demon he had married. At the same time, he was worried that he had done something wrong by looking. But he went away again without making any noise, and then returned to his house.

By the seventh day the pillow had been lowered, and the woman came out carrying a beautiful baby boy. She was weeping. After some time she said, "I wanted to stay here forever as your wife and I bore you a child, but today I must leave you. Why did you look inside the hut after I had asked you so often not to do it? Since you have seen my true form, I can never stay. I cannot remain in human form much longer. I will go back to the pond in the mountains. Please take good care of this child."

Her husband said, "Wait! Wait! It was wrong for me to look when you told me not to, but don't think ill of me. Everything I did was because of my worry over you. If you leave now, there will be no milk for our child. How am I going to care for him? Please stay at least until he is three or four years old!"

The woman replied, "I must go because I cannot stay even a single day after my real form has been seen, but I really pity this child. Let him suck this when he cries." And she twisted out her left eyeball and set it down. She turned immediately into a great snake and glided away to the pond in the mountains.

The man named his child Bōtarō. Whenever the child cried, he gave him his mother's eyeball to suck. Bōtarō carried the eyeball around with him when he played after he grew bigger. But as time passed, the eyeball gradually became smaller until it finally disappeared. After it was gone, Bōtarō cried no matter what was done for him. There was no other way, so the father tied his child onto his back and set out to look for Bōtarō's mother. He asked along the way and finally came to a pond far back in the mountain.

The man stood at its edge and called, "Bōtarō's mother, where are you?" A big snake appeared and asked, "Why did you come?"

The man answered, "I came only because after you left, I let the child suck your eyeball every day. I have taken care of him in such a way until now, but the eyeball is all sucked away. Bōtarō cries and I do not know what to do."

The great snake sighed sadly and said, "I will give you my other eye, Father, but now I will have no eyes and can no longer know dawn and sunset. This will be difficult for me, so please hang a bell on the bank of this pond and strike it six times at dawn and at sunset to let me know." Then she said she was sorry, but that she would have to leave them. She sank into the pond with her face all bloody.

The father realized how helpless his great snake wife was now. He placed a bell in the mountain temple by the bank of the pond. He struck it six times at dawn and six times at sunset to let her know the time. Bōtarō gradually grew up, nourished by the eyeball. He heard that his mother was in the pond. One day he went to its bank and called, "Bōtarō's mother, please come out! Bōtarō's mother, please come out!"

His mother came out then in her human form. She could not see her son because she was blind, and she had to feel his face to know it was he. He put her on his back and took her home. There he built her a room and gave her whatever she wanted to eat every day. He was a good son to her.

Sasaki Kizen
Esashi-gun, Iwate

## 29. The Frog Wife

It was a very rainy night when somebody came to a man's door and said, "Please put me up for the night."

He said, "I can't let you stay." But the person asked again, and he let her stay. In the morning the woman said, "Since you don't have anyone to cook for you, why not let me stay and be your wife?"

The man was a candle peddler and sold candles every day. Day after day the woman did not eat any rice. After thirty or forty days had passed, the woman said, "It is now 100 days since my father died at the home where I was born. Please let me go home."

The husband asked, "What would be a good thing for you to take with you?" She said she didn't have to take anything, but he told her to take some candles and go. He gave her the candles and followed her secretly to her home. She went along until she came to the bank of a pond and there she jumped in with a splash. The man thought it was strange.

When the man went back there the next day at about 10 a.m., frogs were croaking. He thought, "Now I am sure my wife is a frog." He carried a big rock to the pond and threw it in. The frogs suddenly stopped croaking.

That night his wife came home with cakes that had been given her at the memorial service. The man asked, "How was everybody?"

"Everybody was fine," she answered, "but a terrible thing happened. While the sutras were being read, there was a big earthquake. Some people were killed and others were hurt in the confusion. Luckily, I was in a corner and was not hurt."

The man thought, "Yes, it must have been that rock." He looked closely at his wife and saw that she was a frog.

It is better not to take in someone who does not eat rice and who is satisfied without things.

Seino Hisao
Higashitagawa-gun, Yamagata

## 30. The Snake Son-in-law

Once upon a time, when a farmer in a certain place was passing his rice paddies on his way home from work, he saw a big snake trying to swallow a frog. He was sorry for the frog and said to the snake, "I will give you a daughter if you will spare the frog." The snake seemed to understand, for it let the frog go and glided away somewhere.

The farmer was glad to see how happy the frog was, but once he reached home and began to think about it, he worried so much over the foolish promise he had made that be became sick.

The farmer called his oldest daughter to his bedside the next morning and said, "Father felt so sorry for a frog yesterday that he promised a daughter as a bride to the snake. I wonder if you would go for me." The girl went off, saying, "How awful! You had better go yourself, Father."

The farmer gave up and called his second daughter. But when she heard what he had to say, she too answered, "How awful! You had better go yourself, Father." She ran off.

The farmer thought his youngest daughter would refuse, too, but he decided to try asking her. Her eyes filled with tears as she listened to him, but she said, "I will go. Please go and buy me 1000 gourds and 1000 needles."

The happy farmer went to town immediately and bought the 1000 needles and the 1000 gourds and gave them to his daughter.

The snake came in the evening as a handsome samurai, leading a great number of men to receive the girl. The father wept as he packed the 1000 needles and 1000 gourds for her and sent her away with them. The snakes crossed the field, crossed the hill, and went farther and farther into the mountains. They came to the snake's home, where a thousand of his snake comrads were twisting and coiling as they waited to eat the girl.

When it seemed that the time had come for the girl to be devoured, she said, "I came expressly to be eaten by you, but I have just one request before that. Please do as I say. I want you to sink these 1000 gourds and float these 1000 needles."

Then she threw the 1000 gourds and 1000 needles she had brought into the pond. "We can finish that in a hurry," the snakes said, as they plunged eagerly into the water. But gourds are things that float and needles are things that sink, and the snakes became exhausted.

In the meantime the girl started to run home, but she lost her way. While she was worrying about that, she saw a light flickering in a house beyond. She hurried toward it and found an old woman spinning alone there. The girl told the old woman why she was lost and she was allowed to stay there for that night. The old woman seemed happy as she brought out all kinds of good things to eat one after another, and cared for the girl.

The old woman said, "The feudal lord of this land has sent messengers everywhere looking for a bride. You are beautiful and open-hearted, really a girl without faults, so you should go to the feudal lord. I will guide you to his place after daylight tomorrow."

The girl was pleased with this idea and spent a happy night with the old woman. She followed the old woman to the castle town in the morning to see. It seemed to her that all the girls in the land had gathered there, pushing each other around, and each of course said she would be chosen. Presently the head steward came and looked over each girl in line. A sash was too short or an overgarment was too long and no girl looked just right to him. He came to the girl the old woman had brought at the end of the line. He declared that she was a good one, and she became the bride of the feudal lord.

The girl sent for her parents in her own land to come to the castle, and they lived a life of ease there for all their lives. It is said that the old woman was the frog the farmer had saved.

Katō Kaichi
Haga-gun, Tochigi

## 31. The Demon Son-in-law

*Mukashi atta ja.*

There was once a man and woman with eight daughters and many rice paddies. One day when the farmer went to his rice paddies he found a big demon blocking up the water he was flooding them with. The man called to the demon, "I have eight daughters at home. I will give you one if you will let the water flow into my paddies."

The next morning the farmer did not get up for breakfast. His oldest daughter went to him to tell him that breakfast was ready, but he refused to get up unless she would do what he asked her to do. The girl said she would, but when he asked her to go to the demon as his bride, she refused and ran away. The next girl and the next then came in, until he had asked all but the youngest, and each ran away and refused him.

The eighth child agreed to go as the demon's bride. While she was preparing to go to the demon, she was given wild violet seeds and told to drop them along the way. When the time came for them to bloom she would be able to run away from the demon and find her way home. Presently the demon came for the girl and took her away. He was the biggest of the demons.

The girl started to go outside when the violets bloomed. She said, "I just want to go over there and I will come right back." The demon chased her and tried to catch her. She danced for him and called, "Demon! Demon's friends!" And the demon drank water and died.

Yanagita Kunio
Hachinohe, Aomori

## 32. The Kappa Son-in-law

Long ago there was a village official in Kitaarima who had a beautiful only daughter who was at the age to marry. The water supply for only those paddies owned by that official seemed to be cut off suddenly one summer at the most important time for the rice plants. His workers tried hard, time after time, to mend the ditches, but the water did not flow. There seemed to be no help for the official, so he went to petition Ujigami. He had a dream one night after that in which a kami told him, "You have a beautiful daughter of marriage age. The kappa who lives in Arima River wants her. If you give her to him as a bride, the water will flow immediately into your paddies."

The official did not tell this to anyone at home. He set out as usual to his rice paddies the next morning, but he could see that it was true that only his had had no water for several days. The ground was hard and cracked and the plants were turning yellow. He could see, however, that the other paddies had plenty of water and their plants were a lush green.

The man felt helpless. He could bear it if he were tending his fields himself, but this was hard for his helpers. He was sure that if he told them about his dream, they would tell him that if he would give his daughter to the kappa, they would rescue her. He thought of many ways, but finally went to the opening where water was supposed to flow into his paddies.

Sure enough, a kappa was there stopping it up just as the man had heard in his dream. He asked the kappa why it was doing this, and the kappa demanded the man's daughter.

The troubled official went sadly home, but he could not tell anyone of his dream the night before or what had happened that morning. He could not tell his only daughter to go to the kappa, much less give her to him. His daughter noticed him staring vacantly, lost in thought, and asked what was wrong. Finally, he told her about his dream and about the kappa that morning. She said, "If that is what is troubling you, don't worry. Just leave it to me. I will see that water is put into your paddies."

Taking a gourd with her, the girl went to the Arima River. She said to the kappa, "I have come as you wished to be your bride, but you must put as much water on my father's field as there is on the others. I will put my spirit into this gourd which I have brought, and when you have sunk it into the river, I will go any time to your place." She tossed the gourd into the river and went home. Then water flowed into the official's paddies and the plants revived.

From that time there has been a gourd in the Arima River every autumn, floating, sinking, and floating.

Seki Keigo
Shimabara, Nagasaki

## 33. The Monkey Son-in-law

*Mukashi atta ge do.*

Once upon a time there was a farmer. The sun shone day after day one year and his family's rice fields dried up. No more water came, and the soil cracked. The farmer sat on the border of his paddy and said to himself, "If only somebody would come and water my field that can grow 1000 bundles of rice, I would give him whichever of my three daughters he wanted."

Just then a monkey came rustling out of the bamboo grass thicket and said, "If I put water on your paddies, will you give me one of your daughters?"

"Of course I will," declared the farmer. Then the monkey went far above on the hill and lots of water came down to the paddies that could produce 1000 bundles of rice. They filled to the brim before the farmer's eyes. He was delighted. "Day after tomorrow is a good day," he said, "so come then to get my daughter."

The farmer worried for fear that when he went home his daughters would refuse. That night he would not eat his supper before he went to bed. His oldest daughter went to him and asked, "Why don't you eat? Hurry and get up." He said, "I am worried about something. Will you do something for me?"

The girl answered that she would do anything her father said, but when her father said he wanted to send her to the monkey as a bride she got angry. She said, "Was there ever such a fool as Father! Who wants to go to a monkey's place!" She stamped on her father's head as she went off.

Then the second girl came, and when she heard what he had to say, she kicked his pillow and ran away. His third daughter came and said, "Get up quickly, Father. Supper is ready."

When her father told her what was on his mind, she said, "I will go to the monkey's place as a bride if Father tells me to, or even to a snake. I'll do anything you say, so hurry and get up."

That made the old man happy. He got up and ate his supper.

On the proper day the monkey appeared in a red sleeveless coat to get his bride. The old man took out the good clothes his wife had worn when she was young and dressed up his daughter. He gave her to the monkey, who led her far back in the hills. There they lived together on good terms.

Presently spring came again. The girl said to the monkey, "I want to go home for a visit. Please make Father's favorite burdock leaf mochi and carry it for me." The monkey agreed and set about making it while she prepared to go. He steamed the rice and made burdock leaf mochi. He was going to put it into the lunch box, but the girl said, "If you put that into the lunch box it will smell of the box and Father won't eat it."

The monkey asked if he should put it in the kettle, but the girl said it would smell of the kettle and her father would not eat it. The monkey said, "I will leave it in the mortar and carry it on my back." The two started off together, the monkey trudging along with the mortar on his back.

Along their way was a river where beautiful cherry blossoms bloomed on its banks. The girl asked the monkey to pick some of the blossoms to make her father happy. The monkey agreed and started to set the mortar down to get ready to climb a tree. The girl said, "If you put the mortar down, the mochi will smell of dirt and it won't be fit to eat."

So the monkey climbed with the mortar on his back. He tried to break off a branch that was right and asked the girl, but she told him to climb a little farther. He asked, "How about here?" She told him to go farther.

Finally, when she said it was just right, the branch broke off, and the monkey fell into the river with the mortar on his back. As he was carried away by the current, he called:

My life washed away in Sarusawa without a regret;
Later the girl will surely weep.

The girl did not cry at all. She hurried back to her home where her father wept for joy. Her older sisters laughed at her because she returned from the monkey's home. They turned into rats for being disloyal to their father and scurried off into the rafters of the house.

*Tonpi kanko nai kedo.*

Sakenobe Zuihō
Mogami-gun, Yamagata

# 4. *Stepchildren Stories*

## 34. Nukabuku, Komebuku

Once upon a time there was a woman with two daughters, but one of them was a stepdaughter. The stepdaughter's name was Komebukuro.

Girls in their neighborhood came by one day to invite the sisters to go gather chestnuts in the mountains. Komebukuro asked her stepmother, "What shall I take to put chestnuts in?" The woman answered, "Take that old rotten rush bag."

When her own girl, Awabuku, asked, she answered, "Take the new little bag." The two girls obeyed and went off with their friends.

Komebukuro's rotten bag had a hole in it and no matter how many chestnuts she gathered, she could not fill it. Her friends all filled theirs and went home. While Komebukuro was trying to fill her bag she became hungry and went down to a little stream for a drink.

A beautiful white bird came flying to the girl and said, "My form has changed, but I was your mother in my former life. I am glad to see how you obey your stepmother good-naturedly every day. I have brought you this dress. Keep it buried in the ground usually, but you can wear it when there is something special."

The bird gave her a hollyhock flute and a new bag, too. Komebukuro was very happy. She hurriedly gathered chestnuts and went home by sunset.

There was a festival in the neighboring village five or six days after that. The mother dressed Awabukuro in a pretty dress and took her to the festival, but she left Komebukuro behind and told her to spin three skeins of linen. Komebukuro spun the linen as fast as she could. When her friends came by to invite her to go with them to the festival she said she had to do the work or she would be scolded.

The friends all felt sorry for Komebukuro and helped her finish in no time. Komebukuro put on the beautiful dress the little bird had given her and walked along, blowing her flute. It seemed to say:

Whoever hears this little flute—
Birds in flight across the sky,
Rest your wings and listen;
Worms that crawl upon the ground,
Halt your feet and listen.

The girls arrived at the shrine of the neighboring village in this way. They saw Awabukuro and her mother watching dolls dance. Komebukuro tossed the covering of a dango and hit Awabukuro's cheek with it. Awabukuro was startled. She said to her mother, "Komebukuro threw a dango wrapper at me."

Her mother said, "No, there isn't any reason for Komebukuro to have come here. It is just somebody who looks like her. Turn the other way and pay no attention."

Presently Komebukuro tossed the wrapper from a piece of ame at Awabukuro while she was looking the other way. Awabukuro was provoked and told her mother again, but she would not believe her. She just said, "When somebody throws something at you, look the other way."

After a while Komebukuro went home to be there ahead of the other two. She acted as though she knew nothing about what had happened. A villager who had seen what went on came to their house and asked for Komebukuro as his bride. The stepmother wanted him to take her own child, but he insisted he wanted Komebukuro. The stepmother asked him to compare their beauty and then to make his choice, and he agreed.

The two girls went to their room to dress up. Awabukuro asked, "What shall I put on my hair?" Her mother answered, "Put the oil that is in the cupboard on it."

When Komebukuro asked, her stepmother said, "You can put water from the kitchen drain on it if you want to."

Awabukuro's hair was kinky and would catch in the comb, snapping, *pinpara, pinpara*. Her mother sat there watching her and said, "It sounds like the music of a biwa or a shamisen."

Komebukuro's hair was thick and long. Her comb went through it smoothly, but her stepmother sneered and said, "It sounds like turds falling into the privy."

After the two girls finished combing their hair and changing their clothes, the stepchild Komebukuro was by far the prettier. She rode away in a sedan chair as a bride. Awabukuro was so envious that she could not bear it. She badgered her mother over and over, saying, "I want to ride in a beautiful sedan chair like that and go away as a bride, too."

Her mother put Awabukuro onto a cart and pulled it herself. She went around calling, "Anyone want a bride? Anyone want a bride?"

The cart fell over and the girl dropped into a rice paddy. She turned into a mudsnail immediately. Her mother fell into the mill pond and turned into a sluice shellfish.

Kawai Yūtarō
Tsugaru, Aomori

## 35. Benizara, Kakezara

[Translator's note: The two names here seemed unusual to Mr. Yanagita and he opened a separate group, anticipating that a different version would be found. This did not prove to be true, however, and for this reason a tale with these names will not be offered here.]

## 36. Sara-Sara Yama

*Aru tokoro ni atta to sa.*

Once upon a time there were two sisters, but the older girl was the daughter of the husband's former wife. When their father was away hunting in the hills once, the mother sent the girls to get water. The younger girl had a good dipper, but the older girl's was broken. No matter how much she tried, she could not fill her bucket.

A feudal lord's procession came by there, and the feudal lord was attracted by the grace of the older girl. He told one of his men that he would like to take her to his castle and sent him to ask for her. The man went to the stepsister and asked, "Why do you dip water with a broken dipper like that?"

The girl answered, "We are poor and I cannot ask to buy a new one."

The man said, "I will buy you a dipper or anything you wish, so please come to the castle. The feudal lord is asking for you. How about it?"

The girl said she didn't know unless he asked her mother.

The feudal lord's man then went to the mother. She was very fond of her own child and asked him to take her daughter. The man said his master wanted the older girl. The mother, however, would not agree, so the man went back to his master and reported about it.

The feudal lord thought of a plan to try and sent his man back to the mother. He said, "When I told my master, he said he wants the girl who is the more clever. I would like to test them." He told the mother to bring out a tray, a dish, some salt, and a piece of pine. He said, "Put the dish on the tray, the salt on the dish, and the pine onto the salt. Then ask your daughters to compose a poem about it. I will take the one that writes the better one to the castle."

The mother had the younger girl try first. She said promptly:

On the tray there is a dish,
On the dish there is salt,
On the salt there is a pine.

The man nodded and said, "Very well. Let the older girl try this time." She was intelligent. She looked at the things thoughtfully for a while, and then said:

Oh, tray and dish,
Has snow covered your mountain
To nourish the roots of the pine?

The retainer slapped his knee and praised the older girl's lines. He took her in a sedan chair to the castle.

The stepmother was angry. She put her younger daughter into the lower part of a mortar and rolled it around until the girl's eyes popped out and she turned into a mudsnail.

That is why it is said that people with bad eyes should not eat mudsnails.

*Sorede oshimai.*

Arai Yoshimasa
Kitasaku-gun, Nagano

## 37. The Old Woman's Skin

Once there was a very wealthy man whose young wife died, leaving him an only daughter. He married again and had many children. The stepmother hated the child of the former wife and tried to think of some way to get her out of the house.

She told the wet-nurse to take her off somewhere and to get rid of her. The nurse pitied the girl, but there was no telling what would happen to her if she stayed at home. She talked matters over with her master. They decided to give the girl 1000 ryō and to turn her out.

The nurse said to the girl, "You have a lot of money now and you are very beautiful. Unless you are very careful, you may meet with danger." She gave the girl something called a babakkawa [an old woman's skin]. The girl put it on and looked like an old woman as she left her home.

The girl went around here and there and finally hired herself to a gentleman's house in a certain town as their water carrier. She always wore the old woman's skin while she worked. She took her bath only after everyone else, so she had no worry about being found out when she took off the skin.

One evening the young master happened to see the girl bathing without the old woman's skin on. He thought about the beautiful girl until he became sick. His father worried and called in a fortune teller to find out what the trouble was.

The fortune teller said, "There is somebody at this house whom the young man likes. If you bring her to him, his sickness will be over."

Then each maid was sent to the young man to ask if he would take some medicine or drink some hot water. But the young man did not like any of them. He would only raise his head a little and then lie back on his bed. At last it was the turn of the old woman who carried water. She tried to refuse, saying, "What use is it for an old woman like me to go?" But they insisted upon her going.

When the girl went to the young master's room and asked, "Shall I give you some medicine?" he recognized her immediately. Then she took off the old woman's skin and turned into a beautiful girl.

She became his bride and they lived happy ever after.

Fumino Shirakoma [Iwakura Ichirō]
Minamikanbara-gun, Niigata

## 38. The Girl who Tended Fires

A certain beautiful wife who lived far back in the hills gave birth to a baby girl. She knew that she was about to die because of an illness from childbed. She wrapped her baby in heavy paper made from persimmon tree bark, tied her onto the antlers of a deer, and turned it loose.

The deer carried the baby to an old couple living in a little settlement. They called her Deer Maid because she had been carried to them by a deer. She was very beautiful. Since the old couple had no children, they kept the baby and brought her up.

After the old folks died, Deer Maid went down to the edge of the village and became fire tender in the kitchen of a chōja. When the young master in the family saw her, he became ill. The old woman who arranged the match appeared—she might have been an old frog or a deer. She said that if a girl who could complete three tests were taken as his bride, the young master's illness would disappear.

One test was for the girl to break off the twig of a tree on which a sparrow was perching without disturbing it. Another test was to walk across a newly spread sheet of silk batting wearing new straw sandals without snagging the silk. The third test was to walk across the surface of water.

Many girls came from villages around to try, but none could accomplish even one of the three tests. Finally, Deer Maid, who tended fires in the kitchen, tried, and she did them from first to last.

She became the bride of the chōja's son.

Sasaki Kizen
Kamihei-gun, Iwate

## 39. Haibōtarō

Long ago there was a bath heater called Sanpachi at the home of a samurai. One day his master said to him, "There is to be a noh performance today and all of us are going to go to see it. Watch the time and have the bath heated for us by the time we return." Then he set out with all his family.

After they left, Sanpachi heated the bath and got into it himself. He tied up his hair beautifully, dressed in a ceremonial robe, put two swords at his side, and looked exactly like a handsome samurai. He had been a samurai formerly, but because of circumstances, he had assumed the role of bath tender.

Sanpachi set out for the noh. He asked to do an impromptu dance during the performance there. As his samurai master looked on in admiration, he did not dream that the dancer was the bath tender from his house. Sanpachi's dance was especially fine and everybody admired it.

After Sanpachi finished his dance, he hurried home ahead of the rest and changed back into a bath tender. He reheated the bath and waited for his master's return. Presently his master and his party all came back. Sanpachi asked his master, "How did you enjoy the noh today?"

His master replied, "It was all splendid, but an impromptu dance by an unknown samurai was the most splendid of all." Sanpachi knew that his master was talking about him, but he did not show that he knew.

The daughter of the family became ill and she stayed in bed and refused to eat from the next day. A doctor was called immediately, but he could not understand the cause of her illness. When a fortune teller was asked, he said, "This illness is concerned with the heart. If somebody living here takes food to her that she will eat and if he takes care of her, she will gradually get well."

Her parents wondered who it could be. They could not think and none of the rest had any idea. They decided that her parents and everyone in the household should go in turn to try to give the girl food. But regardless of who came, the girl would not take up her chopsticks to eat for anyone.

Finally, only Sanpachi, the bath heater, was left. He was asked to take food to the daughter. Oddly enough, when he took food to her, she ate it. Then Sanpachi was asked to care for her. The daughter's illness gradually disappeared.

Yamaguchi Asatarō
Iki-gun, Nagasaki

## 40. When the Stepchild Gathered Acorns

Once upon a time there were two sisters, but one of them was a stepchild. Their mother sent them to gather chestnuts. She gave her stepchild a bag with a torn bottom, but a new, strong one to her own child. She told them to fill their bags with chestnuts.

The two girls went into the hills together and each picked up chestnuts to put into her bag. The real daughter's bag was a good one, so she soon filled it, and went home first. No matter how many chestnuts the stepchild picked up, she could not fill her bag because it was torn.

In the meantime, the sun set and the worried girl began to cry. She saw a light beyond her and walked toward it. She came to a lonely house in which an old woman was spinning alone. The stepchild told her what had happened and asked to spend the night with her. The old woman said, "Demons live at this house. They are away in the hills now, but they will come back soon. If they find you, they will eat you. Put these on and hide in the corner of the yard."

She gave the girl a magic straw cloak and sedge hat which would make her invisible.

The girl took the cloak and hat and hid in the corner of the yard. Presently a great crowd of noisy demons came back from the hills. As soon as they went into the house, they shouted, "It smells of humans! It smells of humans! Has a human being come, old woman? It smells of humans!" They hunted all through the house. Since the girl had on the invisible hat and cloak, they could not find her.

The old woman said, "Why should a human come here? It's late now, nearly time for the cock's first crow. Hurry to bed." After she hustled the demons off to bed, the old woman took that time to tell the girl to run away quickly. She ran off wearing the magic cloak and hat.

The girl had barely managed to escape with her life and she reached home safely. The feudal lord heard that the stepchild brought home a strange treasure called an invisible cloak and hat. He sent for her and praised her highly.

It is said that she received many gifts from him.

Kamiina-gun, Nagano

## 41. The Bottomless Bag

Once upon a time there was a stepmother. She hated the older girl, her stepchild, and gave her a bottomless bag, but she petted her own girl, the younger one, and gave her a good bag when she sent them to the hills to gather acorns. She said, "Come home when your bag is full."

The older girl walked ahead and picked up acorn after acorn, but she could not fill her bag because it had no bottom. The younger girl followed her and picked up the acorns the older girl dropped. She filled her bag right away because it was a good one.

The younger girl asked her sister to go home, but the older girl said she could not go home because her bag was not full. She told the younger girl to go home alone. The older girl went farther and farther into the hills, trying to gather acorns.

In the meantime, the sun set. She wondered what to do, but she saw a Jizō shrine. She said, "Please, Jizō Sama, let me stay here tonight."

He said, "All right. I will let you stay. Demons will come with treasure in the night, so hide behind me. Don't laugh when they start to dance even if it is funny. After their dance is over, imitate a cock's crow *kokekokko*. The demons will say that it is dawn and rush away, leaving their treasure behind. Gather up the treasure when it is really daylight and take it home."

The girl hid behind Jizō, and in the night the demons came carrying treasure on their shoulders. They were funny when they started to dance, but the girl managed to hold back her laughter even if she wanted to laugh. When the dance was over, she did as Jizō had told her and imitated the cock's crow. At that, the demons shouted, "Look! It's dawn!"

They forgot their treasure and ran away. The stepchild took as much of the treasure as she could carry and went home.

When the stepmother saw the treasure, she asked, "How do you happen to bring that kind of treasure home?" The girl then told all about what had happened. Then her stepmother sent her child to the Jizō shrine. The younger girl went to the shrine and said, "Jizō Sama, please let me stay here tonight." He did not tell her what he had told her big sister, but she knew what had happened. She hid behind Jizō. The demons came again in the night, shouldering their treasure. When they started their dance, they were so funny that the girl could not help laughing at them.

The demons shouted, "That human who fooled us last night is here again!" They dragged the girl from behind Jizō and thrashed her.

The younger girl barely escaped with her life and ran home.

Noda Tarō
Tamana-gun, Kumamoto

## 42. Otsuki, Ohoshi
[Also called "Ogin, Kogin"]

Once upon a time there was a man in a certain place whose wife died when she gave birth to a little girl. He named her Orinko. The man married again after his wife died. The new wife had a daughter named Korinko, and the two girls grew up together.

When the father set out one day for Kyoto, he said to the girls, "Play nicely together, for I will buy you lots of gifts." The stepmother hated Orinko. She was glad to have a chance while her father was away to hire a carpenter to make a box. She put Orinko into it with some riceballs and had her buried alive in the forest.

The younger girl heard what was going to happen. She had some holes made in the bottom of the box and gave Orinko mustard seeds to take.

Orinko dropped a few seeds at a time from the holes in the box while she was being carried into the forest. She ate riceballs a little at a time to keep herself alive in the ground where she was buried.

The scattered mustard seeds sprouted and flowers bloomed all the way from the house to the forest. Korinko followed the path of the mustard flowers into the forest where her sister was buried. When she called her sister, a voice answered from the ground below. Korinko cried as she tried to dig to her, but she didn't have anything to dig with. Her nails were torn and her hands were covered with blood, but she dug as best she could.

A man came along with a hoe across his shoulders. He asked Korinko, "Why are you trying to do such a difficult thing?" She told him what had happened. The man then dug the dirt with his hoe and helped Orinko out. She was pale from being in the ground for a long time. The man took the two girls home to his house to look after them.

Meanwhile, their father came home from Kyoto, bringing many gifts, but his two girls were not there. When he asked his wife, she pretended not to know. He grieved so much that he lost his sight. He tied the gifts onto his back and set out with a cane in his hand and straw sandals on his feet, looking like a pilgrim, to search for his girls. He went from village to village, singing at doors:

Orinko, Korinko, Namu Amida,
I brought you ten boxes from Kyoto.

When he came to a certain village, singing as usual at doors, a girl came out from a big house to give rice to the pilgrim. She was sure that he was her father from whom she was separated. She was Orinko and she said, "Father, here I am." At that, the father's eyes could suddenly see and he wept with joy. Korinko came running out, and the three wept together. They thanked the man at the house warmly and went home.

They all lived a happy life together.

Terada Denichirō
Hiraga-gun, Akita

## 43. The River that Rose Each Day

Once there was an older sister who was a stepchild and a younger sister who was the daughter of the stepmother. The stepmother abused her stepchild, but the two girls liked each other. Finally, the stepmother abandoned the older girl in the river that rose each day. The younger girl carried food to her sister every day and asked how far the water had risen. She would ask, "How far up has the water come today?" The answer would be, "It has come as far as my abdomen." The water gradually came to her chest and then to her neck. Finally she died.

Koyama Masao
Chiisagata-gun, Nagano

## 44. When the Stepchild Dug a Well

A stepmother looked after her stepson, but she hated him and decided to kill him. One day she said, "Tomorrow we will dredge the well together."

When the boy told that to an old man who lived in the neighborhood, the old man asked, "Do you have any money?" The boy said, "I have only a little."

"Then take your money with you when you go down into the well," the old man said. "Each time you fill the basket with dirt, put a coin into it. If you do not dig a hole in the side of the well for as long as your coins last, you will lose your life tomorrow."

The boy did as the old man said on the next day. He went down into the well and each time he sent up a basket of dirt, he put a coin into it. His stepmother was happy over finding that coins were in her well. She continued to raise the basket and send it back down. In the meantime, the child was digging the hole at the side of the bottom of the well. He climbed into it and hid when his money was all gone. His stepmother decided it was time to throw rocks into the well when the coins stopped coming.

The boy was hiding in the hole at the side and was not hurt by the rocks. His life was saved in that way.

Iwakura Ichirō
Kikaijima, Kagoshima

## 45. A Thousand Bundles of Thatch

Long ago there was a mean stepmother in Yahai-mura, Rikuzen-no-Kuni [Iwate]. She decided to kill her stepchild somehow. She set out for town with her own child and her stepchild, and climbed a steep mountain on the way.

She told the girls she would drop them over a cliff. She cut 1000 sheaves of thatch and wrapped her own girl in them, tied securely, but she left her stepchild unprotected. Then she pushed the girls together over the top of the cliff.

The hem of the stepchild's dress caught on the root of a tree on the way down and she was saved, but the weight of the bundle in which the other was tied carried her down to the stream below. She struck a big rock and was dashed to pieces. When the stepmother saw that, she realized for the first time how wicked she was. She leaped from the cliff to her death.

The legend about this remains, and the place is called Senbakaya [Thousand Thatch Bundles] to this day.

Sasaki Kizen
Kesen-gun, Iwate

## 46. The Stepchild Flower

The selfheal flower is also called the stepchild flower. Long ago there was a family where there was a stepchild and another child who was the daughter of the stepmother. When the mother came home from an errand one day, she found the two girls eating rice from the rice chest. The mother was suspicious of her stepchild and she forced her mouth open saying, "You ate lots, didn't you?" But there were only two grains of rice in it.

Her own child's mouth was full of rice grains. The two children turned into selfheal flowers. Inside the lower petal of some of the selfheal flowers there are two white protuberances that look like grains of rice, and under others, there are five or six. The ones with only two are called stepchildren and those with more are called the "True daughters."

Takada Jūrō
Soekami-gun, Nara

## 47. The Stepmother a Ghost

There was once a mean stepmother in a certain place. A boy of about 12 or 13 years of age, who was the son of a former wife, lived at her home. He had done well in his studies, but after his mother died he was always falling asleep in class and he made no progress in his studies. His teacher wondered why. When he scolded the boy, he cried and told the teacher about his troubles. That night the teacher stood secretly outside the door of the boy's home to look things over.

Late in the night, when even the plants seemed to be asleep, the stepmother dressed herself in white and let her hair down, all dishevelled. She held a luke-warm piece of konyaku in her mouth and went close to the child. She said, "I am your dead mother." Then she seemed to lick the boy all over to torment him. The teacher who saw all this informed the police immediately. The stepmother was punished.

Suchi-gun, Shizuoka

## 48. The Stepchild and the Flute

Long ago there was a little girl of about ten years old called Osono in a certain village. Her mother died early and she lived a lonely life with her father. After a while, a new mother came, bringing her girl called Ohana, who was a year or two younger than Osono. Everything was all right at first, but gradually things became unpleasant, and Osono was shy even when her father was at home. But he only heard her say "yes" obediently.

The stepmother decided to get rid of Osono while her father was away, so that her own child could inherit the estate. She called Osono and told her to fill a big kettle with a basket, then made her light a fire under it with flint stones. The child cried and cried but she did her best. Presently the water was boiling.

The stepmother put a single round stick across the kettle and asked Osono if she wanted to see her father. The child nodded with happiness.

The woman said, "Cross the kettle on the stick, and when you come to the middle, look down. You will see your father's face then." The little girl wanted to see her father with all her heart. She started across the stick unsteadily. When she reached the center, the mother suddenly moved the stick and Osono fell into the boiling water and died. The woman buried Osono by the house with the help of Ohana.

Presently the father returned. He did not see his daughter and asked his wife about her. The woman only put him off with all kinds of excuses. When he went out into the yard a nightingale flew up from near where Osono's body was buried. It fluttered and turned toward him. He heard it twitter and listened closely. It seemed to say, "I was boiled in the water I dipped with a basket a thousand times, and I turned into this form."

When the father went back into the house, the nightingale went in with him and perched on his shoulder. It repeated its song. The stepmother was surprised and tried to chase the bird out with a broom, but it continued to sing.

The woman was sent to the authorities after Osono's white bones were found in the yard. The stepmother lost her mind and died in prison, haunted by the spirit of the dead girl. Ohana, too, died out in the wilderness. The father was left to pass his days a lonely man.

[Translator's note: In some versions, a bamboo sprouts from the grave of the murdered girl and it is made into a flute. When it is blown, it sounds the voice of the child telling how she was killed.]

Iwasaki Toshio
Iwaki-gun, Fukushima

## 49. The Father's Gift

Once upon a time there was a mean stepmother at a certain place. She wanted to somehow kill the two girls of her husband's former wife, but it was difficult to find a chance. Then the father had to go to Edo on business. In the evening before he was to start, he said to his daughters, "I want to buy gifts in Edo to bring back to you. What would you like to have?"

The older girl said, "I want a pair of gold scissors." The younger girl said, "Please buy me a little gold box." The father promised to bring them, then he left.

After the father had gone, the stepmother said to the girls, "You must help me with the housework since your father has gone away. Go to the well and dip up water with a basket." The two girls carried the basket between them to the well to dip up the water. No matter how hard they tried, they could not dip up enough water to fill their bucket.

While they were crying about it, a kind little mother from next door came and asked, "What are you crying about?" She felt sorry for them when they told her. She explained, "Take off your dresses and soak them in the water and then wring them out. Then you can dip up the water with them."

After they had dipped up the water and taken it home, the stepmother saw that her plan had failed and she was disappointed.

On the next day the stepmother said, "This time, take the wooden ladle with you to cut bamboo grass for me." The girls did as she said and took the wooden ladle to the hills. They tried to cut the bamboo grass, but there was no way to do it. While they sobbed and cried, the kind little mother from next door came again and asked why they were crying. She felt sorry for them and cut the bamboo grass with her own sickle. The girls carried the bamboo grass home on their shoulders gladly. The stepmother had failed again in her plan and was disappointed.

The stepmother thought if she did not kill the girls then, her husband might come home before she could do what she had in mind. She got out the big kettle and filled it with water. After she had brought the water to a boil, she laid two slender chopsticks across the kettle and hung two ground cherries on the other side. She called the older girl and said, "I will give you those ground cherries, so go get them."

The woman forced the girl to cross on the chopsticks. The sticks broke suddenly and the girl fell into the water and died. Then the stepmother called the younger girl and said, "I will give you those ground cherries, so go get them."

That girl, too, fell into the kettle. That night the stepmother buried the older girl under the shoulder of the bridge that crossed the big river and she buried the younger girl by the well. She acted as though nothing had happened as she waited for her husband to come home.

The father finished his business in Edo, bought the gold scissors and the little gold box, and started home. When he arrived as far as the shoulder of the bridge across the big river, he heard a sad little song coming from somewhere. It said, "Father, we do not need the gold scissors or little gold box anymore, *chin chirori*!"

The father thought this strange as he went on toward his house. When he went to the well to wash his feet, he heard it again, "Father, we do not need the gold scissors and the little gold box any more, *chin chirori*."

This was something out of the ordinary. The father hurried into the house and asked his wife, "Where did my little girls go?" She answered, "They went somewhere to play this morning and have not come back yet."

"If that's true, all right," he declared. He put his hoe across his shoulder and went to the approach to the bridge and dug. There he found the bones of his older daughter. Then he went to the well and dug beside it and found his younger daughter's bones.

He asked their stepmother angrily, "Are you going to lie in spite of this?"

She could not stay after her wickedness had been discovered, and she ran away.

Kato Kaichi
Haga-gun, Tochigi

## 50. The Girl Without Hands

Once there was a happy couple and their sweet little girl named Oharu in a certain place. When the little girl was four years old, her mother suddenly took sick and died and went to the other world.

Her father married again, but the new wife hated her stepchild Oharu intensely. She wanted to find a way to kill her, but the child was intelligent, and the stepmother could not find an excuse.

Days and months passed, then a year and another with her still hating the child, until the spring in which Oharu was a young girl of fifteen. She was lovelier than words could describe, lovelier than any picture. This made the stepmother more bitter than ever. The woman thought, "What a hateful girl! What can I do to her?"

Then a chance came for her to say to Oharu's father, "I cannot live any longer with such a clever girl as Oharu. Please let me go back to my home."

Oharu's father was controlled by his wife. He said, "Don't worry. I will kill Oharu presently for you with a little ax."

Thus the man decided to kill Oharu, who had done no wrong.

On a day soon after that, the father said, "Oharu, let's go to the festival this month." He had her dress in prettier clothes than she had ever worn before and they set out for the festival. The weather was beautiful that day, and Oharu set out with a light heart at the invitation of her father. But as they went deeper and deeper into the hills, Oharu grew uneasy because her father had said they were going to the festival. She asked, "Where is the festival, Father?"

He answered, "It is a festival by a castle beyond one or two mountains." When they had crossed the second mountain and were in a valley, he said, "Let's eat lunch." He took out the riceballs he had brought and they ate together. Oharu was so tired that she began to doze.

Her father took that time to take the little ax he had stuck into his belt and cut off first Oharu's right arm, then the left. He left her crying there and went back over the mountains. Oharu was covered with blood and stumbled and fell as she tried to run after him. She cried, "Wait for me, Father! It hurts, Father!" The only response was the echo in the valley.

"Oh, what misery! What fate could have made my good father do such a thing to me?" Oharu thought, for she no longer had a home to go to. She washed her wounds in the stream in the valley and ate fruit on trees and plants for two or three days to keep alive. Then a handsome young man on horseback came by with a companion. He stared in surprise at Oharu, who was moving in a thicket. He said, "You aren't a bird, you aren't an animal. Your hair looks like that of a human being, but you don't have hands. What sort of being are you?"

Oharu said, "I am ashamed to say, young Sir, that I have been abandoned by my good father, and I am destined to be left in this world without hands." Beyond that she would only weep. But the young man did not understand why it had happened, so he inquired and heard her story. He was filled with pity and said, "How sad! What strange things happen! At any rate, come to my home." He put Oharu on his horse and they went down the mountain.

When they came to the young man's home, he went to his mother and said, "I did not do any hunting today, but I found an unusual girl without hands in the mountains and brought her home. She is a pathetic girl, so please let her stay here." Then he told his mother all he knew about Oharu's story. His mother was a good person, too. She washed the girl's face and combed her hair and tied it up for her. Except for not having hands, the girl was as lovely as a flower. The mother was happy for her and loved her as her own daughter.

After a long time passed, the young man went to his mother. He knelt and bowed low as he said, "Mother, I have the most important request in my life to make. Please let Oharu become my bride."

"When it comes to Oharu, you are not alone in thinking that," said his mother. "I have been thinking the same thing." She agreed, and the beautiful ceremony was promptly performed.

Oharu was loved by her young husband and presently she became pregnant. She and her mother-in-law lived pleasantly together when her husband had to go to Edo suddenly on business. Before he set out regretfully on his journey, he said to his mother, "Please send me word when Oharu's baby is born." His mother assured him there was nothing for him to worry about, and promised to send him a message by a fast courier.

When Oharu's time had come, she gave birth to a boy as lovely as a jewel. "How well you have done," said the son's mother. "Now I must let my son know immediately."

She wrote the happy news and hired the courier next door to carry the letter. He set out, crossing one mountain and next, but he became thirsty as he went. He stopped at a certain house for a drink of water. It happened to be the house where Oharu was born. Her stepmother asked him where he was going. He said thoughtlessly, "The bride Oharu at the chōja's house, a girl without hands, has given birth to a baby, and I am carrying a message to the young husband in Edo."

In this way the stepmother learned that Oharu was still alive. She suddenly became very attentive to the messenger. She said, "It must be very important for you to go to Edo in this hot weather. Please rest a while."

The woman served the courier fish and wine to make him drunk. Then she took the letter out of his box and read it. As she read, she exclaimed, "How hateful! A little boy like a jewel, too lovely to describe, has been born." She wrote, "A monster, hard to describe, a demon or a snake, has been born." She substituted her letter for the one in the box.

The messenger woke up from the nap he had been taking after all he had eaten and drunk. He declared, "Wonderful! What hospitality I have enjoyed!" The stepmother fawned on him to make a good impression. She said, "Please be sure to stop by on your way back and tell me all about Edo."

In Edo, the young father read the letter and wrote his reply, "Even if it is a demon or a snake, take good care of it until I get home." He sent his letter back with the courier.

Remembering the good natured woman's invitation at that house, the messenger thought he would stop in for some more wine on his way back. The stepmother greeted him, "Well, are you on your way back? Please come in." She repeated her former hospitality, leading the man into the parlor and urging him to drink more and more until he was drunk.

After the man had fallen asleep, the stepmother wrote a heartless reply. "I don't want to see the child and I don't want to see that handless Oharu. If you don't drive her and the child out, I'll stay in Edo for the rest of my life." Again, she put her note into the courier's box.

When the messenger had eaten and drunk and slept as much as he wanted, he thanked the stepmother and went on his way over one mountain and another, reaching home at last.

The mother read the unthinkable letter from her son. "Oh, how terrible," she cried. She asked the messenger if he had stopped anywhere on his way. He said, "I didn't stop anywhere. I went as straight as a horse with blinds to Edo and came straight back."

The mother thought even then that she should wait until her son had come home. She thought he might return that day or the next, and she didn't show the letter to Oharu. She waited still another day, but it did not seem that her son was going to return. She made some excuse to call Oharu and wept as she told her about the letter from her son. Oharu could not reply because of her grief. She only cried and cried.

Presently, she said, "I regret leaving without having done anything in return for your kindness in caring for this crippled girl, but if it is the will of my young husband, I will leave without a word of parting." She asked her mother-in-law to tie her baby on her back. She said her farewell and cried as she left the mansion.

Oharu left her home, but she had no place to go. She followed whichever way her steps turned, whichever way the wind blew, going on aimlessly. She became thirsty as she walked around and decided to drink from a little stream she saw. When she crouched to drink, her baby started to slip off her back. "Oh, somebody. . . ." she exclaimed, and tried to push him back without hands.

But a strange thing happened. Both her hands appeared again, and she held her baby from falling.

"How happy I am! My hands have grown back!" thought Oharu, overcome with joy and thankfulness.

In the meantime, her young husband came home on the following day, eager to see his child and hoping Oharu was well, only to find that Oharu and his baby had left in tears. As he listened to what had happened, he became suspicious of the courier next door. He questioned him closely, and the man finally told what had really happened and why—about stopping at the woman's house and how he drank. His mother said, "Oh, what a pity! Don't wait a moment. Look for Oharu right away." So her son set out quickly to look for her.

When the young father came to a shrine by a stream he saw a beggar woman nursing her child as she prayed earnestly. She looked exactly like Oharu from behind, but this woman had two hands. He thought it strange and spoke to her. He said, "I wonder if you could be Oharu."

She exclaimed, "Oh, it is my young husband."

"You are Oharu, after all, and this is our baby?" he asked. "You have had to suffer bitterly, but your hands—how did you get them?"

Oharu wept as she told her husband and he wept as he listened. Beautiful flowers blossomed where their tears flowed, and as the three of them took the road home, trees and plants burst into bloom along the way.

Oharu's stepmother and her father were punished by the authorities for mistreating her. They were led to the crossroads and killed there.

*Dondo hare.*

Hirano Tadashi
Hienuki-gun, Iwate

# 5. Brothers Not Alike

## 51. The Brothers

*Mukashi atta zon.*

There used to be a very deep pond called Akafuchi in the valley where reeds grow at Shimokawara of Kakunodate-machi. Lots of cinnabar lay on its bottom. In those days there were two brothers at Shimokawara who went every day to dive to the bottom of the pond to collect cinnabar. They made a living by taking it to town to sell.

The younger brother, unlike his older brother, for some reason had a bad nature. He began to think about how much he could earn if he went to get the cinnabar alone. One evening he thought of a shrewd plan. He got a lot of red lacquered bowls and strung them together into a big, frightful looking dragon head. He took this secretly to Akafuchi and left it floating there. The next morning his unsuspecting older brother went as usual to gather cinnabar. When he saw the big dragon with its red mouth open, ready to come swallow him, he turned pale and ran home.

The younger brother saw that his plan had worked well. He began to go alone to collect cinnabar to sell, and he became very rich. One day when he set out as usual, it seemed to him that the dragon looked alive when he started to go into the water. There was no reason for that, because this was something he had himself made and set afloat.

When he braced himself and started to gather up the cinnabar, the dragon came at him, really alive. It opened its big mouth and swallowed that bad-natured brother.

That is why one should not try to do something alone for his own profit.

*Naa.*

Mutō Tetsujō
Senhoku-gun, Akita

## 52. The Younger Brother's Success

Long, long ago there were three brothers. The oldest was named Ichirōji, the next was Jirōji, and the youngest was Saburōji. The oldest was good-hearted but rather unsteady in character. When Ichirōji was twenty, Jirōji was eighteen, and Saburōji was sixteen, their father called the three of them to him and said, "You boys are now at the age to succeed, but if you stay around home all the time, it will do you no good. I am going to give you three years in which to go out into the world to make good in any way you want to. Then please come home."

He gave each of his sons five ryō in little gold coins. Jirōji and Saburōji both assured their father that they would come home successful after three years. Only Ichirōji said nothing.

Soon the night of the fifteenth of the month came, and the three brothers set out for distant places. They went along a mountain road past ripening grain nodding in the wind until they came to a three-way crossing. They rested there for the night. Jirōji said in the morning, "It is not good for the three of us to go along together every day. Let's take different roads from here and go home after we are successful. Let's separate here."

When Saburōji heard that he said, "Yes, it is as Jirōji says. Let's do that."

Ichirōji, too, said, "It's a good idea."

The three agreed to meet at that place three years later. As they parted, Ichirōji took the road to the right, Jirōji took the middle road, and Saburōji took the road to the left.

Well, to start with, Ichirōji, who took the road to the right, had no special plan, and he walked along aimlessly for a while after he had parted from his brothers. He was in the mountains, but presently he came to a big pond like Meihire-numa. There were a lot of wild geese there. Ichirōji thought he would like to try to catch one. He looked for a stone to throw, but since he could not find one, he reached into his bosom and took out his gold coins. He threw them one after another at the geese, but his aim was not sure. He could not hit a single goose. All he did was throw his money away.

Ichirōji walked on until nightfall. He was hungry, but he thought that if he kept on walking, he would find something. He was worried because he had no money. He went on until he came to a little shrine beside the road. he went in and fell asleep. In the night he heard something or other calling, "Here, Ichirōji, Ichirōji!" He got up and looked around this way and that, but he couldn't see anything. He thought a fox or a badger was making a fool of him, and he went back to sleep. The same voice called even louder, "Ichirōji, Ichirōji!"

Ichirōji exclaimed, "What's going on!" He looked around carefully and found a broken bowl calling him from the corner of the shrine. He said to it, "So it's you who has been calling me, is it? I thought it was a fox or badger."

The bowl said, "Yes, I'm the one. You might be a man, but look at you—you're going around without any money and with only the clothes on your back. You can't keep that up forever. How about coming and working with me?"

"Well, what kind of work can you do?" asked Ichirōji. The bowl only answered, "If you do as I say, it will be all right." After talking together, they went to sleep for the rest of the night.

From the evening of the next day, Ichirōji put the chipped bowl into the bosom of his clothes and set out for town. He went to a rich man's house after it was quiet and everyone was asleep. He let the bowl crawl through the hole for the cat into the house. Then the bowl opened the door from the inside and let Ichirōji in. He stole money and all kinds of treasures. In this way Ichirōji became a famous robber.

Next, I will tell you about Jirōji, who took the middle road. He was naturally quiet and had the best nature among the three brothers. He lost confidence in himself after he left Ichirōji and Saburōji. He wanted to quickly find a place where people lived. In the meantime night came on. He gave up and sat down disappointed on the grass beside the road. While he was sitting there, thinking vacantly about home and his brothers, something under his seat called to him, "Here, Jirōji, Jirōji!" He was surprised and looked around under where he was sitting. He found a ladle there.

He exclaimed, "What's going on here? Are you the one who called me? You scared me!"

The ladle answered, "Oh, there's nothing for you to be scared of. I'll tell you something good. The fact is, the daughter of a chōja who lives about one ri from here is very ill. Itinerate priests and yamabushi go every day to pray and doctors go to treat her, but such men have no pity for her. They do not cure her and she just gets worse every day. There is no sense in the way they try to cure her. If you turn me over and stroke the girl's seat with me, she will get well right away."

"If I stroke her with your right side, what will happen?" asked Jirōji.

If you stroke her with my right side, that will make her all the worse," answered the ladle. "That's why I want you to take me to the young lady and try stroking her seat. Of course, it's going to be difficult to get the chance to stroke the girl's seat, but as things are she may die any day now, so you must lose no time."

Jirōji was naturally well behaved, and he thought there could be nothing better than to cure somebody of a serious illness. He put the ladle into his bosom hurriedly and set out immediately, even though it was night, to the chōja's house. Sure enough, he could hear the girl groaning from the entrance of the house.

Jirōji entered and said he wanted to cure the young lady. By then the family were ready to try anything, so he was hired. Jirōji sent everybody out of the room for a while, and set up a screen around the girl. Then he took the ladle from his bosom and began to stroke the girl's seat slowly. Although she had been groaning until then, she suddenly became well. The chōja was delighted. The family declared that Jirōji had saved the girl's life and they showed him great hospitality. It followed that Jirōji was married to the girl.

Now I will tell you about the youngest brother, Saburōji. Although he was young, he was the bravest of the three brothers. He strode down the road to the left, but no matter how far he walked, he was still in the mountains at sunset. The evening wind was blowing through the pines as he came to a place that made him feel uneasy. He was tired from walking all day, so he decided to spend the night under a pine tree.

While he rested, a sudden damp, fishy-smelling wind rustled across the grass. Saburōji was startled and looked quickly behind. He saw a great snake stick out its bright red forked tongue and come rolling and coiling toward him.

Saburōji climbed the pine tree in fright. The snake came up to it and looked up, his long tongue darting out. Then it spied Saburōji and began to crawl up the tree. Saburōji wondered what to do as the snake came higher and higher. It was a matter of life or death, and he began to pray, "Nammanda, Nammanda," trembling all the while. He trembled so much that his sash came loose and the money tucked in his bosom fell into the open mouth of the snake below. It stuck in the snake's throat and the strangled snake slid back down.

While Saburōji was feeling relieved about that, a feudal lord and his followers came along and saw the snake in agony. "This is a great deed," exclaimed the feudal lord.

"It is hard to say how many people have been tormented by this snake, and here you have come and saved us by killing it. Come with me!"

He took Saburōji with him back to his castle. Saburōji became a samurai and was given the duty of destroying bad men.

Time goes quickly and soon the third year came. The wind blew through the arrowroot vines, bending the ripe grain and calling out the autumn moon. Ichirōji, who had become a thief, began to think of his home. "Alas, I have spent my time in this way. I wonder what my father is doing by now," he thought.

He was a thief, but he was not really greedy. He had been giving all his money to the poor. He sighed as he sat dressed in poor clothes on a ruined veranda. "That's it," he thought. "I have promised my brothers and I must go home, but I can't go like this to my father. I must steal one more time to take something to him as a gift."

The broken bowl in his bosom agreed. "Sure, tonight we will do something clever."

There was Jirōji, now the son-in-law of the chōja. He had no worries about money, but he used that ladle to cure sick people here and there. Everybody was grateful to the son-in-law of the chōja. He had cured somebody that very day and now he was bathed and sitting on the veranda, looking at the full moon as it rose over the mountain beyond. He thought, "Here it is, the Fifteenth Day of the Eighth month. I promised to go home on the Fifteenth Day of the Ninth Month. I wonder what my older and younger brothers are doing. I must keep my promise and go home."

He got a 500 ryō box ready to take as a gift and waited for the day.

Saburōji was in another place, thinking constantly of his home and even dreaming of his brothers at night. Days passed, one after another, until it was the first day of the Ninth Month. It would be time for him to start home by the next day. Then there was a complaint that 500 ryō had been stolen from the local chōja the night before. The problem conflicted with Saburōji's plan to go home that day, but he put all his efforts into catching the thief.

The result was that he caught a filthy beggar dressed in rags. When he questioned the thief, he proved to be his older brother Ichirōji, and strangest of all, the chōja's son-in-law, who had reported the theft, was his brother Jirōji. The three brothers wept together, their hearts full of recollections. How surprised their father was when they called on him the next day.

In the past, three brothers felt such close ties.

This is a tale told by a zatō, but it is well told.

Momoo-gun, Miyagi

## 53. The Sister and Her Younger Brother

Once there was a poor girl and her younger brother who lived together. The boy went to school. One day his friends at school said, "Let's have a contest with fans tomorrow." The boy went home and told his sister about it. She hunted out the frame of an old fan and pasted paper onto it. Then she drew a picture on it of a plum tree and a nightingale.

When the boy went to school, he saw all the gold and silver fans of his friends. He was so ashamed of his that he was the last to bring his out. When he spread his fan open, the nightingale flew out and lighted on the tip of the fan. His fan took first place.

Then the brother's friends said, "Let's have a boat race this time." The boy asked his sister to make him a boat. She made a little boat and put three little clay dolls into it. The boy's boat was very crude, but when it raced, the three little dolls set up their oars and started to row. The brother's boat won the race.

Iwakura Ichirō
Shimokoshiki-mura, Satsuma-gun, Kagoshima

### A second story:

There once was a girl named Hana-no-senmatsu and her younger brother. The boy went to school and could do anything better than his friends. One day his friends said they would give him a banquet. When he told his sister about it, she warned him to take the lid off the bowls and look at them. He could eat anything that was in a bowl whose lid had steam on it, but not to eat it if there was no steam.

The boy went to where his friends had gathered and the banquet was served. When he lifted the lids to the bowls, there was no steam on any of them. There was no steam on the rice bowl, either, when it was served. The boy did just as his sister had said and did not eat anything, but he unconsciously licked off one grain of rice that had stuck to his hand. He died as soon as he got home.

When his friends came to see, the sister pretended to be her younger brother and looked unconcerned. His friends went back to the banquet and ate everything and died. The sister gathered a thousand kinds of flowers. She extracted their juice and spread it over her brother's body and brought him back to life.

Iwakura Ichirō
Satsuma-gun, Kagoshima

## 54. The Three Brothers

*Mukashi attaja mo na.*

Three brothers were once given 100 ryō each and a storehouse was built for each of them. They were told that they would have three years in which to fill their storehouses. The one who put things of the most value into his storehouse would inherit the estate.

The third son went to Kyoto and bought all kinds of silk to put into his storehouse. The second son started to trade in rice, and he stored a great amount in his storehouse.

When the oldest son left home, he said, "I don't want anything. I just want the ends of three burnt logs to plug up the mouths of fellows who say mean things." He walked off aimlessly.

As the oldest son passed the Kannon temple at Kurokawa, he noticed it was badly in need of repair. He wanted to put new thatch on the roof, so he hired villagers to thatch it. He was pleased with the results, but when he came to Gongen by the gate, that shrine, too, was dilapidated, standing as it did in the wind and rain. He had the villagers thatch that roof, too. The two buildings looked splendid after that, but he saw that people had difficulty when they came to worship because there was no bridge at Kitakamigawa. He decided that a bridge should be built, and hired carpenters to construct it. By then all his 100 ryō were gone.

The man was pleased to see people flocking from nearby places to worship after the bridge was built across Kitakamigawa. He decided to spend the night at the Kannon shrine. He had a revelation in a dream that night that he had received a fishing pole, and when he woke up, there was a fishing pole by his pillow. He took it with him and spent the next night at Gongen's shrine. This time he dreamed that he got a fan that would restore youth and a tin flask of sacred wine. When he woke up and looked around he saw a youth-restoring fan and a tin flask of sacred wine by his pillow.

The man carried them all to the bridge he had made. When he tried fishing, he pulled up a little bag. He opened it to see what was inside, and money came pouring out until the bridge was covered with money. He stuffed it all back into the bag and decided to go home.

At home they were talking about the inspection of the storehouses the next day. The oldest son's wife was so worried she could not sleep. Her husband came back in the night and told her to get up and have a drink of wine. She said, "This is no time for drinking. Tomorrow is the day when your relatives are going to gather to examine the storehouses. Your two brothers have lots of things in theirs. I am worried because your storehouse has nothing in it."

Her husband assured her, "There's nothing to worry about. Get up and have some wine, anyway." He got out his tin flask and poured her some wine. Even though it was a little flask, wine kept coming out, no matter how many times the man poured from it. Then he said his wife should go in front of the storehouse door.

She did so because he insisted. He went to a window and opened his little bag and shook it. Soon the storehouse was full of coins that fell with a clatter. They even began to spill out of the front door where his wife was standing. She held the door as best she could, but coins began to spill out the window. The man stopped shaking the coins out then and the two of them went to bed to sleep.

When the relatives gathered the next day to inspect the storehouses, the oldest son got out his little flask of wine and treated them all. No matter how many times he filled their cups, it did not give out. Instead of serving them food, he gave each of his relatives two coins. They wondered where he got them. Then it was time to look over the storehouses.

They went to the youngest son's storehouse first. It was so full of all kinds of silk that they could not figure its worth. When they went to the second son's storehouse, it was crammed with rice, and that, too, was something great.

They finally came to the oldest son's storehouse. Nobody thought there was any use in looking into an empty storehouse, but they decided not to pass it by. When the relatives tried to open the door, they found it was difficult to move. They thought it strange. Four or five of them forced the door open, and the money came spilling out. The estate went to the oldest son after all.

Later the oldest son got out the little youth-restoring fan he had received at Gongen's shrine. He made his mother and his wife younger with it. His mother wanted to be still younger, so she hunted out the youth-restoring fan one day when her son was away. She fanned herself until she became too young. She turned into a child crawling all around.

*Dotto harai.*

Ogasawara Kenkichi
Shiwa-gun, Iwate

# 6. *Finding Treasures*

## 55. Goro's Broken Bowl

Once upon a time there was a man who had three sons, called Tarō, Jirō and Saburō. He called them to him one day and gave each some money. He said, "I am giving you this money and I want you to go away for three years to do what you want. Come back as a success then."

The two younger sons were hard workers. Jirō became a dealer in cotton goods, and Saburō became a dealer in rice. Only the oldest boy, who was always lazy, put the money into his bosom and set out alone into the mountains. He met a yamauba such as he had never seen before. When she saw Tarō, she asked what he had come for. He told her everything. She said she would hire Tarō for three years, so he stayed and worked for her for three years.

After the three years were up, the yamauba called Tarō to her and said, "You have worked well for three years. I will give you this bowl in payment. Take good care of it." Tarō put the filthy bowl carefully into his bosom and went home.

Jirō and Saburō came home as successful merchants, but Tarō came home in dirty, ragged clothes, and his father was displeased. He looked at Tarō and asked, "What did you learn? You have come home looking filthy." The bowl in Tarō's bosom said, "Tell him you learned thieving."

Tarō said, "I have learned nothing but thieving, and have come home." His father said, "Let's see you try to steal our horse tonight."

In the meantime, the sun set. The father tied his horse in its stall and hired three young men to guard it. He tied a scallop shell onto the dog's mouth. When Tarō put the bowl into his bosom and went toward the stable, the bowl fell out by itself and began to dig a hole. Presently it had dug a hole big enough for the horse to be led out on the other side of the stable. It shouted, "Now's the time to steal the horse!"

The young men in the yard shouted, "The thief has come now." There was a lot of confusion and the dog blew on its shell as it barked. They forgot all about the horse and just milled around. Tarō took that time to lead the horse out of the hole to his father. He said, "Well, I stole the horse!" His father felt better about him and admired him.

Tarō took charge of Jirō and Saburō and they lived in comfort for the rest of their lives.

Noda Tarō
Sannohe-gun, Aomori

### 56. The Power of Treasures

There was an old man and an old woman in a certain place. In the morning, the old man swept his dirt-floored workroom and the old woman swept the inside of their house.

The old woman picked up a bean in their parlor. She said, "I found a bean. What shall we do with it?" The old man told her to put it in the cupboard. But as she was putting the bean into the cupboard, it fell from her hand and rolled into a knothole in the floor.

She exclaimed, "Look! The bean rolled into the knothole. What shall we do?" The old man said, "That's all right. I'll go and get it." So he went into the knothole.

He went farther and farther until he came to a big parlor. One of the Little Folk was standing there. When the old man went toward him, he said, "Old man, imitate a cock's crow." The old man tried crowing loudly, "Kokekko!"

The little man said, "Yes, you do it very well. I will give you this as a reward." He gave the old man a kaburewarashi [a homely little boy like Hyottoko]. The old man said, "I don't want anything like this," and he started to throw it away.

The little boy said with a faint voice, "Don't throw me away." The old man repeated, "I'm going to throw you away." Again the kaburewarashi said, "Don't throw me away." So the old man gave up trying to throw him away and went home, forgetting all about the bean.

When he reached home, the old man said, "I'm home now. I brought a little child home." Since the old woman had never had a child, she wondered what kind of child it was. She said, "Hurry, let me see the child." When the old woman saw the little boy her old man had brought home, he was so ugly that she did not know what to say. He had an even bigger navel than Hyottoko. Besides, he was filthy and his feet were crippled. He was about the size of the Little Folk. He looked so much like a goblin that she nearly fell over in surprise.

She said angrily, "They wouldn't keep him even at a hungry demon's house."

But her old man said, "Well, wait. Since he asked over and over for me not to throw him away, I can hardly do that." He calmed his old woman down and they kept the kaburewarashi and cared for him.

After ten years, the little boy had grown quite a bit, but the old man and the old woman had become more frail. One day the kaburewarashi said to the old man, "I am obliged to you for caring for me all this time, but I have not been able to do anything for you in return. I want to go home now and tell my father about it and repay your kindness. Please have a happy life together." Then he went away somewhere.

After that the home of the old man and the old woman began to prosper until they became the foremost chōja in the village.

Sasaki Kizen
Waga-gun, Iwate

## 57. Hachikoku Yama

Once there was an older brother who was very rich, but stingy. His younger brother was poor, but he had a good character. One year the younger brother went to borrow seed-rice from his brother. The older man put the seed into hot water before he gave it to him.

Not knowing this, the young man planted the seed in his seed-bed, but not a single sprout appeared. Oddly enough, a single calabash came up in his field. There was nothing he could do about it, so he took good care of the calabash. It grew until it covered the surface of the whole field. Many flowers bloomed on it and many calabashes formed.

Since the younger brother had no rice that year, he decided to eat calabash. He picked the first one that ripened and tried to cut it open with his kitchen knife. It was too hard to cut, so he got out his ax and split it open. White rice came pouring out. The young man delighted. He picked another calabash to see what would come out, and more white rice came out. While he cut many calabashes, the heap of rice grew as big as a mountain. Thus the younger brother became a famous chōja.

Sasaki Kizen
Shiwa-gun, Iwate

## 58. "Hold Fast or Stick Fast"

Once upon a time there was a very honest man in a certain place. When he was coming home from the hills along a path one night, a voice shouted from the big tree directly above him, "I want to jump onto you. I want to jump onto you."

The old man was not in the least frightened. He promptly shouted back, "Jump away!" Something came falling onto the old man's back with a jangle. He could not get it off easily, but it seemed to be something like a box. When he reached home, he lifted the lid to see. It was full of little gold coins. His household suddenly became very wealthy.

The bad old man living next door heard about what had happened and wanted to get coins for himself. When he was below that cryptomeria tree, something came flying onto him. He went home smiling and called, "Old woman, bring a light." His old wife lighted a pine torch hurriedly. When she came close, she saw pine pitch on her old man's back. It caught fire and the old man burned to death.

Moriguchi Seiichi
Arita-gun, Wakayama

### 59. "Carry Me on Your Back"

There was an old temple where nobody lived any more because of reports that it was haunted. One day a brave young man went there to destroy the ghost. While he was asleep in the main hall, a ghost came out of the base of the pillar by the main altar. It said, "I'll climb onto your back. I'll climb onto your back."

The young man answered, "I'll carry you on my back, so get on." It said, "See, I am getting onto your back," as something fell with a clatter onto the young man. He looked in the morning to see what it was. It was all big and little gold coins. Life had entered the old coins, and that is why they appeared as a ghost.

Kawai Yūtarō
Tsugaru, Aomori

### 60. Heaven's Blessings and Earth's Blessings

Well, once upon a time there were two old women, one a good one and the other a grasping one, who lived as neighbors in a certain place. The good old woman wanted to go to worship Shaka on the 8th Day of the Fourth Month and she went to her grasping old neighbor to invite her to go along. "How about it?" she asked. "Would you like to come with me to worship O'Shaka Sama?" Her stingy neighbor refused, saying, "I don't get anything out of going to worship O'Shaka Sama, so I don't do it."

There was nothing more to say, so the good old woman set out alone. She found a little bag of money that had been dropped on the way. She wondered who had dropped it as she picked it up and wrapped it around the railing of the bridge. Then she went on to the temple. After she had worshipped Shaka, she went home and told everybody about what had happened. She wondered how to return the money to whoever had dropped it.

The greedy old neighbor happened to go to her house and when she heard about the bag of money, her spirit of greed was aroused. She wanted to get that money somehow. She suddenly decided to go herself to worship Shaka. When she reached the bridge, she found that a scary looking snake instead of a bag of coins was wrapped around the railing. She was provoked and lost her temper. She thought, "A bag of money or whatever it is, my neighbor did a good job of fooling folks. I will get even with her in some way."

She split the tip of a bamboo stick to pick up the snake and carried it off. She took it to her good neighbor's house and threw it through the window. There was the clinking sound of money when she did that, but she could not see the snake she had thrown anywhere when she peeked through a hole in the shōji. For some reason, there was money scattered around the house.

The good old woman was sewing in her house and was surprised to see something come flying through her window with a clatter. It was that little bag that she had left wrapped onto the railing of the bridge that day, and money was coming pouring out and scattering all over her house.

The old woman thought that it was unusual and wanted to show it to her old man. She picked up the money bag and set it aside to show him when he came home. The old man came home presently, and the old woman told him all about everything and showed him the bag. He was surprised, too, but he said, "It looks as if what you tied onto the railing of a bridge came flying here by itself. It must have been its own money. Then it is all right for us to keep it."

The old couple rejoiced together. They went to buy sacred wine to offer to Shaka and invited their neighbors in for a feast. As we might expect, the greedy old neighbor looked on at the festivities dumbfounded. She repented and said, "What was really a money bag looked like a snake to me. It does not pay to do bad things."

*Sore mo sorekkiri.*

Dobashi Riki
Nishiyatsushiro-gun, Yamanashi

## 61. The Snake and the Treasure of Gold

Once upon a time there was an old man living in Otomo-mura. Every time he went to Yokota (now called Tōno), he would buy a chipped clay mixing bowl and go home wearing it on his head. When people asked him what he was doing with it, he would say, "Oh, this! I was thinking of using it for the roof over my bathroom"

This old man had a dream one night in which gold came raining down from the sky. When he was digging in his yard the next day to plant a tree, he struck a jar. He wondered what it was. He lifted the lid and saw it was full of big and little shining gold coins.

He said, "But the dream I had last night was about treasure falling from the sky, and this treasure is in the ground. This is not for me." He put the jar lid back and buried the jar again.

The old man next door was looking on and wondered what the old man was saying to himself and what he was digging. After the good old man stood up and went away, the neighbor crawled under the hedge and turned over the newly dug dirt to see. He found the jar. "That's it," he thought. "The old man was hiding this jar." He took off the lid and looked in. A snake was wiggling around inside. The neighbor complained, "I don't like that old man!"

He carried the jar up onto the old man's roof, ripped a hole in the thatch, and threw the snake from the jar into the house, saying, "Now, look at this!"

In the meantime, the old man was eating his supper unaware of anything. Then big and little shiny gold coins came showering down from overhead. He laid his chopsticks down and exclaimed in delight, "Now, this is it. This is it. It's just like my dream last night. This treasure has fallen from heaven, so it is for me." With that he became a chōja.

Sasaki Kizen
Kamihei-gun, Iwate

## 62. Finding a Treasure

Once there was an old man and an old woman in a certain place who had all kinds of difficulties because they had no children. Since the old man was a wood gatherer, he had to go back and forth to the hills every day.

One day as the old man was walking along a path, he heard something call by the stream in the opposite hills. It said, "Danger, danger!" The old man wondered what it was. He heard it again the next morning.

The old man took the path leading to the river and looked around, but he saw nothing. He decided he had only thought he had heard something and started to leave. He heard something call again, "Danger, danger!" He stopped to listen. He saw a big jar about to fall into the river where the bank was crumbling. That was what it was. When the old man saw that, he thought, "There must be something in that jar that is calling."

The water was deep at the crossing and the old man looked on, worrying about it, but the jar kept on calling. The old man crossed the stream and managed to bring the jar back in his arms to his side of the river. Wondering what was in it that was calling, he took off the lid and looked inside. It was full of large and small gold coins. The astonished old man tied the jar onto his back and went home.

The old man and his old woman were delighted because they could live without any more difficulties. They became chōja.

Sasaki Kizen
Kamihei-gun, Iwate

## 63. The Jar of Gold Coins

Once upon a time there was a poor old man and old woman. They went to the hills to work in their garden patch one day. While they were trampling down the soil to smooth it, they stepped onto a jar that was there. They wondered what was in it. They found that it was full of money that shone blue. They did not want to keep it for fear of arousing the feudal lord's suspicions and decided to take it to him the next morning.

They enjoyed talking it over in the evening and pretended they had received money. The greedy old woman next door overheard them. She decided to dig the money out before they delivered it to the feudal lord.

The old woman next door took her old man with her to dig out the jar in the hills. When they lifted the lid, they were sure they saw it full of money shining blue. They were delighted as they carried it home. They lifted the lid once more at home to count how much money there was. Although there should have been money that shone blue in it, for some reason, a lot of blue snakes came gliding out.

The greedy old woman was angry, for she thought the old man next door had fooled her. She and her old man put the snakes back into the jar and carried it next door. They set up a ladder and climbed onto the roof and threw the jar down where the two neighbors were eating.

This time, instead of blue snakes, lots of blue shining pieces of gold fell with a clatter. As the happy couple picked it up, they said, "This is what is called money that falls from heaven." The two of them became chōja and lived happy after that.

This is why people must be honest.

Noda Tayoko
Aomori

## 64. The Snake in the Jar

A report that something was written is at Kōraji (now Dotō Yakushi) about a treasure has been handed down since long ago. That entry is said to be:

At the base of a mulberry pillar standing where the rising sun and setting sun shine on it, 1000 ryō of gold, 1000 ryō of mercury, 1000 lacquered wine cups, and 1000 bundles of rope . . . .

Many people have wanted to dig out this treasure, but they could not understand the meaning of the entry: "at the base of the mulberry pillar standing where the rising sun and setting sun shine on it." Nobody has found the treasure. (Regarding this, Mr. Mitsukawa, now a member of the village council, has related the following.)

When I was a child, two or three friends and I used to play behind the Yakushi temple. One day we found an old jar sticking out of the ground. Thinking it strange, we dug it up. A snake was coiled in the jar and below it there was a lot of what looked like black lacquer. It surprised us to see the snake, but it was small and really beautiful. We did not dislike it, and we took it home. We gave the jar to the priest at the temple. We gave the snake to the old man next door because he said he wanted it.

The next morning we remembered the cute little snake and we went next door. The old man's wife was there. We asked to see the snake we had found the day before, but she said her husband had taken it away somewhere that morning. Just then the old man came home and we asked where he had taken the snake. He only laughed and would not tell.

The old man's family became visibly prosperous because of this happening. He built a storehouse in a short time and he could buy land to grow rice. Villagers thought it strange and started this rumor. That little snake seemed really dangerous. The night the old man got the snake, he had a revelation about it and he gave it to Benten at Waka-zakura. It was said that later the priest sold an old jar for a good price to a store in town. Rumor says that it could be sold for a high price in Kyoto.

Taniguchi Tetsumi
Iwami-gun, Tottori

## 65. "If Anyone Sees You, Turn into a Frog"

Once upon a time there was a slightly simple novice at a certain temple. He used to go here and there on errands, and each time he would get three mon coins with holes in the centers. He would string these on a straw cord. Even if it was only a little at a time, the coins gradually accumulated until he had many of them. After considering many plans, he dug a hole at the edge of the garden and buried the coins.

When the novice buried them, he said, "If I dig you up, be money. If anyone else digs you up, turn into frogs."

Each time after that, when the novice received money for going on an errand, he would dig in the yard and add to the string. He would say, "If I dig you up, be money. If anyone else sees you, turn into frogs."

The priest noticed that his novice had been acting oddly recently, so one evening he watched secretly what the boy was doing and learned what was going on. He was amused. He went secretly in the night to dig up all the novice's money and in its place he put a frog. The next day the novice earned another two or three mon from somebody. He took them to the garden to bury them, but a frog jumped out of the ground. The boy tried excitedly to push the frog back, but it went hopping away. The boy called in a panic, "Here, wait! I'm not anyone else. I'm me. If you jump that way, the straw will break. Here, wait!" He ran as fast as he could after the frog.

The priest looked on at a distance and held his sides laughing.

Dobashi Riki
Nishiyatsushiro-gun, Yamanashi

## 66. Misokai Bridge

Once upon a time a pious, honest charcoal maker named Chōkichi lived at Sawakami in Niukawa-mura. An old man resembling a hermit appeared by his pillow in a dream one night. Chōkichi woke up just as he was saying, "If you go and stand at Misokai Bridge in Takayama, you will hear something good."

Since it was a dream, Chōkichi promptly prepared charcoal to sell on the way to Takayama and stood a whole day on Misokai Bridge, but he heard nothing special. The second and third day passed without anything good. On the fifth day, the owner of the tōfu shop by the bridge thought Chōkichi looked strange and asked him why he stood on the bridge every day. When Chōkichi told about his dream, the tōfu maker burst out laughing.

"Nothing comes from a silly dream," the man said. "I had a dream myself, a while ago. An old man appeared and said something about a man called Chōkichi who lived in a village called Sawakami or something like that at the foot of Mt. Norikura. He told me to dig at the base of a cryptomeria tree beside his house and find treasure there. I don't know where a village called Sawakami is at the foot of Mt. Norikura, but even if I did, I don't feel like believing such a silly dream. I'm not mean, but I say you should just go home."

When Chōkichi heard what the man said, he was certain that it was like his dream. He hurriedly thanked the man and rushed back to his house. He wanted to dance for joy. As soon as he reached home, he dug at the base of the cryptomeria tree. There it was! All kinds of gold and silver treasures came pouring out. Chōkichi became a chōja because of them.

The villagers called the charcoal maker Fukutoku Chōja, a chōja with great blessings.

Sawada Shirōsaku
Yashiki-gun, Gifu

## 67. The Boy Who Had a Dream

In days before there were schools, a tutor of twelve children said to them on the 2nd Day of the New Year, "Those of you who had a First Dream, tell about it." One after another boy told what kind of dream he had.

One boy said, "I had a dream, but I will not tell it." The teacher said, "It would be rude not to tell us about it."

The boy said, "I'll not tell it, no matter what." The teacher threatened, "If you don't tell your dream, I cannot help you. I will put you into a dugout boat and set you adrift. Do you still refuse?"

The boy still refused, so he was put into a four-sided boat that had metal rods on the four corners to prevent it from coming up onto a beach. Cycad fruit was set in it for food. The dream the boy had was that he was holding hands with two girls on a bridge.

Time went by quickly, and by the 16th Day of the New Year, the boat reached Onigashima. The boat tumbled over on the sandy beach where it landed. Demons found the boat and were going to seize it, but they saw what was written on it.

On the front of the boat was written, "Whoever rescues this will be killed to the seventh cousin," and on the back, "Whoever rescues this will have a happy life to the seventh cousin." The demons began to yell and pull the boat. It split into two and the boy came out. They talked of eating him, but one of them said their leader would be angry if they did.

They reported to the leader what had happened instead. He said, "Fine! Slice him up like a fish on the chopping board and bring him to me."

The boy said, "Wait a bit. It won't do any good for me to be cut up and eaten. I have something to tell your leader. Please take me to him."

When the boy was taken to the leader, he said, "There were three of us. One was to go to the Dragon Palace, one to Hell Paradise, and I was to come here to see treasures. We agreed to meet afterwards. I want to see your treasure before I die. If I see it, I can tell them about it in the Next World after I die."

The demon leader brought out three treasures to show the boy. He explained, "This one is a Thousand-ri Stick. This one is a Life Stick. If a dead person is stroked with it, he will revive. And this is a Listening Stick. You can understand what the birds say with it."

The boy said, "Let me hold them so that when the three of us meet again, I can tell them of something they never saw even if they did return." The demon said, "You can hold them in your hand, but don't say anything."

The boy grasped them and hurriedly said, "A thousand ri, a thousand ri." Off he flew to the land of Osaka.

When the boy came to the gate of a certain house, he saw two crows perched there. He put the Listening Stick to his ear and heard, "The only daughter of West Chōja is about to die. Hurry, hurry!" The boy went quickly to West Chōja's house. About ten women were polishing rice for the funeral.

The boy said, "I am a fortune teller. I would like to see the girl who died. One of the women stopped polishing the rice and led the boy to the chōja. The man was relieved to see a fortune teller and asked him to see his daughter. The boy said, "Even if she died just now, I want to examine her." He set up screens around the dead girl. When he stroked her with the Life Stick, she came back to life. She got up and went into the room.

Everyone said that nothing like that had ever happened before. After they gave supper to the girl who had come back to life, she was just like her former self. The chōja declared, "This boy is the master of my girl's soul." He took him as his son-in-law and he lived there as a married man. In the meantime, the only daughter of East Chōja died suddenly. That chōja said he had heard that the son-in-law of West Chōja could revive the dead. He said he would ask him to bring his girl back to life, but West Chōja refused to let him go. He said, "If I let the young man go there, you will want him for a son."

East Chōja said that he could not hope to have him as his son-in-law. So the young man went to save the girl. After he brought her back to life with his Life Stick, East Chōja kept him and would not let him go home.

West Chōja asked the feudal lord to judge the matter. His judgement was that the boy should be son-in-law in the east for the first fifteen days of the month and son-in-law of the west for the last fifteen days of the month. The boy thus received two households. On the fifteenth day, one girl would give him up and the other would come to meet him on a bridge between the two places. In this way the boy's First Dream came true. He could put his hands on the shoulders of two girls.

Iwakura Ichirō
Koshikijima, Kagoshima

## 68. The Bee and the Dream

Once upon a time there were two merchants in a certain place who set out on a journey to sell things. When they reached Teradomari, they were quite tired and decided to rest for a while. Presently the older man said he wanted to go to sleep.

While the younger was suggesting the older man lie down and have a sleep, he was already asleep and snoring. The younger man was fascinated by how quickly the older one went to sleep. As the younger man looked vacantly at the sleeping man, a horsefly came out of the man's nostrils and suddenly flew off toward Sado Island. When the horsefly came flying back and entered the nose of the sleeping man again, he thought something unusual was going on.

The older man woke up and said, "I just had a strange dream." "Did you? What kind of dream?" asked the young man.

The older man said, "Well, there was a wealthy estate on Sado Island where many white camellias bloomed in the yard. A horsefly came flying up from the foot of one of the trees and told me to dig there. I dreamed that I dug up a jar full of gold coins."

The young man listened intently and then said, "Please sell me that dream!" The older man asked, "What are you going to do with a dream you buy?" "No matter," the younger man said, "please sell it to me."

"How much will you pay for it?" asked the older man. The younger man asked, "Would you let me have it for 100 coins?"

The older man agreed and sold the dream for 100 coins.

After their journey was over, they went home. The younger man pretended to start out again to sell things, but he crossed secretly to Sado Island. He went around looking here and there for a big estate. He told the master there that he was a poor man who had come over from Echigo and asked to be hired as yard sweeper. The rich man said, "You have come at a good time. I have been thinking that I needed a yard sweeper, so please go to work."

Things turned out just right for the young man. He kept busy every day with various small tasks, waiting for spring.

Finally the bitterly cold winter passed and spring arrived. Flowers appeared all over the garden, but not a single white camellia bloomed. There were many red ones, but none that were white. The young man was disappointed, but he decided to wait for the spring of the following year. At last it was spring again, and flowers bloomed in the yard. The young man looked every day for white flowers and finally, one morning, he found a camellia covered with white blossoms.

That night the young man took metal chopsticks with him to the camellia tree secretly and poked around its roots. He heard a clicking sound. When he dug away the soil, he found something like the lid of a jar.

"Here it is," he thought as he lifted its lid. It was a money jar packed full of dazzling gold. The young man dug out the jar and covered the hole carefully once more. Then he hid the jar somewhere so that nobody could see it.

After another half year passed, the young man went to his master one day and said, "I am obliged to you for letting me stay here for a long time, but I must go home for the memorial service for my parents. Please let me stop working for you."

His master said, "You have worked well for a long time. You may go home." He gave the young man money for his passage home. The young man thanked his master warmly. He packed the jar he had found into his belongings and went back to Echigo. He became a prosperous chōja and spent the rest of his life in ease.

*To iu koto dai shi.*

Iwakura Ichirō
Minamikanbara-gun, Niigata

## 69. Chōja from a Straw

Once upon a time there was a man who petitioned Kannon that he might succeed in the world. He received the following revelation from Kannon: "If you take with you the first thing that touches your hand when you stumble and fall the first time after you leave the temple, you will succeed."

The man missed his footing and fell on the stepping stones as he passed out of the gate of the temple. His hand touched a single piece of straw. He went toward the east carrying the straw and caught a horsefly. He tied it onto the straw and continued on his way with it.

He saw a nobleman with a child in his arms, riding a cart coming toward him surrounded by many men. The child began to cry suddenly and they could do nothing to stop it. The nobleman asked the man to give the horsefly tied on the straw to his child. The child stopped crying when he got the horsefly. The nobleman gave the man three oranges as thanks.

The man walked on with the three oranges in his hand. He noticed a dealer in cloth who was very thirsty, and gave him the oranges. The merchant was pleased and gave the man three bolts of cloth in thanks.

The man went on toward the east and came to where a horse had fallen dead by the side of the road. Men were standing around it wondering what to do. The man traded his cloth for the dead horse. After he gave it a drink of water, it came back to life promptly. It was a splendid animal. The man continued on his journey, delighted that one straw had resulted in this fine mount.

One evening the man asked to stay overnight at a wealthy man's home. The owner beckoned to him and said, "I am starting on a long journey, and I do not know whether I can return. If you will lend me the use of your horse, I will let you stay at this place until I come back. If I do not return, the place will be yours." The wealthy man set out and never returned. The man became master of the estate and lived in ease for the rest of his life.

Isogai Isamu
Kure, Hiroshima

## 70. Success Through a Bee

Long ago there was a drifter who had no parents. He had no special skills and he had no work. He only drifted from day to day. He decided to try his luck by setting up a needle and going in the direction it fell. He stuck it into the ground and tossed a coin at it, and the needle fell toward the west.

Saying, "Kami Sama in heaven, point it in the direction in which I can succeed," the man tossed the coin at the needle again. The needle fell to the west again. The drifter concluded that there could be no mistake about it and set out toward the west.

The drifter came to where children had caught a turtle and were tormenting it by the side of the road. The man felt sorry for the turtle and paid money to the children for it. He set it free, saying, "Run away, run away, turtle. If the children catch you, your life will be in danger." The turtle went away somewhere.

As the man continued toward the west, he found children who had caught a bumble bee and were tormenting it. He bought it, too, and set it free. As the man went on and on, he came to where a crowd of people had gathered on both sides of the road.

The man found again that children had found something. He felt sorry for the monkey they had. He pushed through the center of the crowd and said, "Let me have the monkey." The children said, "We will give it to you if you give us money." The drifter reached into his belly band and took out money to give the children and got the monkey. He said to it, "Your life is in danger, monkey. Hurry back to the hills." The monkey ran off looking very happy.

The drifter had rescued a turtle, a bumble bee, and a monkey, but he had spent more than half of the money he carried for his journey. He walked on, feeling uneasy. He met an old woman who lived alone a little farther on. She asked him where he came from, but he said he was just a drifter. The old woman said, "The daughter of the leading chōja in this village is suffering from an illness. If she could eat the fifteen nightingale eggs in a nest in the camphor tree growing in the middle of the stream, she would get well, but nobody has been able to get them. Everybody is worried. They say the chōja is offering to give his daughter as bride to the one who gets the eggs for her."

The drifter left the old woman and went to see the fifteen eggs in the nest in the camphor tree in the stream. There the camphor tree was, growing in the middle of the stream, but the current was so strong that it was impossible to think of getting the eggs. While the man looked worriedly at the tree, the monkey came to him and said, "Master of my life, what are you looking at?"

The man answered, "Could you get the nightingale eggs from the top of that camphor tree for me?" The monkey answered, "That's easy." He went to the bank of the stream and called the turtle. It came out from somewhere and asked the man, "Master of my life, what is troubling you?"

The monkey said to the turtle, "Take me on your back to the foot of that camphor tree because I want to get the nightingale eggs that are in the tree top." The turtle agreed and gave the monkey a ride on his back. The man looked on as the monkey reached the foot of the camphor tree. He climbed it and brought down an egg. Then he got onto the turtle and brought it to the man. He made as many trips as were necessary to get all of the eggs.

The man asked the monkey for the fifteenth egg, but it was stuck in the monkey's throat. The man managed to get the egg out, and after thanking the monkey and the turtle, he set out for the chōja's house.

Along the way, the man met the old woman and told her that he had the fifteen eggs. She was happy for him. Finally, he came to the chōja's house. The chōja came out and asked, "What did you come here for?"

The man replied, "I brought fifteen nightingale eggs." The chōja was delighted. He showed the man into his parlor and served him wine and fish and was very hospitable. When the eggs were fed to the chōja's daughter, her illness disappeared immediately.

But the chōja was worried about taking a drifter who had come from some unheard of place as his son-in-law. He had each of his twelve maids dress like his daughter and brought them with her to where the man was feasting. He turned to the drifter and said, "I will give you as bride the girl to whom you offer a cup of wine."

While the man was hesitating about which one to give the cup, the bumble bee came flying into the room. It flew in front of the chōja's daughter and said, "Offer it here, *bum-bum*. Offer it here, *bum-bum*." The man offered that girl the wine and she proved to be the chōja's daughter. Her father gave her to the drifter, who became the son-in-law of the chōja. The drifter then lived a life of ease.

*Moo nai to.*

Takeda Akira
Mima-gun, Tokushima

## 71. Dragonfly Chōja

Long, long ago in the farthest corner of Ōshū there was a fabulously rich man called Danburi Chōja. His household numbered three thousand, and nearly five bushels of rice were cooked each day at his house. The rice was drained into Yoneshiro river, and even now that river's water is clouded white.

Danburi Chōja went to Kyoto to apply for a chōja's seal. He was told, "To be a chōja, you must possess a treasure which has been bestowed by heaven. The greatest treasure that a man has is his child-treasure. Do you possess such a child-treasure?" He replied, "Through my faith in Dainichi Nyorai of Azukizawa, I was blessed with an only daughter. I brought her with me on this occasion to see the sights." When the girl was called out and presented, she was indeed as beautiful as a rare jewel. It is said that she later became a high ranking consort.

Danburi Chōja was just an honest, hard-working farmer in his youth. He went into the mountains and set up a little hut in which he and his wife lived. They cultivated little patches of garden on the mountainside. One day when they were resting at noon, his wife watched him as he lay asleep with his mouth wide open by the side of the garden. She saw a dragonfly come flying a second and third time from the foot of the mountain opposite, circle above the man's head and around his mouth. She thought it strange.

Then Danburi woke up and said, "I was dreaming just now that I was drinking such good wine. I can't think to tell you how good it was." His wife told him about the dragonfly. They wondered what the meaning could be.

The two of them went around the mountain to look. There they found a clear spring flowing from below a rock. They dipped some up and found that it was a spring of wine. Furthermore, the same mountain yielded an endless amount of gold. They dug and dug it and carried it home. Soon they became great, rich people.

"Danburi" is a word in Ōshū that means "dragonfly." People called him Danburi Chōja because one had showed him how to become a chōja.

Yanagita Kunio
Kazuno-gun, Akita

## 72. The Charcoal Maker Chōja

Once upon a time there were two farmers who were friendly neighbors. They went into the hills to cut wood and stayed overnight at a little shrine for Yama-no-kami. When they compared dreams, they found that they had each had the same dream.

They dreamed that a throng of kami came noisily, discussing something together, to the shrine where they were staying. One of the kami declared, "I don't see Yama-no-kami who runs this place. This is odd. What's going on? I wonder what."

Just then Yama-no-kami came home from somewhere. The other kami all asked, "What happened? Where did you go." Yama-no-kami said, "I'm sorry that I was away. The fact is, there were babies born in the village below here. I thought I could come right back after it was over, but time passed before I knew. At any rate, rejoice that two more human beings have been born into this world."

The kami all said, "That was fine! Were the children boys or girls?"

She replied, "There was one boy and one girl, and they were born to neighbors at the same time."

"What about their property?" asked the kami.

Yama-no-kami said, "The girl has one shō of salt and a wine cup, but the boy has only one shō of rice."

"And what about their marriages?" the kami asked.

"Since they are neighbors, I thought at first of having them marry each other," said Yama-no-kami, "but, well—I will leave it that way for now and think it over."

The two fathers woke up suddenly and compared dreams. They hurried home without waiting for daylight. When they got home, they found that it was just as they had dreamed. At one home a baby girl had been born and at the other, a boy.

When the children grew up, they were married, and their family became noticeably more prosperous. The wife could use one shō of salt a day and the wine cup was never set aside because of callers, just as the kami had decided, for she poured wine generously for anyone who came. There was always something going on at their gate, just as in a city.

The husband looked on all this with displeasure. There seemed an endless supply of everything, just like a spring of water, no matter how much they used. He thought that if only he did not have his wife around, there was no telling how great a chōja he could become. One day he drove his wife away. She wept and apologized, but he would not relent.

The wife left her home with no place to go. She walked around until the sun set. She was hungry and went into a garden patch by the road to pull up a long radish to eat. Water smelling like wine came welling up from where she pulled the radish. She scooped up some to drink and found that it was real wine. She felt refreshed and sang:

There is the scent of old wine
As the spring of wine flows.

The woman took heart and walked along the road toward a red light she saw shining in the mountain beyond. She found an old man working there alone as a blacksmith. She went up to his fire and said, "Please let me stay here tonight."

He replied, "You can see how poor I am. I can't possibly let you stay."

She declared, "If you call yourself poor, then there isn't a chōja anywhere in the world. What do you think these stone stools, the stepping stones, and the table stones are? Look at them!"

The old man said, "They are just stones." "Oh, no, they are solid gold. Take them to town and sell them," said the woman.

The next morning the old man took one of the stones to town, and everyone thought it was wonderful. They told him he was not strong enough to carry the money in payment for the stone, but he put it into a straw sack and took it home on his back. It was the same all around in the mountains around the blacksmith's house. He and the woman suddenly became chōja. When the woman dug in the ground, wine came up as it had for her before. They started a winery, and soon their place in the mountains grew to be like a town.

The former husband of the woman became very poor. He and his son came with firewood on their backs to sell at the town.

Sasaki Kizen
Waga-gun, Iwate

## 73. Potato-Digger Chōja

Somewhere in Chūgoku, I don't know where, there was a woman who was unfortunate. No matter how many times she was sent away as a bride, she could not find a permanent marriage.

One day her father gave her a jewel and said, "It will be best for a girl like you who cannot be married to go where the soil is this color. Consider that to be the place for you and stay until you die." He sent her away from home for her fate to be settled in that way.

The woman resigned herself and went along the Tōkaidō highway to Shichiken-chō in Hamamatsu. She met an old man selling mountain yams there. She showed him her jewel and asked if he knew a place where the soil was that color. He answered that he thought he knew of a place in the hills and told her to come with him.

The woman followed the old man and spent the night at his little shack. The next morning she went with him to the place they were looking for. When they dug, lots of coins came out. They dug frantically and separated the coins from the dirt eagerly. Under the circumstances, there was no question about whether the woman would stay or whether the old man would keep her. They went every day to the hills to dig out coins and to bring them home.

One night Kannon appeared and stood by the old man's pillow. She said, "How about it, old man, you have gathered quite a bit of money, haven't you?"

He answered, "That is quite true. I have gathered quite a bit."

She said, "Well, then, I would like to have a shrine built now. It would be a good idea to send tree cutters into the hills tomorrow, wouldn't it?"

"That is true," he said. "I think it is about time."

Kannon said, "I will count on you to manage the workers."

The old man woke up suddenly. It was nearly day and the clouds were growing a faint white. There he was in his own hut and other than the quiet breathing of his sleeping wife, he could hear nothing and he saw nobody. In the morning a great crowd of tree cutters came flocking to the old man's place. They carried plans with them. They cut one tree after another in the hills.

A few days later, Kannon stood by the old man's pillow again. She said, "How about it, old man, you have about enough trees cut now, so how about hiring carpenters?" He said, "That is true. It is about time."

She said, "Then I will count upon you to manage the carpenters." The next morning, the carpenters came. Plasterers came next. Workers came in succession in that way until in a short time a splendid shrine was completed.

When it was finished, the old man still had 1000 kan of coins and 1000 ryō left over. He buried them at a place in the hills to save for a reserve fund for the shrine in case something unexpected should happen.

Nakamichi Sakuji
Ōchi-gun, Shimane

## 74. The Hearthfire on New Year's Eve

Once upon a time there was a maid called Ofuji. Her master said to her on New Year's Eve, "Tomorrow is the First Day, but don't think that there is nothing to do. See to it that the fire in the hearth does not go out." Ofuji tried to take care of the fire in the hearth so it would not go out, but it died out when she was not looking at it.

The girl was worried and went to borrow some live coals, but all the neighbors had gone to bed. As she walked on and on, she saw a fire burning in the hills. When she came to the house, she said, "The fire in our hearth has gone out and I am sorry for my master. Please give me some live coals."

The girl was told she could have fire, but she was asked to watch a coffin for a little while. It was not convenient for Ofuji to stay and watch the coffin, so the thing to do was to take the coffin with her on her back as she took the live coals home.

After Ofuji started her fire up again, she hid the coffin in an inner corner of the room so her master would not see it. She was uneasy on New Year's morning for fear he would see it.

Four or five days passed without the man who had asked Ofuji to watch the coffin coming for it. She was afraid the corpse was beginning to decay. She lifted the lid of the coffin and found that it was full of gold. She tired to carry it, but she could not move it. She was surprised and told her master all about what had happened. She wanted to give the money to him, but he would not accept it. He tried to have her take it, but she refused.

They decided to use the money to build a temple. On the day before the temple would be completed, the two of them discussed their invitation to attend the completion ceremony. On their way to the temple the next day, Ofuji stepped onto a purple cloud and rode into the temple. There she turned into Kannon. There is this song:

Number Five is the Fujidera in Kawachi.
Pilgrims visit Fujidera to make petitions.
Over the sepals of the flower hangs a purple cloud.

[Number Five is the fifth station visited by pilgrims.]
Ofuji was said to be Toshitokujin, a New Year Deity.

Nishitani Katsuya
Mikata-gun, Hyōgo

## 75. The Guest on New Year's Eve

Once upon a time there was a horse leader in a certain place. He went around until evening on the last day of the year without having a single customer. He gave up trying to get ready for a good New Year's Eve and started home. He came to where a leper lay groaning under a pine tree beside the road.

"I thought I was miserable, but here is this sort of man," he thought as he helped the leper kindly and lifted him onto his horse. He took the leper home with him. The leper was covered with such evil smelling sores that he could not be endured. The horse leader and his wife talked things over. They spread straw matting out on the dirt floor of their workroom and let the leper sleep out the year.

The morning of the 1st Day came and the sun was high in the sky, but the guest of the night before did not get up. The couple thought it was past time for him to wake up and they went to his side. They called him, but he did not answer. He felt so cold and hard they thought he must have died.

When they looked closer, they found that their guest had turned into a big lump of gold.

Hayakawa Kōtarō
Minamishidara-gun, Aichi

## 76. Sedge Hats for Jizō

Once upon a time there was an old man and an old woman. They wanted to buy mochi for New Year which would come soon. They decided to make sedge hats to trade for mochi.

A few days later, the old man started in the snow to town with the hats. Twelve Jizō were standing by the road on the way. They were standing cold and bareheaded in the snow. The old man pitied them so much that he put one of his sedge hats on each one of them. The trouble was that he had only eleven hats, one short of what he needed. He could not possibly leave the last Jizō that way.

He took off his own hat that he was wearing and put it onto Jizō's head. Then he went back home. His old woman came to meet him, asking, "How about the mochi?" Then he told her about the Jizō and said, "We can have a good New Year without mochi."

The old woman praised him for what he did and they were happy about it. She said, "Build up a good fire to get warm before we go to bed."

The next morning they were awakened by shouts outside. When they drew back their wooden doors to see, there was a lot of freshly pounded mochi under the eaves. They looked beyond and were surprised to see the backs of twelve Jizō going away, wearing the old man's sedge hats.

Iwasaki Toshio
Iwaki, Fukushima

## 77. Kōbō's Loom

An itinerant priest came to beg at a house where the housewife was busy weaving. She got down from her loom piously to give him alms. Although he came a second time, she responded, and even a third time, she left her loom good-naturedly.

The priest admired the woman's simple heart. He said, "I will give you a treasure in thanks." He gave her a shuttle that would never give out as long as her loom was threaded. That was really true. Although she wove for three years, the thread in the shuttle was never used up.

The woman had been cautioned never to put her finger into the hole in the shuttle, but she could not see the reason for that. She tried putting her finger in to see. The shuttle disappeared suddenly.

That itinerant priest was said to be Kōbō Daishi.

Yanagita Kunio
Hachinohe, Aomori

## 78. The Magic Towel

Once upon a time a wretched looking beggar stopped at the door of a home, but the lady there happened to be busy weaving. She scolded the beggar and drove him away without giving him anything.

Her maid felt sorry for him and took a riceball secretly to him. The grateful beggar gave her a towel in thanks. When the maid wiped her face with the towel the next day, her face became as beautiful as if she had wiped dirt from it. Everyone was surprised and praised her beauty.

At first she thought they were making fun of her, but when she looked in the mirror, even she was surprised. She told everybody about what had happened on the day before and where the towel had come from.

When her mistress heard about it, she scolded her maid. She said, "I did not tell you to give that wanderer anything. Let me know if he comes again."

A few days later, the same beggar came again. The maid invited him in and informed her mistress. The woman thought this was the time she, herself, would receive something good. She entertained the beggar politely and gave him many things. He gave her a red sash and left. She thought it was a fine obi.

The woman tied it on in a hurry, but the sash suddenly turned into a snake.

Yamaguchi Asatarō
Ikinoshima, Nagasaki

## 79. Water That Restores Youth

Long ago there was a very old man and an old woman in a certain place. They went out to sit on their porch in the sun one bright day in spring. They said, "How nice it would be if we could be young once more."

The old man got up early the next day to cut grass in the hills, but he did not come home at noon and he did not come home when it grew dark. His old woman worried at home as she looked for him. She asked men in the village to look for the old man in the hills. She was so anxious that she went along with them.

They suddenly heard a baby crying far back in the hills. The old woman thought it strange. When she looked closely, she saw a little baby boy lying in the grass, wrapped in the clothes the old man had worn when he set out that morning. It was the old man, who had drunk too much of the "Water of Youth" which bubbled up in the spring there.

The old woman wept with joy and sorrow as she carried her old man who had turned into a baby back home.

Katō Kaichi
Haga-gun, Tochigi

## 80. The Golden Hatchet

A very honest old man who lived in a certain place was cutting a tree by the bank of a pond. His hatchet accidentally slipped from his hand and fell into the pond. With his only hatchet lost, he could not continue to cut trees the next day. If he could not cut trees, he could not support his old wife. He thought he would have to go into the pond to look for the hatchet.

A beautiful girl rose up out of the water just when he was starting to go in. She brought him a golden hatchet and said, "Old man, did you drop a hatchet now?" The old man answered, "Yes, I dropped my precious hatchet and I am going into the water to look for it."

"This is it," said the girl and held out that golden hatchet before his eyes.

He said, "No, it was not such a splendid hatchet. This old man's hatchet was a rusty old iron one." The girl went back into the water and brought out the old hatchet which he had dropped.

"Is this the one?" she asked.

He said, "Yes, that's it."

She laughed and said, "I will give you the golden hatchet, too, because you are an honest old man. Take them home with you." With the help of the golden hatchet, the family became chōja.

The old woman at the house above them heard about how they had become chōja because of the hatchet the Water Spirit in the pond had given the old man. She complained to her old man and nagged the lazy fellow into going to the pond to cut a tree. He went to the bank of the pond to cut a tree, but no matter how long he worked, his hatchet did not fall from his hand.

Finally, the man threw it into the pond on purpose. He stood there, looking at the surface of the water and thinking how fine it would be if the Spirit would come quickly to bring him a golden hatchet. A whirlpool formed and out came a beautiful girl.

She held out the golden hatchet and started to speak, but the old man exclaimed hurriedly, "That's it, that's it. That's my hatchet."

He reached to take the hatchet from her hand, but she said, "Here, you dishonest old man!" She hit him on the head with it and cut it open.

The old man went home covered with blood and crying. He became poorer than ever.

Sasaki Kizen
Shimohei-gun, Iwate

## 81. The Little Boy from the Dragon Palace
[Also called Shintoku Dōji or Nyoi Dōji]

Long ago there was an old man living alone in Mayumi-no-sato. He barely made a living by going into the hills to gather dry wood day after day and selling it at the border town.

One day when the old man had gathered the firewood and carried it on his back to the border to sell, he crossed and recrossed the bridge over the river between the border and the town opposite until sunset, but for some reason he could not sell any wood. If he did not sell wood, he could not buy rice to eat that night. He started across the bridge again, but he was so tired that he sat down half way across. After he had rested a while, he seemed to think of something.

The old man stood up and took the load of wood off his back. He closed his eyes and stood praying to the Ryūjin and then dropped the wood into the river. The falling wood disturbed the surface of the green pool in the river below the bridge into waves that almost reached the bank, and then the wood disappeared. The old man suddenly felt good all over.

A lovely maid, more beautiful than he had ever seen before, was standing on the surface of the water. The man gazed at her as if in dream. She was holding a little child, a really very little child, in her arms.

She said quietly, "Old man, the Dragon Spirit is pleased that you are honest and work hard every day. She wishes to reward you today by leaving this little child in your care. He is called Little Runny-nose Boy. He will grant you anything you wish, but be sure to give him raw shrimp relish every day."

She handed Little Runny-nose Boy to the old man and then disappeared into the bottom of the river.

The old man forgot how tired he was and went home happy. He placed Little Runny-nose Boy by his altar and did not forget to give him raw shrimp relish every day. He would say, "My rice is used up. Please give me some. Or, my money is all used up." Each time the old man asked, Little Runny-nose Boy would make a sound like blowing his nose, and whatever the old man wanted would appear.

The old man no longer went to the hills every day, but asked for all kinds of things. He said, "My house is too filthy. Please give me a cleaner, bigger house." Little Runny-nose Boy gave a little bigger blow than usual, and suddenly the old man felt that his surroundings had changed. He went outside and was surprised to see the house was splendid. In less than a month, the old man had become a great chōja. He had a number of storehouses filled with treasures and rice.

The old man's only work was to go to the border town to buy things for the raw shrimp relish to give to Little Runny-nose Boy. He had been glad at first to do that, but as he prospered, the duty became as troublesome as flies in the Fifth Month. One day he lifted Little Runny-nose Boy down from the side of his altar. He said, "There is nothing more for me to ask you for. Please go back to the Dragon Palace and give Ryūjin Sama my regards."

Little Runny-nose Boy stood up silently and went outside. He could be heard snuffling his nose for a while. The big house that stood there disappeared and only the former dilapidated one was left. The astonished old man hurried out, but he could not see Little Runny-nose Boy anywhere. He could only sit dry-eyed in a daze in front of his home.

Mine Kōsei
Tamana-gun, Kumamoto

## 82. The Golden Puppy

Long ago there was a man named Mafuku at Iwazu-machi. Once when he was crossing the field at Ubino, he saw a group of children by the road. They had caught a little green snake and were tormenting it. It was nearly dead, and Mafuku could not bear to see it suffer.

He gave the children some money for the snake and set it free in the grass. It looked very happy as it escaped. Suddenly a black cloud appeared in the sky. Thunder rolled, lightning flashed, and torrents of rain fell, overflowing the road. People were soaked as they ran indoors, but Mafuku was not wet in the least as he walked home.

Mafuku finished his work and went to bed. At about dawn he saw a beautiful girl standing near his pillow. She said, "I am the one you saved at Ubino yesterday. I am a favorite of the Dragon King. While I was playing, transformed into a small creature, I fell asleep. The children caught me and were about to kill me, for I had lost my power when I was transformed. I was really helpless. I do not know how to express my thanks to you, but I have brought this little dog to give you, my benefactor. It is a sea treasure, but my parents readily gave me permission to give it to you. I want you to feed it three shō of rice every day."

The girl disappeared after she had finished speaking.

When Mafuku awoke, the dog was lying beside him. Mafuku fed it three shō of rice according to his instructions, and the dog disgorged three shō of gold grains. (The place where the dog was kept is said to be called Inukai-no-sato, and there is a settlement called Inubatake even now.)

As the days and months passed, the gold accumulated until the family became very wealthy. People called the man Mafuku Chōja, which means blessed and prosperous chōja.

Nukata-gun, Aichi

## 83. The Boy Magician

I do not know where this story came from, but while a samurai of no special importance was crossing a meadow, a blizzard came up. He saw a forest in the distance and heard a dog bark. A white fox came running from the forest straight to the samurai. It crouched before him and bowed its head several times.

While the samurai was thinking it strange, a hunter came running after the fox. The samurai wondered what he should do, but the fox pushed herself under his divided skirt. The hunter said, "The fox surely hid here. Hunting is my trade and it is how I support my wife and children. Please return the fox to me."

The samurai asked him how much he would take for a fox. He said three ryō. The samurai paid him the money and the man went away happy. The samurai said to the fox, "If you don't want to be caught a second time by the hunter, hurry home now."

The fox bowed its head and went off toward the forest.

The samurai caught a cold and was sick in bed. The fox came as his wife and took good care of him. They grew intimate and she untied her sash. The woman became pregnant and a child as beautiful as a jewel was born. The father thought he had a fine child and slept with him in his arms. When the child was three years old, the man's real wife came home. The fox was surely the white fox who came to care for the man to repay her debt of gratitude for his saving her life. She told her child she was the white fox of Shinoda. She held a brush in her mouth and wrote, "If you long to see me, come to Shinoda forest." Then she went away.

One day when the father was taking his boy to Shinoda forest, they rested near the seashore. The boy suddenly ran toward the beach. A crowd of children were tormenting a tortoise. When he asked them to sell it to him, they asked what he would pay. He offered them his clothes, but they said they did not want such dirty old clothes. One child who belonged to a family who had a secondhand shop said, "What are you saying? The other day we sold a very dirty outfit for a good price. I am sure that even if his clothes are old and soiled, we can sell them for good money." So the boy sold his clothes to them.

The boy became separated from his father while he was getting the tortoise. He set the tortoise free on the beach and sent it into the waves. The tortoise was a lady-in-waiting that had been transformed. She came back in a beautiful boat on the sea. She said, "I will take you to Abenaga-mura where you are going. Keep your eyes closed until I tell you to open them."

When the boy opened his eyes, he suddenly forgot Abenaga-mura and his father. He was wearing beautiful clothes and did not think of going home. Three years passed without his noticing it. When he started home, he was given a tora-no-maki [something to wear next his skin to protect him from cold or heat] and a ryūsengan [something like a wireless set]. The lady-in-waiting took him back to the former seashore. They had thought he was dead at home.

A black bird came from one direction and a white one from the direction of Kyoto and they began to talk in a tree. The boy put the ryūsengan to his ear and heard the birds greet each other. The white bird said, "Well, well, it has been a long time since I have seen you. How are times at the seashore?"

The black bird said, "The carcass of a whale washed up so we are having good times. How is it in Kyoto?"

The white bird answered, "The Emperor is sick and everyone is depressed. Times are bad. Doctors can't cure the Emperor, but Dōjimaru of Abenaga-mura could. Below the pillar at inui, between the west and north corners, there is an earthen jar in which a snake, a toad, and a slug are fighting. I hear that is why the Emperor is ill." The boy Dōjimaru was excited as he listened. He said, "This is fine. What is it about?"

The birds said, "If you go to Kyoto, you will succeed in the world. Hurry! Caw, caw." Then they flew off.

Dōjimaru thought it would not do for anyone to hear about this, so he hurried to Kyoto. Nobody walks around with nothing to say, so every day Dōjimaru went around looking like a beggar and calling, "Tachimachi [suddenly] there will be a great disaster. I pity those who do not know." Presently he was known as Tachimachi Boy.

When an attendant at the palace asked him about the Emperor, Dōjimaru answered, "The illness of the Emperor is caused by the struggle of three animals at the northwest corner. I am hungry, I am hungry. You had better dig them up and throw them into the river to be carried away." The attendant took the word back and everything was done according to instructions. The Emperor's illness was completely cured.

Dōjimaru was called a great man, and he received an official stipend.

Inoue Masafumi
Shimoina-gun, Nagano

## 84. The Visit to the Dragon Palace

Once upon a time there was a man who had no work. People in the village called him a fool because he would go down to the seashore and look at the sea every day.

One day while he was gazing at the sea as usual, Ryūjin came out and handed him a jar. She said, "Here, I will give you this. The water in it is medicine and it will cure any illness. Don't keep it for yourself, but help everyone with it."

The man took the jar home and hid it in the corner of his storehouse. That is why he went to his storehouse many times a day.

The man's wife noticed what he was doing and thought it strange. When he was away one day, she went into the storehouse and found the unusual looking jar in the corner. She wondered what it was. She took off the lid and peered into it. She saw her face reflected on the water, but she thought her husband was going into the storehouse to see that woman's face. That made her jealous. She ran outside to pick up a stone and threw it at the jar, breaking it squarely into two.

When her husband returned, he went straight into the storehouse and saw the broken jar. "This is the work of my wife," he thought. "Women are full of malice and are stupid." He called her to him and said, "Why did you break this jar? The water in it was medicine, and I was curing the illnesses of people with it."

The man gathered up the fragments of the jar and threw them away at the edge of the old pond in his yard.

The man began to go to the seashore to gaze out to sea again from the next day. Then Ryūjin appeared one day and asked, "Why do you come here again?" The man told her about how the jar was broken and how he had thrown the pieces away on the bank of the old pond.

She said, "Go to the place where you threw the fragments away. You will see plants such as you have never seen before. Gather them and dry them in the shade and crumple them up. If you do thus and so with them, you can cure people again with them."

She explained the way to do it in detail for the man. The man parted from Ryūjin and went home. He gathered the plants as he had been instructed and once again he could cure people.

That was the beginning of moxa. The plant was mugwort.

Sasaki Kizen
Kamihei-gun, Iwate

## 85. The Magic Mallet

Once upon a time there was an old man in a certain place who went to sell pine boughs for New Year decorations in the last month of the year. He could not sell a single one. He suddenly decided that it would be better to give them to the kami in the river while he was carrying them home on his back.

He threw the pine boughs into the river from the bridge on his way home. Presently a messenger from the Dragon Palace appeared [the form of the messenger is not clear]. She said she had come to meet the old man and to lead him back with her.

The old man was given a feast. He was given a little magic mallet when he was going to go home. He only had to say what he wanted when he shook the mallet and he would receive it. To start with, he said "rice," and a mountain of rice appeared. Then he said "storehouse" in which to store the rice. A storehouse was set up immediately, and he put his rice into it.

The old man next door wondered how the poor man had a storehouse full of rice overnight. He went to see how it had happened. He said, "Please lend me that mallet for a little while." He took it home with him.

The neighbor was a greedy old man. He thought it would be a bother just to shake out one or two storehouses. He decided to shake out one or two hundred at a time. He kept repeating "ko-mekura" ["little blind man"] instead of "kome-kura" ["rice storehouse"]. Instead of storehouses, a crowd of little blind men came out.

They surrounded the old man and killed him.

Hamada Ryūichi
Yatsushiro-gun, Kumamoto

## 86. The Handmill that Ground Out Salt

Long ago there were two brothers living in a certain place. The older was generous and good, but his brother was a greedy gambler. The villagers were troubled with a continuing famine.

The older brother had some savings, which he drew a little at a time to give to people he found who were suffering. His family became very poor because of that. The younger brother, on the other hand, continued to dissipate and to do nothing.

One day a white-haired man appeared before the older brother. The brother no longer had anything left to eat. He was at the end of his resources and did not know what to do. He said, "Old man, even if you come to me, I have nothing left to give you."

The old man said, "I did not come to ask for anything. You have been helping the people in the village until now, so I have brought you something good. This is a magic stone handmill. Anything you want will come out of it when you turn it."

The old man left as soon as he gave it to the brother.

If the older brother said "rice" or "money" and turned the handmill, a lot of rice or money would come out. He gave what he got, as usual, to people who were in need.

The younger brother heard that his brother had received a good treasure from an old man. He wanted to get it. One day he invited his older brother to bring his handmill along with him in a boat. Then he started to row and killed his brother in the boat. The younger brother had no salt at home. He said "salt" as he turned the handmill, but he did not know how to stop it.

The boat filled with salt and sank with him to the bottom of the sea. The reason the sea is salty is that the little handmill continues to turn.

Takeda Akira
Mima-gun, Tokushima

# 7. Overcoming Evils

## 87. Demon Stories

Once upon a time there was an old man and an old woman. They were always talking about how they wanted to get a child somehow, for they had never had one.

Then one day the palm of the old woman's right hand began to swell. The callus on her hand grew bigger until a baby boy was born from it. The old couple were delighted that they had received the baby they had always wanted. They petted him and called him Kotarō. They took good care of him, but the little fellow did not grow big as time passed. The old couple made him clothes to fit and called him Mamechokotarō [Little Callus Boy].

One day Mamechokotarō said to the old man, "I want a boat!" The old man said, "It is dangerous to get into a boat, so stop asking me." But the boy kept pestering him with, "Buy me a boat, buy me a boat!"

The old man said, "Granny, Kotarō says he wants a boat. Is it all right to get him a little tub?"

The old woman said, "Let's get him one if he wants one that badly."

The old man went to town and bought a little tub and gave it to him. Kotarō was very happy. He took the tub to the river behind the house and played with it as a boat, rowing it with a little oar.

After that, Mamechokotarō played on the river behind the house every day, but one evening he was late coming home. The old man and the old woman were terribly worried. They waited and waited, thinking he would come home any minute, but the old woman worried so much that she sent her old man to go to meet him.

The old man walked back and forth by the river, but Kotarō was not there. He happened to look across the stream and saw Kotarō's tub overturned. Could he have fallen into the river? What should he do? He shouted, "Kotarō, Kotarō," but Kotarō did not answer.

The old man went home dejectedly. He exclaimed, "Granny, something terrible has happened. Kotarō must have fallen into the river, for I couldn't see him. But his boat turned over."

The old woman said, "How awful. Let's hurry and look for him."

"It's no use," said the old man. "I looked all over for him, but he wasn't anywhere. By now he may have reached the Dragon Palace or a fish has eaten him or he has been carried out to sea by the current." The old woman could only agree with him.

The old couple were saying that even if Kotarō's body had not been washed up, they should arrange a funeral for him, when the fish peddler rushed up to their house. He called lustily, "Please buy a fish from me, Grandpa!"

The old man answered, "This is not a day for that. Our precious only child has died and we are planning a funeral for him today. It's not a day to buy fish."

The fish peddler insisted, "Don't refuse, Grandpa. It is a salmon and I have only one. Please buy it. What do you say, Grandma?"

The old woman said, "Well, that was the kind of fish Kotarō liked. Shall I buy it?"

The fish peddler urged the old man so much that he bought the big salmon. He laid it on the chopping board, but when he started to cut it, he heard a faint little voice like an echo underground. It said, "Cut carefully, Grandpa. Cut carefully." The old man felt uneasy, but he began to cut the belly of the fish carefully.

Suddenly Mamechokotarō came jumping out of the fish.

The old man and the old woman were delighted. They kept repeating, "It's Kotarō, it's Kotarō. What happened to you?"

Kotarō said, "I was playing as I always do at the river when my boat suddenly turned over. I fell into the water and a big fish swallowed me. Inside was so dark I couldn't see anything. It was all rough as though I had hit a cliff".

They were all happy and Mamechokotarō grew up safely after that. He was a clever child and dutiful toward the old man and the old woman. One day when he was ten years old, he said, "Grandpa, please buy me a sword." The old man thought it would be hard to find a sword that Kotarō could wear, but the boy teased for it so much that he went to town and bought a needle that was used to sew floor matting. He made a scabbard for it of bamboo and gave it to the boy.

That made him happy. He said, "Now, Grandpa, I'm going to Onigashima to destroy the demons and bring home their treasure to make you and Grandma happy."

The old man was startled. He said, "You're talking nonsense. The demon will eat you in one bite if you go to Onigashima." The old woman scolded him, too. She said, "Don't talk so silly."

But Kotarō wouldn't pay any attention to them and finally got their permission to set out.

Mamechokotarō went to the iron gate at the demon's palace on Onigashima. He looked up to the top of the gate and jumped lightly onto it. When he looked down inside, he saw a crowd of red demons, green demons, and black demons gathering there and watching him in wonder. They shouted, "This is dreadful!" and went to their leader to tell him.

When the demon general came out, he saw the smallest human being that he had ever seen before looking down at him from the top of the gate. Shutendōji was amused as he looked at Mamechokotarō standing haughtily on the iron gate.

"Come on down," he said. "Come on down." He held out the palm of one of his hands and waved to the boy with his military fan with the other. Kotarō leaped down onto the outstretched palm. Shutendōji opened his big mouth and gulped him down. Kotarō began to poke all around in Shutendōji's stomach with the matting needle sword the old man had given him.

"Ouch, ouch," roared the demon as he writhed in pain. "Forgive me, forgive me. Ouch. ouch!"

Mamechokotarō said he would not let him off.

The demon begged, "I'll give you any of my treasure if you will let me off!"

"Well, then, if you will really give me treasure, I'll let you off," said Kotarō. "If you don't give it to me, I will not forgive you."

In the midst of his suffering, Shutendōji told his followers to bring out his treasure. Mamechokotarō said, "Very well, then," and climbed up to the demon's big nose. Shutendōji gave a big sneeze, and out jumped Mamechokotarō.

The demons paid homage to Kotarō and gave him their treasure. He took it home with him and could take care of his old parents in comfort for the rest of their lives.

*Zatto mukashi sakae mōshimashita.*

Takei Takashi
Fukushima

## 88. Picking Nara Pears

Once upon a time there were three brothers named Jirō, Tarō, and Magojirō. Their father had been sick for a long time and did not seem to be able to get well. Somebody said that if they gave him Nara pears that grew back in the hills, he might get well. The oldest brother set out to get them.

As the young man walked along, he met an old woman gathering firewood. He said to her, "I am going into the hills to get Nara pears. Is this a good way to go?" She answered, "This is the right way to go, but there is a monster in those hills. Nobody that went to get Nara pears ever returned. You had better not go."

The young man said, "But I am going because I want to cure my father's illness."

The old woman said, "Then, if you go a little farther, there will be a black bird and a white bird. If the black bird calls not to go, don't go ahead. If the white bird calls to go, then go ahead."

When Jirō went on, he came to the black bird and the white bird. The black bird called for him not to go, but the son's heart was set upon getting a cure for his father, so he went past anyway. He came to a big pond. A big tree loaded with sweet-looking Nara pears stood on its bank. Jirō was happy as he climbed the tree and began to pick the fruit.

Just then the monster came up out of the pond. It said, "I'll swallow Jirō, Tarō, and Magojirō in a twinkling." Down he swallowed Jirō.

Everybody at home was worried because Jirō did not come home. Tarō set out next. As he walked along, he came to the old woman gathering firewood. He asked, "Did you see a young man 22 or 23 years old come by here?"

The old woman said, "There was one that passed by five or six days ago, but I did not see him come back. He might have been eaten by the monster."

But Tarō went on anyway until he came to the big pond where a Nara pear tree stood by its bank loaded with fruit. Tarō climbed the tree, but the monster swallowed him, saying, "I'll swallow Jirō, Tarō, and Magojirō in a twinkling."

Since Magojirō's two brothers had not come back, he decided to go in spite of what his father said. He made a straw figure of a man, wrapped it in a big furoshiki, tied it on his back, and set out. As he went along, he came to the old woman gathering firewood. He asked, "Did a young man about 20 years old go by here two or three days ago?"

The old woman answered, "I saw him go by, but I did not see him come back. He must have been swallowed by the monster. If you came for Nara pears, too, you had better go home."

Magojirō said, "I must get the Nara pears quickly to feed my father so he will get well and I must take revenge for my two older brothers."

The old woman said, "Then, when you go a little farther, you will see a white bird and a black bird. If the white bird calls for you to go, then go, but if the black bird calls not to go, then don't go, but come back."

As Magojirō went along the road he had been showed, there really were a white bird and a black bird. The white bird called for him to go, so he went ahead full of courage. He came to the pond where the tree loaded with Nara pears was growing on the bank. He tied the straw figure that he had carried on his back to the tree and hid himself.

The monster thought the figure was a human being and came out. He said, "I will swallow Jirō, Tarō, and Magojirō in a twinkling." He tried to swallow the straw figure, but he couldn't because it was tied to the tree. Magojirō came out and leaped astride the monster's back and clutched his throat. The monster cried for mercy, but the boy said, "I will spare you only if you disgorge Jirō and Tarō. Let them come out!"

The monster agreed and blew Jirō from one nostril and Tarō from the other. Then Magojirō let the monster free. The three brothers picked the Nara pears and took them home happy for their father.

When the father ate the pears, he got well and they were all happy.

Fujiwara Teijirō
Hienuki-gun, Iwate

## 89. The Gourd That Made Sounds

In a certain place there was a very poor old man who had difficulty caring for his three children. He would dig up a small patch of uncultivated land in the hills and sow buckwheat there. In the autumn his crop would be greater than he had expected. He cultivated more places year after year until his living became easier.

Deer and wild boar appeared one autumn and damaged his crop. His oldest son went to the deer hut to spend the night and look out for deer. He shouted, "Shira-hō, shira-hō," [a hunter's call] to chase the deer off when they came to trample the grain. Each time he called, a voice from somewhere answered:

A gourd in the dell, *chanbuku*,
Mold on the teakettle, *chararin chararin*.

The young man became so frightened that he rushed home without waiting for dawn. (He told what happened there.)

When the second son heard about it, he said, "I never heard of such a silly story. Tonight I'll go to see what is going on."

That son went to the garden plot in the hills to spend the night at the deer hut. He called, "Shira-hō," in the usual way to chase off the deer, but he heard the reply:

A gourd in the dell, *chanbuku*,
Mold on the teakettle, *chararin, chararin*.

The young man was astonished and ran home.

When the youngest son heard all about it, he said, "My brothers are cowards. I'll go tonight and catch that ghost." He went to the deer hut by the garden patch to spend the night. He saw a little gourd bobbing and dancing *chanbuku, chanbuku*, by the dam in a little ditch where the water from the pond was drawn off. He thought that must be a treasure, so he picked it up and put it into his kimono. He took it home and did not show it to anyone. When he would call, "Shira-hō, shira-hō," the gourd in his bosom would reply:

A gourd in the dell, *chanbuku*,
Mold on the teakettle, *chararin, chararin*.

The chōja next door heard this and wanted that singing gourd. He finally traded all his possessions for it. Then the youngest son became the greatest chōja in the village.

Sasaki Kizen
Kamihei-gun, Iwate

## 90. The Flower That Reflected Human Forms

Long ago there was a man called Goyo, who guarded the store of gold of a feudal lord in a certain place. He was honest and diligent, but one night when he happened to fall asleep for a moment, five or six robbers came and carried off a box containing 1000 ryō.

Goyo was worried and searched around, but he could not find the robbers. He reported it to the feudal lord. The feudal lord questioned everybody, but nobody knew anything about it. The result was that Goyo was accused of taking the money and he was put into prison.

Goyo had a little son named Wakamatsu. After a year or two went by, children began to make fun of him, calling him an illegitimate boy. When he told his mother about it bitterly, she explained the reason to him tearfully. He resented that his father had been punished in spite of his innocence. His mother could not dissuade him from setting out to find those robbers.

Wakamatsu wandered around not knowing where to go. One evening he found his way to a single house far back in the hills. When he asked to spend the night there, the old woman said, "I can not let you stay for any reason. Look over there. That flower is called hitobana, a flower that reflects human forms. It blooms when anyone comes. If the men come back and find that person, they kill him."

The old woman saw how sad Wakamatsu was and decided to let him stay. She hid him inside the grindstone.

Presently a crowd of men came back and noticed the flower blooming. They asked, "Has anyone come?" The old woman said, "There was a child here a while ago, but I chased him off."

The men started to drink until they were drunk. They were saying, "Goyo will be executed tomorrow. Ten years had passed since that theft, but nobody has discovered who took the money. It's time we take it into the hills and divide it."

Wakamatsu could not bear to hear them talk in that way. The old woman kept urging the robbers to drink until they were nearly senseless. Then she brought out Wakamatsu. She said, "I told you a lie. There really is a child here." But it was late at night and the robbers fell into a drunken sleep.

Wakamatsu took the money they were dividing and wrapped it in paper. He tucked it into the bosom of his kimono and pretended nothing had happened.

The next morning the robbers decided to go to see Goyo executed. They decided to take Wakamatsu along and set him on their shoulders as they started. A crowd of men was around the place of execution. When it was about to take place, Wakamatsu jumped down from the shoulder of a bandit and ran into the stockade. He hurriedly told what had happened the night before and brought out the package of money. The bandits were caught by the authorities, but the innocence of Goyo was understood and he was spared.

This time Wakamatsu rode home on his father's shoulders. He sang:

Happy is Gokoyo [the royal reign] as Wakamatsu
Whose bough and leaves flourish.

Hiroshima

## 91. **Kozuna, the Demon's Child**
[or The Demon's Laugh]

Once upon a time there was an old man and an old woman who were bringing up a beautiful daughter in a certain place. When she became the age to marry, a demon kidnapped the girl and took her far back into the hills.

Her father searched for her everywhere for fifteen or sixteen years. Finally he found a cave in the mountains and a fifteen or sixteen year old boy near it. He learned that the place was where a demon lived and the demon was now away from home. The boy said the demon ate people who wandered into that place. He urged the old man to go home.

The old man asked the boy if he had a mother, and upon learning that he had, he asked to see her. The boy seemed to realize that there was something special going on and he called his mother. She proved to be the old man's daughter.

The demon was on his way home while the three were rejoicing together. They hid the old man in a closet. When the demon came in, he declared, "I smell a human. Is there a human being around here? Bring him out!"

He began to search around, so they could no longer hide the old man. They told the demon how he had finally found them after many years of searching and they begged him not to eat the old man. When the demon finally agreed, they brought out the old man, but once the demon laid eyes on the father, he could not withstand the urge to eat him. He decided to boil the old man to death and told his boy to heat the bath.

The boy and his mother first led the old man out through a secret tunnel, and then the boy started to heat up the bath. He and his mother decided to run away, too. The demon became impatient and came to urge on the firing of the bath. The boy said, "It isn't ready yet. Please wait a little."

When they thought the old man had gone far enough, the boy put a big rock onto the lid of the tub. He took two dippers, one for his mother and one for himself, and they escaped through the secret tunnel.

When the demon thought the bath would be hot enough, he came to see, but nobody was around. The water in the tub was boiling and he thought the old man should be cooked by then, but when he took the lid off, the old man was not in the tub. The demon was furious when he realized that they had all run away together. He started to chase them. The three had managed to reach the seashore and had climbed into a boat and were rowing away when the demon caught up with them.

The humiliated demon called to them, but it was no use. He put his mouth into the water by the shore and began to drink. The water gradually receded before their eyes and the boat was drawn back toward the shore. It was almost within reach of the demon's hands when the demon's child took out the two dippers he had brought. He rolled up his mother's clothes and stood patting her bottom with the dippers as he called:

Mother, shall I pat your bottom with the dipper?
Mother, shall I pat your bottom with the dipper?

When the demon saw that, he could not hold back his laughter. He burst into a big laugh and spit up all the water he had drunk. The boat was washed back out to sea without any trouble and the three reached home safely.

Ariga Kizaemon
Minamiazumi-gun, Nagano

## 92. Rescuing the Beautiful Girl

A sister and her brother who lived in a certain place went to the hills to gather chestnuts one day in autumn. They were so intent upon gathering the nuts that before they realized it, they wandered away from each other. The girl was carried off by somebody.

The poor boy looked everywhere, calling his sister. While he was searching, he found bits of her dress, a scarf, and the like caught onto branches or twigs of dry wood. He thought they were signs that his sister was not far away.

The boy went farther and farther into the hills to look for her until he came to a big house standing alone. There he found the sleeve of his sister's dress hanging by the pillar of a black gate.

"This is it," thought the boy. "My sister was carried in here and I must go in."

But a black demon was guarding the gate and the brother could not possibly enter. While the boy was wondering what to do, the black demon lay down at the base of the gate and went to sleep. He snored loudly.

The boy took a chance and tried to step over the demon, but he happened to step on one of his feet. The demon shifted his position and muttered, "It must be the field mice. They are such a nuisance I can't sleep." The boy crouched low and crawled on. Luckily, he was not seen.

The brother had succeeded in passing through one gate, but when he went on a little farther, he came to a green gate with a green demon guarding it. He looked at it from behind a tree and he was determined to go through it. Presently, that demon stretched out at the base of the gate and went to sleep, snoring loudly.

The boy tried to step over his legs, but he made the mistake again of stepping onto one of the demon's feet. It complained, "It must be those field mice. They are such a nuisance I can't sleep." The boy managed to get through the gate without being seen.

After he walked a little farther, he saw a red gate with a red demon guarding it. Such a thing was in his way once more. He hid behind a tree to look, and presently the red demon lay down to sleep at the base of the gate just as the others had done. The demon began to snore loudly, and the boy tried to cross his legs, but he stepped on the demon's legs again.

The demon rolled over and complained, "It must be those field mice. They are such a nuisance I can't sleep." So the brother managed to go through danger and was able to go ahead without being seen by any of the demons.

When the boy reached the entrance to the house, he saw his sister's straw sandals there. He called to his sister and she came out to meet him. She hurried him inside and hid him in a bamboo trunk in the corner of the room.

The chief demon came back from somewhere in the evening. As he stood astride the open hearth to warm himself, he said, "Here, little girl, I am sure I smell a human being." She assured him there was nobody there.

"Don't hide anything," he warned as he went out into the yard to look at the leaves of the bamboo grass. "There is a drop of dew on this leaf," he declared. "That is a sign there is a human being in the house."

The demon went back into the house to warm himself again. He turned his eyes this way and that carefully. Then he noticed the end of the boy's sash sticking out of the bamboo trunk in the corner.

"What is that?" he roared. He stood up straight and went over to the trunk. He pushed open the lid and dragged the boy out.

The girl begged, "That is my brother, so whatever you do, please don't eat him." The demon roared with laughter, baring all his white teeth.

At supper time, the demon said, "Now, my fine guest, let's have a contest in eating boiled rice. The one who loses will be taken and eaten."

The sister managed to put a small bowl into her brother's bowl and to pile the rice onto that. She packed a big mound of rice into the demon's bowl. In this way, her brother finished eating his rice first. The humiliated demon said, "This makes a fool of me. Anyway, a winner is decided by three trials. This time we will have a contest in eating parched beans. The one who loses will be eaten by the winner."

This time the sister managed to give her brother ordinary beans, but she gave the demon pebbles. Her brother won again, much to the surprise of the demon.

The demon declared, "Well, well, wait. We will have one more contest. We will have a good sleep tonight and in the morning we will have a contest in cutting down trees. The one who loses will be eaten." He went off to his bed and soon fell asleep, snoring loudly.

In the night, the girl sharpened her brother's hatchet and dented the demon's hatchet with a stone until it was as round as a stick. She called the demon at dawn the next morning and said, "Hurry up to cut trees."

The demon went to call his guest. The boy leaped up and hurried down to the yard to begin to cut trees. The demon and the boy tried to cut a tree of equal size. The boy cut his tree promptly with his hatchet, but the demon's hatchet only cut the bark and could not get to the trunk. The demon tried his best to win because he wanted to eat the boy.

In the meantime, the girl went over to her brother and said, "This is the time, brother. Cut the demon down quickly with your hatchet." The boy went behind the demon unnoticed and cut off his head.

All of the demons came and knelt down before the brother and sister to pay them homage. The sister had all the treasures of the demons loaded onto little demons and had them carried triumphantly to their own home.

Sasaki Kizen
Iwate-gun, Iwate

## 93. The Flight from Onigashima

Once there were two brothers who were made to work hard every day by their stepmother. They worked, however, without complaining, but she hated them and accused them falsely to their father.

She said, "When I send the children out to cultivate the field, they do nothing but play around. We can never make a living with such children around the house."

Her husband believed her and said, "A farmer cannot eat if he does not work in the field." One day the brothers were given a big feast, for the time had come for them to be sent away. After they had eaten well, they left home with good wishes for their parents.

The two boys talked about going somewhere to become good men. The older said he wanted to be adopted by someone in the east. The younger wanted to be adopted by someone in the west. When they parted, they agreed that if the string on one's bow broke, he would know that the other brother had died. Then they set out.

The younger brother hired himself to the watchman in a village. He thought he would be paid a lot of money after he had worked for ten years. He told his master he would like to stop working.

The man said that he had worked well, but he had no money to give him. He asked the young man to take a sword he had. That was not what the young man had expected, but there was nothing he could do about it. He accepted the sword and left the watchman's place.

As the young man went along, he came to a pack-ox lying on the road and blocking the way. The beast died strangely when the young man barely touched its nose with his sword. He concluded that the sword which he had received was a good one. He went on full of courage. But as he continued on his way, he became lost in the hills.

The young man wandered around until he came to a strangely

splendid house. He wondered what kind of place it was. A girl came out when he called. She said, "You have come to a terrible place. This house belongs to demons and when they come home, they will surely eat you."

The young man said, "Fine! I'll kill all the demons when they come home."

The demons returned with a great noise as he waited. The young man took out his sword and jabbed the demons in the nose, one after another, and they fell over dead. The young man said. "Now I've killed all the demons. Tell me where their treasures are."

The girl said, "The most precious treasure of all is their Life Whip. If you stroke a dead person just once with it, you can bring him back to life." The young man took the whip and gave the other treasures to the girl. He told her to hurry back home.

Just then the string of the young man's bow snapped. That was terrible, for it meant his older brother had died. He was surprised and hurried toward the east. When he arrived, the funeral for his brother was just commencing. He pulled his brother out of the coffin and stroked him once with the Life Whip. The older brother suddenly opened his eyes.

After that the two carried out their wishes which they had already had. One was adopted by a feudal lord in the east and the other, by a feudal lord in the west. They lived in ease for the rest of their lives.

Iwakura Ichirō
Kikaijima, Kagoshima

## 94. The Seven Cauldrons

A girl in a certain place was carried off by a demon and finally lived with him as his wife. After seven years had passed, her demon husband said he would have a drinking bout to which he would invite every one of his friends and show them the greatest treasures in his house.

The treasures were seven cauldrons, the second bigger than the first, the third bigger than the second, and so on, each bigger than the one before it. The first was as big as a bath tub that could be set out, and the last was so big that one had to look up to see the top. It was rumored that anyone who looked into the seventh cauldron would be killed by the demon. The girl's father was among the invited guests, and the girl wanted to protect her father because she had heard the rumor.

When the day of the feast came, the father was delighted to see his daughter after a long time. He took his place in the line of guests with demons and ghosts. Then the drinking began. The seven treasures were displayed in an awesome row beyond. The daughter realized that the demon would show them to her father.

While the demons were making a lot of noise with their drinking and singing, the daughter led her father out into yard as though he had something to do there. She told him that the demon would propose he look at the cauldrons presently. She said the first two were safe, but from the third, they would grow bigger. She said that nobody who had looked into the seventh had lived. She asked her father to be careful or his lifeblood would be spilled.

The two returned to their places. Then the demon chief said, "Now, Father, I am glad you came today. I am sorry we have not been able to offer you any special feast, but I would like you to examine these seven cauldrons, which are my family treasures."

He led the father over to the cauldrons. The father had been warned by his daughter. As he looked at the first cauldron, he took a step back and exclaimed, "How big it is!" When he looked at the second, he took another step back, gradually getting farther away. By the time he looked at the seventh cauldron, he was seven steps away from it. The demon admired his cleverness and said, "You are a very smart fellow. I can't help letting you go free." Thus the father was able to go home safely.

Dobashi Riki
Nishiyatsushiro-gun, Yamanashi

## 95. The Thousand Ri Boots

Once there was a poor family where the father had died and left his wife to care for their three little boys eleven, nine, and seven years old. The mother worked as hard as she could, but a single woman could barely earn enough to feed herself, and she could not possibly take good care of the three children. It frightened her to see their misery.

The mother finally decided to abandon her children in the hills. She thought that perhaps an animal would find them there and devour them to settle her problem. One day she took the three little boys with her far back into the hills. She said, "Wait here for a while. Mother will go to buy some cakes and come back soon." She deceived them in this way and abandoned them.

The children believed their mother and waited, but after a while it began to grow dark, and for some reason their mother did not come back. The two older boys could not bear it any longer and they began to sob.

The seven-year-old said, "There's no use in crying, brothers. Maybe we can find a man's house around here who will let us spend the night. I'll climb a tree to look."

He climbed a tree nearby and saw a fire burning beyond. He said, "I see a fire burning over there. Let's walk."

The boy climbed down and urged his two brothers along. They came to a single dilapidated hut in the midst of the hills. An old woman was building a good fire on the hearth.

The children went into the house and said, "We have lost our way. Please let us spend the night here."

The old woman answered, "I would like to let you stay, but my house is a demon's house, and it's about time for him to come home. I can't possibly let you stay. If you take this road, you will meet the demon, but if you take that one, you will be safe. Please hurry." She showed the boys the road to take, but they did not want to leave. They said it was dark and they couldn't go home. They insisted upon staying. She asked them if they were willing to have the demon eat them, but even as she talked, they could hear the tread of the approaching demon.

The old woman was flustered. She said, "Look, while you are wasting time, here he comes. What shall I do? Come, get into here." She put the three children into a pit in the room with a dirt floor, covered it with its lid and a piece of straw matting.

That was just in time, for the demon was coming in by the back door as she finished. He began to sniff around and said, "Granny, I smell human beings! You surely have put somebody up here." He hunted all through the house.

The worried old woman said, "To tell the truth, three human children came to the front door and wanted to spend the night here. Just then you came in through the back door and they ran away. That is why you think you smell human beings. It must be the smell of the children is still around."

The demon believed her, but he couldn't stand to think of the children being nearby. He thought that if he hurried, he could catch up with them. He pulled on his 1000 ri boots and rushed out the back door as fast as a bullet shot from a gun. No matter how far he went, he could not see anything like children. He said to himself, "I must have gone beyond where the children are. They will be along presently, so I might as well rest for a while." He sat down at the side of the road and soon he was asleep and snoring loudly because he was tired.

At the demon's house, the old woman helped the children out of the pit as soon as the demon left. She said, "The demon has set out wearing his 1000 ri boots and he has surely gone far away by now. Take this road quickly and escape."

She sent the boys out the back door and away, but for some reason, the boys made a wrong turn and went onto the road the demon had taken. While they were going along, they heard a big noise like thunder. They wondered what it was. Then they saw a big demon asleep by the road and snoring like thunder. The children were frightened and the two older ones began to sob.

The youngest boy said, "There is no use crying, big brothers. Let's pass the demon while he is asleep." He went ahead to look the demon over.

When the boy looked at the demon who was sound asleep, he suddenly noticed the demon's feet. Those things he was wearing were the things called 1000 ri boots, for sure. He wanted to get them somehow. He tried to pull one boot off carefully without waking the demon. When he got it off, the demon gave a kick and turned over. The boy held his breath.

The demon muttered in his sleep, "Those field mice are setting out for their night's work."

The boy waited until the demon settled down to sleep again, and then he pulled off the other boot. The demon gave another kick and turned over. The boy held his breath as the demon muttered, "Those field mice have come home from their night's work." Then the demon went back to sleep.

The boy took the demon's boots back to his brothers. He told his oldest brother to put the boots on and helped him do it. Then he tied his next brother onto his own back with his sash and he, himself, got onto the back of his oldest brother. "Now fly," he ordered. There was a whirring sound as the three flew away like a shot from a gun.

The demon woke up when he heard them take off. "Have those brats escaped?" he said as he gritted his teeth in humiliation. He tried to chase them, but he could not catch up with them because his 1000 ri boots had been stolen. Even as he watched, the children reached a place where there were people's houses. The demon could only go home dejectedly.

When he reached home, the old woman wanted to know about the fate of the children. She asked, "Did you catch the children?" The demon said, "I went a little too far. Somebody stole my boots while I was resting, so I couldn't catch them." She was relieved when she heard that.

The children were able to reach home safely. They worked hard and helped their mother after that.

Dobashi Riki
Nishiyatsushiro-gun, Yamanashi

## 96. The Water Spirit's Letter Carrier

One evening when a certain man was hurrying along a road by a stream, he saw a man fishing for little fish. The fisherman called him to stop. He said, "There should be a man fishing on the bank of the pool downstream. Please take this letter to him." He gave a note to the man.

The man thought nothing of it as he went around the pool to where a man was fishing and handed him the letter. The fisher opened it and read it silently. He said, "Just wait a minute. I dropped something into the pool." He jumped in with a splash and came out after a little bit. He said, "The truth is that I am the kappa that lives in this pool. That kappa has written that your purple buttocks look good to eat. He told me to catch you and eat you, but you are so honest that I can't do it. I will give you this treasure instead." He handed the man a package of gold and told the man not to tell anyone what had happened.

Then the kappa went back into the pool. After that, the man became a wealthy chōja.

Sasaki Kizen
Iwate-gun, Iwate

## 97. Destroying the Monkey Gods

No matter how many priests were put in charge of Shōhōji temple, they were all destroyed by ghosts. The temple was in difficulties because no priest wanted to take charge of it.

An itinerant priest came begging and asked a priest if he could spend the night. The priest said, "I can not let anyone stay, but there is a vacant temple over there. It would be better for you to stay over night there."

The itinerant priest went there to put up for the night and ate what food people nearby brought him. He was satisfied to sleep anywhere he could be protected from rain. When he was ready to go to sleep, he recalled that his teacher had told him before he set out that when he slept in a vacant house, he should be sure to sleep where there was an entrance.

He looked around the kitchen and crawled under a kettle that happened to be there.

In the night he heard a clatter in the main hall and then some things appeared. They gathered in the kitchen. One of them said, "Let's dance before we enjoy our sweet feast tonight." They all agreed and began to dance.

The priest listened closely to the words of their song. It sounded like:

Don't let Denshōbō in Tanba
Hear of this, *chū, chū, chū.*

After the things had sung and danced for a while, they began to walk around, saying, "It smells of a human, it smells of a human." They could not find anyone so they went outside. In the meantime dawn began to come on.

About the time the priest came out from under the kettle, the villagers gathered gradually. They were astonished to see him, for they had expected that the ghosts would have eaten him down to bones, and there he looked as though nothing had happened. They thought the priest, himself, might be a ghost and started to run away.

The priest said, "I am no ghost. There is no need to run away."

The villagers were relieved. They asked, "Didn't anything strange happen last night?"

He answered, "Some things came out in the kitchen and carried on, but I was sleeping and did not see what they were. They shouted that they smelled a human being and then went off."

The villagers said, "Countless priests have been eaten up here, but you must have great power, for you have not been eaten. Please stay and run the temple for us." The priest answered, "I must go somewhere before that, but I will return." Then he left them. The villagers said, "That priest went off because he was afraid. He just made an excuse to get away."

The priest had heard of Denshōbō in the song the ghosts had sung, so he thought they were talking about a priest. He decided to go in search of him. When he arrived in Tanba, he learned that Denshōbō was a cat and not a priest. He borrowed it and brought it back with him.

The villagers were happy to see the priest and they turned the temple over to him. Denshōbō lived there with the priest, always staying close wherever he walked, never losing sight of him. The priest thought it strange and asked it why it always stayed near him.

The cat replied, "The ghosts in this temple are really old rats. If I left you for a moment, they would eat you."

The priest asked, "Will you destroy the rats for me?" The cat said, "I can't destroy them by myself. If my brother cat would come to help, we could destroy them."

The priest then told Denshōbō to go and ask his brother to come to help. The cat said that if he left the priest, the rats would eat him. He told him to have somebody draw pictures of cats and put them up in the kitchen and for the priest to stay in the kitchen while he was away. Then the cat set out to ask his brother to help him. The rats would come to the kitchen at night but then run off repeatedly, so that place was safe.

Ten days later the big cat returned with his brother. They hid the priest at night and took the pictures down. The two cats hid and waited. The rats came in the night, but since the pictures of the cats were no longer there, they did not expect trouble.

The two cats came out and the fight began. The cats were powerful, but the rats were powerful, too. There was a great struggle for a while, the cats and rats calling at each other.

The priest was huddled up, hiding in fright. When the noise quieted, he came out and found that the cats as well as the rats were dead. He took the rat legs to make a little stand for his sutra and it is still preserved as a treasure at the temple. He hastened to bury the cats and to offer prayers for their souls. In that way the priest became head of the temple.

*Dondo harai.*

Fujiwara Teijirō
Hienuki-gun, Iwate

## 98. Travelers Turned into Horses

[In the form of *Hankyō sanjūshi*]

Once upon a time a priest took six young men with him on a trip over a mountain road. Somehow, they missed their way and the longer they walked, the farther they went into the hills until they were completely lost deep in the mountains. Evening was gradually coming on in the meantime.

Thinking he must find a place to spend the night, the priest noticed a fire beyond. He exclaimed, "This is a lucky chance. Let's go there to spend the night!"

The seven of them gradually made their way toward the fire. When they reached it, they found a single house. They looked in and saw an old man keeping the fire going in his hearth. They said, "We have lost our way. Please let us spend the night here."

He agreed and showed the seven in. He started the fire blazing and invited them over by it to warm themselves.

The old man said, "I really don't have much of anything, but I'll prepare some supper for you." He hung the kettle for the gruel over the hearth and then went into the next room. The priest wondered what he was up to and cautiously followed the old man to get a view through a crack.

The old man was not aware of that. He put some dirt into a tub and scattered some kind of seed onto it. Then he laid a sheet of straw matting over it. Presently, when it was about time for the gruel to boil, he took off the matting to see. The seeds that he had just planted had sprouted into some strange plants.

The priest saw all this and hurried back to his seat, pretending nothing had happened. The old man came back into the room with those plants he had gathered. As he put the plants into the kettle and stirred them, he said, "If I put some vegetables into the gruel, it will taste better."

The old man offered the gruel to them, saying, "Now supper is ready. Please have some."

The six young men were hungry and praised it, eating several bowlsful. Only the priest just pretended to eat it and managed to get rid of it without eating any. After supper was finished, the old man said, "Now, my guests, would you like to bathe your fatigue away?"

They all said, "By all means, let us take a bath!" The old man led them one at a time to the bath.

The priest was suspicious of this. Once more he hid himself and looked on. The old man led each young man to the tub and helped him in. As soon as the young man was in, he turned into a horse. He would get up on his four legs and whinny exactly like a real horse. Then the old man would put a halter on the horse and say "dō-dō" as he hit its rump with a thick bamboo stick and chase it out of the bath to the stable behind. He would tie him up there.

The old man took the six young men to the bath in this way and turned them into horses. He put a rope on each and turned it out. When he counted the horses, he found he had only six. "There should be one more," he thought. "One is missing." He walked around and looked everywhere.

By that time the priest had gone out beyond the hedge. When he saw the old man begin to hunt, he ran away as fast as he could. The old man changed into a demon when he saw that and chased the priest, calling, "Wait, priest, wait, priest!"

The priest tried hard to get away, but he did not know the paths in the mountain and soon got tired. It looked as though the demon would overtake him, but he began to repeat "Namu Amida Butsu" as he ran. Then dawn finally came and the sun rose over the mountains in the east.

Since a demon can not let the sun shine onto him, he gave up and went home. The priest managed to escape and he reached a place where people lived.

Dobashi Riki
Nishiyatsushiro-gun, Yamanashi

## 99. Kōketsu Palace
[Extracting Oil]

Once upon a time a woman who was going alone to a distant place met a strange looking man. He asked her to become his wife. She replied that she had two children and could not be his wife. But he insisted, "If you come to my house, I won't make you work and you can eat as much as you like of good things."

The man finally forced her to go with him. His house stood alone in the hills and it was truly a splendid house. He let the woman enjoy good things to eat every day, just as he had said, and he asked no favors of her as a wife. The man gave her only one strict instruction. She was not to step out of the door of the house.

After several years had passed, the woman was tired of always being in the house. She wanted to go outside to look around. She opened the door and went outside secretly while the man was away. When she walked a little beyond, she came to another splendid house. She was surprised at what she saw when she looked in.

A number of women had been hung upside down from the rafters there to dry. One of them said, "We all were fed well and when we got fat, we had our fat extracted in this way. You will surely be hung upside down and your fat taken as ours has been. Run away now quickly."

The woman thought this would be terrible and started to run away in the mountains without knowing where to go. Unfortunately, the sun began to set, and she worried about where to spend the night. She saw a fire in the distance and went toward it. A white-haired woman was there alone.

The poor woman begged, "Please save me, Grandmother." She told why she had run far away.

The old woman said, "This won't do. I belong to that man's group."

The poor woman said, "If you don't help me here, I can not escape, for the road in the mountain is dark and dangerous. Please save me. Save me!" She begged so humbly and insisted so much that the old woman gave in. She told the woman to hide in the well, for it was about time for the man to come. The woman hurriedly hid above the well.

The man came in as he always did. He said, "Granny, the woman I have been keeping has run away. Has she come here?" The old woman denied it. He said, "Did she really not come?"

The old woman said, "If you think she is here, look through the house."

The man looked all around and could not find the runaway. He scolded as he left. The poor woman thanked the old woman in the morning and managed to reach home. She found that everybody had given her up as dead and they had held a funeral for her.

Since she had really come back, her family and neighbors said, "Let's have a big celebration."

Then there was confusion. At this point the woman woke up. It had all been a dream.

Iwakura Ichirō
Kikaijima, Kagoshima

## 100. The Three Charms

There was a young novice living with a priest at a temple in a little village in the mountains. The novice said, "Please let me go into the hills to gather flowers."

The priest said, "You had better not go into the hills. It would be terrible if a demon came out."

"I will come back right away," insisted the boy.

"Well, then, I will give you these three charms," said the priest. "If you are in trouble, you can toss one of them." He gave the charms to the boy.

The novice went into the hills and while he was breaking off beautiful branches of flowers, an old woman appeared. She said, "Novice, pick some flowers for me, too, won't you?" He agreed and got some for her.

The old woman said, "Come to Granny's house and I will give you something nice." The boy agreed and followed her home. She said, "Stay at Granny's house tonight, boy." He agreed and stayed there for the night.

It began to rain in the night. As the boy listened, the rain dropping from the eaves seemed to say:

Water from the roof falls *tan-tan*,
Get up and look at Granny's face.

The boy stuck his head out from the covers and looked. The old woman had turned into a demon. That was terrible and he wondered how he could escape. He said, "Granny, I have to go to the privy."

The old woman said, "That's all right. Just do it here."

He said, "I can't do it unless I go to the privy." The old woman tied a rope around his waist and fastened it to the millstone that was there before she let him go out. After a while she called, "Are you through, boy?"

He tied the rope from around his waist onto the pillar in the privy and stuck one of his charms onto it. He said, "When she calls me, say not yet!" Then he ran away.

When the old woman called, "Are you through?" the charm would answer each time, "Not yet."

The boy was so slow coming back that the old woman pulled the rope tied to the millstone and discovered he was not there. She roared, "Does that boy think he can get away from me?" And she chased him.

The boy hardly knew what to do when he heard footsteps following him. He flung one of his charms and cried, "Big river, come out here!" Then a big river appeared. The old she-demon swam across the river and came after the boy again.

The boy threw the other charm behind and cried, "Big mountain, come out," and a big mountain appeared. The she-demon tried to climb it, but she kept slipping down in the sand.

While the she-demon was slipping and sliding, the boy ran to the temple. He called to the priest, "I'm being chased by a she-demon. Please hide me!" The priest put the boy into a closet to hide.

The she-demon came running into the temple and shouted, "Did your novice come back yet?"

The priest said, "He hasn't come back."

"Don't lie to me, you silly priest," she yelled. "If you have hid the boy, I'll eat you both, starting with you."

"That's amusing," said the priest. "If you think you can eat me, go ahead and try it. Let's compare tricks. The one who loses will get eaten up. How about it, old she-demon, can you turn into a bean? If you can't, I'll catch you and eat you!"

"Do you think I can't, you turd-covered priest," the she-demon shouted. "Just look at this!" She promptly turned into a bean.

The priest stuck her onto a piece of mochi that he was toasting and ate her in a twinkling.

Sasaki Kizen
Senhoku-gun, Akita

## 101. The Privy at the Demon's House

Two brothers went into the hills. When the sun set, they went toward a light which they saw. They found an old woman living alone and asked to spend the night with her.

There seemed to be many dangerous things about the old woman, so the boys told her they had to go to the privy and asked to be let out. She tied a rope around the boys to keep them from running away before she let them go out.

The boys prayed earnestly to the kami in the privy. Then they tied the rope to the pillar in the privy and climbed through a hole in the plaster wall. (And that is why there has been a window in the privy since long ago.) When the old woman called repeatedly, "Are you through?" there was always the answer, "Not yet!"

The old woman became angry and pulled the rope hard. The privy toppled over at that. She thought the children might have been killed and she pulled the roof and plaster off to see. They were not there and the rope was tied to the pillar. She shouted as she chased the boys.

There was a big river on the way, but the boys crossed it with the help of the kami, and the she-demon was overcome in the river and died.

Suzuki Tōzō
Yoshiki-gun, Gifu

## 102. Eating a Demon in one Bite

Once upon a time a novice went to gather chestnuts. As he went farther and farther into the hills, a yamajii appeared. He said to the boy, "I know where there are heaps of chestnuts. I will show you where."

When the boy went with the man to see, sure enough, there were lots of chestnuts. The sun set while the boy was enjoying gathering them, so he decided to go to the yamajii's house to spend the night. When the boy woke up suddenly in the night, he saw that what had been a yamajii in the daytime had turned into an ōnyūdō, a monstrous ghost, and it was about to swallow him.

The boy started to run away with the ōnyūdō chasing him. He came to a mountain temple and dashed into it. He said to the priest, "Please save me!"

The priest asked, "What's going on?"

The boy told him he was being chased by an ōnyūdō. The priest told him not to worry, for he would save him. He hid the boy in a closet and looked as though nothing had happened when the ōnyūdō came. It said, "Here, priest, that novice who was running away from me must have come here. Bring him out."

The priest said, "If you turn yourself into a flea, I will tell you."

"That's no trouble," declared the ōnyūdō and promptly became a flea.

The priest crushed it in a hurry and rescued the novice.

*Oshimae.*

Katō Kaichi
Haga-gun, Tochigi

## 103. Dan'ichi Whose Ears Were Cut Off

Once upon a time there was a novice at a mountain temple who received permission from the priest to go into the hills. The sun set before he noticed while he was playing there. He tried to go home, but no matter how far he walked, he could not find his way.

In the midst of his worry, the boy heard a voice behind him call, "Wait, wait!" He ran in confusion, but he could not find the road in the dark. He ran toward a light that he saw in the distance, but an old she-demon was chasing him.

The boy came to a river where a ferry boat was tied. He jumped into it and managed to get across the river, but the she-demon turned into a snake and swam over. The boy finally reached a temple. He rushed into it and begged the priest to save him.

The priest wrote "Namu Amida Butsu" all over the boy's body and hid him in the bell that was hanging there. The snake came in and coiled around the bell and pulled it down. Then the boy had to come out. The snake wanted to devour the boy, but she couldn't because "Namu Amida Butsu" was written all over him.

It happened, however, that the priest had forgotten to write on the boy's ears, so the snake ate his ears off.

Iwasaki Toshio
Iwaki-gun, Fukushima

## 104. The Staring Match with a Demon

The castle of Yuriwaka was at Takasaki-yama. One day Yuriwaka asked his father, the owner of the castle, for permission to go to Oni-kai-ga-shima to destroy the demons.

His father answered, "If you can lift the rock at Hachijōjiki, I will let you go." Yuriwaka lifted the rock and threw it into Bungo Bay. Then he crossed over to Oni-kai-ga-shima to challenge the demon. The demon said, "Let's have a staring match. The one who loses will surrender."

Yuriwaka put gongs which he had brought with him into his eyes and outstared the demon. Yuriwaka started a settlement on that island later.

Ichiba Naojirō
Ōita

## 105. "O, Sun, the Chain"

Long ago there were three brothers called Tadakichi, Sankichi, and Magokichi. Their mother called them together one day and said, "Keep quiet until I come home. If you don't the man-eater will come and eat you all up. If she comes, look carefully at her because she will be different from me." Then the mother went away.

Somebody knocked at the door toward evening. Tadakichi went to see if it was his mother, but when he looked carefully, he saw lots of hair on her hands. After he shut the door, the man-eater scrubbed her hands with a potato grater and knocked again. When the boy went to see, Tadakichi thought she was his mother and let her in.

He heard his mother eating something in the night. He wondered what it was and asked, "What are you eating, Mother?"

She said, "I got hungry so I am eating this!" She tossed out a finger she had been gnawing. Tadakichi was terrified. He woke Sankichi up and they ran out into the yard and climbed a peach tree.

After the man-eater had finished devouring Magokichi, she came out to look for the two boys. She saw that they had climbed the peach tree and she started to climb up after them.

Tadakichi and Sankichi were frightened. They called, "O, Tentō-san [O, Sun], save us!"

Then a chain was lowered to them from the sky. Tadakichi and Sadakichi climbed it. When the man-eater started to climb it, the chain broke. She fell to the rock below and was killed. The roots of the corn that was planted near the rock were covered with the blood of the man-eater. From the next year, the roots of the corn were red.

*Mukashi mo mae ni mo, ketchiriko.*

Isogai Isamu
Asa-gun, Hiroshima

## 106. The Ox-leader and the Yamauba

A fish peddler took mackerel to sell in the mountain villages, but he had the misfortune of meeting up with a she-demon on his way back. When she had finished eating the fish that he had left, she threatened to catch him and eat him, too.

The fish peddler turned pale and started to run away. He climbed a tree growing by the edge of a dike. The she-demon came running up all out of breath and saw the reflection of the fish peddler in the marsh. She plunged in, but when she discovered that it was only a reflection, she went home angrily. The fish peddler then climbed down the tree and followed the she-demon to her hut and climbed into the rafters.

The she-demon built up a fire on her hearth, all the while complaining about how much trouble the fish peddler had caused her. Then she got out big pieces of mochi to toast. She nodded and dozed while the mochi was toasting.

The fish peddler picked up the mochi with a piece of thatch and ate it all. When the she-demon woke up, she shouted, "Who ate my mochi!"

The fish peddler intoned, "Hi-no-kami [Fire God], Hi-no-kami." She picked up a piece of mochi that had burned black and declared, "There's no help for it if it is the Hi-no-kami."

Next, she poured sweet wine into a kettle to warm it. She dozed off again while it heated. The fish peddler broke off a long piece of thatch and sipped up all the sweet wine in the kettle. When the she-demon woke up, she heard the voice of Hi-no-kami again. She gave up trying to do anything more and decided that on such a day it would be better to go to bed.

The she-demon muttered, "Shall I sleep in the wooden chest or the metal chest?"

The fish peddler did not fail to say, "Wooden chest!"

The she-demon said, "Well, I'll do as Hi-no-kami says." She climbed into the wooden chest to sleep. Then the fish peddler came down from the rafters and heated a kettle of water at the hearth. He went to the chest and began to drill holes in its lid with a gimlet. The she-demon whispered inside the chest, "Tomorrow will be a good day because the drill bugs are singing."

Then the boiling water was poured through the holes and she was killed.

Toma Rekirō
Minamikanbara-gun, Niigata

## 107. The Wife Who Didn't Eat

*Mukashi attaji mo na.*

Once there was a single man cutting firewood in the hills. He said to his friends, "I would like to have a wife who does not eat anything."

A strange looking woman came to the man's house a few days later and said, "I won't eat anything so please take me as your wife."

The man took the woman in and, sure enough, she never ate anything. But the man's supply of rice in the chest seemed to grow less and less and the bean paste bucket got empty after she came. The man thought it strange. One day he pretended to set out for town, but when his wife went to the privy, he came back and hid in the rafters of the stable.

After the woman came back from the privy, she dipped rice from the chest, washed it, and put it into a one-shō kettle to cook. Then she crushed bean paste in the grinding bowl and made soup. Then she made riceballs and set them in rows on a straw mat and set the soup in the bucket to cool. She took her hair down, and a big mouth came into view on the top of her head. She tossed the riceballs into that mouth and then dipped the cooled soup into it.

When she had finished, she tied her hair back again. The man climbed down from the rafters while she was cleaning everything up. He put dust onto his sandals and pretended he had come back from town and went into his house.

The next morning the man said to his wife, "I am going to send you back home."

She said, "I'll leave, but what are you going to give me?"

He said, "Take that tub that is big enough for two." She looked into it and cried, "Oh, there's a worm in it! Take it out!"

The man went over to the tub and leaned across to see. At that moment, the woman grabbed his two feet and thrust him into the tub head first. She swung it up onto her shoulders and turning into a yamauba, she started to run pellmell back into the hills. She called, "I'm bringing some fish to have with our wine. Everybody come!"

The yamauba climbed up the mountainside, parting the thickets as she went. There were answering calls from the hills beyond. The man lost all hope for his life, but when the tub brushed against a tree, he caught hold of a branch and pulled himself out. He started to run as fast as he could. The yamauba did not seem to miss him and continued to shout, "I'm bringing some tasty fish to have with our wine. Everybody come!"

When the yamauba reached the place where everybody had gathered, she set the tub down and discovered that the man was not there. She concluded he had escaped and she chased him down the hill along the way she had come. It looked as though she would catch up with the man, but he hid among iris and mugwort that were growing beside the path. The yamauba came up and looked into the patch of iris and mugwort. She saw the man, but she knew that if she put her hands among the plants, they would rot. There was nothing she could do about it, so she went back up the hills.

Since the man's life had been saved by the iris and mugwort, he fastened some onto his head and tied it around his waist. When he reached home, he put the plants on his roof and at the entrance to his house. The yamauba never came again because of that.

*Dotto harai.*

Ogasawara Kenkichi
Shiwa-gun, Iwate

## 108. The Wife Without a Mouth
[The Wife Who Didn't Eat]

I'll tell you why iris and mugwort are hung from the eaves and iris leaves are put into bath water at the festival of the 5th Day of the Fifth Month. The reason is that long ago there was a very stingy priest at a mountain temple. He wanted a wife, but she had to be one who did not eat and the kind he wanted the most was one without a mouth. He searched all over and finally found a bride who did not have a mouth.

The woman did not eat rice, sure enough, and the priest was delighted. But as time passed, The priest noticed that his bride cooked lots of rice every morning. He thought that if his bride did not eat rice, there was no reason for her to cook that much. It seemed strange to him.

The priest pretended to go away one day, but he hid in the corner of the yard to look on. When the woman thought there was nobody around, she took down her sidelocks and began to stuff lots of rice into a big mouth where the part was in her hair. The priest was terrified when he saw her. He let out a cry.

His bride rushed toward him and picked up the tub the priest was hiding in and started to run off with it. She decided to eat the priest along the way. She set the tub down where the grass was thick, and it rolled away and dropped into a pond. She came running after it, but fortunately there was a thick growth of iris and mugwort there, and she could not go into it.

That is why iris and mugwort are hung from the eaves and put into bath water to keep ghosts away at the festival of the 5th Day of the Fifth Month.

Kanno Norisuke
Tome-gun, Miyagi

## 109. The Younger Sister a Demon

Once there was a man and a woman who had two children, a boy and a girl. The girl slept with her parents until she was 12 or 13 years old, but after that she slept with her brother, who was older than she.

Shortly after they started sleeping like this, the sister examined her brother one night to see if he was asleep and then slipped out of the house. He only pretended to be asleep and wondered where she was going. He followed her to the edge of the village to the house farthest out in a place like Megunda. There his sister gave herself a shake and her face turned into something frightful with a huge mouth wide open, showing fangs.

His sister gobbled up a horse and started back home. Her brother ran as fast as he could to get there first. He went to bed, but when his sister got back, she looked at her brother's eyes once more. He snored. The girl's breath smelled unspeakably vile.

The next morning somebody passing the house said, "Nothing like this has ever happened before. A horse disappeared from its stable. Something strange is going on."

When the mother and father heard the talk, they said it was just a rumor. The same thing happened a second and a third night. On the fourth night, the girl set out after examining her brother, but this time she went to the east side of the village to eat a horse. The brother watched secretly again and reached home before his sister. Once more, she looked at his eyes.

The girl slept late because she was tired in the morning. Her father and mother heard talk by somebody passing again, but they said it must be just a rumor. The brother spoke up and said, "That was not a human being. It was my sister."

His parents were angry. They asked the boy if he wasn't a human being, too. And here he was talking about his sister! They turned their son out of his home.

The young man made himself look like a beggar and went off to a place like Katanoura to beg and just lived from day to day. He went to a place like Aose and arrived at a certain house where a man and his wife and their daughter were eating breakfast. They said, "This young man looks refined. He's not a real beggar."

They told the young man that he could see what kind of family they were, just the three of them. They asked to take him as their son. So the young man was adopted and became the son-in-law at a wedding ceremony in the fifth year after he had left home. On the exact day in the fifth year after he left home, he said, "Father and Mother, I have something to ask of you. I want to see my parents in my home town." They gave him permission to go.

The young man handed a mirror to his wife and said, "If this mirror becomes clouded, you will know that I am in mortal danger. Please set the pair of male and female hawks in our yard free." With that he set out.

When the young man looked down upon his village from the mountains, it was a vine-covered ruin. He went down to it and could not find a single house. His sister was there alone, lying on her back asleep in a frightful form. The brother thought he must do something before he returned. He cleared his throat and spoke to his sister.

The sister woke up and changed back into her usual form as she said, "Oh, my brother, it has been a long time since we saw each other. A terrible sickness came to our village and everybody died. I am the only one left. Please beat this drum for the comfort of their souls while I prepare a feast for you." She left him to go to wash the rice.

While the brother beat the drum, a black rat and a white rat came out. They said, "Hurry away! We are your father and mother. Our daughter ate us because we paid no attention to what you said, and we turned into this form. We will beat the drum for you, so run fast. Your sister is not polishing rice. She is polishing her teeth by chewing one shō of salt."

The brother ran as fast as the wind, but his sister noticed that the drum beats had changed. She came back to see and found the rats beating the drum. "I'll catch you," she cried as she chased the rats, but they went in and out of their holes and she could not get them. That took time. She declared, "I can't bother with you any more. No matter how far my brother goes, in one stride . . ." And the demon sister chased her brother.

She had almost caught up with her brother when he came to where three pine trees grew in a row. He climbed one, but his sister began to dig at the foot of the tree and felled it. The brother jumped to the next tree, but she dug around it. When he changed to the third tree, his wife noticed that the mirror was clouded. She exclaimed, "My husband is in danger!"

The wife freed the male and female hawks. That was just as the third tree was about to fall. The demon was digging with all her might. The two hawks came flying and clawed the sister's face. They flew at her alternately until they put out her eyes. But the demon's breath had touched the hawks and they died.

The brother looked at the demon and said, "You told me that all the villagers died from a terrible sickness, but our father and mother who turned into rats told me you had eaten them. Now I am going to take revenge for our parents and for the villagers."

He split the demon's head and body into two and he broke her legs. He dug a grave for the two hawks and stood the scabbard of his sword upon the grave of the female hawk and its blade upon the grave of the male hawk.

When the young man reached home, his wife and parents came to meet him. They led him into the house together and offered a memorial. His wife's parents became like his own from that time and they lived on together.

Iwakura Ichirō
Koshikijima, Kagoshima

## 110. A Thousand Wolves

A certain dry goods merchant of Kōshū went to Fuji-gun in Suruga on business. The sun set when he reached Tōppara, a three ri broad plain at the foot of Mt. Fuji at the border between Suruga and Kai, on his way home.

There was not a single house in sight. It grew dark on the road as he wondered what to do. Since it was the end of autumn, there were a number of sheaves of straw stacked around tree trunks. The merchant decided to make them do and crawled into a stack to stay until dawn. In the middle of the night, a pack of wild dogs which had scented the man gathered around where the merchant was. They circled him, sniffing and growling dreadfully. The frightened merchant got up in a flurry and ran to a tree nearby and climbed it. All the wild dogs came chasing him, but animals can't climb a tree. They only milled around and growled.

No matter how much they circled around the tree, they could not accomplish anything, so they began to talk over what to do. Then they said, "Let's send for Old Lady Magotarō and ask her to help." Two or three dogs went flying off while the rest stayed to guard the merchant. He wondered what sort of thing Old Lady Magotarō was. He waited and the dogs that had been sent came back leading an old tiger cat.

All the dogs went to meet her. They said, "Thank you for coming, Old Lady Magotarō. You see, a man has climbed that tree and we can't possibly reach him. What shall we do?"

The tiger-cat lowered her head and seemed to think it over for a while. Presently she said, "A good way would be to set up a dog ladder."

While the merchant was wondering what a dog ladder was, he looked down and saw one of the dogs crouch at the base of the tree. Then another dog climbed onto him, and another climbed onto that one. In this way the dogs climbed one over the other until they almost reached the feet of the merchant. The frightened man tried to climb higher into the tree, but unfortunately there was a big nest in the top branches and he could not go higher. In the meantime, the dogs were gaining on him and almost had reached him.

The desperate man drew his sword and thrust it blindly with all his might into the nest overhead. The nest happened to belong to a bear, whose comfortable sleep had ended with the pain of the sword jabbing his rear. It jumped up in fright and tumbled to the ground. The bear rushed off, not knowing what it was all about. The dogs saw it and thought they had succeeded in knocking the man out of the tree.

They broke their ladder in confusion and started to chase the black thing that was running off. They realized it was a bear only after they had run a distance. The dogs were dumbfounded. They declared the man must still be up the tree and ran back to it.

By that time, the sky in the east was gradually turning light. Old Lady Magotarō said, "Dawn is coming on so we can't go on with tonight's work. We can try again tomorrow." The wild dogs all agreed. They went off somewhere looking disappointed. The merchant, who had been trembling all the while in the treetop, came down and broke into a frantic run.

Dobashi Riki
Nishiyatsushiro-gun, Yamanashi

## 111. The Cat and the Teakettle Lid

There was a hunter in a certain place who prepared to make his first trip into the hills after New Year. While he counted out the bullets he would take in the morning, his three-colored cat seemed to be asleep by the hearth, but she was watching him.

The hunter was unaware of that and left for the hills. Presently he met a frightful monster, the likes of which he had never seen in the hills before. It was a big, one-eyed monster. No matter how many times he shot it, it seemed unconcerned. Presently the hunter used up all the bullets he had brought.

The monster then turned into a big cat and came leaping at the hunter. The man pulled out his hidden charm bullet and brought the cat down. When he went up to the cat to examine it, there was the copper lid of a teakettle beside it. The cat had held the lid in its mouth to protect itself from the bullets.

The hunter thought that the cat looked like the one kept at his house. He took the lid of the teakettle home with him to make sure. When he reached home, sure enough, the lid was missing from the teakettle and the cat was nowhere around.

Sasaki Kizen
Kamihei-gun, Iwate

## 112. Cat Mountain
[Nekomata]

A certain man thought he would cross the mountains from Osarusawa to go to Kemanai. He went as far as Shinden, but missed his way from there and found himself in an unknown mountain. The sun set while he was still in the mountains and he was worried.

The man saw a light in a big house beyond and went toward it to ask to spend the night there. A great crowd of women and children were chattering in the kitchen. When he asked to spend the night, they led him into the living room. He heard the crowd go out behind the house.

Presently, the sliding doors behind him were drawn open and an old woman entered. She said, "It has been a long time since I saw you, Sir. Please do not be surprised. I am the old cat your grandfather kept for a long time. This place is called Nekomata [Cat Mountain], a place where unwanted cats of the village gather. They have gone to get bedding for you now, but they will eat you if you stay. Please run away quickly. There is a hole in the corner of the alcove. If you crawl through that, you will come out below the porch. You will see a river when you go out of the gate. Once you get across that, you will be safe, for the cats can not follow you. Please hurry."

The man recalled that in the days of his grandfather there had been an old three-colored cat around that came up missing. He concluded that this cat must be the one. He followed her directions and left the mansion. He tied his clothes onto his head and started across the river as a great throng of cats came howling after him. He was frightened, but he managed to cross to the bank on the other side.

The cats did not follow the man. While he climbed the mountain, dawn came on. He looked from the top of the mountain and saw how much he had strayed from his way. He finally found his road and reached home.

Uchida Takeshi
Kazuno-gun, Akita

## 113. Cat Mountain and Cat Island

Once a lady and her maid who had a pet cat were living together. The maid loved the cat, but her mistress abused it. Then one day the cat suddenly was missing. The maid felt bad and cried every day because the cat was gone.

A pilgrim came by after a while and said to the maid, "That cat is on Cat Mountain of Inaba in Kyūshū." The maid was happy to hear that and asked permission from her mistress to look for it. Then she set out to the mountain in Inaba.

When the maid reached Inaba, she could not figure out which mountain she was looking for. In the meantime, the sun set and she was worried. She asked somebody she met and was told it was only a little farther. She saw a splendid house after she had gone a little way. It looked strange to her, but she decided to ask to spend the night there.

When the maid asked, a beautiful woman came out. The maid explained, "I am looking for my lovely cat, but I have lost my way. I came to ask to spend the night here."

The woman seemed to smile to herself. She said, "Did you come to be eaten alive?"

That frightened the girl, but just then an old woman came out. The old woman said kindly, "Please excuse that woman for being rude. It is all right for you to stay here tonight." So the maid stayed there.

When the maid was trying to sleep, she heard voices in the next room in the night. She thought it strange and drew back the sliding door to her room a little. She saw two beautiful women lying and beyond them in the next room, another beautiful woman asleep. The girl felt uneasy and trembled. She was sure she had heard talk and she stood still to listen. Someone was saying, "The woman who came today said she was looking for her precious cat. That is why we can't attack her." The maid was terrified.

Just then the door to her room was drawn open and her beloved cat came in. She appeared as a woman, but she had the face of a cat.

Her cat said, "Thank you for coming to look for me. However, I came here because I was old and could no longer serve at my house in the village. Coming here means success for a cat, so please do not worry. This is no place for you because this is where cats come from all over Japan. I will give you a treasure. Please hurry home. You must not open this until you reach home. If you meet cats along the way, wave this at them. In that way they will let you past." Then she gave the maid a white paper parcel.

The maid set out very happy. There was a big crowd of cats around, but when she waved the parcel as she went, they moved aside to let her pass. At home she told her mistress all that had happened. She opened the parcel and found the picture of a dog. It was holding a real 10 ryō gold coin in its mouth.

The mistress was envious when she saw the coin. She said, "It isn't right for a maid to receive 10 ryō. You can live for the rest of your life on that much. I am going to see. Since I was the mistress of the cat, they will probably give me more money." Then she set out.

When the lady arrived at the mountain in Inaba of Kyūshū, sure enough, a splendid house was there, just as her maid had said. She went to the door and called. When a young woman came out, the lady told her why she had come. A dirty looking old woman then came out from an inner room.

The lady demanded, "Let me stay here tonight. Let me meet my cat."

The old woman answered, "All right, I will let you stay."

And the lady was put up for the night. While she was asleep, there was a sudden disturbance in the next room in the night. She drew her sliding door back a little and saw two big speckled cats. The lady was surprised and looked into the next room. Two more fierce looking cats were there. The lady was completely terror stricken. Just then the door to her room opened and the cat that had been at her house came in.

The lady said, "Let's go home, cat! There's no telling what will happen in a place like this." She wanted to take the cat home with her.

The cat leaped upon the lady fiercely and bit her windpipe open.

Miyamoto Tsuneichi
Suō Ōshima, Yamaguchi

## 114. The Ghost of Treasure

*Mukashi ataru koto ni.*

If travelers came to this island [Keraji], they found a house where they could sleep at night. Kettles were set out so anyone could stay overnight, but for some reason, nobody would stay for two days. A certain man came to the island and went around asking for a place to spend the night, but nobody let him in. Finally, he was directed to that house, so he tried staying there.

A beautiful woman came out in the night and disappeared after saying a word or two. The next night a snake came out and disappeared after a few words. On the third night, a man came out and disappeared after saying a few words.

The first woman reappeared on the fourth night. She asked the man, "Where do you come from and what is your name?" The traveler told her about himself.

She said then, "No matter where men come from, they never spend two nights in succession here. They have not been your sort. I have a request to make for this reason. I am really money which has been hidden under this house for a long time. I have wanted to go out into the world quickly and to be given to men for their enjoyment, but I do not have the power to do it. This has made me suffer for a long time. I beg of you to dig me up quickly."

The man hastened the next morning to ask the villagers to help dig under to house to see. A great amount of money came out. He gave half of it to the villagers and took the other half for himself. Money that has been buried for many hundred years can transform itself and talk.

Iwakura Ichirō
Kikaijima, Kagoshima

## 115. The Ghost of the Mountain Pears

An ōnyūdō came out in the autumn while a novice was alone at a temple. It said, "Get the big grinding bowl out, boy." The novice was frightened, but he got out the grinding bowl.

The monster straddled it and defecated a big pile into it. It said,

"Now eat it, boy." The novice did not know what would happen if he refused, so he tried to eat it. It had the flavor of pears and really was delicious.

Whenever the priest was away, calling upon patrons, the ghost would be sure to come and make the novice eat his feces. The boy was truly frightened and finally told the priest what was happening. The priest listened to him.

He said, "This is very strange. The next time the ōnyūdō comes, follow it and mark the way it goes." The matter was left that way.

The next time the priest was away, the ōnyūdō came again. He defecated into the grinding bowl as usual and left after he made the boy eat it. The boy was frightened, but he followed the ōnyūdō as he had been told. It went into the mountain behind the temple and disappeared. The novice marked the place with a little branch he broke off and then went home.

He and the priest went the next day to where the stick had been set to look around. There was an odor of decaying pears coming from somewhere. This seemed unusual, and they went farther into the mountain to search. They found a huge old mountain pear tree with fruit that had fallen year after year and lay in a decaying mound at its base. It had transformed itself and had come to the temple.

The priest and his novice cleared up the place, sweeping below the tree and then purifying it. The ōnyūdō never came back to the temple after that.

Sasaki Kizen
Shiwa-gun, Iwate

## 116. The Man-Eating Mushroom

A certain poor drifter had a hard time making a living. He went to town and bought masks which he carried around to sell at various places. The sun set one evening just as he reached a certain village. He asked to spend the night at a house by the road, but the man said, "Things are all in disorder here. There is a vacant house next door. Please go there to stay. We will send food to you presently."

The mask peddler then went to the vacant house for the night. He was happy to find furnishings ready when he went in. He went over to the hearth to warm himself. Then he decided to set out his masks to see what he had sold that day.

Just as he was doing that, he heard a scary step of something approaching from the inner parlor. The partition door was pushed open and a big voice shouted, "Hey! Is there a human being there?" The surprised peddler looked over his shoulder and saw a huge face as big as a floor mat staring at him. The peddler picked up one of the masks beside him on the impulse and held it to his face as he yelled a response. He shifted his position so he could look in the direction of the face.

The Thing beyond burst into a roar of laughter. The peddler quickly picked up another mask as he looked at the Thing. Then he changed to another and another.

The Thing beyond suddenly stopped laughing. "Just what are you?" it asked.

The peddler replied, "I'm a ghost. As for that, what are you?" The Thing said, "I'm a ghost, too."

"Is that a fact," commented the man. "Are you a ghost that is only a big face?"

"Yes," admitted the ghost, "but I can turn into a face any number of times." The man said, "You don't amount to much if you don't have a variety of transformations. A real ghost can appear as a number of things. You saw me, didn't you?"

"I did, I did," answered the ghost. "You certainly are clever."

"If you are impressed with this little display, I feel sorry for you," boasted the man. "I have lots of disguises I can put on. Let's pass the time with a contest in disguises. Come on over by the fire to warm yourself."

The ghost said, "It makes me feel bad when I go near the fire, so I can't." The man broke into a laugh. "How your looks belie your spirit," jeered the man. "Have you always been a ghost?"

"No," said the ghost as he started to tell about himself. "There was an old peach tree that stood for many years beyond a lot of ponds far back in the mountains. It withered naturally at last and decayed. I am a mushroom that sprouted on the trunk of that tree.

"After many years I matured on the tree trunk and I can say I became a fairly large mushroom. One day a beautiful little bird flew to the branch of the tree and sang sweetly. At first I only looked at it, thinking what a lovely thing it was, but then I began to want to eat it. I kept thinking how I wanted to eat it—wanted to eat it—and fixed my sight on it until eyes and a mouth appeared on my body. Quick as a flash, I tell you, I sucked in the bird and ate it. How sweet it was! From that time I could eat living things any time I wanted to. For many years I continued to eat in this way, but the peach tree decayed completely in the meantime and toppled over. I was dislodged from its trunk.

"While I moved around, folding and sliding, I grew hands and a foot and learned to walk without any trouble. When I could do this, wasn't I really a fine ghost? Instead of living only far back in the mountains, I wanted to try coming down to the village. There wasn't any place for me to hide, so I crept under the foundation beam of this house. Here, I tell you, I could eat rats or snakes or toads. Presently I was able to push up the trap door in the back room. From there I could go into the inner parlor, and I have been there for a number of years, you see."

The man exclaimed, "Then it has been your doings, the men who have been killed and eaten in this house!" "No, that's not true," protested the ghost. "I get tired of staying in the damp, dark back parlor all year. I like to slip out sometimes to find company. When I call to men, it is strange how one after another drops dead. I tell you, if I eat his corpse, that isn't killing him."

"Well, you have explained everything now. Come on over by the fire and we can talk together until dawn," urged the man.

"No, it's like I said before," refused the ghost. "I am a mushroom and heat and salt are poisonous for me. When I am touched by them, I melt. Those boards around the hearth have been saturated with salt for many years and I can't go any nearer than here, I tell you. It's getting late now, so I will go back. I'll come out again tomorrow night to talk. Please stay here every night." Then the ghost dragged itself back into the inner parlor.

When it was morning, the people from next door came to the vacant house, wondering what had happened to the guest. They found him in the midst of eating breakfast. They asked in surprise, "Didn't anything happen last night?"

The peddler replied, "There certainly was something going on. Something frightful appeared. I think we should plan together to destroy it."

Word was sent around and a crowd of villagers gathered. They made two or three big kettles of salty bean soup and heated salt water. They poured it into buckets and set out plenty of dippers. All the men in the village came to the peddler, and he led them into the vacant house. They hunted in every corner, but they could not find the ghost of the night before. As they gathered dumb-founded in the middle of the parlor to talk things over, they heard the sound of loud snoring coming from somewhere.

That certainly was suspicious, so they hunted here and there again. Finally they found a big mushroom leaning against the pillar in the alcove and snoring loudly. The men winked at each other and each took a dipperful of soup or salt water to toss onto the mushroom. It billowed up into a huge thing, spreading all over the room and looking like a big, astonished mushroom. It slid this way and that, trying to suck in someone, but the men all dashed salt water onto it. It was completely weakened at last and died from fatigue.

The men bound the mushroom with ropes and dragged it to the crossroads to exhibit it. The mask peddler was praised by everybody. He was given the house and became a chōja.

Sasaki Kizen
Kamihei-gun, Iwate

## 117. The Haunted Mountain Temple

*Attaji mo na.*

An itinerant priest came to a certain village and asked to be put up for the night. He was told that no traveler was allowed to stay over night there, but he could stay at a vacant temple at the foot of the mountain nearby.

When the priest reached the temple, several villagers were already there. They had built a fire and seemed glad to let him stay. They said, "Here is wine and cooked rice. Please help yourself and stay the night." Then they left him and returned to the village.

The priest warmed himself at the fire and then settled down. He heard strange footsteps in the main hall in the night. He put the kettle over his head and waited. An ōnyūdō with three eyes and two sets of teeth came out from the inner room.

"Let's hear how you sound, priest," it said and whacked the kettle on the priest's head. It said, "What a hard head!"

The priest said, "It's my turn now." He picked up a big stick of firewood from the pile by the hearth and hit the ōnyūdō on its head and split it open. He picked up the ghost and tossed it outside.

Presently, the priest heard the same kind of steps again, and another ōnyūdō came in. It said, "Let's hear how you sound, priest," and it whacked the kettle.

The priest said, "It's my turn, now!" He split that ghost's head with a piece of firewood and tossed it outside.

And once more, those heavy steps came and an ōnyūdō entered. "Let's hear how you sound, priest," it exclaimed and whacked the kettle on the priest's head. It exclaimed, "What a hard head!"

The priest said, "It's my turn now." He split the head of that ōnyūdō with firewood, picked it up, and tossed it outside. After that nothing more came out.

The next morning the villagers came to the temple to see. They thought the itinerant priest of the night before had surely been killed and eaten. But the priest was sitting by the fire as though nothing had happened. The villagers asked, "Wasn't there anything going on last night?"

He said, "Three ōnyūdō made a noise in the main hall and came in here. They said they wanted to hear how I sounded, but I split their heads and tossed them outside. Look at them when the morning sun shines on them because the real form of ghosts can be seen then."

The villagers went to see and found the three dead ōnyūdō with their heads split open. When the morning sun reached them, they found that they were old disguised wooden clogs.

The villagers said, "This has been a haunted temple. No matter how many priests have come to take charge of it, they have all been eaten. That is why it is a vacant temple and we look after it every morning and evening. Please stay and run this temple." The itinerant priest stayed and took charge of the place.

*Dotto harai.*

Ogasawara Kenkichi
Shiwa-gun, Iwate

## 118. The Ghost in the Deserted House

A traveler going beyond Toyomane-mura became tired and was glad to see a light in the home of a friend. He asked to rest a bit there, and his friend welcomed him.

The friend said, "Someone has died here. Please sit by the corpse for a while." The traveler was annoyed, but there was no way to refuse. He went over to the hearth to have a smoke. The corpse was that of an old woman lying farther back in the room. When the traveler happened to glance that way, he saw her stir and start to rise. The startled man kept control of himself and looked around quietly.

He saw something like a fox had its face at the hole of the drain below the sink. Its eyes were fixed upon the dead woman. The man shifted his position cautiously and eased himself out of the room. When he went around behind the house, he saw a fox standing on its hind legs with its head stuck through the hole in the drain. He picked up a handy stick and beat the fox to death.

Yanagita Kunio
Shimohei, Iwate

# 8. *Help from Animals*

## 119. The Listening Hood

There was an old man in a certain place where Inari was the Ujigami [tutelary deity]. The old man was always wishing he could offer fresh fish to Ujigami, but he was too poor. One day when he went to the shrine, he pressed the palms of his hands together and prayed, "I am so poor that I can not offer you any fresh fish, Ujigami Sama. Just eat me in place of it."

Ujigami replied, "I don't want you to worry over such a matter, old man. I know very well what difficulties you have. I will grant you some good fortune. Look, I will give you this magic hood. Try putting it on. When you wear it, you can understand anything birds or beasts say." Then Ujigami gave the old man a soiled old red hood.

"Thank you very much. Can it be true," exclaimed the old man. He took the red hood gladly and went shuffling off to where a big pine tree stood by the road.

The old man dozed off as he rested beneath it. Just about the time he thought he had dozed off, a tired crow came flying from the direction of the seashore and rested for a while on a branch of the tree. Then another crow came flying from the direction of Arima (the region of Waga and Hienuki) and perched on the top of the tree.

The old man decided this was the time to try out the hood he had received from Inari. He put it onto his head and suddenly heard strange voices overhead. The two crows were talking. The crow from Arima said, "It has been a long time since I saw you. Where did you fly from just now?"

The crow from the seashore answered, "I have been over by the seashore, but there aren't any fish these days and times are hard. That is why I came flying this way. And where did you fly from?"

The other crow said, "I came from Arima. Hard times seem to be everywhere. Have you heard of anything unusual going on?" The crow from the coast replied, "It isn't especially unusual, but it has been five or six years since the chōja in a certain village near the seashore built a storehouse. When they were thatching the entrance to it, a snake crawled up for some reason. It was not noticed and a board was laid over him and nailed down. It can't move and is hovering between life and death. I admire the way the female snake continues to bring it food all these years to keep it alive. They both are really suffering and their resentment has built up until it has affected the daughter in the family, causing her illness. If they don't take that board off the snake in the storehouse and save the snake, both it and the girl will die. I fly to the roof and call time after time, but men have no pity."

The other crow said, "Yes, men are really like that. They don't understand when such things happen. Well, I'll see you again sometime." The two crows parted and one flew off to the east and the other to the west.

The old man thought he had been lucky to have heard what the crows had said. He wanted to hurry to the chōja's house to save the snake and the daughter, but he could not set out without being prepared.

The old man walked around the village until he found a broken, round wooden box that had been thrown away. He pasted paper over it and set it on his head as he set out to the chōja's house by the seashore. He walked by the house calling, "Fortunes told! Fortunes told!"

The chōja was worried about learning a good way to cure his daughter. He called, "You, there! Come in quickly and lay out your divining sticks." The old man went in and asked, "What do you want me to find out?" The chōja said, "My daughter has been sick for a long time. It looks like any day will be her last. Please lay out your sticks to see what we can do to make her well."

The old man said, "Then take me to where your sick girl is." He went in and sat by where she was lying. He chanted over and over, "When arrowroot leaves that spread twenty ri spread twenty ri," and then told in detail the story he had heard from the crow.

The chōja declared, "It is just as you say, Fortune Teller! Five or six years ago I built a storehouse. That could have happened. We must save that snake and get rid of it right away."

The chōja called a carpenter who lived nearby to lift the board over the entrance to his storehouse. Sure enough, there lay the snake, white and almost half decayed. They lifted it carefully into a basket and lowered it. Then they set it by the drain in the kitchen and gave it things to eat. They turned the snake loose when it was well.

In the meantime, the daughter's illness gradually disappeared until she was completely cured. The happy chōja gave the old man 300 ryō. The old man went home a rich man. He rebuilt the Ujigami Shrine immediately and bought fresh fish to offer. Then he celebrated a finer festival of thanksgiving than ever before had been seen.

The old man set out again on a journey, but this time wearing good clothes he had bought. He went back to the same big tree. While he rested, crows came flying from the east and west again and lighted on a branch of the tree. They began to talk about what was going on. One crow said, "I get tired of always staying in one town."

The other agreed with him. Then he said, "This is what has been going on in the town where I have been. The chōja in town is so sick that he may die any day. The reason is that when he had a teahouse built in his yard five or six years ago, a camphor tree that had grown in the yard for a long time was cut down. Its stump is just below the eaves where the rain drips off onto it. Since its roots were not cut so it could die, it keeps sending out shoots as long as it lives. It does its best to grow, but as soon as its shoots come out, they are cut off. The stump can't die even if it wants to and neither can it live. It's resentment has rested on the master of the house, causing his illness. Besides, friendly trees from the mountains around come to call upon the ailing camphor stump nearly every night. They worry about it, saying that it should be allowed to live if it wants to, but if it wants to wither, its roots should be dug up completely."

When the old man heard this story, he set out for the house of the chōja in town. He called, "Fortunes told! Fortunes told!" Somebody came out of the chōja's house and asked him in to tell a fortune.

When the old man went in, he found that the house was even more splendid that it had appeared to be from the outside. He asked, "What fortune do you want me to ascertain?"

The man on the staff of the house said, "The master of this house has been suffering from an illness for many years. No matter how many doctors or hōsha we hire, he never gets well. If you have any idea from your fortune sticks, Sir Fortune Teller, please let us know."

The old man agreed. He said, "I can find the exact cause of your master's illness, and beyond that, how to cure it, so please do not worry any more." He then repeated what he had heard about the teahouse from the crow. He said, "I think that a teahouse was built here five or six years ago. Let me stay in it."

The man at the house said, "Why, Sir Fortune Teller, how do you know about the teahouse?"

The old man answered, "I learned it from my fortune sticks. Just leave me there three days and three nights, and I can show you clearly the cause of your master's illness." So the old man went into the teahouse. He said, "Let nobody come into this place until I say the word." He stayed up all night to make sure of everything.

In the middle of the night, something approached with a rustle and a voice asked, "How are you, Camphor Tree?"

A ghostly voice answered from deep in the ground, "Oh, the one who asks must be the willow tree from Rokkōzan. I am sorry you come from so far every night. I can only go on suffering."

The willow tree said, "Don't give in that way." It tried to comfort him as it left.

Presently something came swishing along. A voice said, "How are you, Camphor Tree?"

The stump answered, "There is no help for me. I am sorry you come every night this way to see me. You must be the creeping pine from Hayachinezan."

"Yes, I am," it answered. "But it is no bother, so stop worrying. I am on my way to Goyōzan, so I can see you. This is not a long way around. You should be all right by spring. Just wait for the right time and don't give up." The creeping pine went away with the same sound as when he had come.

The old man heard all this with the magic hood on his head. He waited impatiently for dawn.

The next morning he said, "Take me into the sick man's room." He went beside where the master was lying. He intoned his usual chant about arrowroot leaves and then told in detail how the trees had worried the night before. He said, "It is not only the suffering of the camphor tree in your yard, for trees in the high mountains all around are worrying. Have the roots of the old tree dug up immediately."

After the stump was dug up and worshipped as Ki-no-kami [Tree Deity], the master's illness was gradually cured. Everybody was grateful to the old man. He received another 300 ryō and went home.

The old man had no more desires after that and gave up fortune telling. He became a chōja.

Sasaki Kizen
Kamihei-gun, Iwate

## 120. The Golden Fan and the Silver Fan

Once upon a time there was a man called Gonemon who was always poor, and he wore such tattered clothes that people called him Ragged Gonemon.

The man finally could no longer endure his poverty and went to the shrine of Kangamo Myōjin to begin a petition lasting three times seven or twenty-one days. He prayed earnestly, "Please make me a rich man."

On the twenty-first day, the final day of petition, the deity appeared in the form of a white-haired old man. He said, "Since you have offered your prayers faithfully, I will make you rich." He held out a gold fan and a silver fan and said, "If you fan with this gold fan, you can make the nose of anyone you wish long, and with the silver fan you can make it short again. You can use these fans any way you want, but you must never use them improperly." He gave careful instructions.

Gonemon was delighted. He waited for a good chance to use the fans. Then he heard that the chōja's only daughter was going to see cherry blossoms. Gonemon went there ahead of the girl and stood behind a cherry tree. He fanned the girl's nose two or three times with his gold fan. The girl's nose lengthened two or three feet in plain sight of everybody.

No doctor they hired could cure the girl's nose. She could only weep for shame. The chōja and his wife and everybody wondered how such a strange illness should befall their precious girl. They were overcome with grief.

The family finally decided to take as son-in-law anyone who could cure their girl. They had a notice to this effect written on a tall sign and set up in front of their house. After three days had passed, Gonemon walked by the chōja's house, calling "Massage treatment for noses! Massage treatment for noses!"

He was called in hurriedly. He made the girl eat grains of rice with flour on them, saying that it was medicine. In the meantime he fanned the girl's face a little from a distance with his silver fan. Her nose began to get shorter a little at a time. After a day or two, it looked like it always had. The chōja then recalled his promise and reluctantly made the filthy man his son-in-law. From that time Gonemon wore good clothes and ate good things all the time. He lived a life of ease without any effort.

One day Gonemon remembered the fans that were by then in the cupboard and covered with dust. He had only used them on somebody else until then, but he wondered what would happen if he tried them on himself. He sprawled out on his back and began to fan his nose with the gold fan. It felt good as it lengthened out, so good that he dozed off as he fanned it.

His nose lengthened until it reached the sky and pierced the clouds. It happened that they all were in the midst of toasting mochi at Thunder's house. They saw a strange looking soft round horn come pushing up through the ashes. The people were uneasy about it. They heated one of their metal chopsticks red hot and poked it through the thing that looked like a horn. Gonemon below could not endure the pain.

He screamed, "It's hot! It's hot!" and hurriedly fanned with his silver fan, but the tip of his nose was held fast by the metal chopstick. As his nose shrank, Gonemon's body was drawn up higher and higher. Finally he reached a place below the floor of Thunder's house. He could go no farther up or down.

He is probably still hanging there in the sky. He will have to stay there until Thunder decides to pull the chopstick out.

Dobashi Riki
Nishiyatsushiro-gun, Yamanashi

## 121. The Magic Ladle

At a certain place there once was a man who was a great liar. He had no friends because he was always telling things nobody could believe. He realized this, finally, and thought, "It won't do. I must be able to make friends of ordinary folk." He repented and secluded himself at the Kannon Shrine in the village for seven days and seven nights.

He prayed, "Please, Kannon Sama, make me an honest man like others." He prayed for one night, two nights, and on until the morning of the seventh day. That night his petitions would be complete, but he had received no sign.

He went down the hill from the shrine a little provoked. He

chanced to see a little red ladle that had been dropped below the gate to the grounds. "Could it be this sort of thing!" he thought. Well, there must be some use for it, so he picked it up and tucked it into the bosom of his clothes. He walked slowly across a broad meadow.

Suddenly the man felt that his bowels would move and he stepped into a thicket by the road. When he had finished, he tried to find something to use and felt near his hips. He happened to touch the little ladle. Since that was all there was, he used it to wipe his bottom. When he did, a sudden sound came from his butt:

*Oppoko koppoko otten nenjiu*
*Hakuyaku Genji no sanganka*
*Kiyomizu Kannon no Rokkakudō*
*Naraba nare, naraba nare*
*Taketsu shitehiri yoitsumuro tsuppai*
*Tatabichi gatabichi*

The liar was astonished. It really was terrific. He thought there must be some way to use the ladle, but he could not decide. He was speechless and dumbfounded, but he noticed that one side of the ladle was red and the other was black. There should be some reason for that, he thought, and he tried giving himself a pat with the black side. The big noise suddenly stopped. This was certainly an unusual object.

The liar strolled into town carrying the ladle. A mare was urinating profusely at the edge of town. The liar tried his ladle on its butt. Sure enough, but there was an even bigger noise because it was from a horse.

*Oppoko koppoko nenjin*
*Hakuyaku Genji no sanganka . . .*

The horse leader was sitting in front of a little shop eating his lunch of fried noodles. He leaped up in surprise. "Something has possessed my horse," he cried. "Something terrible has happened. I must take my horse to a yamabushi or a hōin!"

The liar said, "Don't make such a fuss about a little thing like this. I'll cure it." He went around to the other side of the horse and stroked it with the back of the ladle and the big noise stopped abruptly. The owner of the horse was delighted. He thanked the liar and bought him some wine. The liar went home happier than ever over the thing he had found.

The chōja in the village where the liar lived happened to have a beautiful daughter. The liar had been in love with her for a long time, but, much to his regret, he never had a chance to speak to her. He had been wanting to be taken by her family as her bridegroom. One night he hid in the snow-covered grounds of the chōja's house and waited for the girl to come out for "a little run." He was tired of waiting and came out of the shadows to pat the girl's white little bottom with his ladle.

There was a burst of "oppoko koppoko sutten nenjin gatabichi gatabichi. . ." The girl was astonished and ran into the house crying. She could not stop breaking wind from that time, day or night. All her laughter stopped, she grew pale, and she never left the house.

Doctors and hōin were called, and all kinds of treatments were tried, but nothing took effect. There was nothing left to try. The chōja had a tall sign erected before his gate on which was written, "Any wish will be granted to the one who can cure the strange illness of the only daughter of this family."

Men who saw the sign came every day, each one thinking he could be the one, but none was successful. All the relatives gathered at the house to sigh and to try to think of what to do. Then the liar came along. He said, "I came because I saw the sign in front. I'll show you that I can cure the young lady."

The chōja had seen one after another come with no results, but the sign was still up, so he allowed the liar to go into the other room for a try. The liar found a gold screen set up and doctors huddled together looking pale. They glared at the liar as if to say that when they could not cure the girl, how could such an amateur as the liar do anything. The liar was so amused he could hardly hold back a laugh. He went to the girl's side confidently. He moved the gold screen around them so that they could not be seen from anywhere. Then he patted the girl's little bottom with the ladle. The loud noises that had been going on until then suddenly stopped as if a lid had been put on them.

The girl cried, "Oh, I'm cured!" She went running and dancing out of the inner room. The chōja and his wife were delighted and broke into a dance, too, exclaiming, "By your help! By your help!" The men who had gathered there looked downcast and rushed away.

That is how the liar became the son-in-law of the chōja and became successful. It was all because of the little ladle. It was worshipped later as a deity called O-hera Daimyōjin [The Great Manifestation in the Ladle].

Sasaki Kizen
Kamihei-gun, Iwate

## 122. Bumbuku Teakettle

Once upon a time there was a junk dealer in a certain village. He was always poor, no matter how hard he worked. One day he thought of a good plan.

He hurried off to the home of a badger nearby in the middle of the day. He said, "I want to ask a favor of you, Badger, so please listen."

The badger replied, "I'll listen to anything you have to say. What is it?"

The junk dealer said, "Well, this is it. I wish you would transform yourself into a teakettle for me, Badger."

The badger said, "I was wondering what you wanted of me. There's nothing to turning into a teakettle. I'll do it any time. Look, are you ready?" The badger promptly turned into a teakettle.

That settled things for the junk dealer. He wrapped the teakettle immediately in a furoshiki and tied it onto his back to carry to the priest at the temple. There he said to the priest, "Oshō Sama, I came priest at the temple. There he said to the priest, "Oshō Sama, I came across a rare teakettle recently. I'll make it cheap for you, so please buy it."

The priest responded, "Let's see it. What kind of teakettle is it?" He untied the furoshiki to look at it. He said, "This is really a good teakettle. How much is it?"

The junk dealer said, "Since it is for you, Oshō Sama, I will make it very cheap. It will be three ryō." The priest thought that three ryō was cheap and he bought the teakettle.

The priest called his novice and said, "Take this teakettle to the river and scour it with sand, boy." The novice took the teakettle to the river obediently and began to scour it vigorously.

The teakettle said, "It hurts! Scour more gently, boy!" The surprised novice ran to the priest and told him what had happened.

The priest said, "I'll go and try scouring it." The priest went then to the edge of the river and began to scour the teakettle with sand.

It cried, "It hurts, Oshō! Scour gently!"

The priest said, "This is strange. Fill the teakettle with water and set it on the fire to boil."

The novice did as he was told. He filled the teakettle with water and built a fire under it. Presently the teakettle said, "It's hot, boy. Build up the fire more slowly." The fire gradually burned higher and hotter.

The badger suddenly stuck his face out of the kettle and then his feet and then to the amazement of the novice, out came the big fat tail. The teakettle turned into a badger and ran off to the mountains. In that way the priest lost his three ryō.

Shimoina-gun, Nagano

## 123. The Fox Harlot

Once upon a time there was a poor old couple. One day after the old man had sold a few vegetables and was on his way home, he saw a group of mischievous children by the river who were about to tie up a little fox they had caught.

The old man felt sorry for the fox and tried to stop the children, but they paid no attention to him. He finally took out the little money he had and bought the little fox from them. He turned it loose and said, "You are going to get into trouble if you play around in a place like this. Hurry home now."

When the old man had gone a little farther, he met a small, beautiful woman who looked about forty years old. She said to the old man, "Thank you for what you did just now. That was my daughter. She went out to play because the weather was good today, shifting from rain to sunshine, off and on. Human children caught her and she was in danger when you saved her. I really have no way to thank you, but I will do what I can. I am going to circle this cherry tree three times now and turn myself into a pretty young girl. Take me to that greedy Kanjyamu at Ozaka-machi and sell me for 400 ryō."

you?" That woman said, "I will sing an amusing song as I run away. There is nothing for you to worry about."

The old man led the transformed fox. She was a little girl dressed in a kimono with long sleeves and a sash tied like a harlot's. They came to the gate of Kanjyamu at Ozaka-machi. He paid 400 ryō for the girl without any objection because she was so beautiful. The old man took the money and went right home.

The girl asked the attendant where the privy was. After she went into the privy, she slipped out of the window and climbed onto the roof. There she clapped her hands and mocked Kanjyamu as she sang:

Kanjyamu of Ozaka-machi,
See the fox you bought for 400 ryō.
*Konkon chiririn, konkon chiririn.*

People who heard her voice were astonished. They looked this way and that, but could not see anyone. Then somebody said, "The voice is from the roof!" They went outside to see. There on the roof was a small girl with her sash tied like a harlot's but with the face of a fox. She clapped her hands and sang as she went leaping lightly from roof to roof.

Hasegawa Tamae
Sado, Niigata

## 124. Animal Gratitude

Once upon a time a courier was surprised on his way home to see a wolf. He looked at it closely and saw that it seemed to have a problem with a bone stuck in its throat. He felt sorry for the wolf and removed the bone. The wolf looked happy as it went off.

The courier reached home that night without anything happening. He met the wolf in the mountains every day after that but nothing special happened.

One day, however, the wolf appeared when the courier was on his way home and took hold of his garment. It tried to lead him away.

Thinking this strange the courier shook his garment and asked, "What are you trying to do?"

The wolf only caught hold again and tried to lead him away. This went on until the courier finally gave up and went along with the wolf. It took him to its own cave. In a short time a pack of 1000 wolves passed by. The courier's life had been saved by the wolf.

Kinosaki-gun, Hyōgo

## 125. The Dog, the Cat, and the Ring

Long ago there were two homes on the opposite banks of a river, one on the east bank and one on the west bank, and an old couple lived in each.

The house on the east bank belonged to a very honest old man. He had a cat, but could not feed it well because he was poor. One night the old man had a revelation from the Dragon Palace. It said, "I will give you a monkey farthing. Hang it behind the well and worship it." When the old man woke up the next morning, there really was a monkey farthing by his pillow.

After the old man hung it up behind the well, his family that had been so poor began to prosper more and more each day. On the contrary, the family of the stingy old man on the west bank of the river began to fail more and more each day. Since women are gossips, the old woman from the east bank told the old woman on the west bank that her old man was prospering more and more each day because he had received a monkey farthing. The old man on the west bank heard about it and promptly crossed over to the east bank to borrow that monkey farthing.

The old man on the east bank was honest by nature. He said, "I can't lend it to you for a long time, but you may have it for a little while."

After the old man from the west bank took the coin home and hung it behind his well, his fortunes that had been growing worse changed. They became better day by day. The old man on the east bank who had loaned the coin began to get visibly poorer once more.

The old man on the east bank crossed over to urge the old man on the west bank to return the coin he had loaned him, but that old man put him off with one excuse and another and refused to return it. The old man on the east bank became more and more troubled. His old wife thought of many plans, but she finally told their pet cat to go to get the coin.

The cat was willing enough, but she could not cross the river when she came to it. A dog happened along and she told him about things. She asked him to take her across the river on his back. The cat could then cross the river. When she reached the house on the west side, she heard a rat squeaking. She caught the rat without any difficulty. She said to it, "I will spare you if you go behind the well and drop the coin that hangs there to me." The rat climbed behind the well and, got the coin and brought it to the cat. The cat carried it back to the dog and asked it to carry her back across the river.

When they reached the middle of the river, the dog said, "Don't drop what you got."

The cat said, "Yes," but when she spoke, she dropped the coin into the water. She cried as she tried to think what to do. Just then a kite came flying down from the sky. The cat caught onto it and said, "I will spare you if you look for the coin I dropped in the river."

The kite could see anything below when it flew up, but it could not see what was on the bottom of the river. The kite caught a cormorant that was playing around the river. The kite said to it, "You can catch a trout swimming at the bottom of the river, so pick up the farthing that has dropped to the bottom of the river."

The cormorant went to the bank of the river and looked up and down the stream. He caught a big trout and said to it, "I am not going to kill you. Please get the monkey farthing that has dropped to the bottom of the river. You do well there, for you catch little crabs and crayfish for food that do not move on the bottom of the river."

When the trout went down to look, it saw the monkey farthing. It picked up the coin and gave it to the cormorant. The cormorant gave the coin to the kite, and the kite handed it over to the cat. The cat was so happy that she burst into song:

From the cat to the rat and to the kite
And to the cormorant that caught the fish in the river.

Although the dog had helped the cat cross the river, it had made her drop the precious coin. That is why it was not mentioned in the song. The cat took the coin back to the old man on the east bank, and he began to prosper once more.

*Sorede potchiri.*

Ushio Michio
Ōchi-gun, Shimane

## 126. The Tongue-cut Sparrow

There was an old man and an old woman who kept a sparrow in a cage. One day the sparrow ate all the dango the old woman had made and left to dry on the roof. She was angry and cut the sparrow's tongue. The old man heard about what happened when he came home from the hills.

He set out, calling, "Sparrow, sparrow, where have you gone?" He came to a bamboo cutter and asked, "Do you know where the sparrow went?"

The man answered, "If you cut bamboo for me, I will tell you." So the old man cut bamboo. Next the old man came to a man who was spreading fertilizer, and he helped dip that up . . . The rest is the usual story.

[Translator's note: Sugiwara gives seven different beginnings to this well-known story but omits the latter episodes. The "usual story" might be something like this:

Eventually the old man arrived at the sparrow's house and said he was sorry for what had happened. The sparrows entertained him and gave him a feast. When the old man was about to leave, they gave him a choice of baskets as a gift. He modestly chose the smallest one to take home. He was told not to open it before he reached home. When he opened the basket, he found it full of treasures. His old wife decided that she would see what she could get. She was entertained by the sparrows and given a choice of gifts. She chose the biggest basket. It became so heavy on her way home that she set it down. She was too greedy to wait and she opened the basket. Frightful snakes and monsters came out. She barely escaped and ran home.]

Sugiwara Takeo
Sakai-gun, Fukui

## 127. The Sparrow with a Broken Back

Long ago there was an honest old woman and a stingy old woman in a place where there were farmers in the mountains.

One day when the honest old woman was working by her porch, she saw a little sparrow come flying in great pain into her yard. Children had thrown stones at it and had broken its back. The old woman ran up to it and cried, "Oh, you poor thing! What happened!" She picked the sparrow up carefully and took it into her house. She fixed a soft, warm nest lined with cotton in a cage for it. She fed the sparrow good things and cared for it.

The sparrow's injury was completely healed after three or four days. The old woman no longer worried about it. She opened the door to the cage and said, "You are all right now, so I will let you go. Be careful not to let children catch you and hurt you again." Even though a sparrow may be a bird, it lowered its head and listened, realizing the kindness of the old woman. It then flew away into the thicket.

The next day the old woman heard a sparrow chirping by her door. She thought it must be her sparrow as she opened the door. Sure enough, it was. The old woman wondered why it had come back. When she looked closely, she saw that the sparrow had dropped something white from its anus. She thought its bowels were runny, but she picked the dropping up.

It was a gourd seed. The old woman planted it to see if it would grow. It grew and grew until a big gourd vine spread all over her yard. The gourds looked so good that the old woman wanted to eat one. It was delicious. She ate some every day, but she decided she should not eat them alone. She took many of the gourds to her neighbors and to people in the village.

She decided to hang seven or nine of the largest gourds that were left under the eaves to dry. Presently the gourds looked heavy. She took one down and shook it to see. Rice came flying miraculously from it. The happy old woman said, "Thank you, sparrow." She pressed the palms of her hands together and turned reverently toward the thicket. The old woman was able to eat rice every day after that. She grew plump in her easy life. As soon as the gourd was empty, it would fill again. Her family became very prosperous.

The old woman next door was very greedy. She was envious when she heard what had happened. She thought, "I would like to have a prosperous, easy life like that. I wonder if there is a sparrow with a broken back somewhere."

The neighbor looked all over for one, but she could not find a single sparrow with a broken back. She was so jealous that she caught a sparrow that was near her and broke its back on purpose. Then she put it into a cage. She waited four or five days for its back to heal and then took it from its cage. She gave it a toss as she set it free.

The old woman craned her neck every day to see if the sparrow had come back. The little sparrow came to her window after five or six days. The greedy old lady danced with joy as she hurried out to see. Sure enough, the sparrow dropped a little gourd seed, just as she had expected. The old woman planted the seed in a corner of her yard. Presently the seed sprouted into a beautiful vine. The old woman thought that many gourds would form, but only seven or eight small ones appeared. She was disappointed, but she was a thoroughly selfish woman. She decided, "I can't help it if lots of gourds don't grow. I'll keep all of these so I can get plenty of rice." When children in the neighborhood came to ask for some, she would not give them any.

The old woman hung all of the gourds under her eaves to dry. She looked at them and thought, "I broke the sparrow's back and took care of it until it was well and it should be grateful. It will surely give me lots of rice as it did for the old woman next door." The old woman started to take one gourd down, wondering if it was full of rice, but it was almost too heavy for her.

The old woman was happy as she thought, "I'll be the greatest chōja in Japan." She hurried to cut the gourd open. My goodness! There wasn't a single grain of rice! What came out were vipers, centipedes, toads, and monsters. The greedy old woman was speechless with fright and died.

*Oshimai koppori.*

Suzuki Kiyomi
Usa-gun, Ōita

## 128. Kokōjirō

An old man brought a crab from the hills and put it into the cupboard to take care of it. His old woman looked in to see how big the crab had grown while the old man was away. It was running across the bamboo basket in the cupboard. The old woman could not help wanting to eat it. She cooked it in a kettle and ate it.

When the old man came back from the hills and asked about the crab, the old woman pretended she knew nothing about it. She said it must have run away somewhere. A crow in a tree called:

The shell on the roof, the claws in the garden,
The meat in Granny's belly, *gaa-gaa.*

The old man caught the old woman. She apologized and said, "I ate it! I ate it!"

Nakaichi Kenzō
Kamikita-gun, Aomori

## 129. The Temple Patron Who was a Cat

There was an old priest who was nearly ninety years old at a certain mountain temple. He was so old that he was always tired and dozed night and day. The temple seemed abandoned for this reason, and nobody was concerned about it. The old priest had a scrawny yellow cat called Tora as a companion.

It was very old, too. It was always dozing by the hearth just as the priest did. One day the cat said to the old priest, "Oshō Sama, nobody helps you because you have become quite old. You have looked after me for a long time, so I want to repay you for your kindness in some way, but I can't think of how to do it."

The priest was a little surprised to hear his cat talk, but he answered, "Now, Tora, it is better for you and me just to stay here without trying to think."

The cat said, "I can't agree, Oshō Sama. I heard something good recently and I want to tell you about it. I want to restore this temple and to be sure of your comfort in the future. You see, the only daughter of the chōja here is going to die in a short time. I will raise her coffin into the air at her funeral. I will hold it there and not let it down. You must read sutras then and put "Namu Tora-ya" into the sutra. When I hear you say that, I will lower the coffin."

Presently the chōja's only daughter really got sick and died. She was so precious to her father that he asked priests from all the various sects around to come to read sutras at her funeral. Everybody forgot the sleepy old priest at the mountain temple, so he was not invited. Anyway, a funeral procession of unheard of splendor formed and proceeded to encircle her oval grave.

Then for some reason the beautifully decorated coffin suddenly rose and was suspended high in the air. Everyone exclaimed in surprise. The throng of priests began to chant sutras and to rub their rosaries with all their might when they saw that, but it was to no effect. At last, each one in turn recited the secret traditional formula of the temple of his sect as he gazed upward, but the sun only dazzled him and there was no remedy.

The chōja wailed in his misery and complained about the spiritless efforts of the priests. He said he would furnish rice for a lifetime, he would repair the temple, he would erect a gate and a bell tower according to wish, he would contribute anything to the priest who could lower the coffin. When the priests heard that, they raised their voices even louder as they looked up, but it was to no avail.

The chōja wept and sent a man running this way and that to ask everyone, "Can't you lower the coffin?"

He asked, "Have we invited every single priest from hereabouts?"

The villagers assured him that all the heads of temples around had come. The chōja asked again if there wasn't somebody missing.

A voice in the crowd answered, "The only one who is not here is that sleepy old priest at the mountain temple. It would do no good to bring him here."

The priests there all agreed. They said, "When we can't do anything, that sleepy old priest would only be in the way if he came."

The chōja declared, "That's not true. Hurry and call that priest." Somebody rushed away to bring him.

The sleepy old priest from the mountain temple, dressed in his tattered vestments, arrived quietly with the help of his cane. He took a seat on the grass and looked up at the sky as he intoned his sutra quietly. At a suitable time, he included the words his yellow cat had told him, "Namu Tora-ya, Namu Tora-ya."

The girl's coffin, which had been motionless, came gliding down and rested on the ground. Everyone lifted his voice in praise of the old priest. They all knelt before him to pay him reverence. The other priests stole away to their temples crestfallen.

That is why the old priest concluded the service alone. The chōja wept tears of gratitude. He prepared a red lacquered sedan chair to send the old priest home from the funeral to his mountain temple.

The temple of the sleepy old priest was immediately beautifully rebuilt. A gate and a bell tower were erected for it as well. The old priest was revered as a living Buddha. Throngs of people came continually to the temple daily until a town grew outside its gate.

Sasaki Kizen
Kamihei-gun, Iwate

## 130. Cat Temple
[The Cat's Power]

Long ago there was a chōja in a certain place whose daughter suddenly became ill. It was strange how she would groan at midnight, but those beside her could not help her. They could only feel sorry. Matters could not be left that way. Doctors and hōsha were asked to try various remedies, but there was no change in the way she suffered in the night.

Her mother tried everything to help her daughter. She noticed how the pet cat never left the girl's side. She thought it was strange how it would not leave even when she tried to chase it away. The mother finally thought, "The cat must be in love with my daughter. How terrible!"

It was a big cat. The mother worried about it as the sun set, and that night she was talking to the cat in her dreams. She asked it as though it were human, "Why have you fallen in love with my daughter? We have taken good care of you until now, and here you are doing something to worry us."

Toward dawn the mother had another dream. The cat seemed to come to her sobbing and saying, "I have not fallen in love with your daughter at all. If I were not there, your daughter would be killed. That is why I stay by her. If you talk this way I will be resentful. The trouble is that I can not destroy the tenko by myself. I have a brother cat many miles from here. Please send somebody for him. If you do that, we can destroy it." The mother sent somebody to see if it were true.

After a few days went by, he came back with a cat that looked like the one at the girl's home. The mother set out good things to eat for the cats. That night she asked her cat what it wanted her to do. The cat told her in a dream what day of what month and at what time she was to put him and his brother cat into the storehouse.

Then the woman woke up. When that day came, she put the two cats into the storehouse and waited. Nothing happened for a while, but then a big noise broke out. There seemed to be a scuffle for some time, and then everything was quiet. Then the big noise started again. The woman opened the door because she thought everything would be safe by then. The other cat came running out first, followed by her own that was biting a silvery colored tenko to death.

Both cats died after a short time, but the girl's illness suddenly disappeared. A tomb was built for the cats to prevent a curse upon the family.

Imamura Katsuomi
Tomata-gun, Okayama

## 131. The Forbidden Room

After the rice harvest was finished in the autumn, a young farmer in a certain place set out to go to Edo to look for work. The sun set quickly beyond the western mountains as he neared the wild region of Mikuni Pass. The day was gone by the time he came to a little shrine half way through it.

That meant trouble, for the young man realized that he could not cross the pass before dark. He barely managed to reach it after crossing one more hill. He found a splendid house there surrounded by mountains. He called and asked, "I am sorry to do it, but please let me ask you to let me spend the night here."

A beautiful girl came out and said, "I really have nothing to offer you, but please come in and stay."

The young man entered a beautiful room. Many dishes unusual for a mountainous region were served to him. He was admiring them when the girl asked, "Where are you going?"

He answered, "I thought I would go to Edo to get work."

She said, "Then how about working for me for a year? All you have to do would be to look after things when I have to be away."

The young man said, "It really makes no difference where I work. I never heard of anything easier than to be a caretaker, so please hire me." So that is how it happened that he worked at that house.

The next morning the girl got ready to set out for somewhere on a horse. She said to the young man, "There is everything in the cupboard for you to eat, so eat what you want when you are hungry. Only please do not open the door and look into the room farthest back in the house." He agreed.

Then his female employer went off happy. It was just as his mistress had said. When he was hungry, he could open the cupboard door and find anything he wanted to eat. No matter if it snowed or if the wind blew, his young mistress rode away each morning on her horse and came back in the evening. The young man had an honest nature. Although he thought it strange, he took good care of things every day and obeyed the instructions never to open the door to the inner room.

A whole year passed while the young man kept busy. One day he said to his mistress, "I have been obliged to you for a long time, but I think my family at home is worrying about me. Please let me go back."

She said, "You have taken good care of things while I have been away. It is not much to offer you, but please take this home as thanks." She gave him what seemed to be only a little money wrapped in paper and a bolt of white cotton cloth.

The young man thanked her and went down from the pass to his home. He and his wife opened the wrapping around the money and found a single strange coin. "I worked a long time, so there is no reason for this," declared the young man. He decided, anyway, to ask the village head to look at the coin.

The official was astonished when he saw the coin. He said, "This is a nightingale farthing, a very rare coin in the world. Please sell it to me for 1000 ryō." The young man sold it gladly and suddenly became very rich.

When the man next door heard about what had happened, he thought he would like to come by some easy money, too. He asked the way and set out for Mikuni Pass. He stopped at the house standing alone in the mountains and had the good fortune to be hired there. He, too, was asked not to open the door and look into the room at the back. He thought there must be a lot of good things in it.

One day when his mistress was away, the man opened the sliding door to the room and found it completely empty. He could not understand why. When his mistress came home, he acted as though nothing had happened. His mistress went as usual to the room in the back and returned in a daze. She said sadly, "You have done something terrible. All the hokekyō [a Buddhist sutra or the call of a nightingale] that I have gone around the mountains to collect for a long time were in that room. Now they have all been let out."

She dismissed the man, and he went home without any pay.

Fumino Shirakoma [Iwakura Ichirō]
Minamikanbara-gun, Niigata

## 132. The Monkey Farthing

An old man and an old woman who had no children had a pet cat and a pet dog they loved. When the old man was on his way to a neighboring village one day, he saw children teasing a little monkey they had caught. He bought the monkey from the children and set it free.

He met an old man who was the transformed father of the little monkey on his way home. The stranger gave him a monkey farthing as thanks for his kindness. When the old man reached home, he said, "We have plenty of money. I'll put this coin onto our money box."

When he did that, it turned out lots of money. When he put the coin on the rice chest, it turned out lots of rice.

The old woman next door heard about the coin and asked to see it. She took it home with her, and from that time her house grew rich.

The pet dog and the pet cat decided to get the coin back, but it was the cat that got it and it won over the dog. That is why cats and dogs are unfriendly.

Takata-gun, Hiroshima

## 133. Rat Jōdo

*Mukashi attaji mo na.*

Once an old man set out for his garden patch with a toasted buckwheat cake for his lunch. A rat came out while he was digging busily.

The old man broke off half of his cake and tossed it to the rat. It ate it and ran back into its hole. After the old man started to dig again, another rat came out of its hole. The old man tossed half of what he had left to the rat. The rat ate it and ran back into its hole. The old man went on digging away.

This time the father rat came out. He thanked the old man for giving his children good things to eat. He said, "Please follow me to my home."

The old man said, "How am I going to follow you?"

The father rat said, "You can do it if you close your eyes tight. Keep them closed until I tell you to open them."

When the old man opened his eyes, he found himself in a splendid room. The little rats he had seen came in and thanked him. They gave him good things to eat, and when he started to go home, they gave him money to take.

The greedy neighbor of the old man heard about what had happened. He had his old woman make him a toasted buckwheat cake. He took it with him as he set out for his garden patch. He started to dig busily there. A little rat came out and he tossed half of his toasted cake to it. The rat ate it and ran back into its hole. The old man started to dig again, and another rat came out. He tossed it half of what he had left over. The rat ate it and ran back into its hole.

This time the father rat came out and said, "Thank you for the good things you gave my children. Please follow me."

The old neighbor was happy. He closed his eyes and followed the rat. Soon he arrived at the rat's home. When he opened his eyes, he saw little rats come out. They thanked him, but since the old man was greedy, he looked all around as he ate the feast they served him.

He saw rats pounding gold in a mortar in the corner of the room. While they worked, they sang, "We don't want to hear the voice of a cat." They continued to pound the gold. The old man wanted that gold. He suddenly called out, "Niyagon," imitating a cat loudly.

The rats all scurried away and everything turned pitch dark. This was terrible. The old man was frightened. He struggled with his head stuck into the rat hole in the middle of his garden patch.

*Dotto harai.*

Ogasawara Kenkichi
Shiwa-gun, Iwate

## 134. Jizō Jōdo

Once upon a time there was a hard working old man and his old woman. The old man went to the hills to cut firewood. Noon came as he worked away.

When the old man sat down at the foot of a tree to eat the riceball he had brought, it rolled away for some reason, and dropped into a hole beyond. He was sorry about that and wanted to get it. As he crawled farther into the hole, he came to Jizō, who was eating his riceball.

The old man said, "Please, Jizō San, I am a poor man and that riceball is all I have for my lunch. If I do not eat it, I will be too tired to work. Please give it back to me."

Jizō said, "I'm sorry. I did not know. Well, a demon will come here presently. Crawl under my seat and when I shake it three times, imitate a rooster's crow."

The old man was terribly frightened, but he crawled under Jizō's seat. Soon a demon shouted, "Jizō, I smell a man!"

Jizō declared, "There is nothing like a man around here."

"Yes, there is a man," insisted the demon. Jizō shook his seat three times, and the old man called, "Kokekokko!"

Jizō said, "There, the paradise bird has crowed. It's dawn, so go back, go back!" The demon ran away without looking around. Then the old man came out relieved.

Jizō said, "The demon ran off leaving his metal rod behind. It is the kind that will give you anything you want when you shake it. Take it home with you."

The old man accepted the rod and went home. When he shook the rod, he thought, "I want rice." Lots of sacks of rice came out. When he thought, "I want money," a heap of money came out. Suddenly he became rich.

His bad neighbor saw what was happening and wanted to get a metal rod and to be rich, too. He made a riceball and took it to the hills. Although he started to eat the riceball, it would not roll off. He was angry and threw the riceball.

Then it rolled down into a hole. The old man was satisfied and crawled in after it. Just as had happened before, Jizō was eating the riceball. The old man said, "Please, Jizō San, I am a poor man and that is the only riceball I have to eat. If I don't eat it, I will be too hungry to work. Please give it back to me."

Just as Jizō had done before, he said, "I'm sorry. I did not know. Well, presently a demon will come. Crawl under my seat. When I shake it three times, imitate a rooster's crow."

The old man crawled under Jizō as he was told and soon the demon came. It shouted, "I smell a man, Jizō, I smell a man around here!"

Then Jizō shook his seat three times. The old man was so amused that he started to snicker. The demon was furious. He shouted, "See, there is a man here after all. You fooled me yesterday, didn't you!"

He pushed Jizō out of the way, thrust his metal rod through the old man, and took him off to Hell.

Isogai Isamu
Saeki-gun, Hiroshima

## 135. Dango Jōdo

Once upon a time there was an old woman. When she was cooking dango broth, the kettle fell, for some reason, and the soup spilled.

A dango rolled into a rat's hole in the corner of the hearth. The soup spilled and the rat hole became larger. The old woman ran down it after the dango, calling, "Wait for me! Wait for me, dango!" Finally she reached Rat Paradise. When she looked around, she saw many rats who were singing as they worked at their mortar:

If only no cats would come to Rat Paradise,
This world would be full of bliss!

The old woman tried saying "niyaan" like a cat. The rats scurried away somewhere at that. The old woman went in farther and found lots of gold and silver and treasures the rats had stolen. She gathered them up and took them home.

When the old woman next door heard about it, she decided she would get treasure, too. She busied herself grinding flour and making dango soup. She hung it from the hook to boil. She became angry because the kettle did not fall. She knocked it off the hook and the dango spilled. One of them happened to roll into the rat hole that was in the corner of her hearth, too. She followed it, calling, "Wait for me! Wait for me, dango!" At last she came to Rat Paradise. She looked around and saw the rats working and singing:

If only no cats would come to Rat Paradise,
This world would be full of bliss!

The old woman said "niyaan," but the rats knew that a cat-like human had come the day before and had carried off treasure. They gathered around the old woman and beat her. She managed to get home half dead.

That is why one should not be jealous. Even now the rat's bite is poisonous.

*Mukashi kappo komen dango.*

Abe Michinaga
Hayami-gun, Ōita

## 136. The Old Man Who Made Flowers Bloom

[The Old Man Above and the Old Man Below, The Old Man Who Scattered Ashes, or The Old Man Who Caught Geese, and other such stories]

There were two old men at a certain place, one who lived upstream and the other downstream. They went together to set fish traps in the stream. Only a little dog was caught in the trap upstream, but the trap downstream was full of fish.

The old man from upstream went first to look and he was angry about what he found. He tossed the little dog into the other trap and took all of its fish. Then he went home as though nothing had happened. When the old man from downstream went later, he found a cute little dog had fallen and was hurt. He lifted it up and took it home. He kept it and tended it carefully. The little dog grew bigger gradually—as big as a bowl when it was fed from a bowl, and then as big as a basin when it was fed from a basin. After a month went by, it was big enough to carry the old man's tools on its back, and it went with him every day when he went to work in the hills.

One day when the dog went into the hills with the old man, he told his master to call, "Deer from there, come here! Deer from this way, too, come here." Many deer came from all directions when they were called. The dog killed them one by one by biting them. He brought them home on his back.

The old man and the old woman cooked the deer and the dog ate deer soup with them. The old woman from upstream came and exclaimed, "Well, where did you get the deer to cook?"

The old couple said, "The dog at our house caught them and brought them to us so we could cook them to eat this way."

The old woman from the upper house said, "We would like to eat deer soup, too. Please lend us your dog." She borrowed the dog and led it home.

The next day the old man upstream decided to take the dog to the hills. Although the dog did not tell the old man to do it, he put his hatchet and ax onto its back and hurried it into the hills. He misunderstood the word for "deer" as "bee" and shouted, "Bees from there, come here! Bees from this way, too, come here!" All the bees in the mountains came flying and stung the old man's balls.

That made the old man frantic. He beat the dog to death and buried it under a rice-tree. No matter how long the old man downstream waited, the old man upstream did not return the dog. Finally, he went to ask for it. He found the old man there groaning in bed. He shouted, "What kind of a dog was that! Because of that beast my balls got stung and here I lie in bed. If you want your dog, go look for it below the rice-tree in the hills."

When the old man from downstream heard that, he was sad. He went to cut the rice-tree down and he made a handmill of it. As he and his old woman ground out rice, they sang, "Money come out for Grandpa, rice come out for Grandma." Then just as the song said, money came out in front of the old man and rice came out in front of the old woman. In no time they became prosperous chōja. They could wear good clothes and cook rice to eat. The old woman from upstream came again. She asked, "Where did you get such good clothes to wear?"

The old man answered, "Oh, these! The old man at your house killed our dog. I cut the rice-tree where he buried it. When we turned the handmill we made of the rice-tree, we asked money and rice to come out. That's how it was." The old woman from upstream borrowed the handmill.

The old couple upstream turned the handmill with all their might, but they forgot the words of the song. They sang, "Turds, come out for Grandpa, urine come out for Grandma!" Lots of smelly stuff came dropping out, just as the song said, turds in front of the old man and urine came pouring out in front of the old woman.

They were dumbfounded. They chopped up the handmill and burned it all up. No matter how many days passed, the old man upstream did not return the mortar, so the old man downstream went to get it.

The old man upstream said angrily, "That handmill spread turds and urine all over. We could not put up with it. We split it up and stuffed it into our stove to burn."

The old man from downstream said, "Well, the ashes will do, so let me have them." He brought a basket and took the ashes home.

The old man took the ashes to his garden patch. Geese came down there onto the pond by the embankment. The old man scattered the ashes onto them as he sang. "Ashes, go into the eyes of the geese! Ashes, go into the eyes of the geese!" The ashes really fell into the eyes of the geese and they toppled over dead. The old man gathered up the geese and took them home. The old couple made goose soup and ate it.

The old woman from the upper house came again. She asked, "Where did you get the geese to make that good-smelling soup you are eating?"

"Oh, that!" exclaimed the old man. "I brought the ashes back from the mortar we loaned you and you burnt up. In the night when the wind was blowing hard, I took them to the roof and told them to fly into the eyes of the geese. The geese fell dead when the ashes went into their eyes. I brought them in and that is how we are eating this."

When the old woman from the upper house heard that, she wanted some goose soup right away. She said, "Please divide some of the ashes with me." She took the ashes home with her. On a night when there was a strong wind blowing, her old man climbed up onto his roof to scatter ashes, but he forgot the words to make the ashes fall into the eyes of geese. As he scattered them, he shouted, "Ashes, go into Grandpa's eyes! Ashes, go into Grandpa's eyes!" The wind blew them into the old man's eyes and blinded him. He went rolling off the roof.

The old woman was waiting eagerly for the geese to fall. She thought he was a goose and hit him with a big mallet and killed him.

Sasaki Kizen
Esashi-gun, Iwate

## 137. The Old Bamboo Cutter

Long ago a feudal lord heard the sound of bamboo being cut as he passed a bamboo thicket. He demanded, "Who is that fellow cutting bamboo in my thicket?"

The man cutting the bamboo replied, "The greatest at breaking wind in all Japan."

The feudal lord thought he must be an amusing fellow. He said, "Come out and let's hear you!" The man came out and let go—"chinpui goyo no sakazuki o-chichin pu." The feudal lord was impressed and gave him a big reward.

A bad old man in the neighborhood heard about that and decided to earn some easy money himself. He went to the feudal lord's thicket and cut bamboo as he waited for the procession. Presently the feudal lord heard the bamboo being cut. He demanded, "Who is that fellow cutting bamboo in my thicket?"

The bad old man thought this was his chance. He answered, "The greatest at breaking wind in all Japan."

The feudal lord said, "Come out and let's hear you!" The old man came out, but all he could do was "chichin buppu." He failed miserably.

The feudal lord declared, "You are a fake!" He promptly had him arrested.

Mitamura Kōji
Takashima, Shiga

## 138. The Old Man Who Swallowed A Bird

Once upon a time there was a good old man and a bad old man in a certain place, and the good old man was praised in the village because he was a hard worker.

He decided to work in his garden because the snow had melted. He went to the foot of the mountain with his hoe over his shoulder to work in his field. After he had worked for a while, he decided to rest. He sat down on a stump, took out his pipe from his hip, and started to smoke.

As he did that, he heard a bird sing with a voice like a little bell being shaken: "aya chūchū, koya chūchū, nishiki sara-sara, goyō no matsu, tabete mōseba, pipira piin."

It was such a lovely song that the old man wished the bird would come and perch on the hazel bush to sing. The little bird then flew to the hazel bush to sing. It started its song again, "aya chūchū . . ." The old man admired it even more, but he could not see the bird. He said to himself, "It would be fine if the bird came flying right over here and rested on the handle of the hoe!"

Then the little bird flew right over and rested on the handle of the hoe. The old man saw that it was a small, beautiful bird. He admired it and wondered where the voice came from. He said to the little bird, "Come and sing on the tip of my tongue!" The little bird flew over and perched on the tip of the old man's tongue. It began to sing again, "aya chūchū . . ." It was such a lovely song that the old man gulped and swallowed the little bird.

The old man was sorry he had done such a thing. He started to rub his belly so the bird would come out, but it didn't. The little bird said from inside the old man's belly, "There's nothing to worry about, old man. Go to the crossroads and climb the cherry tree now. The feudal lord's procession will come by. If you pat your belly, I will sing for you. The feudal lord will think you are the best singer in all Japan and give you a big reward."

The happy old man went to the crossroads and climbed the cherry tree to wait. The feudal lord's procession approached with calls of, "Down on your knees! Down on your knees!" The old man hurriedly patted his belly, and at that signal the bird inside started to sing, "aya chūchū . . ." The feudal lord thought it was a beautiful song. He looked up and saw the old man. He asked, "Who are you?" The old man answered, "The best singer in Japan." The feudal lord said, "Sing again!" The old man give his belly a couple of pats, and the bird sang again, "aya chūchū . . ."

The feudal lord praised the old man and declared, "You are a fine singer. I'll be coming again tomorrow, so sing for me again." He had two boxes brought out and let the old man choose his reward. The old man said, "I am old so I would like to have the light one." He took one of the boxes home and found that it was full of gold and silver and treasures. He and his old woman gazed at it in delight.

The bad old man next door came and found the two looking at their treasure. He asked, "Did you steal that or pick it up somewhere?" The good old man told him how he had gone to work in his garden that day and how he had swallowed the little bird. The bad old man decided he had heard something good. He got up early the next morning and took his hoe with him to his field. There were weeds growing all over it because he was lazy. He sat down on a stump to wait for a bird without doing any work. Then he heard a bird somewhere sing "fukkurafu kintama ki."

He thought an amusing bird had come. Then the same thing happened for him as had happened for the other old man, but he insisted on swallowing the bird. He hurried to the crossroads and climbed the cherry tree to wait for the feudal lord's procession. When it came along with calls of, "Down on your knees! Down on your knees!" the old man thumped his belly. It sang, "fukkurafu kintama ki." The feudal lord thought that was a stupid song. "Try singing again," he ordered. The old man thought he would get rewarded, so he thumped his belly hard.

All the bird sang was "fu-fu-fu-fu."

"What's the matter? Hurry up and sing," urged the feudal lord. The next time the old man thumped his belly, no sound came out. He thought there should be no reason for that and tried thumping his belly with both hands, but he fell from the tree.

The feudal lord thought he was a fake and ordered his men to beat him. The old man ran home covered with blood and fell with a thud at the door of his house. When his old woman heard that sound upstairs, she thought her old man had set down the reward he had brought home.

She hurried down, but missed her footing on the stairs and fell, breaking her leg.

Watanabe Kōichi
Minamiuonuma-gun, Niigata

## 139. Monkey Jizō

Once upon a time there was a good old man who went to the hills one day to cut wood. He saw a crowd of monkeys on the sandbar of the river beyond carrying a stone image of Jizō across to the other side.

He was amused. He went to the sandbar, covered his body with rice flour, tipped a mortar over, and stood on it to look like Jizō. When the monkeys found him, they said, "Here's a Jizō, too." A big crowd of the monkeys carried the old man off on their shoulders, singing:

Who is riding on our shoulders?
Jizō Sama is on our shoulders.

When they came to the deep part of the river, they sang:

Even if our balls get wet,
We can't let Jizō's balls get wet.

After they all got across, they set the Jizō down and paid him reverence. The old man said in a disguised voice, "Set rocks in a row for pillows with a mallet ready. Then go to sleep." The monkeys hurriedly obeyed Jizō and set out the stones for pillows, put a mallet by them, and lay down. After the old man was sure they were all asleep, he picked up the mallet and hit each monkey on the head.

He killed them all and took them home to eat monkey soup with his old woman.

Uchida Takeshi
Kazuno-gun, Akita

## 140. The Old Man Who Got a Tumor

Once upon a time there was an honest old man and a bad old man. One day the honest old man went to the hills to cut wood, but a big rain started when it came time for him to go home.

That worried the old man, but he found a big cryptomeria tree with a hole at its base and he crawled into it to rest. He woke up at midnight when he heard things come noisily. All kinds of ghosts came jostling each other. The monkey came shaking a bamboo rattle, the wolf came riding a mortar, the fox came dragging a tree stump, the badger crawled into a tenjō, all in a jolly confusion.

While the old man looked on, all sorts of ghosts came, too. There was a one-eyed monster, a three-eyed monster, a long-armed monster, a long-legged monster, and others. The rain had stopped and the full moon was shining. The ghosts started to drink in front of the hole in the tree, and when they were drunk, they began to dance. The old man could hear them laugh and shout. They danced boisterously, calling for the first dance, the second dance, the third, the fourth, and so on.

The old man liked to dance. By the time the second dance was over, he forgot all about being scared. Since they were calling for a third and a fourth dance, he came out and asked to dance. He cut in on the fifth dance. The ghosts all circled around him. They were not sure that he was deformed, too, but they gave him wine and let him dance. Their dancing went on until dawn. Then the ghosts shouted, "Here, now, it's nearly dawn. Let's go back!"

As they got ready to leave, they said to the old man, "You are such a jolly fellow, come back tonight!"

They decided to keep something of value as a pledge and took the big tumor off the old man's left cheek. The old man loaded his wood on his back and went home.

His old woman was astonished. She asked, "Where did you stay last night?" Then the old man told her all that had happened and how his tumor had been taken off. She was delighted.

It happened the old man next door had a tumor on his right cheek. When he heard what had happened, he decided to go to get his tumor taken off, too. He hunted for the cryptomeria tree with a hole at its base in the hills. It grew late while he waited. The ghosts came again at midnight and started their drinking bout and dance. The bad old man was so frightened that he started to tremble. The ghosts missed the old man who had come the night before and looked for him in the trunk of the tree. They found the bad old man and dragged him out. They tried to make him dance, but he couldn't. The ghosts declared, "This old man has no talents at all." They stuck the left tumor onto his face. There he was, with a tumor on each cheek.

That is why trying to imitate others is like the crow who tried to imitate the man or the stupid crow that tried to imitate a cormorant and fell into the river.

*Tonpin yanko nai to wa.*

Sakenobe Zuihō
Mogami-gun, Yamagata

# 9. *The Power of Words*

## 141. A Dialogue with a Ghost

A traveler came to a certain village in the mountains and said, "I am a doctor. Please let me live here."

It just happened that the villagers were worried at that time because they had no doctor. They thought this was a good chance and gladly let him stay, but they really had no good place for him to live. They asked him to stay at a vacant temple a little apart from the village. The doctor was busy since he was the only one and people came to him from here and there.

One night after the doctor had returned from the village and was preparing his supper at the hearth, he started to doze off from the warmth of the fire and from his fatigue. Just then he heard a rustling in the bamboo grass behind the temple and the steps of what seemed to be an animal. Presently the boards on the porch creaked as the thing climbed up onto it.

The doctor was alone at the temple. He gave up eating and hurried to bed, crawling deep under the quilts. The thing that climbed onto the porch began to shout with a voice like a broken bell, "*Suteten koten* on the doctor's head! *Suteten koten* on the doctor's head!" It pounded on the wooden doors until they nearly broke.

The frightened doctor huddled under his quilts and prayed, "Namu Amida Butsu, Namu Amida Butsu!" The thing stopped abruptly with only the two shouts and seemed to go off somewhere. That was all that happened.

When the doctor crawled out from under his quilts in the morning to look, he found big footprints of an animal all over the porch. He hurried down to the village very agitated to tell everything that had happened.

The villagers said, "That must have been that badger's doings. A successful badger has been living around here lately and he bothers us with his violent pranks."

They talked together about ways to control him, and they finally decided that several young men should spend the night together at the temple. They gathered there that night, shut the doors carefully, and waited with poles ready. The young men sat around a blazing fire in the hearth and exchanged stories about the mountains, expecting the badger any moment.

At about the same time as on the night before, the group heard a rustling in the bamboo grass thicket. The thing came up onto the porch and pounded hard enough to break the doors in. The young men braced the doors. In a voice that sounded like a broken bell, the thing started its shout, "*Suteten koten* on the doctor's head!"

But that night those inside felt brave because they were in a crowd. They shouted back, "*Suteten koten* on the head of what says that!"

The thing on the porch knew then that there was resistance inside. He raised his voice louder, "*Suteten koten* on the doctor's head!" The response inside was louder to match it.

Since they were in the temple, there would be a drum used in services. The young men got it out to pound to accompany their shouts. A great clamor began as those on both sides of the doors exchanged shouts. The contest continued for some time, the voices on the inside matching the one outside.

By midnight the thing outside gave up completely and was silent. When dawn came, those inside went out to look. They found a big badger that had torn its belly open from humiliation.

He died because he had lost out. They all made badger soup to eat.

Dobashi Riki
Nishiyatsushiro-gun, Yamanashi

## 142. A Dialogue with a Crab

A famous itinerant priest was overtaken by sunset in the mountains. He found a wretched looking woodcutter's hut and asked to spend the night. The man said, "I can not let you stay. There is an old temple a little farther on, but it is rumored to be haunted."

The itinerant priest went there to stay. At midnight he heard a loud clatter and an ōnyūdō came out from somewhere. It said angrily, "If you don't solve the riddle I tell you, I will eat you. Here it is: Little legs eight legs, big legs two legs, red in color, two shining eyes like the sun and moon look up to the sky."

The itinerant priest struck the ōnyūdō on the head with his staff and replied, "A crab!"

The ōnyūdō withdrew with a clatter and nothing more happened before morning. When the priest went out to look in the morning, he found a big dead crab under the porch. It is said the ghosts never came out at that temple after that.

Suzuki Tōzō
Kawagoe, Saitama

## 143. The Poem about Ashes

Once upon a time a house was vacated. The man living next door would let people stay in it overnight, but nobody would stay a second night because they would say that a ghost appeared.

One night a brave man came along and said, "I came to see the ghost." He went into the house and built a good fire in the hearth and waited. He heard a sound over by the inner room around midnight and a ghost came gliding into the room. The ghost sat down by the fire. The man waited, wondering what it would say. It began to rake the ashes as it said, "Raked ashes are the color of the seashore. . ." and then it burst into tears. It continued to repeat the line and to weep.

The brave man thought, "If I don't add the last line, the ghost will come out every night." The next time the ghost repeated, "Raked ashes are the color of the seashore," the man said promptly, "At the hearth I watch the open sea (live coals)."

The ghost said, "I have tried to think of a closing line, but couldn't. Now that I have heard one, I can rest and will no longer come out." Then it vanished. It never came again to that house.

Suzuki Kiyomi
Naori-gun, Ōita

## 144. The Carpenter and Oniroku

There was a big river with a swift current at a certain place, and no matter how many bridges were built across it, they would be swept away. The troubled villagers gathered to discuss what to do about it. They finally decided to hire a very famous carpenter who lived in a village not far away to build the bridge.

Although the carpenter had great skill and agreed to do the work, he was uneasy about it. He went to the edge of the pool in the river where he would build the bridge and hesitated as he stared into the current. Foam came floating to the surface of the water and a big demon suddenly appeared.

The demon said, "Master Carpenter, you are famous around here. What are you thinking about?"

The carpenter answered, "I have been hired to build a bridge here and I am thinking over what I am going to do about it."

The demon laughed. It said, "No matter how good a carpenter you are, you can never build a bridge here. I am willing to build it for you if you will give me your eyeballs." The carpenter agreed and went home.

When the carpenter went to the river the next day to see what was going on, half of the bridge was up. On the next day a fine bridge was already finished. While the carpenter gazed at it in astonishment, the demon came out. It demanded, "Now give me your eyeballs."

"Just wait a bit," exclaimed the carpenter and he fled to the hills, not knowing where he was going. As he went here and there, he heard children sing in the distance:

> If only Oniroku would hurry with the eyeballs,
> What fun it would be!

The carpenter came to his senses when he heard that. He went home and to bed. In the morning he went again to the river and the demon appeared.

It said, "Hurry up and hand over your eyeballs." The carpenter asked him to wait a little.

The demon said, "If you are unwilling to give me your eyeballs, guess my name!" The carpenter agreed and purposely made a mistake. That delighted the demon. It said, "That is not right. Demon's names are not easy." The carpenter tried another and the demon shouted that was wrong.

Then the carpenter said, "Oniroku!" The demon disappeared at once.

Sasaki Kizen
Isawa-gun, Iwate

## 145. The Warning in the Lullaby

Once upon a time an itinerant priest was going to a place in Gōshū. The sun set while he was in the mountains, so he stopped at a teahouse to spend the night.

The owner was a bad man. He and his neighbor decided to kill the priest and talked over their plan. While the host was gone, the old nurse came with a baby on her back. She sang repeatedly by the priest, "If you try writing it in words. . ."

The priest thought it strange that she repeated a nursery song without meaning, but he tried writing it in characters.

The priest discovered that she was saying, "If I tell you what the neighbor and my master say, it is that they will kill the itinerant priest. Go away quickly." He realized that the woman was kindly warning him. In that way he was able to escape. He thanked her in his heart and left immediately.

The place came to be called Nyūba-no-chaya [The Nurse's Teahouse] after that and it is still called that today.

Chikujō-gun, Fukuoka

## 146. Zuitonbō

Once upon a time there was a priest named Zuiton at a temple in the mountains. A badger came out nearly every night to annoy him.

When the priest would think it time to go to sleep, the badger would come outside the wooden doors and shout, "Zuiton, are you there!" This vexed the priest beyond words. He determined to get even with the badger somehow. One night he prepared a lot of wild yams and long radishes to eat, got out wine from his store, and waited to outdo the badger.

The badger arrived at the usual time and began to shout, "Zuiton, are you there?"

Not to be outdone, the priest shouted from inside, "Yeah, I'm here!"

They exchanged shouts—"Zuiton, are you there?"

"Yeah, I'm here!"

"Zuiton are you there?"

"Yeah, I'm here!"

"Zuiton, are you there?"

"Yeah, I'm here!"

The priest was eating his food and drinking his wine to keep up his spirits as he matched the badger's shouts. But he began to shout louder than the badger, "Yeah, I'm here!"

"Zuiton, are you there?"

"Yeah, I'm here!"

"Zuiton, are you there?"

"Yeah, I'm here!"

The badger was becoming tired and his voice started to falter, "Zuiton, are you there?" The priest continued to eat and drink as he shouted, "Yeah, I'm here!" (a strong voice). "Zuiton, are you there?" (a weak voice).

"Yeah, I'm here!" (the voice became stronger and stronger). Finally, the badger's voice was weaker and weaker "Zuiton . . . Zuiton . . . Zuiton!" It could hardly be heard.

The voice of the priest inside was as strong as ever, "Yeah, I'm here!" At last the badger's could no longer be heard.

The priest decided the contest was ended and he went to bed for a good sleep. The next morning he got up early to open the doors. He saw a big dead badger dead with its belly split open from shouting.

Shimoina-gun, Nagano

# 10. *Cleverness at Work*

## 147. Destroying the Fox

A fox used to come out at night in the pine grove in Shirasu. If a man came along, it would appear as a woman, and if a woman came along, it would appear as a man, and it played all sorts of pranks.

When Ichibei was returning from Taigahara one night, a woman came walking toward him at the pine grove. He was sure she was a fox, but he continued walking as though he knew nothing. The woman broke into a smile as she came nearer and greeted Ichibei in a sugary voice. She said, "You must be tired."

Ichibei responded, "You must be tired, too."

The woman said, "I have to go as far as Kyōraishi, but I'm afraid to go alone since it is late. Please let me walk with you."

Ichibei said, "Oh, come along!" He watched closely as he asked, "It is a simple request, but tell me where you are going in Kyōraishi."

The woman said, "The second house from the last at the edge is my mother's place."

Ichibei secretly spit three times and put some spit on his eyebrows as he said, "Lady, I saw something interesting a little while ago. I saw a big dog near where I entered the pine grove. It was holding two mountain foxes in its mouth as it ran along. They must have been young foxes that belong to that fox that lives in the grove. I suppose by now the mother fox is crying and making a big fuss."

The fox-woman suddenly turned pale. She said she was dizzy and seemed to drop back a step. Then she vanished. She went back to her nest when she heard her children had been carried off by a dog.

Ichibei knew that and had a big laugh. He said, "Ichibei is the only one in the world to fool a fox instead of being fooled."

Nakata Senpō
Yamanashi

## 148. The Fox in the Straw Bag

Two young men went to meet their father one evening when he was coming home from town. (There is no part about the wrong eye. They just noticed that there was something different about his looks.) The young men got out the straw bag they had ready and said, "When we meet our father, we put him in a straw bag and give him a ride home on our backs. Wonder what has happened to him tonight!"

The old man climbed hastily into the straw bag. He said, "Let's go! Let's go!"

After the boys put him into the straw bag, they said, "Father always tells us to tie up the end of the straw bag after he gets in. Wonder what has happened to him tonight."

The fox oldster in the bag said hurriedly, "Tie it up! Tie it up!"

The young men lifted the straw bag up onto their shoulders and beat the fox to death.

Yanagita Kunio
Hachinohei, Aomori

## 149. The Wrong One-Eye

There once was an old man and an old woman in a certain place, and the old man could only see with his right eye. When he was late coming home from town one night, his old woman waited anxiously. Then he arrived and said, "I'm home now, Granny!"

She noticed that it was his left eye that was good. She thought he was surely a fox. She said, "You came home drunk again, Grandpa!"

"Yes, I came drunk," he answered.

The old woman said, "When you come drunk, you always get into the straw bag, Grandpa."

"That's right," he agreed and climbed into the straw bag.

Then the old woman said, "And after that you tell me to tie you up with a rope, Grandpa!"

"That's right," he agreed.

The old woman did as she said. This time she said, "Then you tell me to set you on the mortar."

"That's right," he said.

The old woman said, "Then you tell me to put you on the shelf by the fire to smoke you."

"That's right," he responded.

So the old woman put him tied in the straw bag onto the shelf by the fire and began to smoke him. The fox had a bad time. The old woman got out fish and things and let him smell them as she ate supper. Presently the real right-eyed old man came home. The old man on the shelf became fox soup.

Sasaki Kizen
Kamihei-gun, Iwate

## 150. The Fake Image of Buddha

Ten young men in a neighborhood gathered at a home one night in winter to work with straw, making straw sandals and such. The son of the family spoke up, "It would be fun to catch a fox on a night like this."

But in the end, the young man had to set out alone to catch the fox. He led a horse from the stable and put a load rack onto it to prepare to leave. He went where foxes usually appeared and pretended to be waiting for somebody. He said to himself aloud, "It's about time for Grandma to come home."

At that, an old woman showed up. The young man appeared to be happy as he said, "I'm glad to see you come back. Now get onto the horse."

The young man helped the old woman onto it. He said, "This is a very wild horse," and tied the old woman securely with a rope and led the horse home.

The young man said to his friends in front of the stable, "This is a fox, so all of you gather around." He untied the ropes after they had all gathered around.

Then the old woman turned into her true form and escaped as a bewildered fox into the house. The young men searched through the house, but there was no sign of a fox. They were perplexed. The son in the family put his horse in the stable and came in. He sat by the hearth alone and started to smoke his pipe. He said without addressing anyone in particular, "We have two statues of Amida Sama at our house, and they wave their hands at each other."

Suddenly the statue on the altar became two statues and one waved its hand. "There you are," shouted the young man as he pulled down the image that waved. He knocked it over. It turned out to be the fox. They all made fox soup of it together.

Then somebody had to test it for poison, but the young men decided that the one who caught the fox should do it. The young man from the house was the first to taste it. He cried out in sudden pain. He seemed to be in agony with pain in his stomach. Somebody said Chinese herbs sold by itinerants would help, another gave a different remedy, but nothing seemed to relieve the young man.

The young friends were worried. First one and then another slipped away and went home until they were all gone. When the young man was sure nobody else was there, he stopped pretending to be sick and ate the fox-soup all by himself.

Moriguchi Tari
Isawa-gun, Iwate

## 151. Admitting Defeat

Long ago there was a teahouse at the pass on a certain mountain in Mimasaka. A man named Kihei lived there with his wife. An itinerant samurai stopped there to rest late one evening.

When the couple looked closely, they saw that the guest was a disguised fox. His divided skirt, his kimono, his two swords were correct, but he seemed to be an inexperienced fox. A little hair was still on his pointed face and his three-cornered ears stood up. The samurai himself was not aware of this and acted very haughtily thinking that he was well transformed.

Kihei was so amused that he could hardly control himself, but he managed to keep from laughing. He decided to see what the samurai would do, and brought him a metal basin of water and set it before the fox-samurai. He said politely, "Please make use of this."

After a while the fox decided to use the water. He leaned over it and for the first time he saw in his reflection that his disguise was not complete. He let out a shout of surprise and jumped out of the teahouse and went off somewhere.

Kihei went alone to cut wood in the hills the next day. As he was starting home, somebody called, "Kihei san, Kihei san!" Although he could not see anyone, he answered. The voice said, "Wasn't it funny last night, Kihei?" Kihei realized it was the fox of the night before.

In olden days people living in the mountains thought that foxes were this honest and that they could laugh with people.

Yanagita Kunio
Mimasaka (Okayama)

## 152. Kōkōzaka

There was a very filial daughter living in the country. She and her father led a lonely life there. They talked things over and decided the girl should go to work for a family living in a village a little over two miles away.

The girl missed seeing her father every night and morning because she had always been devoted to him. One day when she went on an errand to market for her master, she stopped at a toy shop and bought a mask that resembled her father. She placed it above the cupboard in the kitchen when she got back. She prayed to it every morning and evening that her father would be safe from fire and calamity.

The manner in which the girl prayed made her look crazy to those around her. A mischievous maid working there bought a demon mask and switched it secretly with the mask the girl had bought. Then she pretended that nothing had happened as she waited to see the look of surprise on the face of the filial girl when she noticed it.

That girl did not dream of such a thing. One evening as she unconsciously paid her respects to her father's mask as she passed it, she happened to look up at the mask. She was surprised that her beloved father's mask had suddenly turned into a demon mask. "This is no ordinary happening," she thought. "My father must be in danger."

The maid was so frantic with worry that she had a headache. She told her master what had happened and asked for permission to hurry home that night, promising to be back early the next morning. She insisted so earnestly that he finally agreed to let her go, but since it was already late, he advised her to go on the next day. The girl would not agree. She said, "My father is precious to me. He is only one ri away, so you need not worry." She made preparations immediately, tucked the demon mask into her bosom, and set out at dusk for her home town.

Night was coming on as the girl climbed a hill. The cold night wind blew through her light clothes, and her hands and feet were cold as she hurried on miserably. She noticed a bonfire burning on the hill beyond and decided to go up to it to warm her hands and feet and to rest a little. She drew near bravely, but she had happened unexpectedly onto two or three men sitting cross-legged and gambling. She started to draw back at first, but she braced herself after hesitating.

The girl resolved, "I don't have any ill will toward the men and I am not doing anything wrong, so they should not harm me." She went up to the men and explained politely why she was there. Then she went up to the fire to warm herself. The smoke from the bonfire was blowing into her face and bothering her. She took the demon mask out of her bosom and put it on. The gamblers sitting around the fire were arguing about who won. They, too, could no longer endure the smoke in their throats and glanced unconsciously across the bonfire.

What they had thought was a girl was then a demon. They shouted in surprise, "Look, a demon has appeared tonight. A demon has appeared!" They ran off like mad men, leaving everything.

The girl was not only free from the danger of bad men, but she gathered up the money they had scattered and trampled and she hurried home with it. She was happy to find that her father was in good health. She gave him all the money, not keeping any for herself. The father and daughter slept well until morning and then the girl returned to her master's house.

Ukiwa-gun, Fukuoka

## 153. Comparing Disguises

*Sore wa mukashi.*

Once there was a bad fox called Osan at Enami and a badger equally bad at Sanuki on Shikoku Island. They met one time to compare which was the more clever at transforming himself. First, the badger put some grass on his head and turned into a beautiful bride and then into a footman and such.

"It's my turn now," said Osan. "Day after tomorrow a feudal lord's procession will come through the pine grove on the highway. Just have a look!"

The badger agreed and they parted. The badger went on the appointed day to the highway and saw a splendid procession approaching. He admired it and went up to the sedan chair of the feudal lord and said sincerely, "You have done fine! You have done fine!"

The samurai in the accompanying guard cut him down. The procession was a real one, and Osan had known three days before that it would pass. She made a fool of the badger.

Isogai Isamu
Hiroshima

## 154. The Magic Hood with Eight Disguises

Long ago there was a little Inari Shrine at the edge of a pond. A fox called Osami, who was very clever at transformations, made her home there, but after a skin for transformations has been stolen by a human being, it is easier for the man to do the tricking.

A yamabushi went there one day and said, "I am the real top-ranking Inari Daimyōjin of Kyoto. I hear that your skin for disguises had been touched by human hands. That won't do, will it? Bring out that skin for disguising and let's see. I can restore its magic power."

Osami was impressed. She brought out the skin and said, "I really am ashamed that my transformation skin was defiled by human hands through my fault. Please help me."

The yamabushi snatched the skin for disguises and went off. Osami regretted that she had been fooled again by a human being, but she resolved to get the skin back.

The yamabushi was a good friend of the shōya in the village. Osami borrowed the skin for transformations from a badger. She disguised herself as the shōya and went to call upon the yamabushi. She said, "I hear you took Osami Fox's transformation skin away from her. Please let me see it. I never have seen a transformation skin of a fox."

Since the yamabushi thought it really was the shōya, he brought the skin out promptly and showed it to him.

The shōya said, "Let's see. I'll try putting it on." He put it across his shoulders. "This is great," he exclaimed and went off with it. The yamabushi was humiliated, but there was nothing to do.

The yamabushi then went to Osami again and said, "Are you in, Osami? I am the genuine top-ranking Inari Daimyōjin. I hear that your transformation skin is frequently touched by human hands. That won't do. I have my gold purification staff with me. I will take away the defilement for you, so bring the skin out."

The fox was fooled again and brought out her transformation skin. "I'm the yamabushi," he shouted. "I'll take it with me!" And off he went with it.

After that Osami became like a dog and stole things to eat.

Yamaguchi Asatarō
Ikinoshima, Nagasaki

## 155. Exchanging Treasures

Once a child in a certain place packed his lunch in a wooden box and went into the hills. A tengu was perched above him while he rested in the shade of a thicket. The boy decided to try fooling the tengu.

After he finished eating his lunch, he held up the box to his eyes like spectacles and began to prance around as though enjoying himself. He said to himself, "I see Kyoto! I see the five-story pagoda!"

The tengu looked on from overhead and wanted to see, too. He shouted, "Boy, lend that to me for a little so I can see, too!"

The boy pretended to refuse. The tengu grew impatient. He said, "I will lend you my invisible straw cloak and hat if you will. Please lend it to me!" That was what the boy wanted. He pretended to hand his lunch box over reluctantly to the tengu in exchange for the cloak and hat. The tengu held the box to his eyes, but he could not possibly see anything. He concluded that he had been fooled and looked down for the boy, but he had put on the tengu's invisible straw cloak and hat and could not be seen.

The boy went home confidently and said to his mother, "I'm home now." His mother could not see him. The boy then realized that his body was invisible because of the cloak and hat. He went to the cake store and stole things to eat. Things began to disappear strangely from homes in the village, but nobody could find out whose doings it was. Everyone became uneasy. The boy's tricks gradually grew worse until everyone was annoyed.

The boy hid his straw cloak and hat in the drawers of his mother's chest, but one day when he was away, she found the dirty straw cloak and hat. She stuffed them into her kitchen stove and burned them up. When the boy came home and wanted to get them out, they were gone. He asked his mother about them and heard that she had burned them. He thought about it for a while and then took a dip in the river to get wet all over. Then he rolled in the ashes of the cloak and hat.

Suddenly the boy's mother could not see him. While she was staring perplexed, the boy flew out of the house to the wine shop. There he began drinking wine, but the ashes fell off his mouth and only that was visible. The wine dealer declared, "A ghost that is only a mouth is drinking my wine!"

Everyone started to chase it. While the boy was running away, he stopped to piss, so the ashes fell off that place, too. The villagers were excited and said, "That mouth-ghost and the penis-ghost are running together."

A samurai came from the opposite direction, swinging his sword, which left the boy with nowhere to run. He had to jump from the bridge into the river. All the ashes were washed off and the boy became visible.

Ariga Kizaemon<br>
Kamiina-gun, Nagano

## 156. The Invisible Straw Cloak and Hat

Once upon a time a notorious drunkard came selling straw mats at a village. He spent all his earnings on drinks and went walking home unsteadily. He saw a persimmon seed that had fallen on the ground as he started across a meadow.

The drunkard picked it up and held it to his eye, remarking, "With such a treasure as this, I can see any tengu right off in spite of his invisible straw cloak and hat."

It just happened that a tengu was there. He felt humiliated and made himself visible to the man. He said, "Please give me that treasure." The drunkard was a bit startled over stumbling over such a stroke of luck, but he talked matters over with the tengu and traded his persimmon seed for the straw cloak and hat the tengu was wearing.

The tengu tried out the seed he held in his hand, but saw nothing special. He thought he had made a big mistake, but when he looked around for the drunkard, the man had already put on the straw cloak and hat and could not be seen anywhere.

The drunkard went to the privy after he reached home. While he was there, his wife found the dirty straw cloak and hat he had taken off by the hearth. "How do these things come here?" she thought as she stuffed them under the kettle for kindling.

Her drunk husband scolded her, but there was nothing that could be done about it. He happened to stick a finger into the ashes and the tip of his finger suddenly became invisible. That was encouraging. He mixed water in the ashes and plastered his body everywhere with them, not missing a single place. Then it was impossible for anyone to see where he was. His wife was amazed.

Then a bad notion came into his head. He set out for the storehouse at the winery. He drank all he wanted there without being seen. In the meantime, he became sleepy and fell asleep. While he was lying there, he wet himself. Where he pissed became visible and that surprised the workers at the winery.

The man woke up presently and ran home in a flurry. He caused a great uproar in town.

Toyama Rekirō
Minamikanbara-gun, Niigata

## 157. The Bird Fan

Once upon a time a mischievous boy climbed to the top of a hill carrying a one-mon coin with a hole in its center. He held it up to look through it and said to himself, "When I hold it right, I can see Isahaya. I can see Nagasaki! Isn't this a great thing. Nobody else has anything like this."

Then the boy heard a rustle in the tree behind him. When he looked around, he saw that a big, scary tengu had come.

It asked, "What is that you are holding up and looking through? Let me have a look!"

The boy answered, "I can't let anybody but a human being look through this sort of thing."

"Please lend it to me for a little while," urged the tengu.

"No. I can't lend it," said the boy.

"Well, I'll trade it for my most precious bird fan," offered the tengu. "You can make anything you want happen with this bird fan."

The boy agreed and traded his coin for the fan. Then he ran down the mountain to his home quickly.

The boy tried fanning his nose with the bird fan and said, "Nose grow high." Then his nose grew high. He said, "Nose, go down." And his nose came down when he fanned it. That was truly a fine object. The boy tried to think of a good way to use it. The lovely daughter of the rich man in town came riding a sedan chair at the festival for Jizō in the village. "That's it, that's it," decided the boy as he ran up beside the sedan chair. He looked below its bamboo curtain. He said, "Nose, grow high," as he fanned the girl's nose.

There in the sight of everyone, the girl's nose grew higher and higher until the end of it stuck out of the sedan chair. The people accompanying the girl were dumbfounded and confusion broke out. They carried her home in her chair quickly. Everybody in the house hustled around, trying to help because the nose of the precious daughter of the rich man had grown long. They put her to bed and set up a gold screen around her and would not let anyone see her. They inquired everywhere for medicine that would help her.

In the midst of their worry over not finding a suitable cure, they heard somebody passing the house and calling, "Nose treatments! Nose treatments!" Her father heard that and said, "Call in that man who says he treats noses now!"

The boy was called in. The father said to him, "You say you treat noses. Can you cure my daughter's high nose?"

The boy said, "I can't say unless I see it."

The boy was led into the room where the girl was. The boy took advantage of the moment when nobody was there to get out his fan. He said as he fanned her, "Nose, grow higher. Nose, grow higher." Her nose stretched all the way to the ceiling. He left it that way and said to the family, "It will cost extra money for me to get this nose down."

They said, "In that case, we will give you any amount of money if you can bring it back to where it was before."

The boy said, "Well, then, I will give it a try. I will ask you to bring me 300 ryō for medicine."

The money was brought to the boy and from the next day he lowered the girl's nose a little at a time with his fan. After it had improved considerably, the boy said he had used up most of his money for medicine and needed another 300 ryō. After he received it, he brought the nose down to where it was before.

The girl's parents were delighted and gave the boy more money as thanks.

Yūki Jirō
Kitatakaku-gun, Nagasaki

## 158. "What Are You the Most Scared of?"

*Tonto mukashi ga atta gena.*

An old woman lived in a little hut made of firewood at a place back in the hills. She would warm herself at night by building a fire.

A tengu with a cross looking face called to her. It sounded so much like a human that the old woman opened her door. A scary looking tengu with a big nose came in. The old woman was frightened, but there was nothing she could say, so she let him come over to her fire.

The old woman asked the tengu, "What are you the most scared of?"

It replied, "I'm most scared of dense brush growing in a thicket. What are you the most scared of, Granny?"

The old woman said, "I'm the most scared of botamochi and little gold coins."

Then nothing more happened and the tengu went out. The old woman decided to stack green boughs all around the walls of her hut so such a dreadful thing would not come again. She waited impatiently for morning when she could put up the branches.

The next night the tengu came again and found the brush stacked all around, but there was none on the roof. He said, "I'll get even with you, you hateful old thing."

He went to a certain house and had a lot of botamochi made for him and he got a lot of little gold coins. He brought them to the old woman's hut to get even with her. He called from above the roof, "I'll get even with you, Granny!" Then he threw in the botamochi.

The old woman cried, "Oh, I'm afraid!" When the tengu's botamochi was gone, he began to throw in little gold coins.

He called, "Are you still alive?"

When all the cakes and coins were thrown in, he thought the old woman must be dead, so he ran away. The old woman ate the bota-mochi, but she decided there was no telling who she would meet up with if she lived there. She went down into the village and lived in comfort with the money.

*Sono mukashi yo na.*

Iwakura Ichirō
Okinoshima, Shimane

## 159. Tanokyū

There was a mother and her son living together in the village called Ubaguchi in Higashiyatsushiro-gun. His name was Tanukiemon and he was an actor. He traveled all around putting on plays.

He crossed the high pass to put on plays once when he was hired to perform in a village on the other side of Ubaguchi Pass. After he had been working for two or three days, a message came toward evening for him to go home quickly because his mother had taken ill suddenly. He had always been a dutiful son and this worried him. He got ready to go home immediately.

The villagers said, "Wait until tomorrow morning to go home. There is a monster serpent at the pass. It comes out at night to catch men to eat. It is dangerous to cross the pass at night."

They tried to stop Tanukiemon from leaving, but he answered, "I can't take my time when my mother is ill."

Tanukiemon set out alone for the pass in good spirits. The monster appeared before him disguised as a man when the young man reached the summit of the pass. He looked at the young actor and said, "I am glad to see you. I have not had anything to eat for several days and I am getting to be hungry."

The young man trembled as he said, "Please spare my life."

The monster asked, "What is your name?"

"It is Tanukiemon," he answered.

"So you are a badger ["Tanuki" means "badger"], are you?" remarked the monster. "Badgers know a lot of transformations. Show me some."

The young man took some wigs and masks and things he used in acting from the baggage he was carrying on his back. He put on one after another, changing many times. The monster was quite impressed. He said, "You really are clever after all. I can't match you. Well, what do you dislike the most?"

"I hate coins the most," answered the young man. "And what do you hate the most?"

The monster said, "I hate tobacco juice the most. You are not to tell anyone about meeting me here tonight, see? If you promise, I will spare you. Hurry on home." With that, the monster went off somewhere.

The young man hurried down to the village. He told all the men about what happened and he took good care of his mother. The villagers gathered all the tobacco juice in the village and carried it up to the pass in a big barrel. They stuffed it into the cave where the monster lived and destroyed that great serpent at the pass.

Dobashi Riki
Nishiyatsushiro-gun, Yamanashi

## 160. Kashikobuchi

Once upon a time when a man was fishing at the pond in Handayama in the summer, he caught an unusual number of fish. The day was hot, and he took off his sandals to soak his feet in the pond. A water-spider came across the water from somewhere and fastened its thread onto one of the man's big toes. It soon came back a second time and fastened another thread on the same toe. The man thought it strange. He unfastened the thread on his toe quietly and wound it around a willow stump that was beside him.

Presently, somebody shouted from the bottom of the pond, "Jirō, Tarō, and all of you come here!" All the fish in the man's basket jumped out and got away, much to his surprise. Then a lot of voices called "En-to-en-yara-saa" and the spider's thread began to be pulled. While the man looked on, the thick stump was broken off at its base.

From that time to even this day nobody ever has gone alone to fish at that pond again.

Yanagita Kunio
Date-gun, Fukushima

## 161. The Eighth Leg of the Octopus

Once upon a time while an old woman was washing beside the seashore, an octopus appeared right in front of her. It stuck a big leg out toward her although it did tell her to cut it off. She promptly cut it off and took it home. She enjoyed eating it.

When the old woman went to do some washing the next day, the octopus she had seen the day before came out again and offered her another leg. The old woman felt a little uneasy about that, but it was so delicious that she cut it off and took it home. The next day and the next the same thing happened. It went on for seven days. Then came the eighth day.

The old woman set out in the usual way and waited, intending to get the head as well as the last leg of the octopus. It came and stuck out its one leg, but as the old woman was about to cut it off, the octopus came dancing up to her and wound its leg around her neck.

It dragged her down to the bottom of the sea.

Seki Keigo
Minamitakaku-gun, Nagasaki

## 162. The Secret of the Big Tree

Once upon a time a feudal lord decided to build another exorbitantly extravagant mansion although he already had a splendid one. It was to have a single roof beam. He insisted that the boards in the ceiling be camphor wood.

He sent his men in all directions to look for a big camphor tree. A great camphor tree was found at last in the woods on the grounds of a shrine in a certain village. The feudal lord sent a number of woodcutters there with orders to cut the tree. When they arrived to see the tree, they found it was so big that ten or even twenty men could not reach around it together.

The men set about cutting the tree with all their strength, but their axes only bounced back without making a dent in the wood. Several days went by in the same way while couriers came from the feudal lord asking, "Aren't you finished? Aren't you finished?"

Finally, the head man sat down below the tree at a loss with his face in his hands, trying to think what to do. He was not even aware that night had come as he sat plunged in thought. Then as he dozed a bit, a throng of Little Folk came out and began to talk.

They said, "No matter how many woodcutters try, they can not cut this tree. How silly they are! It isn't the kind of tree that can be cut blindly. The only way is to boil seaweed and pour the water over the roots of the tree. There is no other way at all. Men are such fools that it is funny they do not know this." This was how the Little Folk talked among themselves.

When the head man woke up, he realized that he had heard something good. He hastened to have the seaweed boiled and poured the water over the roots of the tree. Then in a single night ants came swarming out and gnawed the roots of the tree, heaping up worm droppings. They hollowed out the wood. The axes of the woodcutters then cut the great tree without any difficulty.

As might be expected, the tree was felled. The men presented it to the feudal lord hurriedly. He was so pleased that he gave them a great reward.

Dobashi Riki
Nishiyatsushiro-gun, Yamanashi

## 163. The Satori and the Hoop
[A Dialogue with a Yamabushi]

Once upon a time there was a man who went far into the mountains to make charcoal. He gathered his wood and started to bake it. He was uneasy because he had gone far back into the hills alone.

He thought, "I'll be all right unless something scary comes out."

Just then a voice from somewhere said, "I'll be all right unless something scary comes out," and a tengu appeared.

The man was so frightened that he did not know what to do. He thought, "How shall I get away?"

The tengu said, "How shall I get away?" It continued to repeat everything the man thought. The poor man became completely befuddled.

Presently the rod he used to guide his ox fell from his hands and sent sparks flying onto the tengu. It tore off pellmell saying, "Men do things they don't think about."

Nishitani Katsuya
Kinosaki-gun, Hyōgo

## 164. The Mountain Where Old Women were Abandoned

Once upon a time there was a feudal lord in the land of Shinshū who disliked anything old. Since people who were old grew feeble, he sent out an order to kill all of them.

A man whose mother was growing old received the notice to kill her. This troubled him greatly because he was a filial son. He could not refuse to kill his mother, but at the same time he could not kill her. He decided to hide her far back in the hills.

The mother broke off twigs along the way so her son would not get lost on his way home. He was able to return without any mistake because of that. Then he took his mother things secretly every day.

When the feudal lord heard about it later, he was so impressed that he became a good feudal lord.

Hakoyama Kitarō
Chiisagata-gun, Nagano

## 165. A Thousand Bales of Rope

Long ago, anyone who reached the age of 60 was sent to Deederano [the place where spirits go]. But there was a very devoted son at a certain place who could not bear to send his father to Deederano. He hid him secretly under the floor.

It happened that at that time a feudal lord came from China to Japan for some reason to match accomplishments. He demanded as tests a thousand bales of ash rope and a hole bored through a tree that had seven bends in its trunk. Since nobody at the Japanese feudal lord's place could accomplish these tests, he published a decree throughout his land that a prize would be given to anyone solving the problems.

When the dutiful son who had hidden his father asked him about the tests, he replied, "There is nothing to such silly problems. For the thousand bales of rope, make an iron box, put the thousand bales into it, and sprinkle them with salt. Then light up a fire and bake them. As for the hole in the tree, spread honey on the top of the tree with the seven bends. Tie a copper thread around the waist of a red ant and turn it loose in front of the tree. It will naturally make a hole through the tree and come out at the other end."

The instructions were carried out and the feudal lord of Japan won in the contest. The wish of the son was to be permitted not to send his 60-year-old father to Deederano. The edict was lifted because of that.

Sasaki Kizen
Hienuki-gun, Iwate

## 166. The Wife's Cleverness

A certain merchant set out for Edo to sell flowers used in dyeing. When he stopped overnight at a certain inn on his way, the woman who ran it came to him and said, "The picture scroll hanging there is unusual. The cock painted on it always crows in the morning."

The merchant said, "There is no reason for a cock painted on a picture to crow."

The woman then proposed that they wager whether it would or not. The agreement was that if the merchant lost, he would give the innkeeper all his load of flowers, and if the innkeeper lost, she would pay the price of the load.

The next morning the cock on the scroll crowed, just as the innkeeper had said it would. The merchant went home to his wife in tears because all his load of flowers was gone. When his wife heard what had happened, she said, "Then I will go to get even."

The wife took with her a load of flowers twice as big as the one her husband had taken. She put up at the same inn as where her husband had been and the innkeeper made the same wager with her. The wife secretly sewed up the throat of the cock on the picture scroll in the night. It could not make a single sound in the morning.

The wife took the price of her load in this way and went home.

Fumino Shirakoma [Iwakura Ichirō]
Minamikanbara-gun, Niigata

## 167. The Wife Who was a Thief

*Attan koto ni wa.*

There once was a wife who was a thief. She would order her husband every day, "Get out and steal. It makes no difference where you take things from."

If the man brought home a cow, his wife would rub oil on its horns and burn them to change those that were bent forward to ones that bent back. No matter how often officers came to arrest them, they could not catch them.

Since his wife was always annoying the man with orders to go to get something, he decided one day to give her some trouble. He dug up a dead man in the graveyard and brought him home. He wondered what his wife would do with it. She stuffed the corpse into a rice chest and put it out on the porch. Then she went off to visit at a friend's house as though nothing had happened. Two robbers of her gang lived there.

After about the right time had come, the woman cried out, "Oh, I have forgotten something. I came off and left something valuable of ours in a chest on our porch. I must hurry back to take care of it!"

The woman and her husband left the friend's house. When the thieves heard about something valuable, they flew to the woman's house ahead of her. One of them put the chest onto his shoulders and the other followed as they ran away. But the one behind noticed what was in the box. He shouted, "It's a man! It's a man!"

"That's why I am running," the first one called back as they broke into a run and got away as fast as they could.

Iwakura Ichirō
Ōshima-gun, Kagoshima

## 168. The Thief's Gambling

Once upon a time there was a chōja who had many 1000-ryō boxes. He slept with one under his head as a pillow every night. Thief after thief would come to steal a 1000-ryō box, but there was such strict watch that nobody could get a single one. The mansion had two or three inner gates so that it was not easy to go through to the interior.

The chōja announced one day that he would give a 1000-ryō box to anyone who could get the one he used as a pillow without letting him know. An ordinary thief tried to enter the house, but he was noticed immediately and was caught before he got inside.

Another man came one day and said, "I'll break in tonight. Is that all right?"

The chōja said, "I'll give you the 1000-ryō box from under my head if you do, so come on in." The man looked over the place and went home.

Since the people at the house knew that somebody was coming that night, they made more sure than ever that the locks were secure.

The thief prepared three riceballs, a sheaf of straw, twenty or thirty dango, thread, and a wooden pillow and waited until nighttime to start out. When he crossed over the first gate, a big steer came at him, shaking its horns. The thief immediately gave it the straw he had ready and the steer started to eat it.

When the thief went through the second gate, three dogs as big as calves came leaping toward him and barking. The thief was startled although he had expected that. He gave each dog a riceball and they ate tamely.

In this way the thief overcame two difficulties and entered the house. A number of men servants were sleeping in a row in the entrance room. Starting from the first, the thief tied each one's hair to the hair of the next with the thread he had brought. He found a number of maid servants sleeping in the next room. He reached under the quilts of each and stuck a dango onto her butt.

Then the thief went into the kitchen and picked up the bamboo fire blower. He played on it as though it were a flute. At that, all the servants woke up. The men shouted, "Whose pulling my hair? What are you up to? Stop pulling my hair!" There was a big uproar.

The maids called to each other, "What's on my butt? What's sticking to my butt? It better not be a turd!" They shouted from one side of the room to the other.

In the midst of this confusion the thief went without any trouble into the room where the chōja was sleeping. As the clamor of the servants grew louder, the chōja turned over in his sleep. He raised his head a little at that time, and the thief exchanged the wooden pillow he had brought with the 1000-ryō box he had been using as a pillow. By then the servants got up and declared that the thief had entered. They went into the kitchen to light up the fire, but when they went to blow it, the bamboo let out sounds like a flute.

While all this was going on, the thief strolled away with the 1000-ryō box. Then, according to the agreement, he was able to live for the rest of his life just eating and sleeping.

Seki Keigo
Nagasaki

## 169. The Clever Man

When a certain man came home one night, he heard somebody talking with his wife. He thought it must be a vile man and he went in and gave him a whack on the back. He killed the visitor without intending to.

The man looked more carefully and discovered it was the gentleman of the village. The husband and wife worried about what to do. They decided finally it would be best to talk things over with a clever man and sent for him.

When the clever man arrived, he said, "All right, I'll take over from here," and carried the dead man off on his shoulders. He leaned him up against the wooden doors that were closed at a house where young men were gambling. He rattled the doors a little and went away.

When the young men inside heard the noise, they said, "Somebody has come to spy on us." One of them took a stick and went around outside. He hit the man standing there on the back. He fell with a thud. All the young men came out to see and found the gentleman of the village there. They said, "We certainly have done something foolish. We have killed the gentleman."

The young men were worried and went to the clever man to talk things over. He said, "All right, all right, I'll take over."

This time, the clever man carried the corpse of the gentleman to his home and said at the door, "I'm home now. Open up!"

His wife said, "A fellow like you who goes out sporting at night doesn't need to come home."

Then the man said, "I'll jump into the well and die then." He took the corpse to the well, threw it in and ran home.

The wife thought that her husband had really killed himself. She opened the door and began to cry, "If I had opened the door and let him in, this would not have happened." She decided to go to the clever man for advice. He let on he would never hurt a flea. He said, "I'll tell you what to do, so stop worrying."

The clever man told the woman to heat a kettle of water and put her husband into the bath tub to steam him up. He then went to call the doctor. He said, "The gentleman of the village is sick with a fever." The doctor came rushing over and took the man's pulse. He said, "I am sorry to say he has already stopped breathing." At last a funeral could be arranged for the gentleman.

The clever man received many gifts of thanks from everyone and profited greatly from all that had happened.

Fumino Shirakoma [Iwakura Ichirō]
Minamikanbara-gun, Niigata

## 170. Yakushi in the Straw Bag

Once upon a time in a certain place there was a very unfilial son who was a liar. His father took him along one day to cut trees in the mountains. The boy worked hard for a while, but he soon became bored. He tried to think of a good way to fool his father so that he could go home to play. He began to cry suddenly, "My stomach aches! My stomach aches!" His manner seemed so sincere to his father that he said, "Go home and go to bed then."

The boy went home in high spirits. When he reached home, he said to his mother, "Something terrible has happened, Mother. Father was injured badly in the mountains and has died. You should become a nun quickly and offer prayers for his soul."

His mother said, "What a pity that has happened. I'll become a nun right away." She shaved off all her hair and turned into a nun and sat in front of the family altar, offering prayers with all her heart. She was astonished when her husband came home carrying a big load of wood on his back. She told him what their son had done, and he was furious.

The husband declared, "We don't want such an unfilial son. He should be tied up in a straw mat and be thrown into the river." He hurriedly made a big straw bag and put his son into it. Then he set the bag out under the eaves.

A blind masseur came along and stumbled on the straw bag. The boy asked crossly, "Who has stumbled on me?"

The blind man said, "Please forgive me. I am blind and could not see the straw bag."

"So you are blind, are you?" answered the boy. "I was blind, too, but once I got into this straw bag, I could suddenly see. You can be cured, too, so climb in." He fooled the blind masseur and traded places with him in the straw bag.

When the father had finished eating his lunch, he came out and picked up the straw bag. He took it to the river and threw it in, and it was carried away by the current.

The boy hid in the mountains for five or six days. He said to a fish peddler who came along, "I live in the neighborhood. Please let me have a salted fish. I will bring you the money right away." He lied to the peddler and took the fish home.

The boy said, "Although you threw me into the river, I was rescued immediately. I found this salted fish in the river. You go and get some, too." He forced his father and mother into a straw bag and threw them into the river.

*Oshimae.*

Katō Kaichi
Haga-gun, Tochigi

## 171. The Horse That Dropped Coins

Once upon a time a horse dealer came leading a cow and said, "This cow drops gold. Would you like to buy it?" A man who heard him thought he could make money on the cow and bought it for a big price right away. Several days went by without the cow's dropping gold. Then the buyer went to the horse dealer to see about it.

The dealer said, "If you do not feed the cow gold, it will not drop gold."

Kashiyama Kaichi
Kumano, Wakayama

## 172. The Golden Eggplant

There was a certain king who had a one-year-old son. He and his consort were taking loving care of the child, but one day the consort broke wind in the midst of a crowd.

The king was furious. He declared, "I can no longer keep such a woman as my consort." He had a dugout boat prepared and set the mother and child adrift in it. They were carried off on the tide without any place to go. Finally the boat arrived at an unknown island. Their life changed from what it had been before, for they were pitifully poor. When the boy grew bigger, his playmates teased him and called him an illegitimate. He went home crying and asked his mother, "Don't I have a father?"

At first the mother kept her secret, but the boy asked so often that she finally told him the whole story. When the boy became 13, he said to his mother, "Please let me leave for a while." She asked, "What do you want to do if I let you go?"

He answered, "I must go to my father's kingdom to meet him and to ask him to restore you to your former place." His mother gave him permission reluctantly to go.

The boy crossed over to the island where his father was. After he inquired where the king lived, he walked by the gate calling, "Does anyone want seed that grows golden eggplant?" He did not go to any other house, only to the gate of the palace every day and called the same thing.

The guard at the gate told the king about the boy. The king thought it strange. He said, "Ask again if golden eggplant will really grow."

When the guard went out to ask the boy, the boy said, "They really grow."

The king ordered, "Bring that boy before me." The boy stood before the king for the first time. The king said, "You say you have seed that grows golden eggplant. Is it true?"

The boy replied, "Yes, such eggplants grow, but the seed must be planted by someone who does not break wind."

The king exclaimed, "Is there anybody in the world who does not break wind?"

The boy realized this was his chance. He related the story about his mother and said, "It is as your majesty says. Since there is nobody in the world who does not break wind, please take my mother and me back as we formerly were."

The king was moved and took the boy immediately. He declared, "It will be safe to take such a wise boy as my heir."

Iwakura Ichirō
Ōshima-gun, Kagoshima

## 173. The Child of the Sun

There was once a child who was bestowed by the Sun. He was brought up by his mother until he was seven years old. He was playing outside on the day he was seven and his playmates teased him, calling him an illegitimate.

When the boy told his mother, she revealed to him what she had kept secret until then. She said, "You really are the child of the Sun."

Upon hearing that, the boy said, "I must climb to the Sky to meet my father, the Sun."

The boy received permission from his mother to leave and he climbed that day to the Sky. When he presented himself before the Sun, the Sun was very angry. He declared, "I have no recollection of siring a son in the world below. Take this child and feed him to the demon."

The Sun's men led the boy off as they were told to do. The demon was delighted and prepared to eat the boy in one bite, but the child was of such noble rank that he could not draw near him. He knelt, instead, and pressed the palms of his hands together in reverence before him. This surprised the Sun's men. They returned hurriedly to report it. The Sun realized upon hearing about it that the child was his. He said, "I will take care of you and your mother. Go down to the earth below for the present."

The child became a cowherd on earth. One day when he led the cow out to the meadow for it to graze, a letter came floating down from the Sky. Just as the boy noticed it, his cow ate up the letter and then spit it out. The writing turned red at the time because of the cow's blood. This resulted in the beginning of the term *osōwata* [intestine of the letter] for the first stomach of the cow. According to the command from the Sky, the boy became the first *osōshi* [oracle] and his mother became the first *yuta* [female shaman].

Iwakura Ichirō
Kikaijima, Kagoshima

## 174. A Thousand Ryō for a Saying

Once upon a time a man left his wife and mother at home while he set out to earn money in another region. He saved his earnings and after several years he decided to go home. He thought he would take some good sayings home as gifts. He went to the head of a local temple and asked for some.

The priest told him that it was a good idea and taught him three. The first was "Even if men pause, I should not." The second was, "A small tree rather than a big one." The third was, "A short temper loses." The man learned the three and kept them carefully in mind as he set out for home.

Along the man's way a crowd of men had gathered by the side of the road. He wondered what was going on and started to look, but he remembered, "Even if men pause, I should not." He passed them by. After he had gone thirty feet or so, he heard a big noise behind. All the men who had been looking where there was digging going on after a landslide were buried alive under the dirt. The man realized that he had been saved by the priest's saying.

The sky suddenly clouded over as he went on. Rain began to fall hard and thunder rolled. Men traveling on the road were frightened and took shelter under a big cryptomeria tree. The man who was going home said to himself, "A small tree rather than a big one." He went under a small tree.

Suddenly thunder struck the big tree and everyone standing under it was killed. [The Japanese concept is that thunder rather than lightning strikes.] The homeward bound man was saved again by a saying from the priest.

It was evening of that day when the man neared his home. He started to enter eagerly, but he noticed the shadow of a shaven head like a priest's on the paper window. Somebody was talking intimately with his wife. He suspected they were doing something wrong. He flew into a rage and ran to the outshed to grab a scythe. He started to sharpen it, but then he remembered the saying, "A short temper loses." He tossed the scythe aside and went into his house, saying quietly, "I'm home now."

The man saw his wife greet him with delight. He asked, "Who is the bald-head here?"

His wife answered, "It is your mother. She has been troubled with dizziness lately and has had her hair shaved off to relieve it. I have been telling her she should sleep with me because it is cold tonight."

The man rejoiced over how dutiful his wife was toward his mother, but he thought the sayings the priest had taught him were the best gift of all.

Kawano Masao
Shōdojima, Kagawa

## 175. Two Bolts of White Cloth

One day when a bride and her mother-in-law were talking, the bride declared, "That deity riding a horse on the mountain is called Atago Sama."

The mother-in-law said, "Oh, no, Atago Sama is not a deity that sets out on horseback. Women should be careful about saying such things."

The two women argued till the end of the day, but they could not settle the matter. They decided to take the matter to Judge Ōoka for arbitration. That night the bride and the mother-in-law each went secretly with a bolt of white cloth under her sleeve and slipped it to the judge. Each begged, "Please decide it the way I say it is." He agreed with each of them.

The two of them appeared before the judge together on the next day. When the bride asked, "Judge Ōoka, the deity Atago Sama sets out on a horse, doesn't he?" He shook his head as in denial.

The mother-in-law then took her turn. She said, "Judge Ōoka, the deity Atago Sama does not ride a horse, does he?" But the judge did not agree again. The bride and her mother-in-law thought he had not kept his agreement.

The woman asked, "Then what deity is that on the mountain?"

Judge Ōoka replied, "That is Nitan-no-shiro Tadatori Kō Sama [a play on the name of a popular hero, "Nitan-no-shiro" and words meaning "two bolts of white taken for nothing."]

Sasaki Kizen
Kamihei-gun, Iwate

## 176. The Child Judge

A bride and her mother-in-law gave birth to babies at the same time. After they had put them in the same tub at the same time to wash them, they could not decide which baby was which. One baby was a boy and the other was a girl, but each woman said she had given birth to a boy.

Since the women could not agree, they took the matter to Judge Ōoka to arbitrate. The judge was puzzled over a good way to solve the dispute. He went on an impulse to fish at the river. Three children were playing there. He went near them to see what they were playing. They were playing court.

The child who was a little bigger than the others was playing Ōoka and the other two were the disputants. They were arguing about there not being ten "tsu" in counting from one to ten because tō [ten] did not end in "tsu". This was in the form of a riddle. The child who played judge said the itsutsu [five] had two "tsu" so the extra one could be given to tō. Then there would be enough "tsu" for each.

Next, the children played bride and mother-in-law. They pretended they had delivered babies together. They had washed them hurriedly in the same basin, and discovered one was a boy and the other a girl. Each woman declared her baby was a boy. They brought their dispute to Ōoka to arbitrate.

The judge agreed, "Each of you milk your breasts and bring me what you have."

The children pretended to milk their breasts. They took turns using the same bowl. The judge weighed each bowlful and said, "The mother-in-law's milk is heavier than the bride's. The mother who gives birth to a son has heavier breasts, so the boy baby belongs to the mother-in-law."

The real judge looked on at this from the thicket where he was hiding. When the children stopped their play and went away, he wondered where they lived and followed them far back into the mountains. They went into a big house there.

The judge went in, too, to see, but there was no sign of the children who had just gone in. He thought it strange as he looked around the place. He noticed that although the house was large, it had only a single pillar in the center. This surprised him. Although he called, nobody answered, so he went home. He went to the bride and her mother-in-law who had the problem and settled the question as the children had done.

The judge recalled the house with a single pillar later and invented the umbrella. The three children were deities.

Sasaki Kizen
Iwate

## 177. The Badger's Nest

*Mukashi mukashi no koto desu.*

There was a nest of something in a tree growing on the little border between rice paddies. Two men walked by it, discussing what kind of nest it might be.

One said, "That must be a badger's nest."

"No," said the other, "it must be a chicken's nest."

"No, it's a badger's nest!"

"No, it's a chicken's nest!"

The two continued to argue. They finally decided to ask a wise old man about it, but each went secretly to try asking. The old man answered each, "Of course, there's no doubt about it."

Each one thought he was right and the men started to quarrel. The old man came along then. When one man asked, "Is this a tanuki-no-su [badger's nest]?"

The old man said, "Of course it is a ta-no-ki-no-su [a tree nest by the field]."

The other man asked, "Is it a mistake to say it's a niwatori-no-su [a chicken's nest]?"

The old man answered, "Of course it is a ni-wa-tori-no-su [a two-winged bird's nest]."

Yamaguchi Asatarō
Ikinoshima, Nagasaki

## 178. The Famous Judge

There were three brothers at a certain place. When their father was about to die, he called each of them to him and gave him a gourd. He said, "Cherish this, for by it you will learn who is to be my heir." He made his will in this way and died a short time after.

The brothers found out after their father had died that he had given each of them a gourd and had said the same thing. An argument broke out as to which was the heir. They went to the priest at the local temple to settle the matter.

After the priest heard what the brothers said, he declared, "I can understand this. The son who received the first gourd is to be the heir. If I can weigh them, I can decide right away."

Each son put his gourd on the scales, and the oldest son's was the heaviest. He became the heir after all.

Sasaki Kizen
Iwate

## 179. Red Rice and the Child

Once upon a time a poor man lived with his child in a little rented hut. They ate only red rice (a rice of poor quality that matures early) because they could not afford the ordinary kind.

When the child went to play at the landlord's house, he was asked, "What do you eat at home?"

The child replied "red rice." [Red rice is the name given glutinous rice steamed with red beans for festive occasions.]

The landlord said, "My red beans are disappearing a little at a time these days. It must be your father's doings." He went immediately to the poor man's hut to drive him out. The father finally cut open his child's stomach to show what was in it to prove his innocence. Only a poor quality of red rice was there. The landlord was so full of remorse that he committed suicide.

Nobody grew red rice again in that place.

Takatori Teruō
Okayama

## 180. Improving the Omen

A certain couple had been childless although they had wanted one for many years. Then a child was born and the father set out to take the good news to his wife's home.

The man picked up a priest's robe and surplice and a rosary that had been dropped on his way. That worried him, for he thought it was a bad omen to find such things on the morning his child had been born. He went to the local priest to ask for advice the next morning. He related what had happened and asked what to do. The priest said, "Nothing better could have happened. If you are uneasy about it, I will give you a poem to improve the omen:

The child will live as many decades as beads on the rosary
That was picked up on the 13th Morning of the Eleventh Month."

[The poem has puns on rosary beads, surplice, and robe.]

The father was completely reassured and went home happy.

Dobashi Riki
Nishiyatsushiro-gun, Yamanashi

## 181. The Zatō's Cleverness

Once an old man and an old woman were talking one evening about making kaimochi [sweet rice cakes] for supper when a rokubu came along and begged to be put up for the night. The old man said, "It is not convenient to let you stay tonight." But the man insisted so much that they finally let him in.

The old man and old woman talked over a secret plan after they put the rokubu to bed. They would tie a string on the old man's toe, and when the mochi was ready, the old woman would pull the string to wake him up.

The guest, however, eavesdropped and decided he had heard something good. He waited until the old man had gone to sleep and then carefully switched the string to his own toe, put on the old man's clothes, and waited for the string to be pulled. Presently the string was pulled and the pilgrim got up and ate his fill of the mochi in the dark.

Then the old woman said, "Let's put what's left over in the cupboard. There is some sweet wine left, too, in the jar. After the rokubu leaves, you and I can eat all we want."

The pilgrim took all the mochi that was left in the cupboard and wrapped it up in his straw cloak in the night. He drank up the sweet wine and smeared dregs on the rim of the jar. When the rokubu was leaving the next morning, the old man asked him, "What region are you from?"

The guest replied, "I'm from Mino-ni-Kaimochi, Kurumi-no-Kōri [the country of the straw cloak wrapped around what was left of the kaimochi]."

The old man asked, "What is your name?"

The rokubu replied, "Kamekasu Nurinosuke [the man who smeared wine dregs on the rim of the jar]."

Then he left.

Fumino Shirakoma [Iwakura Ichirō]
Minamikanbara-gun, Niigata

## 182. Stories with Riddles

A zatō came along tapping his cane. A cowherd came from the opposite direction leading a violent steer, the kind that might gore a man.

The cowherd said, "Please step aside a little." When he heard that, the blind man asked, "What are you?"

The cowherd answered "hito-tsuki" [one month or man gorer].

The zatō asked, "What color?"

The cowherd answered, "The color of the lower leaves on greens in October."

The zatō responded, "Oh, *akage* [red hair or red leaves]."

Nishimura Jirō
Aki-gun, Hiroshima

## 183. The Priest and his Novice

### a Picking up everything the horse drops

A novice on foot followed a priest on horseback whom he accompanied. Presently a wind started up and blew off the priest's hat. When they arrived at their destination, the hat was gone. When the priest asked his novice about the hat, he answered, "I thought you threw it away because you did not need it so I did not pick it up."

The priest said, "No, I was on horseback and could not pick it up. You were following me and should have picked up what fell. Now go and get it."

The novice ran back and picked up the hat. The horse had left droppings along the way they had come. The boy picked up the droppings, too, and put them into the hat to take to the priest. The priest shouted in surprise and anger.

His novice said, "You told me to pick up what had dropped, so I picked up everything."

Koyama Masao
Chiisagata, Nagano

### b Kwan-kwan kutta kutta [Hotoke Sama ate the red beans]

The priest always ate good things that were brought as gifts by himself, and never shared them with his novice. One day the priest laid the good food before the altar as an offering and went away somewhere, luckily for the novice. He thought this was his chance and he ate everything up. He left a bit of boiled food stuck to the edge of Hotoke's mouth.

The priest found all the food gone when he returned. "You ate it all while I was away, didn't you?" he accused the novice angrily.

The boy said, "No, I didn't."

The priest declared, "There is no reason for food to disappear unless somebody eats it."

The boy suggested, "Since you offered it to Hotoke Sama, the main image probably ate it."

"Who ever heard of a metal image eating food?" exclaimed the priest. He picked up his staff that was beside him and hit the main image angrily. There was the sound *kwan-kwan* [I didn't eat it! I didn't eat it!].

The priest said, "See, it says it didn't eat it, doesn't it?"

The novice said, "Our main image has said that he did not eat it although he ate it, so we should knock him down to Hell and boil him in the cauldron." The priest went to the kitchen with his novice to put water into the big kettle. Then they put the main image into it and built up the fire. The water gradually became hotter and Hotoke was being boiled. When they looked in, they heard the sound *kuta-kuta* [I ate it! I ate it!].

The novice said, "Now you see, Oshō Sama, it is finally confessing that it ate it."

Koyama Masao
Chiisagata, Nagano

## c The calabash wife

Once upon a time there was a priest who painted a face on a gourd, fixed it up with woman's clothes, and set it in the alcove as an ornament. Whenever he went out, he would always say to it, "I am leaving now." Then he would pull the cord attached to it and the lady would always lower her head in response like a real wife. When the priest returned, he would go to it and say, "I'm home now," and pull the cord to make the gourd bow. He had pleasure in doing this every day.

The novice thought one day, "Oshō San is always talking in the inner room. I wonder what he is up to." He went to see and there sat the gourd lady. Thinking that he had found something amusing, the novice pulled the cord. The gourd's head lowered. This was so much fun that the boy continued to pull the cord and then to slacken it to make the gourd bow. Suddenly the lady's head dropped off.

When the priest came back and found the lady's head had fallen off, he concluded that it was due to the work of the novice. He called the boy to him and said, "There isn't anyone as mean as you. I will never forgive you now."

When the priest started to grab the boy, he ran as fast as he could to the garden patch behind the temple. The priest chased him calling, "Wait, boy!" But the boy hid in the gourd patch.

When the priest saw that, he said, "My novice has gone to my mother-in-law's house today. I will have to forgive him." He returned to the temple.

Fumino Shirakoma [Iwakura Ichirō]
Minamikanbara-gun, Niigata

### d The novice gets his name changed

Once there was a priest and two novices at a certain place. After the priest sent his two novices to bed every night, he would drink wine, exclaiming, *kyūkyū* [the sound of blowing hot wine], and he would knock the ashes off the mochi, *bata-bata*, which his wife toasted for him.

One night as the two boys in bed listened to the priest drinking, *kyūkyū*, and patting ashes off the mochi, *bata-bata*, they could hardly stand it because they wanted some, too. But they could not get up unless they were called.

The boys talked matters over and went the next day to the priest. One of them said, "Please call me Kyū-kyū from today." The other said, "Please call me Bata-bata from today."

The priest agreed and changed their names. That night when the priest began to say *kyūkyū* as he drank his wine, one of the novices went into the priest's quarters and said, "Yes, what is it you want?" When the priest began to pat ashes of the mochi, *bata-bata*, that his wife had toasted, the other novice went into his quarters and said, "Yes, what is it you want?"

They managed in this way to get wine and mochi given them.

*Too gatchiri.*

Isogai Isamu
Hiroshima

### e Standing the pillar up and finding mochi

A priest who liked toasted mochi would send his novice on errands so that he could eat it alone. The novice knew this and he wanted to eat mochi, too, but he didn't have a chance.

One day the priest sent the boy on an errand as usual and started to toast mochi for himself. The boy made up his mind he would get some that day. He returned at about the right time and walked louder than usual as he called, "I've returned now!"

The priest hurriedly buried the mochi in the ashes of the hearth and tried to look as though nothing was going on. The novice began to report about his errand. He said, "The ceremony for beam raising was great today." The priest asked, "What went on?" The novice reached for the metal chopsticks used in the hearth and drew a general plan of the building on the ashes with the chopsticks.

Then the boy said, "The Daikoku Pillar was set about here." As he said that he pushed the chopsticks deep into the ashes and cleverly stuck them into a piece of mochi. When he drew up the chopsticks, the piece of mochi came out stuck to them. He said to the priest, "Look at what was there."

The priest said, "Oh, yes, I toasted a piece and put it there to give you."

The boy said, "Thanks, I'll eat it." After he ate the mochi, he continued his account of the celebration, "And another pillar was set about here."

The boy stuck the chopsticks into another piece of hidden mochi, and receiving the same response, he accepted it and ate it. He went on with his story, standing the chopsticks in the far side and center of the hearth until he had picked up all the mochi and ate it casually.

The priest did not eat a single piece that day.

Koyama Masao
Chiisagata, Nagano

### f A slip of the tongue when buying tōfu

Long ago there was a priest and his novice at a temple in the mountains. The priest was very fond of tōfu and sent his novice to the tōfu shop day after day to buy it.

There was a rice store along the way to the shop. The old man who ran the store would ask, "Where are you going today?" The boy would answer, "To buy tōfu." This was repeated every day until the boy became annoyed.

One day when the priest told the boy to go to buy tōfu, the novice said he did not want to go.

"Why don't you want to go?" asked the priest.

The novice replied, "The old man at the rice shop below here asks me every day where I am going and that is why I don't want to go."

"Well, then," said the priest, "I'll tell you what to answer. If the man asks you where you are going, tell him you are going to Saihō [toward the West or Paradise]. If he asks you why you are going to Saihō, tell him you are going to Gokuraku Jōdo [Paradise]."

The boy set out in a hurry, thinking he would have a good answer that day for the rice dealer. As usual, the old man asked, "Where are you going, boy?" The novice said, "To Saihō."

"What are you going to Saihō for," asked the old man.

"To buy tōfu," responded the novice.

Isogai Isamu
Hiroshima

### g The trials by the priest

One day a priest called his novice to him and give him some Indian cotton cloth. He said, "Take this to the dyer and have him dye it the color of a fox's call."

The boy said, "Yes, certainly." He set out to the dyer's with the cloth. Since the fox called *kon* [also meaning dark blue], he had the shop dye the cloth dark blue and brought it back. When he reached home, he said, "Here it is," and handed the priest the Indian cotton cloth that had been dyed dark blue.

The next day the priest said to his novice, "Here, boy, go somewhere today and look for a thing called dōmo-kōmo naran [no way, that way nor this]."

The boy said, "Yes, certainly," and flew out on his errand. He saw a beehive on the branch of a fir tree as he walked along. He asked the tree cutter working there, "Will you please give me that beehive?"

The man said, "Please take it away. The bees sting me and are a bother as I work here."

The novice brought a sack and climbed the tree with it. He put the sack over the beehive without any trouble and took it down. When he returned to the temple, the priest asked, "How about it? Did you find something called no way that way nor this?"

"Yes, I found it," answered the boy, "but I can't show it to you here. Please go into the inner room and shut the door. Wait there with your clothes off."

The priest did as the boy said. The boy took off the sack and tossed the beehive into the room, shutting the doors tightly afterwards. The bees flew out and stung the priest all over.

The priest cried out, "Come quickly, boy. The bees are stinging me and there is no way this nor that to get away."

Sasaki Hiroyuki
Kitashidara-gun, Aichi

### h Hand signals

[The first episodes will be omitted.]

One day the priest explained to his novice, "If company is here when it is time to cook rice, I will lift one finger to signal you to cook one shō of rice and if I lift two fingers, cook two shō of rice."

Once when the priest went to the privy, he missed his footing and fell into it. He stuck both hands up and waved, calling the boy to come quickly. The novice caught sight of his ten fingers waving and withdrew hurriedly to cook ten shō of rice.

"What a fool that boy is," muttered the priest as he climbed out of the privy. When he found the *to* [ten shō] of rice cooking, he was astonished for the second time.

Kurate-gun, Fukuoka

### i Overhearing private matters

Every night when the priest was in bed with his wife, they used to say, "What's this . . . big mountains . . . what's this . . . little mountain . . . and this . . . that's *jira-jira* [hair?] . . . what's this . . . that's the red hole . . . and this . . . it is *muka-muka* . . . and this . . . it's the black entrance, hondō . . . "

The novice learned their whole conversation by heart. Then on the next day the novice said to the priest, "Last night I had a funny dream."

"What kind of a dream? Try telling it to me."

The novice started out with, "At the top were big mountains and below a little mountain and below that *jira-jira*, and below that a red hole and below that *muka-muka*, and at the very bottom, the black entrance hondō. It was a strange dream."

The priest declared angrily, "Don't talk nonsense!"

[The rest of the episodes are omitted.]

Iwakura Ichirō
Kikaijima, Kagoshima

### j Substituting words

A priest wanted to forbid his novice to eat ame [a sweet]. He made sure by saying, "Anyone who eats ame will die."

The priest set out on an errand. The novice wanted to eat the ame so badly he couldn't bear it. He took one lick and then another until the jar of ame was empty. Then he dropped a good teacup and broke it. He cried loudly when the priest came home.

The priest asked, "What's the matter?"

The boy said, "I broke one of your good teacups carelessly. I felt so bad I wanted to kill myself as an apology. I ate a little ame, but I didn't die, and I kept on until I ate it all, but still I didn't die. That's why I am crying."

Koyama Masao
Chiisagata, Nagano

### k A story with a comic verse

There once was a priest who liked mochi, but he hid it to eat alone without giving his novice any. The boy felt slighted and wanted some himself.

One night he peeked into the priest's room just as the priest was toasting half a round cake of mochi at the hearth. The boy took his chance and hurried into the room after he opened the door. The flustered priest drew the piece of mochi up quickly.

The boy said, "Shall I give you a line of poetry?"

While the priest sat there holding the half piece, the boy said, "On the night of the full moon, it should not be broken."

There was no choice left for the priest. He responded with the line, "Here is the half hidden in the clouds."

In that way the boy managed to get the other half of the mochi.

Yamashita Hisao
Enuma-gun, Ishikawa

# PART TWO
# *Derived Tales*

# 11. *Stories about Destiny*

## 184. Singing Bones

Once upon a time there were partners in a trade—I'll try to tell this so it can be understood—who went together from here to a place like Katanoura, doing some sort of work. One of them earned a lot of money and the other was coming home empty-handed.

When the men came to the pass at the top of Yokei-no-Obane, they rested and talked under a goyō pine tree. The man who had not earned anything thought, "This man says he has earned a lot, but I would like to do something to him." He drew his sword and cut off the other man's head.

The murderer took the money from his companion and went home. He stopped his trade for three years, but three years later he passed Obane on his way to Katanoura. He stopped to rest where he and his companion had rested formerly. A fine voice sang from the thicket:

It's happened, it's happened,
What I thought has happened,
At last a stork, a turtle,
And the goyō pine!

[The stork, the tortoise, and the pine are congratulatory symbols.]

"This is strange," thought the man. "I hear singing in the thicket although nobody is around." When he went to see, he found a skull singing. He thought it was a remarkable skull.

The man asked it, "Are you the one who is singing that way?"

The skull answered, "Yes, I am singing."

"Will you sing anywhere you are taken?" asked the man.

It replied, "Yes, I will sing anywhere I go."

The man thought that would be a fine way to make money. He wrapped up the skull and put it in his sleeve and went home.

The man went to a certain rich man's house. He was asked, "What do you trade in?"

The man answered, "I have a skull that sings."

"You have a skull? I never heard of a skull that sings," declared the rich man.

The merchant took out the skull to show him and said, "Here it is. This is the skull that sings."

The rich man asked, "What will you do if it does not sing?"

The merchant replied, "If it doesn't sing, you can cut off my head, but if it sings, what will you do, Sir?"

The rich man said, "At that time I will give you all my wealth."

And so it was agreed. The merchant said, "Now, sing, skull, sing," but even when he rolled it around or hit it, the skull did not sing. "Well, will it sing?" asked the rich man impatiently. But it did not.

The rich man declared, "There never has been a skull that sang since long ago. Here, present your head according to the bargain." There was no way out for the merchant and he bowed his head. The angry rich man cut it off. At that time, the skull sang:

It's happened, it's happened,
What I thought has happened,
At last a stork, a turtle,
And the goyō pine!

The rich man regretted what he had done, but there was no way to undo it. He said, "If you had sung sooner, I would have given all my wealth to that man and I would not have suffered in this way."

The skull said, "This is my revenge for what happened three years ago."

Iwakura Ichirō
Koshikijima, Kagoshima

## 185. Stories about Forecasting Fortunes

[Translator's note: The first of the three subtypes to this story, which is close to the "Charcoal Maker Chōja," and to "Miidera," which follows, has been omitted.]

**Type II:**

A man whose wife was pregnant went to Koyase Jizō on Tanba hill to pray for her safe delivery. While he was spending the night at the Jizō Shrine, a Jizō from somewhere else came and said, "There is to be a birth somewhere else, so please go for me."

Koyase Jizō answered, "I have a guest and can not go. I wish you would go."

The other Jizō came back toward dawn. Koyase Jizō said, "I'm sorry to have put you to a lot of trouble."

The other Jizō said, "I settled his life for eighteen years. The Water Spirit of Katsura River in Kyoto will take him then."

"You have done well," came the response.

The man wondered if it could be about his family. He went home worried and found that his wife had given birth to her child. He learned in that way that Jizō had been talking about his family that morning. He kept his worry to himself and did not tell his wife. They had no more children after that.

The father became a watchman at the rapids of Katsura River, and his son was a dutiful child. The father loved his boy greatly and grieved alone over the fact the boy's life would end when he was eighteen.

It happened that in the year the boy was eighteen, there was a great flood at Katsura River. The son asked his father to let him go to the rapids for him, but his father was counting the days and was not inclined to let his son go.

The boy got up anyway and set out without his father knowing. He went without his breakfast. When the father found out, he was sure his son would be carried off by the Water Spirit. He told his wife to call the relatives and to prepare for the boy's funeral. His wife argued with him and said it was stupid to say such things, so the father went ahead with the preparations at home because his wife would not obey him.

Since the eighteen-year old young man had set out without breakfast, he was hungry and he stopped at a mochi shop to eat. A beautiful girl came and sat beside him.

The young man said, "Here, Sister, won't you eat some, too?" She replied that she would accept some, but she ate and ate an awful lot of it. In the meantime the weather cleared. The young man decided to go out on watch and asked for his bill. The girl had eaten 100 kan of mochi, but he did not have any money with him.

He said to the shopkeeper, "I will leave you my umbrella to keep until I come back. If I get killed, keep the umbrella to pay for the 100 kan of mochi." Then he went to his station. The girl went with him.

At the bank of the Katsura River, the girl said, "I am the Water Spirit here. You say you are taking the watch for your father and you ignored the fact I ate that much mochi I will extend your life from eighteen to sixty-one years."

The young man thought that something wonderful had happened. He stopped at the teahouse on his way home. He said, "Just because I am a dutiful son I was told my life would lengthen from eighteen to sixty-one years. I am glad that girl ate so much."

The owner said, "Since you were spared, you don't need to pay for the mochi. You told me to take your umbrella on your bill, and I wrote it off because I thought you got killed." The man excused him from paying the bill for the mochi

When the young man reached home, preparations were going on for his funeral. His parents were overjoyed when they heard what had happened.

Nishitani Katsuya
Mikata-gun, Hyōgo

**Type III:**

Once upon a time a rokubu came to a certain village, where he put up at the shrine of Yama-no-kami. He was awakened in the night by voices. It proved to be two Yama-no-kami.

One was saying, "You didn't go tonight, did you?"

The response was, "No, I couldn't because I had a guest tonight. How were things?"

The first one said, "The mother and the child are both all right."

"And how long will he live?"

"He will be killed by a hand ax when he is seven years old."

The rokubu wondered what it was all about.

When he went to the same village seven years later, he found that the carpenter at a certain family had been working beside his sleeping child. A horsefly had come flying around the sleeping child's face, and the man had tried to drive it off with the hand ax he was holding. The ax had slipped and split the child's head open. There was great confusion everywhere.

The rokubu recalled the talk of the Yama-no-kami at the shrine seven years before. He realized for the first time what they had been talking about.

Sasaki Kizen
Iwate-gun, Iwate

## 186. Miidera

*Mukashi sō na.*

Once there was a man who was a hunter by trade at a certain village. There was a big shower one evening when he was out hunting. It lasted for a long time and he wondered what to do.

The man decided to take refuge in a little shrine in the mountains. He was tired and started to go to sleep, but just then he heard heavy footsteps on the road in front of the place. That could mean danger, even a bear, so he picked up his gun to be ready. A huge person, not an animal, came into the shrine. The hunter looked on, thinking here was no ordinary person.

The one who came was Kannon and the deity at the shrine was Jizō. They began to talk. Kannon said, "The delivery was easy because I went. Sometimes, Jizō, the success of boys and girls depends upon the time they are born. The place I was asked to go had a baby boy, and next door a little girl was born. They were born at about the same time, but their fortunes turned out different. The girl next door is born to a good life, but the boy is born to poverty. The boy really has hard luck."

Jizō asked Kannon, "How can it happen that when they were born at the same time, there is such a difference?"

Kannon answered, "I would say it is like a cock's crow. The first part of his call will be full of spirit and the last part will be spiritless. The boy's fortune is three bamboo and the girl's fortune is a thousand bags of rice."

The man listening to Kannon and Jizō realized that it was exactly the time for his wife's delivery. He hoped that his child was the girl. When he looked outside, he saw the weather had cleared and stars were shining brightly. He went home walking across the evening dew.

When the man reached home, he heard a baby cry. He asked if it was a boy or girl baby and learned that it was a boy. What miserable luck he had! He began to tremble and his wife asked the reason. Then he told her all that he had heard.

Their fortune certainly was bad, but the girl had been born next door. The parents decided to arrange an engagement for the babies, but not to tell the reason. When the hunter went to his neighbor the next day, the man was feeling sorry that he had a girl. The couple next door were quite willing to arrange the engagement of their daughter.

When the two children grew up, they were married, but the man only made bamboo baskets and they were always poor. All that poor people can do is to make baskets and live on that. The man had no luck after he married that woman. Finally, things were so bad that he no longer worked. Their plans had failed and it was miserable for them to have to separate because of poverty, but they decided that rather than for both of them to die, it would be better to leave each other alive.

The woman decided to go without telling her parents and to find work somewhere. She went to the town of Ōtsu and found work at a wealthy home. The man's wife had died and he was looking for a second wife. He found this woman to be honest and he took her to be his wife. The former husband's health improved after his wife left, and he concluded that it really had been a bad idea to marry that woman. As he grew stronger, he began once more to make bamboo things and to go around selling them.

One day when the man went to Ōtsu to sell bamboo winnowing baskets, he looked into a big house and saw the mistress there. She seemed very much like his former wife. Then she noticed him, and they exchanged glances. She had become the wife of a man of good standing.

The woman pitied the basket seller and bought all he had. She bought some each time he came. Finally, she thought it would not be wrong to use some money without telling her husband. She spread bean paste over a lot of coins and gave them to the basket seller.

The man took the bean paste home. He never had anything to eat with his rice, and the woman had felt sorry to see him eat his lunch every day without anything to go with the rice and that was why she had given the bean paste to him. When he stuck his chopsticks into the bean paste, he heard a click and decided there must be something in it that could not be eaten. He saw the little coins, but a beggar bought the bean paste from the basket seller. The man went home and died a short time later.

A fire broke out at the Kannon temple in Ōtsu. Since there was a shortage of water, everyone went to the wealthy man's home to get winnowing baskets [*mii*] to put the fire out. Ever since that, the temple has been known as Miidera.

*Mō nashi shan shan.*

Takeda Akira
Shishijima, Mitoyo-gun, Kagawa

# 12. *Ghost Stories*

### 187. The Tiny Hakama

Long ago an old woman living alone in a hut in the mountains was spinning late as usual when a little man came out from somewhere. He was an angular little fellow wearing a tiny, neat hakama [divided skirt]. He said, "You must be lonely, Granny. I'll do a dance for you."

He danced as he sang:

Tiny, tiny hakama
And a wooden sword at my side,
Look, Granny, *nen-nen*!

Then he disappeared somewhere.

The old woman was amused, but felt uneasy as dawn came. She searched all around in the morning, but found nothing unusual. When she looked under her porch, she found an old wooden pick used in blackening teeth. It was a clever looking little thing. The old woman promptly burned it to get rid of it. Nothing unusual happened again that night.

There is a tradition from long ago that picks used in blackening teeth were gathered and burned to get rid of them.

Suzuki Tōzō
Sado Island, Niigata

---

* Translator's note: The Japanese word "bakemono," translated here as "ghost," refers to something transformed.

## 188. Destroying the Ghost

Long ago there were two brothers in Gōshū who shot with guns. One day when they went far into the mountains to hunt, they came to a big valley. It did not seem worthwhile to just walk together, so one of them went to the left and the other to the right of the valley as they climbed.

When the older brother had gone farther into the mountains, he suddenly heard a shot from his younger brother, who should have been on the other side of the valley. He thought his brother must have found something, for the shots continued one after another, and they kept on. The older man thought, "There must be something bigger than usual over there. I must go see." But the valley was deep and it was not easy to cross to the other side. Besides, trees and plants grew thick and there were many cliffs and boulders. He was ultimately unable to see his brother's side of the valley. The shots continued and then stopped abruptly.

The older brother was worried for fear his brother had run out of bullets. If he could only reach him! He tried harder than ever, and reached the head of the valley at last. He crossed a steep place to the other side. He called his brother many times, but could get no answer. Then he noticed a white-haired woman sitting at the foot of a tree about 75 feet away. She was turning her spinning wheel, spinning. She was a frightful sight. The man thought she must have done something to his brother. He aimed his gun at her and shot her squarely. The old woman did not seem scared, she didn't run away, she only looked at him with a grin on her face.

The man realized for the first time that she was a ghost. The bullet had certainly hit her arm, but she went right on spinning and grinning at him. The older man became angry. He shot her head, he shot her hands, he shot her side with his bullets, but she ignored them all. At last there were no more places to shoot except the spinning wheel she was turning, but that did not seem to be important.

Finally, the man had only two bullets left. He thought, "When these two bullets are gone that ghost will catch me and eat me. This is humiliating!" He looked the old woman over closely to see if there was something he had not yet shot. There was a box as big as a three shō measure beside her into which she was putting her thread. He decided to try shooting it, and took careful aim. The old woman, who had acted so deliberately, disappeared suddenly. The happy man went close to see and found a baboon struck at a vital spot and dead.

The brother might have been overcome by the creature and eaten, or he might have wandered off somewhere. The man went all around looking for his brother, and calling him, but he found nothing. There was nothing left to do, so he put the baboon over his shoulder and went down the mountain.

News of this spread around until the feudal lord at Hikone heard about it. He put on a big hunt in the mountains, but the fate of the younger brother could not be learned. The feudal lord bought the hide

### 189. The Mochi and the White Stones

The mountain road on Hayachine was constructed because of a certain hunter at Tsukimaushi-mura in the early days of the Nanbu Daimyō family. Nobody would go into the mountains in the region until then.

A hunter opened a road about half way and built a temporary hut. One day when he was there, he toasted mochi and set the pieces ready in a row. Somebody passed and stared into the hut when the hunter was about to eat the mochi. When the hunter looked closely, he saw that the man was a big priest.

The stranger came into the hut presently and watched the mochi being toasted with interest. Finally he reached out and took a piece to eat. The hunter was frightened. He himself had not had a piece to eat, but the stranger seemed to enjoy eating the mochi and did not leave until he had eaten every piece of it.

The hunter espected the priest would come again on the next day, so he found two or three white stones that looked like mochi and put them on to toast with the mochi. They grew hot as fire. Just as the man had anticipated, the priest came again and started to eat the mochi as he had done before.

After the mochi were gone, the priest put a white stone into his mouth. He rushed out of the hut in great astonishment and disappeared. It is said that he was found dead in the valley below.

Yanagita Kunio
Kamihei-gun, Iwate

### 190. The Old Woman's Three Moles

My great grandfather liked stories. This is one he told.

Long ago several officials came to the home of Shinemon (but that is not certain) in Yoshinoya of Ōmo-mura one evening in autumn. They said they had to have the three moles that were on the old woman's bottom.

She said, "My husband is away now. Please wait until he comes back and I can talk with him."

When her husband came home from the fields, he heard the story but he was a little suspicious. If it was the demand of the feudal lord, however, there was no way to refuse. He took thread and wound it around one of the moles to prepare to remove it.

The old man had to go to Nagamine in Honjōji-mura. As he passed a pine grove, he heard a silly song in the thicket. He didn't think it should be going on at that time of night. He listened and heard:

The three moles on Shinemon's old lady's seat
Are lucky moles for us.
*Bunbuku-bunbuku, bunbuku-bunbuku.*

Shall we wager today?
Shall we wager tomorrow?
*Bunbuku-bunbuku, bunbuku-bunbuku.*

The old man concluded that it was all a trick of foxes and went home without finishing his errand.

The officials came again the next day to demand the three moles. The old man greeted them and said, "It looks as though the three moles will come off soon, but please stay here tonight." There was a great odor of fried rats coming from the kitchen where the husband was preparing them.

The fox-officials could not resist the invitation and went into the house. They were led into a room where they were feasted with serving after serving of fried rats and rice with red beans in it. When it came time for the officials to go to bed, the husband said, "I am a poor man and have no pillows for you. Please forgive me, for I must offer these gourds for pillows." He had stuffed fried rats into the big gourds.

A great uproar broke out in the sleeping room during the night. The young people of the village came with a pack of dogs to see. Just as had been expected, the officials had turned back into their true forms and had stuck their heads into the gourds to get the fried rats.

The pack of dogs attacked the foxes in the midst of their distress and killed them.

Toyama Rekirō
Minamikanbara-gun, Niigata

## 191. The Spider Web

When a yamabushi went to a certain village and asked to stay overnight, the villagers said, "According to regulations at this village, we can't put up any itinerant. There is a temple in the mountain behind here. If that will do, you could go and stay there."

The yamabushi went to see and found it was a vacant temple with weeds growing thickly around it. But he was tired, so he went around behind the storehouse to go inside and lie down.

In the night an ōnyūdō came from the main hall and called, "You, there, Guest!"

When the yamabushi got up to see what was going on, the ghost said, "I'll play my shamisen for you." As he said that, he tightened the strings, *kiri-kiri.*

At the same time, the yamabushi's throat pained him, *kiri-kiri.* He took his sword from his side and cut toward his throat, and the strings on the shamisen snapped strangely.

When the ōnyūdō started to tighten the strings again, the yamabushi's throat pained him again. He cut toward his throat again. In this way his throat was gripped with pain a number of times, and the strings on the shamisen snapped each time he used his sword.

said, "I'll play my shamisen for you." As he said that, he tightened the strings, *kiri-kiri.*

At the same time, the yamabushi's throat pained him, *kiri-kiri.* He took his sword from his side and cut toward his throat, and the strings on the shamisen snapped strangely.

When the ōnyūdō started to tighten the strings again, the yamabushi's throat pained him again. He cut toward his throat again. In this way his throat was gripped with pain a number of times, and the strings on the shamisen snapped each time he used his sword.

The ōnyūdō started to withdraw in astonishment, but the yamabushi called, "Wait, nyūdō!" He flung a piece of firewood lying there at it, and split its head open. He had killed it.

The yamabushi picked up the corpse and threw it into the room with the dirt floor. He held it up where the morning sun shone on it in the morning and found it was the body of a huge old spider.

Sasaki Kizen
Shiwa-gun, Iwate

## 192. The Notions Peddler and the Badger

Once upon a time when a notions dealer was hurrying home along a mountain road toward evening, he saw a light shining beyond him. He went up to see and found a house there. He stopped and asked, "Will you please let me stay here tonight?"

The woman who was alone there consented immediately. The grateful peddler went in by the fire to warm himself. After he had finished the supper that the old woman gave him, he went over by the fire again and sat down. The old woman asked, "Do you have any needles?"

The notions peddler took needles out of his bundle and said, "I have plenty of needles, so please look them over." He showed her his finest pointed needle first.

The woman said, "This is a good needle, but it is too fine."

The woman returned it to him. He took it and stuck it in the straw mat.

Just as the peddler did that, the woman cried out, "Ouch! It hurts!"

The man thought that strange, but he took out a coarser needle to show her next.

The woman said, "I don't care for this one, either."

The peddler stuck the needle into the straw mat again, and again the woman cried out, "Ouch! That hurts!"

This seemed really unusual to the peddler. He took out his biggest needle, one like mat makers use, to show her. The woman said, "This is too big. It won't do."

The notions peddler took a firm grip on the needle and jabbed it with all his might into the matting. There was a big shout, and the woman, the house, and the fire all disappeared. The notions peddler found himself alone, sitting on a pitch black mountain.

That was a mountain where there was a badger who bothered people time after time. When it disguised itself to the peddler, the man had pricked its balls and it died because of that. Nobody was bothered by the badger from that time.

Shimoina-gun, Nagano

### 193. Failing to Destroy the Fox

There was a bad fox at Onnyada Nakazawa of Yonezato-mura. A man boasted that no fox could fool him. When the man was on his way home from Hitokabe, a fox appeared at the foot of the mountain beyond.

It picked up an ordinary leaf that had fallen on the path and held it up to its head. It kept on stroking its forehead with this leaf, and waving it around. While the man looked on, wondering what the fox was up to, it pressed the leaf lightly onto its back and then stood up. The fox suddenly turned into a young woman with a baby on her back.

The man concluded that was the way things like foxes transformed themselves. The fox pretended that it had not noticed anyone looking on. It went on down the path, across the bridge the man was standing on, and toward Nozato. It stopped at a little house by the road. The man wondered what the fox was doing. He set his load down on a rock beside the path and went to the house.

Somebody was saying, "Why if it isn't Sister! Hurry and come in!"

The man thought, "So that's it. I understand. The fox has transformed itself into a girl that has gone away from that house as a bride." When he thought about it, he recalled that he had heard that the girl had recently had a baby.

The fox certainly was clever at disguises. The man decided to tell the folks there that this wasn't their daughter, but a fox. He rolled up the bamboo blind at the door quickly and shouted, "That's not your daughter! That's a fox!" He stood looking at the butt of a mare.

The woman in the house said to an acquaintance passing by, "Why, what is that man doing! That's our mare. We tied her up because she is going to foal."

When the man heard the talk about himself he found he was holding up a horse's tail and shouting with all his might. He was staring at its butt in a daze.

It goes without saying that there was nothing left of his load with food in it that he had left on the rock.

Sasaki Kizen
Esashi-gun, Iwate

## 194. The Hōin and the Fox

Long ago a yamabushi at a certain temple in the mountains was called Daigakuin. He was skilled at writing and fond of wine, so he was asked for assistance in writing here and there in villages. He usually carried a conch shell when he went from village to village.

The yamabushi strolled out of the temple on a certain day with his big shell hanging at his side because he had been asked for help in a village. He saw a fox taking a nap comfortably by a stream along the way. The hōin was fond of playing pranks. He tiptoed near the fox and, lifting the conch shell by his side, he let out a shrill blast. The fox leaped in surprise and fell into the stream.

After the hōin had finished his errand and had drunk plenty, he started home feeling fine. He had thought when he left the village that there was plenty of time until sunset, but it suddenly became pitch dark while he was on the road. As he stood there perplexed, he happened to see a light beyond him. He thought he would ask to borrow a lantern and ask his way.

The man at the house said that unfortunately he did not have a candle just then. He asked the yamabushi to wait a little while he went to buy one. Then he left the house. The hōin sat down on the porch to wait, but no matter how long he waited, the man did not return. He grew tired of waiting and gave a big yawn. Just as he did that, he fell over backwards and landed in a stream with a big splash.

Suddenly the surroundings that had been dark became light.

Iwasaki Toshio
Fukushima

## 195. The Feud Between a Man and a Fox or a Badger

Long ago there was a clever fox living on Hichiyama in Iwami-gun. Young men of the village started a discussion one time. One of them said, "Can a fox fool a man or not?"

Another said, "Foxes have been fooling men from the beginning. Isn't the fox living at the pass above our village one that fools men?"

Another said, "What are you talking about? There is no question about whether a fox can fool a man or a man being fooled by a fox. If a man keeps his wits about him, a fox can't fool him."

The argument went on and on without coming to any conclusion, so they all finally decided to take anything handy and set out for the pass above the village to destroy the fox.

The men hid there to wait for the fox to come out. Presently an old fox came out of the shadows by a little stream flowing in the valley below them. It began to dip water over its body many times. Then it picked tree leaves and stuck them onto itself and got bamboo for a load as it prepared to transform itself into a man.

The young villagers watched everything. They boasted, "We aren't the sort that are fooled by such a disguise, however clever it might be. Just wait and see. We will catch you and give you a bad time. Don't cry then!"

Just then a fellow called Lazy Tasuke, from their neighboring village, came climbing up the road from the other side of the pass.

The young men said, "Look, we were wondering what that old fox would turn into, and here he is as Tasuke. That's clever, isn't it? But we aren't fooled." They waited for him to come up.

Presently Tasuke drew near and asked, "What are you all doing here today?"

Since the villagers thought they would overcome the fox, they said to Tasuke, "You generally are loafing, but we think it's great that you are coming over the mountain today, carrying a load of bamboo baskets with such spirit."

"Thanks," said Tasuke. "I should not be lazy always, so today I am making a little effort."

The young men said, "We have met here today, but we are ready to go home now. We have a sedan chair here. We like seeing you working for a change, so how would you like a ride?"

The real Tasuke answered sincerely, "Thanks, I will get in." He put his load into the sedan chair and then climbed in himself without any hesitation.

The villagers thought they had done well at fooling the fox that day. They had been fooled by it countless times, but they were happy that now they would be able to pay it back at last. They took turns guarding the sedan chair so that the fox could not get away while they went down from the pass.

As the young men approached the dwellings in the valley, one of them said, "It's safe now. No matter how much power the fox has, he can't get away. Hurry and get the fox out and tie him up." They all agreed. They pulled fox-Tasuke out and tied his arms and legs.

Tasuke was surprised. He cried, "What are you doing? I got into the sedan chair because you offered me a ride. What are you tying me up for?"

The young men answered, "What are you trying to say, you old fox? We saw you pour water over yourself by the mountain stream at the pass and transform yourself. Don't talk nonsense. Just stick out your tail!"

Tasuke was more surprised than ever. "This doesn't make sense," he declared. "I'm not a fox. I am Lazy Tasuke from the next village. Please let me go free!"

The young men shouted, "This is how this fox is going on, trying to fool us. They say you are an impudent thief. If you don't reveal your true form, this is what you get!" They tied him securely and began to beat him with sticks.

They hurt Tasuke so much that he cried, "Spare me! Spare me! I'm not such a bad fox!"

They answered, "You silly fox, you're tough, aren't you! We are going to wrap you in bamboo strips and toss you into the river."

Tasuke realized that they would soon bundle him up in a bamboo wrapper and throw him into the river. He began to plead miserably,

"Please spare me. I really am a fox, but I will never do anything bad again. I'll never fool men any more. If you will spare me, I will show you magic that transforms tree leaves into paper money."

The young men talked it over. They said, "The fox has confessed at last. When it comes down to it, we feel sorry for him. Shall we spare him and let him teach us magic?"

They decided to let the fox off and untied the ropes. The fox picked up some leaves and put them into his wallet. After he chanted a formula over them he took them out and they were genuine looking pieces of paper money. The young men learned the formula and turned the fox loose. Then Tasuke who had been turned into a fox thanked them and hurried back toward the pass.

The next day the young men recalled the formula they had learned from the fox and they decided to try it out at the next village. It was where Lazy Tasuke's family owned a winery. They went into his place to drink wine and to talk about what had happened, how the fox had disguised himself as Tasuke the day before. After they had drunk their fill, they said, "This is in payment," and put three leaves out to pay their bill.

The clerk at Tasuke's winery asked, "What is this?"

The young men said, "They're one yen bills."

"You're talking nonsense. These are tree leaves," retorted the clerk.

A fight broke out and Tasuke came rushing out from the back room. "Wait, friends from the next village, I'm the one who taught you the fox's magic formula yesterday," he said. "You kept saying that this Tasuke was a fox and treating me roughly. I pulled out real money to show you my magic. It wasn't a tree leaf at all. Now, what is going to finish up yesterday's doings?"

The young men were dumbfounded. They realized that the fox of the day before was really Tasuke. They apologized, saying, "We are sorry about what we did. So the fox fooled us after all, and we didn't fool him."

The quarrel about the bill ended. Lazy Tasuke reformed and became a good worker. He became a great wine dealer and it is said that he became very prosperous.

Iwami-gun, Tottori

## 196. Surprised Twice

Late one winter evening a certain night school teacher finished at school and was walking home alone. The moon was dim that night.

As the teacher crossed through a lonely rice field on the narrow path, he saw a beautiful girl on the dam beside the path. She was looking down, reading a book. The night school teacher didn't even think that she might be a ghost, he wanted to get a look at her face. He asked, "Are you studying?"

The girl looked up silently. Her face was frightful—something like a demon or a snake with its mouth open to the ears, fangs bared, and ghastly eyes glittering.

At one glance the teacher's hair stood on end. He threw his coat over his head and ran home.

"I'm home now! Hurry! Open the door," he shouted.

His wife wondered what was up as she hurried to the door. She saw her husband outside, pale and panting for breath. "What happened?" she asked.

The man said hurriedly, "It doesn't matter. Light up the fire and make some tea."

"There is fire under the kotatsu now," his wife said. He rushed into the house and sat at the kotatsu to get warm.

His wife persisted and asked again, "Just what happened?"

The man said, "There's no way to explain it, but on my way home I met a woman with a frightful face. It's the first time in my life that I have been so terribly frightened."

His wife asked, "What kind of a frightful face was it?"

The man exclaimed, "It is more terrible than can be described in writing or in a picture. I can't explain it in just a word or two. My hair is still on end."

His wife insisted, "You could at least imitate any kind of a face, couldn't you?"

The poor man said finally, "It was so frightful that I can't speak of it no matter how much you ask. I can't possibly imitate it. If you want to know that much, go see for yourself."

The wife asked, "Then, was it like this?" She faced her husband.

The man was horrified to see the exact face he had seen on the woman before. He gave a cry after one look at it and fainted as he tried to hide in the kotatsu.

The teacher woke up the next morning in the bright sunshine. He found himself lying face down at the dam in the middle of his field.

Dobashi Riki
Nishiyatsushiro-gun, Yamanashi

### 197. Two Mouths, an Upper and a Lower

A man from Yonezato was coming home from Kesen with a load of fish on his horse. The sun set when he had gotten as far as Ōmata in Ubaishi. He wondered where he could put up for the night.

The man took his load down from his horse and built up a fire. Although it was still early in the evening, a young woman walked by with a bundle tied in a furoshiki on her back. She looked like somebody from his neighborhood, the girl who had gone as a bride to Kesen.

The man asked her, "What happened?"

The girl said, "My mother-in-law is so mean that I cry all the time. I can't stand it any longer, so I'm running away tonight."

The man felt sorry for her. He tried to comfort her, and gave her what was left of his food.

In the meantime, the girl's behavior began to seem strange. She sent amorous glances toward the man. He did not recall that she was that sort, and he thought it was unusual that she should be acting like this, but he did not show how he felt. The girl came up to the fire and exposed her white shins, then her private parts, and then lay down on her side.

This was becoming too suspicious for the man to endure, but he still looked on without showing how he felt. He noticed that her private parts were strangely formed. As he looked, they moved. A mouth opened and yawned two or three times.

Then the man caught on. He grabbed a burning stick from the fire and struck the woman with it. She rolled over and shrieked as she got up. Suddenly the part with the bundle began to run away and the part below was knocked over.

The girl had been two badgers disguised.

Sasaki Kizen
Esashi-gun, Iwate

## 198. The Cat and the Squash

Long ago there was a boatman who came every year to stay at a big inn in a place like Morioka. He was treated with consideration at the inn because he was a regular customer. They would set aside good things for him to eat in the cupboard, but sometimes things would disappear.

The people at the inn thought this strange. One night when the boatman was on his way to the privy, he passed the kitchen and saw that the cat had opened the cupboard door and was eating the good food that had been left in it.

The next morning the boatman told the innkeeper about the cat, and the cat listened silently from the corner of the room. The boatman found the cat on his boat when he went back to it. It seemed to try to get even with him by doing all sorts of bad things.

The men on the boat finally beat the cat to death. The boatman explained to the innkeeper why it had been killed and asked to have the cat buried under the plum tree in the back yard.

The boatman returned to the inn at about the same time the next year. The people at the inn were expecting him, for it was about time for him to come. In the meantime, a squash plant had sprouted from a seed that had been dropped under the plum tree, and a single big squash had formed on it. It had grown out of season, but they decided to serve it to the boatman because he liked squash.

When they picked it and cut it open, they found it was full of cat hairs. Everybody at the inn was astonished. It seemed that the cat had wanted to kill the boatman by having the squash fed to him.

Noda Tayoko
Sannohe-gun, Aomori

## 199. The Cat's Secret

There was a fine gentleman living in a village called Izumi who liked cats and roosters. He kept a cat that was 30 years old and a rooster that was 18 years old.

One day the cat said to the rooster, "The master at this house eats the good part of the fish by himself and has never fed me any of it even once. Someday I'm going to kill him and eat it myself."

The rooster said, "Is that a fact? I am always outside during the daytime, and at night I'm shut up in the shed, so I don't know anything about it. How are you planning to kill our master?"

The cat said, "I have some poison under my tail. If I shake my tail three times and shoot it at the good part of the fish and our master eats it, he will die. Then I can eat the good part of the fish."

The rooster valued his master and wanted to tell him about this in a hurry, but he had no chance to warn him because the cat never left his master's side. The rooster tried crowing one evening, but the master said it was a sign of good luck and invited everyone to a celebration. This was not what the rooster had intended by crowing, so he crowed again the next evening. The master did not understand. Then he crowed the next evening.

The master was angry. He said, "When a rooster crows three evenings in a row, that is a bad sign." He ordered some young men to abandon the rooster in the mountains.

When a medicine peddler from Toyama was going through the mountain one day he heard someone call, "Medicine man! Medicine man!"

The medicine peddler wondered who might be calling him in that mountain. He looked around and saw the rooster. He asked, "Are you the one calling me?"

The rooster said, "Now, medicine man, I am 18 years old and belong at the house of the gentleman in Izumi. There is a 30-year-old cat there who says he wants to eat the good part of the master's fish himself and is planning to kill our master in four or five days. I tried to warn my master by crowing in the evening, but he said that was a bad sign and had me abandoned. I don't mind being abandoned, but I am telling you this so you can tell my master soon and keep it from happening."

The peddler said, "So that's how it is. I'm glad you told me. Wait here for me, for I will surely come to get you."

The peddler went immediately to the gentleman's house in Izumi and asked to spend the night there. He saw the cat really aim at the fish breast that was served to his master and wave its tail three times. It hit the piece of fish exactly.

The peddler said, "Look, calico cat, now you can eat the fish breast!" The cat was surprised and ran away somewhere.

The medicine peddler told the gentleman the whole story, and then he went into the mountains and brought the rooster home.

Iwakura Ichirō
Minamikanbara-gun, Niigata

## 200. The Cat's Jōruri

One evening an old woman was left alone to look after things at home. She said as she warmed herself by the fire, "It's boring to be alone."

The cat beside her suddenly began to speak. It said, "I will sing for you, Granny, but don't tell anyone about it."

The old woman agreed. Then the cat broke into a fine voice and sang for the old woman. The old woman's son came home presently. He could hear a fine voice singing as he approached. He stood outside and listened. He went in after the song was over and said, "I'm home now."

But when the son looked around only the grandmother was there. He asked, "Who was that singing, Grandmother?"

She said, "I was the one."

"Oh, no, it was not an old woman," he declared. "That was a fine voice. Who was it?"

The old woman kept silent at first, but because her son kept insisting, she finally said, "Well, it was the cat just now."

At that the cat beside her leaped up and bit through the old woman's windpipe.

Uchida Takeshi
Kazuno-gun, Akita

## 201. The Fish that Ate Things

Long ago there was a big pond in a certain village. Everybody in the village knew that lots of fish were in it. The young men met together once to talk over ways to catch the fish. The pond was big and very deep, and they could not decide how to go about it.

One of the young men who was clever said, "If we put poison into the pond, we can catch fish."

Everyone agreed, and that was what they decided to do. Just then a priest appeared from somewhere. He said, "There is no harm in catching fish, but give up the idea of putting poison into the pond to kill them all."

The young man said, "Just keep still and watch. Eat one of these sticks of dango."

The priest ate the dango and suddenly disappeared. The young men paid no attention to whether he was there as they busied themselves putting poison into the pond. The fish all died and came floating to the surface. The young men gathered them in and rested for a while.

Presently a very big fish came to the surface of the pond. They all pulled it in together. When they cut its belly open to see, they found the five dango on the stick and that was all. The young men turned pale and ran home.

Nobody put poison into the pond to catch fish after that.

Karita-gun, Miyagi

# 13. Humorous Stories: Exaggerations

## 202. An Exaggeration

A certain man happened to swallow an orange seed and it sprouted in his stomach. It grew and grew until it came out his head. When the fruit appeared and ripened on the tree, children came clamoring to pick the fruit.

They were such a nuisance that the man declared, "It's all because of that tree that there is such a fuss." He pulled up the tree.

That left a big hole in his head into which rain fell and finally formed a pool. When that happened, the children came again, this time to fish. Their lines caught in the man's ears and eyes.

The man declared, "I can beat this by dying." He leaped into the pond and drowned.

Iwakura Ichirō
Kikaijima, Kagoshima

## 203. The Cucumber in the Sky

Long ago a gourd sprouted in the corner of the hearth of an honest young man. He watered it and fanned it until the vine grew through the roof to the Sky. The young man climbed the vine to the mansion in Tenjuku. He found green cucumbers growing there.

A heavenly maid came out and warned him, "Don't touch these

cucumbers or the world will quake, and you and this shrine will fall from the Sky." The young man obeyed her. He received a pile of coins eight inches high from the maid. He climbed back down the vine and celebrated a feast with wine and fish.

The young man next door saw that and envied him. He planted a gourd seed in his hearth and fanned and watered it with great care. That vine, too, reached to the Sky and the young man climbed it. But he paid no attention to the warning of the maid. The cucumbers looked so delicious that he touched them. Suddenly the world began to shake, the building fell over, and the young man plunged from the Sky and was killed.

This is why there is a teaching that we should not imitate others.

Yanagita Kunio
Hachinohe, Aomori

## 204. The Bean Story

An old man found a bean while he was sweeping his dirt-floored room. He talked over with his old woman what to do with it. He decided to parch it and put it into the parching pan. When he shook the pan, the bean began to fill the pan. Then he put the bean into the mortar. When he pounded the bean, it filled the mortar.

The old man told his old woman to go to the neighbor to borrow a sieve.

She said, "I don't think she has one and I don't want to go. Use your loin cloth."

There was nothing else to do, so the old man pressed the bean flour through his loin cloth as he sang, "Half fleas, half lice; half fleas, half lice."

The question then was where to store the bean flour. If they put it over the cupboard, the rats would get it. If they put it inside, the cat would get it. If they put it below the cupboard, the weasel would eat it.

There was nowhere else to put it but between them in the quilts. The old man broke wind in the night. That blew the bean flour all over the old woman. The little dog from next door came and thought the bean flour tasted sweet here on her butt and tasted sweet there, too, and he licked her all over, wherever the bean flour landed.

*Toppin parae no puu.*

Mutō Tetsujō
Akita

## 205. Rat Sutra

There was a very pious old woman at a certain place who had strong Buddhist faith. She went to a temple to learn a sutra from the priest. The priest sat in front of the altar, thinking he would teach her a special one. He closed his eyes as he thought, but nothing came to mind. The old woman sat thinking with her eyes closed, too.

When the priest happened to open his eyes, he saw a rat come out by the altar. The priest began to intone, "On-choro-choro [you come cautiously]," and the old woman repeated "On-choro-choro."

The rat heard voices and crouched. The priest continued, "Sora fukudanda [there you crouch]."

The old woman responded, "Sora fukudanda." Then the rat started to run away because of the voices, so the priest added, "Nige yō tatte nigashiwasen do [even if you try, you can't get away]," and the old woman responded "Nige yō tatte nigashiwasen do."

The old woman repeated the words all the way home so she would not forget them, "On choro-choro, sora fukudanda, nige yō tatte nigashiwasen do." [Translator's note: With proper inflection, this sounds very much like a real sutra.]

That evening she repeated her sutra three times before her altar before going to bed. A thief broke in during the night. The old woman had tried so hard to remember her sutra that she was saying it in her sleep.

Just as the thief was coming into her work room, the old woman was saying, "You come cautiously," so he hid behind the vat.

She continued, "There you crouch."

The thief thought, "If I stay here, my life is in danger."

He started away as the voice continued, "Even if you try, you can't get away." At that, the thief rushed off while he still could get away.

That is why sutras are such precious things.

Gotō Sadao
Hayami-gun, Ōita

## 206. The Origin of the Room

There was an old woman living with her son in a certain place. Since the young man had reached that age, the old woman thought she would get a bride for him. About that time, somebody came and said, "Let me arrange a marriage for your son, Granny."

That delighted her and she answered, "Please help me out." She was happy to receive a bride with so little trouble, but after four or five days, the bride grew pale and lost all her energy.

The worried old woman asked, "Don't you feel well, girl?"

The bride replied, "It is only that I am trying to keep from breaking wind, Granny."

The old woman said, "There is no reason for you to hesitate about doing such things. Please break wind any time you feel like it."

The happy girl said, "But grab the edge of the hearth firmly, Mother!"

Then she let go a terribly big blast. There was such a gust of wind that the old woman was blown up to the ceiling, and the skin on her scalp was scraped off.

When her son came home, the old woman talked things over with him. She said, "Keeping a bride like this is dangerous." They decided to send the bride back to her village.

The old woman said to her, "You break wind too much, girl. We can't keep you, so please go home."

The girl could not help it and she left the old woman's house. When the girl got as far as the edge of the village, she saw a crowd of children milling around. She asked, "What are you fussing about?"

They said, "We want to pick the persimmons on this tree, but it is so tall we have no way to reach them."

The girl said, "I'll break wind toward the tree and blow them down for you." The children all laughed and that flustered the girl a little, but she let go a big blast. The persimmons were scattered as far away as sparrows on the wing.

The girl continued on her way to a river. A boat loaded with rice was stuck in the river and the boatmen were trying with all their might to push it with their poles. The girl asked, "What are you trying to do?"

They replied. "Our boat is stuck and we can't move it."

She said, "I'll get it loose for you with a blast when I break wind."

"If you really can get it loose, we'll give you all the rice," the men said.

The girl asked if they really meant it and they assured her they really would give it to her. This time she rolled up her dress and let a huge one go. The boat was freed without any difficulty and the girl got the promised rice.

The girl got so much rice that she took it back to the old woman's house and asked to be accepted again. The old woman and her son decided that the girl was a precious treasure and took her back. They built a special little hut for her to stay in. That is how it is called a **heya** ["he-ya," a house for breaking wind, or "heya," originally a separate house in the yard, but later a room].

Fumino Shirakoma [Iwakura Ichirō]
Minamikanbara-gun, Niigata

## 207. "Who Is It?"

Long ago robbers were getting into a shōya's house at night. The master declared, "We must do something to prevent robberies." They decided upon a plan.

An old man in the neighboring village was good at breaking wind which sounded like "dare ka, dare ka" ["who is it, who is it"]. They decided to hire him and went to the neighboring village to ask him to sleep at their house.

The thief came that night, but when he started to crawl in, he heard somebody say, "Who is it?" But when he listened closely, it did not sound like a man's voice. He decided it was safe and jumped in. He found somebody breaking wind. He decided to plug up the one who was breaking wind and went farther inside to steal a 1000 ryō box. He had a feeling of relief as he picked up the 1000 ryō box because he had stopped the noise.

But when the thief started to leave, he had to pass the old man breaking wind who was asleep on the porch by the front entrance. The plug the robber had used was too long and he stumbled on it. When it came loose, all the accumulated wind came out at one time—"dare ka, dare ka, dare ka."

The robber was so astonished that he threw the money box away and rushed off. The old man received an excessively big reward from the shōya.

Isogai Isamu
Hiroshima

## 208. Stories about Breaking Wind

Long ago an old man and an old woman in a certain village dried wheat one fine day. Geese came flying there and alighted. The old man had eaten so much buckwheat mochi that his stomach bloated. He wanted to break wind so much that he bought a plug and lay with it plugged in. He wanted to break wind so much he could not endure it any longer and let one go.

The plug flew out and hit a goose and killed it. That night the old couple cooked goose soup and ate it.

The old woman from next door came over and asked for live coals. The old couple said, "We will give you some live coals, but have some goose soup." They even gave her some to take home to her old man when she left.

The next day the greedy old woman made buckwheat mochi and fed it to her old man. She plugged him up and put him to bed while she hung wheat sheaves to dry. She waited for the geese to come, but not a single one came and alighted. There was nothing to do about it, so she scratched around in the wheat. Her old man thought geese were there and let fly a blast. The plug flew out and hit the old woman and killed her. The old man went outside, calling, "Granny, Granny, I caught a goose," but when he looked around, he found his old woman dead.

A flood carries away greedy folk who imitate others.

*Dotto harai.*

Noda Tayoko
Aomori

## 209. Rokubei Who had Occult Sight

There was a very jealous man at a certain place. He had the habit of saying to his wife whenever he came home, "You, there, I saw you. So and so came today, didn't he?" And he was usually right.

His wife would be surprised and say, "You fake fortune teller!"

It happened that just at that time somebody had broken into the storehouse of the feudal lord in Sendai and had stolen ten 1000 ryō boxes of money. The thief could not be found, no matter how carefully the matter was investigated. The feudal lord sent inquiries into neighboring regions to ask if a good fortune teller was anywhere.

One of his men said, "The fortune teller in Nanbu is said to be good."

The feudal lord said, "Waste no time. Get that fortune teller to come to lay his fortune sticks here." A group of important men set out together to the fortune teller's home.

The fortune teller and his wife were talking together at home one day when a group of splendid samurai came riding up in front in sedan chairs. As they came in, they asked, "Is the famous fortune teller of Nanbu at home today?" The astonished couple said he was.

The samurai said, "We will speak to him. A thief has broken in and taken ten 1000 ryō boxes of money from the storehouse of the feudal lord of Sendai this time. We decided to ask you to read the fortune and we have come to get you. Make ready quickly and come with us."

His wife complained, "You did not have to make false fortunes," when she heard what was said. But there was no way to change matters. She helped her husband get ready and as she bade him good-bye, she said, "Keep up your courage and lay your sticks carefully and come home."

Then the fake fortune teller set out in a sedan chair for the castle town of Sendai.

The sedan chair the fake fortune teller was riding was set down for a rest at Gorin Pass at the boundary between Nanbu and Sendai. When the sedan carriers went to the shade of a tree, they said, "That man is no ordinary fortune teller. He certainly is possessed by a deity. The money boxes will surely be found when he gets there. I would like to see the criminal punished soon."

The head samurai overheard them talk. He went over to the sedan chair the fake fortune teller was in. He said, "I have a little favor to ask you. Please listen."

The fake fortune teller asked what it was.

After the samurai sent the men away, he said, "Now, Master Fortune Teller, it is just as the men have been saying. When you go, the money boxes will be found for sure. My head is not going to stay on my neck when that happens. That's why I am making this request. I know exactly where the 1000 ryō boxes are. You can keep one of the boxes and I will take one, and you can find eight boxes with your fortune telling and return them to the feudal lord. How about it? If you do not agree, it's a pity, but I will take your life right here."

The fake fortune teller turned pale when he heard that. He

replied, "Yes, I agree to what you say, but where are the boxes hidden?"

The samurai said, "They are buried in the dirt of the embankment behind the castle."

The man said, "All right, I will tell it that way." The pleased samurai said, "I am saved with your help." The fortune teller was carried in fine style after that into the castle of the feudal lord of Sendai.

The fake fortune teller laid out his fortune sticks in the feudal lord's palace. He announced, "The stolen boxes of money are hidden in the embankment of the castle, but two of the ten boxes have already passed into the hands of men and have been taken to the western country. It will be of no use to look for them. Dig up the eight boxes quickly."

The feudal lord said, "If only it were a little sooner, we could have gotten all ten boxes back. We were a little late asking you. But we are lucky to get the eight boxes back. Where did the robbers come from?"

The fortune teller said, "It is just as I said now. The thief is a great robber from the western country and he has gone back there. It is useless to hunt for him."

The feudal lord said, "Then there is no help for it. Let's have the other eight boxes dug up before they are stolen. (Two boxes were not there because the samurai and the fortune teller had dug them up and hidden them the night before.)

The feudal lord was delighted. He said, "There is no other fortune teller as great as you in the world." He gave the man one 1000 ryō box as thanks. The fake fortune teller went home gaily with two money boxes such as he had never seen before. His happy wife declared, "I did not realize you were a man with such talents." They lived together happy.

Sasaki Kizen
Kamihei-gun, Iwate

## 210. Famous for Scenting

*Hanashi aimōshita.*

A certain wealthy man set out for Bizen with a load of salted fish to sell. One of the sailors working on the boat was a poor man called Magojiee who lived in a hut in the hills. When the sailor was leaving home, he said to his wife, "I am coming back on the 15th Day of the New Year. Set fire to our house and burn it down on that day. Be sure to burn it."

It was decided then the boat would sail in the last month of the year and return on the 15th Day of the New Year. Shortly after the boat sailed out of the harbor of Bizen, Magojiee climbed onto the roof of the boat and declared, "Master, my house is on fire!"

His master asked, "How do you know what's happening more than 150 miles away?"

The man said, "I can smell it."

"Don't talk nonsense," exclaimed his master. "How can you smell it?"

The sailor said, "Then let's make a wager."

"Right," said the master and he put it in writing. If the house was burned down, the master would turn over his place completely, and Magojiee and his wife could come with just their umbrella. If the house had not burned down, Magojiee and his wife would become servants of the master for life. The boat pulled into the harbor of their island. Magojiee's wife came running up, weeping false tears. She was asked, "Did it really burn?"

"Yes, it really burned," she said. Then Magojiee took over his master's house.

The news of this came to the ears of the feudal lord of Bizen. He heard that Magojiee of Koshikijima in Satsuma was so accomplished a scenter that he could smell fire more than 150 miles away. It happened that the feudal lord's famous sword was missing at that time. He was worried about it and said, "We must ask Magojiee to come and to scent it out." So Magojiee was brought to him. Things were at a dangerous point.

Magojiee said, "The truth is, I have a cold now and I can't smell anything. Please give me a month's time."

There was nothing to do about it if Magojiee was sick, so the feudal lord had to wait. Magojiee was too worried to do a thing. Since it was in the Ninth Month, he made sweet wine to offer the kami and made his petition to him. Then he drank half of the wine and went to sleep in the shrine.

The priest came out and said, "Somebody has drunk some of the offering wine. It's probably the doings of the fox at Shiroyama who stole the feudal lord's sword. I know that he stole it, but if I say so, I will be accused of doing it. I can't tell anyone. The fox is the one who drank the wine for sure."

Magojiee heard what was said. He hurried to the feudal lord and led many men into Shiroyama and brought the sword back safely. The feudal lord was delighted. He said, "Is there anything you want? Tell me what you wish."

Magojiee said, "No, I have no wish."

The feudal lord insisted, "It makes no difference what you want."

"Well, then," answered Magojiee, "I have been known as Scenter Magojiee until now, but please let me be called Not-scenting Magojiee from now."

Even though Magojiee did no more scenting, he still lived comfortably for the rest of his life on the money he received.

Iwakura Ichirō
Koshikijima, Kagoshima

## 211. The Lucky New Samurai
[Tail Shot]

When Hachibei went to cut grass at a certain place, he found a dead samurai by the road. He was happy to see that. He took the armor, the helmet, and the sword from the body and changed clothes, turning himself into a samurai. He walked along briskly.

At sunset he arrived at a samurai's house. He was allowed to spend the night there and they showed him great hospitality. After Hachibei went to bed, his host came to him and said, "Please meet a neighboring samurai for me at the contest tomorrow." That surprised Hachibei, but he agreed to do it. He had never drawn a bow in his life before. He took the bow and arrow setting in the alcove and tried them out in the night. The arrow shot through the door and hit a thief who was about to break in. Hachibei was not aware of that and worried over losing the arrow.

When the maid at the house got up the next morning and went outside, she said that the guest of the evening before had shot a thief. Hachibei was delighted when he heard that. He went to see and the man was really dead. His reputation rose among those around him, but the time drew near for the contest.

Samurai from all around gathered to see the event. The first contest was on mounting horses, and Hachibei was told to enter it. He had never ridden on a horse and fell off, but he landed in a pheasant's nest. He held the bird up in his hand, and the spectators thought he was very accomplished. It would be too hard to challenge him, so the contest was called off.

The story reached the ears of the clan chief, and he used Hachibei in many ways to perform feats. It happened that a demon was a great nuisance to the chief, so Hachibei was ordered to destroy it. He agreed and promptly had a big bag of flour prepared to take with him to the mountains.

Presently the demon came out, but Hachibei fainted when he saw him. The demon decided to eat the flour before he ate the corpse. The flour stuck in the demon's throat and he died.

Hachibei came to and saw the dead demon. He was delighted. He picked up his bow and arrow and sent a shaft into the demon. Then he gave it to the clan chief. The clan chief was pleased and Hachibei became very important.

Kurate-gun, Fukuoka

## 212. Catching Sparrows

There was a father and a son in a certain place. The father heard one day that sparrows could be sold for a high price in Higo. He talked it over with his son, and they decided to catch a lot of sparrows and take them there by boat. They did not have a good way to catch the sparrows. After they thought of many ways, the father bought wine dregs and his son gathered camellia leaves. They took everything where there were many sparrows. The son spread out the camellia leaves, and the father put some wine dregs onto each. The father and his son rested in the shade of a tree after all their preparations were finished.

Many sparrows came and ate the wine dregs. Each of them got drunk and went to sleep on a camellia leaf. The sun came out and dried the leaves, which then curled and wrapped around the sparrows. The father and his son were delighted. They said, "After all, it's wisdom that makes for success in this world. Nobody can succeed without wisdom."

The two swept the sparrows up and put them into sacks they had ready. They loaded them onto a boat and took them to Higo. When word got around that the sparrow boat had arrived, a crowd gathered, and suddenly the price of sparrows went up.

When the sacks were opened at last, the sparrows flew away. They had been drunk, but they were sobered up and were glad to fly away when the sacks were opened. The father and his son had only fatigue for their efforts.

Seki Keigo
Nagasaki

## 213. The Lucky Hunter

There was a poor hunter in a certain place whose little boy had reached the age of seven. The father had to celebrate with a feast the ceremony in which his son would be given a loincloth to wear. He had no money to buy fish, so he set out to hunt.

He saw a badger and shot it right away. He hit it in a vital spot fortunately, and as it thrashed around, it dug up three long mountain yams. The hunter gathered up everything to take home. Along the way he saw wild ducks floating on a pond. He shot one, and it fell into the water. The hunter went in after it, and when he came out, he found fifty or sixty little fish in his baggy pants.

He went home very happy with everything and celebrated a fine feast for his little son's loincloth ceremony.

Mimakata-gun, Fukuoka

## 214. Gengorō's Trip to the Sky

There was an only son in a certain place whose mother sent him to buy some eggplant shoots. He paid 100 mon for a single plant, the price asked by the old man selling it. His mother was dumbfounded.

She asked, "Why didn't you bring home a lot of cheaper plants?"

Her son replied. "The man said that even if it cost 100 mon, we could get hundreds or thousands of eggplants from this. It's better to get a good one than to get many poor ones, so I decided on this."

The son planted the shoot in his garden and fertilized it eagerly every day. The plant grew fast. Soon it was a big tree they had to look up to. Finally, it grew until it pierced the Sky. The beautiful purple flowers that blossomed on the eggplant hung like a cloud on it. Presently each flower turned into an eggplant.

In the meantime the 7th Day of the Seventh Month came. The mother said to her son, "It's Tanabata tonight, so let's pick eggplants to make an offering. Climb the tree to get some for me."

The son brought the ladder on his shoulders and set it up and climbed the eggplant tree. He climbed and climbed until he reached the Sky. He thought he had come to a strange place, for there was a splendid palace. He looked around and noticed a white-haired old man in a beautiful room.

The young man said, "I came from Japan to gather eggplants. They have grown this far and there are many of them. May I gather these, too?"

The old man seemed to notice him for the first time when he spoke. He turned around and smiled as he said, "Oh, is this eggplant tree yours? We have been enjoying eating eggplants every day because of it. Please help yourself to what you want. But since you have come this far, come in and talk for a while before you go home."

The young man accepted the invitation and went into the room. Two beautiful girls who looked like sisters came with all sorts of unusual dishes to serve him. He was completely at ease and enjoyed the food.

In the meantime it was afternoon. The old man had been enjoying his unusual guest so much that time passed without his noticing. As he stretched and stood up, he said, "Now, girls, get ready." They left the room. The old man went into another room and when he came out presently, he was something completely different looking. He was naked except for a tiger skin loincloth at his hips, two horns were growing from his head, and his mouth was opened all the way to his ears, making him look just like a demon one might see in the world.

The young man cried out in fright when he saw him.

The old man laughed. He said, "Here, now, I am sorry if I surprised you that much. I am the same old man, but I have some work to do now and have to change clothes for it."

The young man asked, "What is the work you are going to do? Are you going to catch men to eat?"

The old man answered, "All that is the work of demons. I don't roast men on a spit. The fact is, I am Raijin [Thunder God]. I must go now and send some evening showers down or crops won't grow. How about it? Would you like to help me a little? You don't know how to make it rain, but it is lots of fun."

The two girls came out looking ready for work and they urged the young man to join them. He felt like trying and said, "I don't know whether I can do it or not, but I'll try. What is my duty going to be?"

The old man said, "The nicest work is to make rain. I will let you try that." He handed the young man a tin pan. He said, "That pan is full of rain water. If you just scatter that, it will be fine."

If that was all, it would not be difficult, so the young man took on the job of making rain.

Raijin held his seven drums that were strung together and a cloud hung from his horns as he started running ahead. His girls followed him carrying mirrors and flashing them. The young man came last, carrying his basin and scattering water from it. They went frolicking and leaping over clouds. A Tanabata festival was going on at the Chinju Shrine in all the villages in the lower world. Everyone was dancing to drums. When the shower began to fall, people broke into great confusion.

Presently Raijin led them above the young man's village. A festival was going on there, too. Most of the folk gathered there were friends of the young man. He decided to have a little fun with them. He asked the old man to beat his drums harder and the girls to flash their mirrors brighter and he scattered rain before him and behind, left and right, without any sense.

The people in the village were drenched in such a downpour and they scattered like little spiders from a spider's egg. The young man enjoyed it and had a good laugh. He happened to look at the girls. They were shaking their mirrors with all their might. Their clothes fell away showing their breasts and their white legs were exposed.

The sight amused the young man so much that he stepped off a cloud. He plunged down to earth and was impaled on a mulberry tree growing by the garden patch.

Those in the sky, especially the two girls, felt sorry for the young man, but they could not do anything about it. The father Raijin saw how his daughters felt. He said, "I will never send a bolt of thunder down near a mulberry tree again because I am sorry for the young man."

That is why, even now, people break off little branches of mulberry and hang them under their eaves when it thunders.

Sasaki Kizen
Esashi-gun, Iwate

## 215. The Shrimp and the Big Bird

Long ago there was a big bird in a certain place. Other birds kept praising him over what a big bird he was until he decided that he was the biggest in all the world. He set out to tour various countries to show off. He became tired while flying over the sea and went down to rest on a pile he saw sticking up.

Somebody asked, "Who is that resting on my whisker?" The bird answered, "I'm the biggest bird there is."

The voice said, "I am the Ise shrimp. If you are the biggest bird, there is not likely anything as big as I am."

The shrimp then set out to tour many islands to show off. He became tired on the way and went into a cave to rest. A voice asked, "Who has come into my nostril?"

The shrimp then noticed that the cave was the nostril of a great fish. The fish sneezed and blew the shrimp out and it hit a cliff. The Ise shrimp's back has been bent since that time.

Yamaguchi Gōsuke
Kitauwa-gun, Ehime

## 216. Matching Strength

A strong man called Daikoku went from Japan to China to match strength with the strong man called Dairikibō. He went to Dairikibō's house and said, "Is the head of the house in? I am Daikoku from Japan and I would like to match strength with him a little."

The wife of Dairikibō came out and said, "You are welcome. My husband had some business and has gone out for a little while, but he will come back soon. Please come in and rest."

The woman picked up a six-foot square fire box and brought it over and set it down beside him. Daikoku wondered how there happened to be such a big fire box. He tried pushing its corner, but he could not budge it. He decided it must be very heavy, so he tried to lift it with both hands, but the fire box would not move. But a mere weak woman was strong enough to lift such a thing easily and to carry it!

There was no telling what would happen when the real strong man Dairikibō came back. Daikoku fled while he had time to get away.

When Dairikibō came home, his wife said, "A strong man called Daikoku has come from Japan to match strength with you and he is waiting." They went to the front entrance, but there was no sign of Daikoku.

"The fellow ran away, did he?" declared Dairikibō. "He can't get away from me. I will chase him no matter how far he has gone." He called up a cloud and in a single leap he reached the seashore where Daikoku was on a boat ready to cross back to Japan.

"You think you can get away, do you?" shouted Dairikibō, and he caught the boat with a long metal hook. He started to draw the boat back, but Daikoku could not allow that. He got out a file and cut the hook. He managed in this way to get back to Japan, but there was no place for him to hide. He went around with bloodshot eyes looking for one. He came to a single temple in a certain village and ran in to beg the priest to hide him.

The priest at the mountain temple was troubled. He said, "You can see that this is a small temple and there is no place I can hide you. But we must think of various ways at a time like this. Climb into the bucket at the well and hide in it."

While Daikoku hid, Dairikibō came flying with the wind and searched everywhere. He came to the well and saw Daikoku's reflection in the bottom. "So that's where you are hiding, is it?" he shouted and leaped into the well with a splash.

This was Daikoku's chance. He stepped out of the bucket and broke off stones from the wall to throw down into the well to fill it up. As you might know, Dairikibō was overcome and could not get out of the well. It is said that occasionally he would give himself a shake from humiliation, and that would cause an earthquake.

Since Daikoku had been saved by the priest at the temple, he served there for the rest of his life in thanks. It is said the word "daikoku" [wife of the priest] originated in this way.

Sasaki Kizen
Shiwa-gun, Iwate

## 217. Fooling Each Other

Once upon a time there was a man named Kichigo in Nakatsu and one named Kichigo in Kokura. One day Kichigo of Kokura said to Kichigo of Nakatsu, "Come to my house, Kichigo San, and see my squash vine that stretches out go-ri [five ri] and is bearing squash."

When Kichigo went from Nakatsu to see, he found the vine was climbing gōri [the usual way]. He did not want to be outdone. He invited Kichigo of Kokura. He said, "Come and see my squash vine that stretches eighteen ri."

Kichigo went from Kokura and found the squash vine covering two chestnut trees. [Kuri is chestnut or "ku ri," nine ri. Two "ku ri" would be eighteen ri or two kuri, two chestnuts.]

Miyako-gun, Fukuoka

## 218. Matching Tricks

Once upon a time three robbers, Sankaku of Kyoto, Sankaku of Edo, and Sankaku of Echigo, broke into the house of a wealthy man. Several young servants caught them before they could take anything.

The robbers begged, "We have just entered the house and haven't stolen anything, so please free us."

The young men answered, "No, we won't let you go." They would not consent to freeing them.

The robbers said, "Then we will show you an entertaining trick. Please let us go free then." The gentlemen of the house came along and agreed. The three robbers borrowed a bamboo pole, which they stood up in the yard.

To start with, Sankaku of Kyoto turned into a kite and perched on the end of the pole. Then Sankaku of Edo turned into a rat and Sankaku of Echigo turned into a bean. The rat picked up the bean and ran up the pole. The kite took hold of the rat and flew off somewhere.

*Ichi ga poon to saketa.*

Fumino Shirakoma [Iwakura Ichirō]
Minamikanbara-gun, Niigata

## 219. Dōmo, Kōmo

Long ago a great doctor called Dōmo lived in our village. A famous doctor called Kōmo lived at the same time at Kirei-dōri, 5-chome, Hana-machi in Edo. Both men were famous for curing without fail any kind of injury or ulcer with their medicines.

One day Dōmo of our village thought he would like to match cures with Kōmo of Edo, and Kōmo of Edo wanted to match cures with Dōmo of Kyūshū. He set out to meet him. In fact, they both set out on the same day at the same hour.

Should we call it strange or marvelous that the two of them met on Kawagishi-dōri, Kawachi, Osaka. (They probably met at the tea-house there and happened to discover this while exchanging remarks.)

"Well, Kōmo," exclaimed one, and "Well, Dōmo," exclaimed the other. "Let's match skills. Will you, the doctor from Kyūshū please begin."

Kōmo showed deference, as might be expected.

Dōmo of Kyūshū then said, "I accept your courtesy. The medicine I use is really a secret family prescription handed down. It is an ointment that both draws out blisters and heals broken bones. I will demonstrate this for you." He took some medicine from his medicine basket and spread a little on a paper and stuck it to the table by the door of the teahouse facing the sea. Oddly enough, the sea receded and a thousand-bushel capacity sailboat came into view, drawn to the shore.

Dōmo turned proudly to Kōmo and asked, "How is that, Doctor Kōmo?"

Kōmo smiled and said politely, "The secret medicine I carry is exactly the same as yours. I will show it to you."

He took out some ointment quietly and spread some on a paper and stuck it to the desk toward Kobe. How strangely, how miraculously, before their eyes the passenger cars and baggage cars on the Sanyo Tōkai line were drawn to the depot at Umeda in Osaka.

"Now, Doctor Dōmo, how about this?" asked Kōmo. The splendid medicines of both doctors were equally fine and no difference could be found.

Then the two decided to try the effectiveness of the ointment on broken bones. Dōmo concealed his hand but drew his sword quickly from his side, turned to Kōmo, and cut off his head and gave it a roll. The clerks at the inn were dismayed by the fresh blood that was spilled. Dōmo calmly picked up the head, put some ointment on the neck, and strangely, miraculously, the neck was healed and the head was as it was before.

Kōmo performed the same feat on Dōmo. He replaced his head beautifully. The winner of this match could not be decided either.

Since the two doctors could not display any superior medicines, they decided to try matching strength by pulling their heads. They each had a towel two feet five inches long. The towel of each was passed around the other's head with the ends held firmly by the doctor opposite. After the preparations were inspected, both heads uttered a shout, but as you know, the doctor's heads were matched. With a one, two, three they fell off at the same time and there was no help for Dōmo, Kōmo. [A play on words meaning "no way, this or that."] The testing of medicine, though dangerous, was possible to do, but they erred in this match. There should have been a limit to their contests.

*Medetashi, medetashi.*

Chikujō-gun, Fukuoka

## 220. Matching Boasts

Once upon a time the feudal lords of Owari, Nanbu, and Kishū compared boasts. The feudal lord from Owari began by saying, "At my place the daikon ["long radish," or "taiko," a drum] grows twenty-five feet square."

The feudal lord from Nanbu said, "We have a horse that spans two and a half miles."

Not to be outdone, the feudal lord from Kishū said, "There is an orange tree at my place that spreads across seven and a half miles."

When the feudal lord of Owari heard that, he said, "Let's cut that orange tree and spread the horsehide from Nanbu over it as a drumhead. We could beat it with the big radish from Owari, couldn't we? The drum would sound *tempo, tempo* [boast, boast]."

Yamashita Hisao
Enuma-gun, Owari (Ishikawa)

## 221. Matching Exaggerations
[The Lie's Skin]

Three men happened to meet one time. One said, "My cow can drink all the water in a two and a half acre square pond at one time."

The second man said, "I have a cowhide big enough to cover a drum one block big."

The first man said, "There surely isn't any cow hide big enough to cover a drum that big."

The second man said, "It's from a cow that can drink a pond two and a half acres square dry." That silenced the first man.

The third man spoke up. He said, "In the hills near my house there is a vine 357 feet long."

The second man said, "There surely isn't any vine that long."

The third man said, "It's used to tie the head on that drum one block big." That silenced the second man.

Iwakura Ichiro
Koshikijima, Kagoshima

## 222. Matching Long Lives

Once upon a time three monkeys went to pick chestnuts on Kuriyama in Tanba. But chestnuts were scarce and they found only one. At that, they could not each have one. They talked over who would eat it and decided the one who was born first could have it.

One monkey said, "I was born when there was no more water in Lake Ōmi than in the bottom of a newly cut tea cup."

The second monkey said, "I was born when Mt. Fuji was still as low as an offering in a bowl."

When the third monkey heard that, she began to sob and cry. The other monkeys noticed that and one asked, "What's the matter?"

The third monkey replied, "When I hear you talking, it recalls my baby born at about that time and who died. It makes me feel sad."

This meant that little monkey was born first and she could have the chestnut.

Seki Keigo
Nagasaki

## 223. Lies
[Dreams]

There was a lazy man living in a certain place who only wanted to eat sweet things and to play around. He went to Kannon to make his petition for seven nights and seven days. Kannon appeared to him in a dream on the night of the final day.

She said, "I grant your petition. Get up tomorrow morning and cross the meadow in front of here. Keep on straight ahead and see what happens."

The lazy man thought the matter was settled. He got up earlier than usual the next morning and walked straight across the meadow in front of the Kannon shrine. He kept going until he came to the seashore. A wretched looking hut was there.

The man looked in and saw a white-haired old woman sitting by the hearth. He asked, "Is there a place around here where one can just eat sweet things and play around, Granny?"

"That there is," the old lady answered. "A boat is just ready now to take off to cross to such an island. Get into it and go."

The man looked around and saw a boat tied up by the shore. The old woman got up from the hearth and called, "Captain, captain!"

The captain came out on the boat and asked, "Is this the passenger? Hurry up. Get onto the boat."

As soon as the man boarded the boat, it shot across to an island as quick as an arrow. A big building with an iron gate and an iron wall around it could be seen there. When the boat docked in front of the gate, a man came out to meet it. He said to the lazy man, "You are welcome." He repeated that as he led him inside.

That night the lazy man was served many unusual dishes at a feast. He was put to bed in silk comforters and shown all kinds of hospitality. He was pleased with everything and stayed on and on.

One night, however, the lazy man woke up in the middle of the night and heard a man groan in the next room. He peered through a crack in the sliding door and saw a man hung upside down from a crossbeam.

A hot charcoal fire was burning below him. A frightful man was beside him, holding out a big dish to catch the human oil that was dripping from the man's eyes, nose, and mouth. The man hanging there was already black and blue and nearly dead.

The one who was collecting the oil said to himself, "It's about time to get the oil from the man in the next room. His turn will be tomorrow night."

The lazy man was terrified when he heard that. He ran frantically from the house that night. Men on the staff of the house heard him go and five or six of them chased him. The lazy man sent dust flying like a badger as he fled. Luckily, he found a boat moored when he reached the shore. He leaped onto it, untied it, and rowed far out to sea.

The man rowed and rowed until at last he reached the mooring place on the other shore. He dashed into the hut he had seen before and told the old woman by the hearth what had happened. He begged, "Please hide me. Anywhere is all right." She refused. She said, "The truth is, this old woman makes her living from day to day with the help of the men on that island who buy men. I can't save you."

But because the man wept and begged so desperately, the old woman finally said, "All right, get into the bag of chestnuts on the shelf to hide. The man crawled into the bag and had barely hid when the men chasing him came rushing into the hut.

They shouted, "Granny, a man got away and came here, that cry baby! We are sure we saw him run into this place. We are here to get him. Bring him out!"

The old woman said, "I didn't see anyone like that."

The ruffians shouted louder, "You retching, dung-covered hag, if you don't bring that cry baby out, we won't let it go at that!"

Their voices were so loud and scary that the man hiding wondered what the men looked like. He opened the chestnut bag a little so he could see, but one of the big, round nuts rolled out and landed on the head of one of the men who was doing the shouting. He yelled and looked up into the eyes of the man in the bag. "What's that," he roared.

The lazy man drew his face back in, and at the same time the bag fell from the shelf . . . At that point, the man woke up from his dream. At the same time, he fell head first from the porch of the Kannon shrine where he had been making his nightly vigil.

*Dotto harai.*

Sasaki Kizen
Kamihei-gun, Iwate

## 224. Matching Laziness

A very lazy man went to town on a disagreeable errand. He got hungry along the way. It was such a bother to take down the riceballs in his lunch tied to his back that he endured his hunger and kept on walking.

A man came from the opposite direction with his mouth hanging wide enough open to show his gullet. The man with the lunch thought he hung his mouth open because he was hungry. He decided to get the man to take his lunch down and share it with him.

He went up to him and said hopefully, "You look pretty hungry. I have my lunch on my back, but it's such a bother to get it down that I am going along enduring my hunger. Please take my lunch down and we can share it together."

The other man said, "It's such a bother to tie the strings on my hat that I am going along with my mouth open to hold them under my chin."

Sasaki Kizen
Shiwa-gun, Iwate

## 225. The Silence Match

Once upon a time a couple was living near Hiroshima in Akinokuni. They liked mochi very much and they received 15 pieces of it from somebody one day. They each ate seven pieces for supper and agreed that the one who did not speak for the longest would have the piece left over. They put it into the cupboard and went to bed silently with the light on.

A robber with a long sword at his side broke into the house that night. He went up to the set of drawers where their clothes were put away. The couple lay quaking but silent under their bedding. They were scared, but they were thinking about that piece of mochi. The robber took out all their clothes and all their money. Then he went towards the cupboard.

The wife, looking on from under the covers, forgot and cried, "Father, that man is going to take our mochi." The husband threw off the covers and got up. He took the piece of mochi from the cupboard and knelt as he held it up to the robber. He pointed to it and said, "Please leave at least this much."

The silence was broken and the robber burst out laughing.

Ishii Kendō
Hiroshima

## 226. A Treasure Match by Two Chōja

Once there was a rich man and a poor man. Although the rich man had plenty of money, he had no children. The poor man was completely without money, but he had seven children. They decided to have a treasure match one day.

The rich man had bags of rice brought out from his storehouse and stacked into a wall. Within the wall he only sang and danced and played around. He asked the poor man, "How about it? Are you envious?"

The poor man came with his seven children and climbed onto the wall of rice bags to watch. He said, "Look, even if you can stack your bags of rice, my children can walk on them."

The rich man concluded that he had no treasures greater than children.

Iwakura Ichirō
Koshikijima, Kagoshima

## 227. Matching Stinginess

A very stingy man lived in the next village. When he got up early one New Year's Day to go to Kitano Shrine to worship, he happened to see a piece of firewood that had dropped by the road on his way home. He may have thought it had been granted him from heaven or not, but he started to pick it up.

However, the man was dressed in his crested coat and divided skirt and it hardly seemed suitable to carry home a piece of firewood. He stood with folded arms, pondering what to do about it. "That's it," he declared as he slapped his knee.

And what did he do? He kicked the stick along. When he was nearly home, one of the clogs on his wooden geta broke off. The man seemed stunned and fainted. People at his house heard him fall and they tried all sorts of treatment in their confusion until he finally started to breathe again.

One of them tried to give his master some medicine he had brought, but the man kept his mouth firmly closed. Another helper had a bright idea. He said, "The medicine does not cost anything."

Then his master opened his mouth for it and swallowed it.

Hayashi Itsuba
Mii-gun, Fukuoka

## 228. Squirming through Questions and Answers

[Translator's note: Due to the difficulty of conveying humor through the play on words, only the first episode of this tale will be translated.]

There was an illiterate priest at a certain temple. Although he did not know a single Chinese character, he was very clever. Somebody died at the home of a patron in the village and a messenger was sent to the priest. He said, "Please write us a name for the ancestral tablet for the altar and one for the grave."

The priest got out his inkstone and brush and looked at the paper for the altar tablet, but he could not think of a posthumous name and he did not know how to write one.

His eyes happened to light on a tax receipt from the village office. "San-bu go-rin" ["three bu, five rin"] was written in large characters on it. He thought that was good and promptly copied the receipt, "Sanbu gorin," for the tablet.

Next, he had to write something for the grave tablet, but he was at a loss for anything and how to write it. He glanced around the room and into his workroom where there was a hoe without a handle, a winnowing basket, and a mallet. They gave him a good idea and he drew a picture of them for the grave tablet.

The messenger from the patron's home accepted the altar tablet and the grave tablet, but try as he might, he could not understand what they meant. Finally he asked, "Oshō San, is this 'sanbu-gorin' on the altar tablet a receipt or a posthumous name?"

The priest answered offhand, "What a silly question! How could it be a receipt. It is a splendid name, Gorin Funsan." [He reversed the order in the style of Chinese reading. It had no meaning, but sounded good.]

The man had to be satisfied, but he handed the tablet for the grave and asked, "What is the meaning of the picture of the hoe with its handle off, a winnowing basket, and the mallet? I never have seen such a picture on a grave tablet in all my life."

The priest said with assurance, "Don't ask silly questions. That isn't just a picture. It means **kuwa** ["hoe" or "suffering"] **nuketa** ["removed" from handle], **mi wa** ["winnowing basket" or "body"] **tsuchi** ["mallet" or "earth"]." ["Removed from suffering, the body returns to earth."]

The priest said it was an auspicious teaching. The man from the patron's home had to accept it and he withdrew with the two tablets.

Dobashi Riki
Nishiyatsushiro-gun, Yamanashi

## 229. The Sandals Three Feet Long

The bride was spinning flax, and the old mother-in-law was warming her back at the hearth. Jirō and Tarō were weaving straw sandals in the corner beyond.

The bride started to doze as she worked, and the old woman glared at her, not noticing that the hem of her garment was scorching.

Jirō and Tarō enjoyed watching that so much that they continued weaving the sandals until they were three feet long. This surprised them and they woke up the bride.

That was lucky for her, but what happened to the old woman and to Jirō and Tarō could not be helped.

Yamashita Hisao
Enuma-gun, Ishikawa

## 230. Three Crying Together

An old woman living in a certain place received a letter from her son. She took it out to the street to wait for somebody passing to read it for her. A samurai came along.

The old woman said, "Please read this for me." The samurai took the letter and looked at it. Tears began to roll down his cheeks presently.

The old woman asked, "Please, Sir, what is written in the letter? Is there something unusual, some change that has happened? I won't be frightened. I won't cry, no matter what it is. Please tell me right now."

The samurai went on crying and paid no attention. The old woman concluded that something terrible had happened to her boy and she began to cry.

A parching pan peddler came along carrying his wares. When he saw the two crying, he set down his load and began to cry as hard as they were. The next person who came along tried to find out why the three were crying. He asked the parching pan peddler first.

The peddler said, "I set out to earn money by the end of the year by selling parching pans, but I broke them. The year is passing without a chance to cry. I have been too busy to cry, but while I was going around today, I saw these two folk crying. Then I recalled my broken parching pans. It made me feel so bad that I began to cry."

The questioner asked, "Why are you crying, Granny?"

The old woman said, "I got a letter from my son. I asked this samurai to read it, but he only stands there crying without saying anything. I think something has happened to my son. I am so sorry for him that I can't help crying."

The man turned to the samurai and asked about him.

The samurai said, "I am ashamed to say I am ignorant, for I never read books when I was little and I can't read this letter. I am regretting it."

Imamura Katsuomi
Mitsu-gun, Okayama

## 231. The Doctor and the Sedan Chair

There once was a quack doctor in a certain village. He was unhappy—not because he did not have plenty of patients, but because nobody ever sent for him with a sedan chair. He was always saying that he wanted to ride in a sedan chair sometime. Finally, somebody came to ask for help early in the morning of New Year's Day.

The doctor thought this was a good time to get his wish. He said, "A doctor should ride a sedan chair instead of walking. I have decided that this year I will go only where a sedan chair is sent to meet me. If you want my services, send a sedan chair shortly."

The man who came thought the doctor was putting on airs to the limit that day, but considering the sick one at home, he could not refuse to ask for his services. It was just that at the village in the mountains a sedan chair could not be had just for the asking.

He decided to go to the home of an important man to borrow the Chinese style round sedan used for carrying prisoners. He had men carry it on their shoulders to the doctor's house. The doctor did not know a Chinese sedan from any other kind. He was just happy to get his first ride in a sedan chair. He got into it with a flourish.

When the sedan chair reached the next village, the villagers pointed at it and said, "Look, a Chinese sedan chair is being carried by this early on New Year's morning. There must be a dangerous criminal in it."

The doctor in the sedan chair heard that and it made him angry. He shouted repeatedly, "I'm not a criminal. I'm the doctor."

The people looking on declared, "Well, he doesn't seem to be a criminal. He seems insane. What a pity."

That made the doctor angrier. He shouted, "I'm not insane. I'm a fine doctor!"

The talk continued. "He certainly must be crazy."

The doctor could not stand it any longer. He stuck his head out of the sedan chair and glared around. He said, "You can see, can't you, I am quite sane."

The people said, "He's pretty bad off. Let's get away before he hurts us." And they started to run away. The doctor was completely dumbfounded. People only shouted the more over what he did, so he fastened the doors of the sedan tightly and rode along silently. Then people looking on as he passed said, "My, my, a corpse carried by this early on New Year's Day. What a pity."

The doctor kept his mouth shut when he heard that. He decided that riding a sedan chair was good enough if one's station in life warranted it, but anyone as low class as he should not ride a second time.

Dobashi Riki
Nishiyatsushiro-gun, Yamanashi

## 232. The Three Derelicts

Once there were three friends, a man with bleary eyes, one with his head covered with scabs, and one covered with lice. The blear-eyed man had the habit of rubbing his eyes, the one with scabs on his head had the habit of scratching, and the one with lice had the habit of shrugging his shoulders and twisting his back. People were always making fun of them.

The three talked things over and decided to stop their bad habits. The three sat silently by the hearth warming themselves. They endured matters at first, but as time passed, the blear-eyed man's eye began to itch like fire, the scabs on the head of the scabby man were so itchy they throbbed and made him dizzy, and the one covered with lice looked ready to grab a piece of firewood to scratch his back.

They could not endure matters any longer. The man covered with lice got up and said, "Look where I'm pointing! The deer on the mountain over there are going along shaking themselves like this." And he shook his clothes to scratch the itchy places on his back.

The blear-eyed man said, "Sure enough. I'll take my bow and aim the arrow this way before they run away." He rubbed one arm across his eyes, pretending to aim repeatedly.

The scabby man's head itched like fire and he could not endure it any more. He took the opportunity to say, "If those deer got away, I would be truly sorry." And he scratched his head as he said so.

Sasaki Kizen
Kamihei-gun, Iwate

## 233. Wagering on Stopping Bad Habits

An old man who liked stories very much lived in a village called Nozuichi. It was well enough for him to like stories, but nobody liked to tell them to him because he had the bad habit of saying, "There ain't no such thing," as he listened to stories. One day he urged Kitchyomu to tell him a story.

Kitchyomu said, "There's nothing I hate more than having somebody talk back."

The old man said, "I promise not to talk back. If I happen to talk back, I'll give you this bag of rice."

This is the story Kitchyomu told:

Long ago when a certain feudal lord was on his way to Edo to take his turn at the Shōgun's court, he noticed at a certain place that a lot of kites had gathered and were circling and calling, *bii-piyoro-piyoro*. He thought that was unusual. He had his sedan chair halt and he alighted and looked up to the sky. Droppings from a kite came falling and landed squarely on the feudal lord's divided skirt. He called to an attendant, "Bring me a new divided skirt!" One of his followers brought him a divided skirt respectfully. The feudal lord changed into it and got back into his sedan chair.

"A feudal lord has any number of changes of skirts, and he wasn't daunted in the least, was he?" explained Kitchyomu.

The old man was wrapped up in the story. He said, "That's a good story. What happened next?"

After the feudal lord had proceeded one or two ri, he heard kites crying up in the sky again. He got out of his sedan chair again and looked up to the sky. This time kite droppings landed squarely on his sword. His accompanying men were aghast because a samurai can get angry if his honor is stained, but the feudal lord only said, "Here, page, bring me a new sword." He changed to his new sword and the sedan chair moved on.

Kitchyomu asked, "Wasn't he dauntless?"

"Well, I declare, he was quite dauntless. What happened next?" asked the old man.

After he proceeded another two or three ri, kites were crying again and the feudal lord thought it strange. He got out of his sedan chair for the third time and looked up to the sky. It's hard to be sure whether it happened or not, but this time the kite droppings landed squarely on the feudal lord's head. The feudal lord drew his sword dauntlessly from his side and cut off his own head and ordered, "Here, page, bring me a new head." The page got a new head out of the big chest and brought it to him. The feudal lord stuck it firmly onto his trunk by himself and got back into the sedan chair. They started on again.

"Wasn't he dauntless?" asked Kitchyomu.

The old man gulped as he listened, but he exclaimed, "There ain't no such thing! No matter what kind of feudal lord he was, he couldn't have changed his head!"

Kitchyomu stood up promptly and said, "I'm sorry, Grandpa, but I'll take that bag of rice home as we agreed." He put the bag of rice onto his shoulder and went off without looking back.

Miyamoto Kiyōshi
Ōita

## 234. The Child with a Long Name

Once when a child was born to a couple, they talked over what to call him. They decided that a short name would be easy to call, and they called him Chotto ["a short time"]. But he died in a short time. He must have died soon because his name was too short.

The parents decided, "Next time we will give a long name. That way our child will surely live a long time." They named their next child Itchōgiri-nichōgiri-chōnai-chōsaburō-gorogoro-heiji-atchiyama-kotchiyama-tori-no-tokkasa-tate-ebōshi-tongarabyō.

Then one day while the child with a long name was playing in the yard, he stumbled and fell into the well. A little child who saw him fall in wanted to rescue him. He went to a house nearby to borrow a ladder.

He said, "Itchōgiri-nichōgiri-chōnai-chōsaburō-gorogoro-heiji-atchiyama-kotchiyama-tori-no-tokkasa-tate-ebōshi-tongarabyō has fallen into the well, so please lend me a ladder."

The old woman here was hard of hearing and he had to repeat that long name for her before he could bring the ladder. By that time the child with a long name had swallowed water and drowned.

Fumino Shirakoma [Iwakura Ichirō]
Minamikanbara-gun, Niigata

## 235. How the Mole Chose a Son-in-Law

The father mole had a fine daughter. He declared that although he had found many suitable followers, he wanted to select the best man in the world to give his daughter to as a bride. Everybody advised him.

One said, "The Sun in the Sky is the best. If we did not have the Sun, we could not get along. That's how great he is."

That is why the mole went to the Sun and asked, "Will you please take my daughter as your bride?" The Sun replied, "I'm great, when it comes to that, but one greater than I is present. I can shine, but the thing called a Cloud can hide me. The Cloud is the greatest in the world."

The father mole said, "Is that a fact?" He went to the Cloud. He said, "I hear that you are the greatest in the world. Please take my daughter as your bride."

The Cloud said, "That is ridiculous. I may win over the Sun, but there is the Wind Deity. Marry her to him."

The father mole went to the Wind Deity next and asked the same thing.

The Wind Deity said, "Oh, that's it, is it? No matter how heavy the Cloud is, I can send it flying, but there is one I can't match. That is Jizō Sama at Sakai-no-hara. No matter how hard I try, I can't tip him over. Marry your daughter to him."

The father mole went to Jizō.

Jizō said, "I never lose a match with the Wind, but there is one I can not match. A little more and he will topple me. It is the mole who burrows under my seat."

Finally the father mole selected a mole to marry his girl.

Iwakura Ichirō
Minamikanbara-gun, Niigata

## 236. Kahei's Hoe

A farmer called Kahei at a certain place set out one day in autumn with a towel tied over his head to dig in his garden patch. There were several crows in the woods beyond him as he went. They began to call, "Kahei! Kahei!"

This made Kahei angry. He threw stones at them as he said, "What's going on, you fool crows! Don't make fun of a man!"

The crows called all the more, "Kahei, kuwa [hoe]! Kahei, kuwa!" When Kahei reached his garden patch, he found that he had forgotten his hoe.

"That's it," he thought. "Those fool crows knew I forgot my hoe and they were talking about me. Now, what'll I do!"

When he looked over at the woods, the crows began to call, "Ahō [fool], ahō!" They flew over Kahei's head and let droppings fall.

Shimoina-gun, Nagano

## 237. The Uneasy Old Man

Once there was a farmer who had a hard time because he was always uneasy about everything. One day when the weather was fine, he decided it would be the right time to plant seeds for long radishes. He set out with his hoe over his shoulder, but he met a child who was crying. The old man asked, "What's the matter?"

The child said, "My tooth [ha may mean tooth or the blade of a hoe] aches so much, it may come out."

If the only blade the old man had for his hoe came out, he couldn't do any work. He decided that rather to plant seed on a day when there was a bad omen, he would wait for another, better day and he went home.

The next day the farmer decided, "The weather is fine today, so I will plant seeds for sure." He set out again with his hoe over his shoulder, but two men were fighting by the road along the way. He went up to stop them.

They both said, "Habakari-sama [an apology or "only leaves"]." And they went away.

The old man heard them and thought, "This is bad. Long radishes with only tops are of no use." He went home again without planting radish seeds. That is why it does not pay to be uneasy.

Katō Kaichi
Haga-gun, Tochigi

# *14. Humorous Stories: Profitless Imitation*

## 238. Learning Gained on a Journey
[Red Dishes and Shaking Salt]

There was a young man whose vocabulary was poor and he could not be taught anything. He set out on a journey to learn. He learned that **going up** to Kyoto was "jōkyō" and **coming down** (back) from Kyoto was "kakō"; a **red bowl** was "shuwan" and to **bleed** was "shio," and many other words. A man along his way was exclaiming "yongiyarasa" as he carried a stone on his shoulder.

One day the young man's father climbed a persimmon tree and fell suddenly from it. He was bleeding badly and his life seemed to be in danger. The young man wrote a note to the doctor, asking him to come quickly. It read: "My father **jōkyō** a persimmon tree and he suddenly **kakō** and struck his head on a **yongiyarasa** and **shuwan shio.**"

Koyama Masao
Chiisagata-gun, Nagano

## 239. Blundering Sōbee

A certain excitable man decided to go on a pilgrimage to Ise. He told his wife in detail what preparations to make for him the night before and he went to bed early. The next morning he got up while it was still dark, but his wife was not interested. She stayed curled up under the quilts and did not help her husband in the least.

When he asked, "Where is my lunch?" she replied without getting up, "It's by [under] my pillow."

He asked, "Where is the furoshiki?" She said, "It's behind where I am lying."

He asked, "Where are my sword and hat?" She answered, "They are below the shelf."

The man got his lunch box from under his wife's pillow, took the furoshiki from where she was lying and wrapped his lunch in it, and took the sword for his trip from where it was hanging below the shelf. He fastened his sword under his belt, put on the sedge hat that was there, tied on his sandals and his leggings, and set out in a happy mood.

As he went along, people would laugh and point at him, saying, "Look at that man!"

He thought it strange and began to look himself over. He discovered he had a wooden pestle stuck into his belt, his lunch was wrapped in his wife's underwear and tied to his back, and he was wearing a winnowing basket on his head. His sandals were tied on upside down and he was wearing only one legging. He had been so excited when he started out that he had tied the other around the door post. He realized how badly he had blundered, but it made him angry to think of going home without accomplishing anything. He decided to go ahead to Ise.

Noon came as he walked along and he decided to eat his lunch. He unwrapped his wife's underwear to get out his lunch box, and it proved to be his wife's sweaty, soiled pillow stand [full of hairpins and such]. That provoked him, but he decided to go on to the shrine and say his prayers and to stop in at a store to buy something to eat afterwards.

He endured his hunger as he stood before the Grand Shrine. He had brought 150 mon in coins for the trip and decided to make an offering of three mon. He divided his money, but he got excited and instead of the three mon, he tossed the remaining 147 mon into the offering box. When he noticed, all he had left in his hand was the three mon.

He realized that he could not buy a lunch with only that much. He walked along and came to a mochi shop with lots of pieces of mochi on display. The sight made the poor man so hungry he could not stand it. He went into the shop and asked the owner how much one piece of mochi cost. The owner said it would be six mon.

"Won't you please cut the price to three mon?" asked the hungry man.

"I certainly won't cut the price in half," answered the storekeeper.

As he was haggling about the price, the man noticed one especially big piece of mochi in the row on display. He repeated, "Come down to three mon," as he reached for the big piece.

He started to run off with it and pretended he did not hear the storekeeper shout, "Here, wait a minute!" He ran as fast as he could. When he thought he had reached a safe distance, he tried to bite off a piece of mochi.

His teeth hurt so badly he jumped with pain. He took a good look at the mochi and found that it was a painted wooden block set out as an advertising display.

One blunder after another had humiliated the poor man more and more. Besides, he was getting to be hungrier and hungrier. He arrived home in a rage over the memories of the day. He found his wife turning the stone handmill at the back entrance.

He gave her a whack on her back as he yelled, "You are good at making trouble for folks!" The woman cried out in pain and turned around. She was the wife of the rich man next door. The flustered man ran off, but he realized that he should at least apologize as best he could. He went back with his head hanging. He knelt with his hands down on the floor and apologized.

As he raised his face and looked around, things seemed a little different. He found that he was apologizing to his own wife.

Dobashi Riki
Nishiyatsushiro-gun, Yamanashi

## 240. A Slip of the Tongue

The landlady at an inn heard that if anyone ate ginger, he would forget things. She prepared a dish with it for a guest, but he was so stunned that he left. The woman thought her guest had surely left his purse or something behind and chuckled as she went to his room to look, but she could not find anything.

She rushed out into the street and asked everyone she met, "Did you see where the furoshiki carrying a round-eyed old man about fifty years old with stripes on him went?"

The landlady herself had tasted some of the ginger cooking and had forgotten to ask for pay for his lodgings.

Uchida Kunihiko
Chiba

## 241. The Man Who Ate Brewers Grains

Once upon a time there was a basket maker who was poor, but he had a wife. He liked wine although he was poor.

His wife once said to him, "If we buy rice, we can't buy wine. From today, how about buying brewer's grains and eating them instead of buying wine? You will have color in your face and your stomach will be filled."

Her husband thought it over and said, "Buy brewer's grains, wife."

So from that time she bought them and he ate them. The basket maker's friends asked, "How many gō did you drink today?"

He answered, "Three hundred grains."

They laughed and said, "You're eating brewer's grains these days, aren't you?"

He felt ashamed. When his work for the day was over, he said to his wife, "You told me to eat brewer's grains, but my friends make fun of me."

His wife said, "That is just like you to say 300 grains. You should have said, three gō. If you are asked tomorrow, say you had three gō if you ate 300 grains. Instead of saying you toasted them, say you warmed them."

The husband thought that was a good idea. He ate brewer's grains again the next morning before he set out for work. His friends asked, "How many gō did you drink, Chōbei?"

He remembered what his wife had told him and said, "I had three gō."

"Don't put on airs," said a friend. "How did you prepare it?"

He said, "Well, I toasted it."

His friends laughed again and said, "You ate brewer's grains, didn't you, Chōbei?"

Yamashita Hisao
Enuma-gun, Ishikawa

## 242. Part of the Song Left Over

Kitchyomu attended a family gathering, but the sun set before he started home. He asked for a candle to carry. He was so grateful for the way the candle lighted the dark road that he did not want to blow it out. He walked past his house until the candle was used up.

Nakata Senpō
Kyūshū

## 243. Tea-Chestnuts-Persimmons

*Tonto hitotsu atta toi.*

Once a stupid man went to town to sell tea and chestnuts and persimmons. He went around calling, "Chakurikaki [tea-chestnuts-persimmons]!" People along the way thought he must be selling unusual wares. They stopped him and found that it was tea and chestnuts and persimmons.

One man said, "You had better try selling them by calling each exactly—tea exactly and chestnuts exactly and persimmons exactly."

Then the peddler went on, calling "Tea-exactly, chestnuts-exactly, persimmons-exactly!"

*Tatte mo katarai demo sōro.*

Tamura Eitarō
Munakata-gun, Fukuoka

## 244. Sieves and Old Metal

One day a tea peddler went around with a load of new crop tea on his back, calling "Shincha [new tea]!" But a sieve peddler followed right behind him, calling "Furui [sieves or old]!" People who heard did not know whether the tea was new or old and nobody bought the tea.

The tea peddler lost his temper and grabbed the sieve peddler. He said, "You rascal! I'm no fool. When I'm trying to sell new crop tea as something special, you come along behind me and call that it is old. How can I sell my tea!"

The sieve peddler declared, "I'm a sieve peddler. Don't be silly. I have to call my wares. I'm not saying your tea is old. I'm just calling furui as I go around and I'm not hindering you. It makes no difference to me whether you sell your tea or not."

Neither man would give in until a real fight broke out between them. Then a man came along selling old metal ["furukane" could mean "old metal" or "it's not old"]. He carried a basket on the scales hanging from a pole across his shoulder. He saw the other two men quarreling and asked, "What are you fighting about?" He separated them and heard each one tell his story. Then he said, "That is nothing to fight over. I have a good idea. Let's all three of us go together to sell our wares."

Then they set out, the tea peddler leading. He called, "Shincha [new tea]." Next came the sieve peddler, calling "Furui [sieves or old]." Last came the old metal buyer, calling "Furukane [old metal or not old]."

In that way each of them was able do business for himself, selling tea or sieves or buying old metal. They went around as friends all the time after that.

Dobashi Riki
Nishiyatsushiro-gun, Yamanashi

## 245. What the Boiling Kettle Said
[Butsu Stories or Butsu Dialogues]

There was a mother living alone with her two boys. The name of the younger was Butsu. They were happy together, but the mother got sick and died.

Butsu went to ask for the services of the priest. The older brother explained to Butsu, "The priest is somebody who wears a black robe."

As Butsu went on his way, he saw a crow that had lighted on the road. He thought it must be a priest and said, "Please come to our house because our mother has died—he used the honorific "o-kaa" for mother.

The crow called, "Kaa-kaa"—the humble form which Butsu should have used for his own mother. The crow flew off.

When Butsu got home and told his brother what happened, his brother said, "That was a crow wearing black. It should have been somebody with red on."

Butsu set out again and along the way he saw a rooster with a bright red comb. He thought it surely was the priest and asked him to come, but it only crowed, "Koketsuko [she's sunk]!"

Butsu went home and said, "I told the priest our mother had died, not sunk, but he would not come and I came home."

The older brother then put rice on to cook for the priest and went himself to call the priest because there was no more use to try to insist on Butsu doing the errand. He told Butsu to watch the rice.

While Butsu was feeding the fire under the kettle, the rice began to boil, *butsu-butsu.*

He thought the rice was calling him, so he answered. But it kept on calling *butsu-butsu* and he got angry.

He put some firewood into the kettle and then it started to say *bukkuta-bukkuta* ["Butsu ate it"]. He was angry because the rice kept saying he ate it and he hadn't. He threw the rice out.

Just then the older brother came home and found they had nothing to serve the priest to eat right off. They had some honey in a jar up in the rafters.

The older brother brought the ladder and climbed up to get the honey. When he started to lift it down, he said, "Butsu, hold [the] bottom. Be careful not to let it fall."

Butsu held his own bottom and the jar fell, breaking it to pieces.

The big brother asked, "Why didn't you hold it?"

Butsu said, "Look, I'm holding my bottom!"

There was nothing left to serve the priest. The big brother decided to heat the bath so the priest could bathe. There wasn't much firewood to keep it hot for him, so Butsu asked his brother what to burn.

He said, "Just anything there."

Then Butsu picked up everything, including the priest's robe to stuff into the fire. The priest had to go home naked.

Takeda Akira
Mima-gun, Tokushima

# *15. Humorous Stories: Tales of Foolish Villages*

## 246. A Series of Instructions

*Mukashi attaji mo no.*

A foolish son was once sent to the home of a relative to borrow an iron kettle. He tied a rope to the handle and dragged it home over a frozen road. The kettle was completely battered to pieces. The boy went home crying and his mother asked the reason. He showed her the kettle and told what had happened. He said, "I'm crying because it was borrowed from our relative. It broke when I tied a rope to it and pulled it home."

His mother comforted him and explained that when he borrowed a kettle, he should carry it on his back.

The next time, the son went to the home of a relative to borrow an earthenware chopping bowl. He tied it with a rope as his mother had told him and put it on his back, but it fell and broke to pieces. He went home crying. When his mother asked why he was crying, he said, "I went to our relative's home to borrow the earthenware bowl, and when I tied it to my back, it fell and broke."

His mother said, "You should have tied it up in a furoshiki to carry it."

The next time, the son went to get the old woman who tended fires. He tied her up in the furoshiki hurriedly, but she got angry and hit him on the head. He went home crying.

When his mother asked him why he was crying, he said, "I went to get the old woman who tends fires, but when I tied her up in a furoshiki, she hit me on the head, and that's why I am crying."

His mother said, "It's a very hot day today and you should have led her home with a smile."

The next time the son went on an errand to the home of a relative, he passed a house that was afire. He went up and said, "It's very hot today" The fireman got angry and hit him on the head. He went home crying.

His mother asked, "What are you crying about?"

He said, "There was a fire on the way and I just said it was a hot day and smiled as I went by. The fireman got angry and hit me on the head. It hurt, and that is why I am crying."

His mother said, "You should have helped put water on the fire."

The next time the boy went to the home of a relative, he passed the blacksmith shop. He saw the fire burning brightly. He hurriedly got a bucket of water and threw it on the fire. It was blacked out in an instant. The blacksmith hit the boy's head angrily and the boy went home crying loudly.

His mother asked, "What are you crying about this time?" He said, "I put water on the blacksmith's fire and he hit me on the head."

His mother said, "At a time like that, you should take a hammer and help him pound."

When the boy set out for the home of a relative again, he met a blind itinerant. The boy thought this was his chance, and he hit the blind man on the head with the blacksmith's hammer. The blind man then hit the boy back with his staff so hard that he saw stars. The boy cried loudly since he was hit back and he went home.

His mother wondered what would happen if she sent him on any more errands. She felt sorry for her boy and kept him home after that.

Ogasawara Kenkichi
Shiwa-gun, Iwate

## 247. The Foolish Son-in-law

A bride said to her husband, "When you go to my father's house, you will see a knothole in the post of the alcove in the parlor. You should say that you think it would be a good idea to hang a decoration over it."

When the young man went to his father-in-law's, he was taken into the parlor, just as his wife had said. He remarked, "Father-in-law, I think it is a pity to see that knothole. Wouldn't it be a good idea to hang a decoration over it?"

This delighted his father-in-law. He replied, "Yes, I have been thinking so, too. You've been very observant."

The son-in-law felt proud of himself for being praised. His father-in-law took him out to show him his horse in the stable. He seemed to be going to feed his horse, but he lifted its tail up to show the son-in-law. The young man noticed the "knothole" below the tail. Hoping to be praised again by his father-in-law, he said, "This is certainly a fine horse, father-in-law, but there is a knothole where it was injured. Why don't you hang an ornament over it?"

The father-in-law went back into the house glaring. He said, "He's a foolish son-in-law! I can't let my precious daughter stay with him." He insisted upon bringing the young bride home from his son-in-law.

Sasaki Kizen
Shiwa-gun, Iwate

## 248. The Son-in-law's Oral Instructions

A foolish son-in-law had to call upon his father-in-law. He was racking his brains over what to say when he got there. As he walked along the bank of a stream, he saw a man absorbed in catching little fish. The son-in-law asked, "What is something good to say to my father-in-law when I go to see him?"

The fisherman misunderstood and thought he asked how many fish he had caught. As he raised his basket of fish high, he said, "Only this much before breakfast."

The son-in-law thought that was fine and went home. On the day he was to call upon his father-in-law he set out in fine spirits carrying a basket. When he arrived at his father-in-law's house, he raised his basket high and said respectfully, "Only this much before breakfast."

His father-in-law decided the fellow was a fool after all and took his daughter back. The son-in-law went home with tears on his face.

Kunohe-gun, Iwate

## 249. The Son-in-law on a String

The family of a girl who had married a foolish man wondered how he would prove to be as they waited for him to visit with his bride. The bride was clever and did not want her husband to appear foolish. She tried to teach him good manners and all sorts of things to say.

The girl said, "When you go into the parlor there, you are not to keep still. I will tie this string onto your loincloth and I'll pull it when it comes time to talk. If I pull it once, you must say, 'Indeed.' If I pull it twice, say, 'It is certainly as you say.' If I pull it three times, say, 'No, that's not so.'"

The couple went together on good terms to her home. The time came at last for her bridegroom to go into the parlor, so the bride tied the string onto her husband and drilled him on what to say.

The relatives were all seated with dignity in the parlor. The son-in-law, too, sat at his place with his hands resting politely on his knees. Everyone was expecting him to do something foolish, but he sat there calmly erect. He smoked sometimes, but he held his posture.

The relatives said to each other, "He hardly acts like a fool. He certainly is a substantial man." Then all sorts of talk started.

One relative said to the young man, "I dug a wider dam for irrigation this year and I have plenty of water."

The bride in the corner pulled the string once and her husband replied politely, "Indeed."

Then another said, "This is the fifth year of good crops, so we are enjoying it very much."

This time the bride pulled the string twice and he said, "It certainly is as you say."

Then still another said, "Everyone says that you are a good worker and we admire you very much."

The bride pulled the string three times and he said, "No, that is not so." His replies were given precisely and everybody was delighted.

In the meantime, the bride wanted to go to the privy. She tied the end of the string to a fishbone to hold it before she left. Then a cat came in and tried repeatedly to pull the bone away. The young man began repeating what his bride had taught him, "Indeed, it is certainly as you say, no, that is not so."

The foolish son-in-law was a foolish son-in-law after all.

Kunohe-gun, Iwate

## 250. The Dango Son-in-law

The oldest son in a family who was a little foolish received a bride. He went to spend the night at his father-in-law's house during the Fifth Month.

He forgot the greeting for the morning and said, "Congratulations, you have waked up." His bride told him to cool the hot water put into his rice bowl with a pickle, so when he went into the hot bath, he asked for a pickle to be brought him to cool it.

In the evening, dango were served at supper. He thought they were very good and wanted to have them made at home, too. On his way home he kept repeating, "Dango-dango-dango!"

The young man came to a little stream and jumped over it with an exclamation, "Ottoko-shō." After that he kept repeating, "Ottoko-shō, ottoko-shō," until he reached home. He said to his bride, "Make me some ottoko-shō."

His bride laughed and asked, "What do you mean by ottoko-shō?"

That made her husband angry. He reached over and whacked her forehead with the stem of his pipe. A big lump appeared where he hit her. She said, "How mean a man you are! The lump is as big as a dango!"

"That's it, a dango, a dango," the young man exclaimed. "Hurry and make me some dango."

*Dotto harae.*

Kunohe-gun, Iwate

## 251. Rice Cakes Are Ghosts

A foolish son-in-law was invited to the autumn celebration at his father-in-law's home. All the women were in the kitchen preparing mochi with sweet red beans. The children kept going in and clamoring for some mochi, and the women would say, "This is something scary and not anything to eat."

The son-in-law in the next room overheard the talk and it frightened him. The food was served after the mochi was prepared. Somebody said, "Now, son-in-law, please have some mochi."

He was served that scary stuff they brought in. He remembered the talk and stuffed all of it under the mat on the floor after pretending to eat it.

The next morning the young man woke up hungry and said he would go home right away. He insisted he would go although his father-in-law tried to get him to stay. The amazed old man gave up, but he had the mochi that was left over from the night before wrapped in a little woven straw mat and given to the young man as a gift.

The son-in-law wondered what was in the package on his way home and opened it to see. There it was, that scary stuff he had seen the night before. He threw it out onto the snow and hit it with a post he pulled up there. When he did that, the bean paste came off and the white mochi showed. The young man thought it was showing its fangs and hit it all the harder. He concluded the scary stuff was weak after all and he went home feeling he had overcome it.

"I'm hungry, Mother," the young man said when he got home. "Hurry up and give me something to eat."

His mother asked, "Didn't they give you anything to eat at your father-in-law's?" Her son said, "They tried to get me to eat something scary last night. They urged me to eat it, but they couldn't fool me."

His mother was surprised. She asked, "What was that scary thing?"

Her son described it and said, "I took it out of the bowl and stuffed it under the mat on the floor. This morning they called it a gift and gave some to take, but when I beat it with a post, it showed its teeth and came at me. I beat it down and left it scattered in the snow."

His mother said, "That was nothing scary. They just said that to stop the children from teasing for it. Perhaps it was mochi. I'll go to look for it and pick it up. Where did you throw it away?"

"It's over there."

"Then I'll go and see."

His mother went to look for it and brought back the mochi wrapped in the little straw mat. Instead of being scary, it tasted good.

Sasaki Kizen
Shiwa-gun, Iwate

## 252. The Jar and the Little Stone

Once upon a time a son-in-law went to visit his father-in-law, and the mother-in-law said, "Our son-in-law has probably never tasted dango made with sweet red beans, so I'll make some for him." They were very sweet.

The son-in-law watched for where the leftovers would be put. He saw them put into the cupboard and in the night when everyone was in bed, he got up and took the jar out. He thrust his head into the jar, but it got stuck.

In the meantime, the young man had to go to the privy. He went out to it and crouched. His father-in-law came with very little on and looked around. The son-in-law climbed into the box of wood chips to hide. The old man was not aware of that. When he finished his business, he could not find a woodchip around the box, so he picked up a little stone at hand to wipe himself. Then he gave it a toss, but it happened to land on the jar on the son-in-law's head and break it.

The son-in-law said, "I won't blab about how you broke the jar if you don't tell about me."

The old man agreed. The two parted as though they knew nothing and slept till morning.

The two of them were invited to the home of a relative at a later time. The father-in-law, as a representative of the family, was asked to sing. He sat very correctly and began, "At the margin of the lake, the tsuru kame . . . [stork and tortoise, but **kame** may also mean jar]."

The son-in-law burst out indignantly, "You have your nerve! It happened because you wiped your butt with that stone."

Sasaki Kizen
Kamihei-gun, Iwate

## 253. Tying the Pillow On

When a foolish son-in-law went to visit his wife's family, his bride told him he should not sleep without a pillow. She told him to tie it to his head so it would not slip away. He tied the pillow on his head with his loincloth that night.

When he went to wash in the morning, the pillow was still tied to his head. His father-in-law saw that and decided he could not leave his daughter with a man like that. He insisted upon her leaving him and coming home.

The bridegroom got his friends in the neighborhood to go to call on his father-in-law at New Year and to spend the night there. Several of them went and tied their pillows to their heads with their loincloths at night. They went that way to wash their faces.

The bride said to her mother, "That is the custom where my bridegroom comes from. They don't do it just because they are stupid."
At that, the girl was allowed to rejoin her husband.

Iwasaki Toshio
Iwaki, Fukushima

## 254. The Three Sons-in-Law

Long ago three daughters were married. One went as a bride to the hills, one went as a bride to a village, and one went as a bride to town. The three of them came home with their husbands at New Year to spend some nights.

The son-in-law from the village brought lots of sweet bean cakes and all sorts of other cakes as gifts. The one from the town was a dealer in dress goods and he brought yardage of several kinds.

The son-in-law from the hills was poor. He said to his wife, "I don't have anything to take as a gift." His bride said, "My father will be glad just for us to go and he does not expect us to bring anything. You don't need to take anything." So they went without gifts.

That night there were lots of good things to eat before bedtime. The son-in-law from the hills had to piss in the night. When he went outside, he saw a bow hanging on the porch. He was a hunter, so he picked up the bow and let an arrow fly. His father-in-law got up in the morning and found two wild geese caught on a single shaft. They had fallen into his rice-seed bed. He called, "Who did this big deed this morning?"

The bride of the son-in-law from the mountains said, "Last night when I had to go out, I brought the bow and arrow back with me and told my husband to shoot it. He shot it." The son-in-law from the mountains suddenly became very important.

The next night there were a lot of good things to eat again before they went to bed. In the night the son-in-law felt he had to defecate. He asked his bride, "Where is the privy?"

She said, "Just do it in the corner of the porch. I'll get up early in the morning and clean it up." So he went out onto the porch and came back after he had finished. The bride forgot all about it in the morning, and the pile was still there on the porch.

When the father-in-law saw it, he exclaimed, "Who did the big deed this morning?"

The son-in-law from town and the son-in-law from the village wanted to be praised this time, for sure. They both spoke up, "I did it. I did it."

In this way the son-in-law from the hills appeared to be the most important and the other two were considered fools.

*Konde yontsuko montsuko saketa to ya.*

Momoo-gun, Miyagi

## 255. The Foolish Bride

Long ago a girl reached that age and it was decided that she was to be married. Since the priest at the temple knew all sorts of things, she went to him to inquire what to do when she went as a bride. The priest was just getting ready to go to a memorial service.

The girl asked him, "What is the proper thing to say when I want to go to the privy when I am at somebody else's house?"

The priest had not paid attention to what she said. He said, "I'm going to a memorial service. I'm going to a memorial service."

The girl concluded that when she was away somewhere and had to go to the privy, she should say, "I'm going to a memorial service."

During her wedding celebration, the girl had to go to the privy. She said to the one beside her who had arranged the wedding, "I have to go to a memorial service. Please let me leave."

The lady refused and said, "I never have heard of going to a memorial service during a wedding. Go after it is over."

But the girl could not wait. She said, "I have to go."

The one in charge would not agree, but the girl finally got up and went. The lady followed her anxiously and saw her go into a patch of burdock. The owner of the garden shouted angrily, "What are you doing in my burdock patch?"

The girl replied, "I'm going to a memorial service. I'm going to a memorial service." She was scolded angrily again.

Seki Keigo
Nagasaki

## 256. Wanting to Go as a Bride

A woman in a certain place had grown quite old without marrying. Then somebody came to ask for her and to arrange a wedding. But the family said, "Our old woman has bad eyes and she isn't very bright."

The woman came out and said, "I'm sorry, but the black ants and the red ants are wrestling on the top of that mountain over there, and I can't see . . . "

It was obvious that she wanted to go as a bride.

Sasaki Kizen
Kamihei-gun, Iwate

## 257. The Foolish Village

A village called Yokoo in Ōya-gō of Tajima-no-kuni has the reputation of being the source for stories about stupidity. Even now on a snowy night, people recall such tales around the hearth and recite one after another for amusement. . . .

Once upon a time a lot of men from this village were invited to a fancy banquet. A man called Chōkichi in the village seemed to be the most informed about things. Before they set out, they decided to sit by him and imitate everything he did.

Chōkichi took the lid off the bowl that had mountain yams in it and was going to pick up a piece with his chopsticks, but it fell onto his lap. Then one after another picked up a piece of yam and rolled it around in his lap.

Chōkichi hastily poked his neighbor with his elbow and said, "This is a mistake." Then one after another did the same. The last one in line asked, "Where do I poke my elbow, Chōkichi?"

Otagaki Ubana
Yabu-gun, Hyōgo

## 258. Mochi in the Bathroom

Once a man who knew little about the world went to Edo and put up at an inn. He was invited to take a bath. When he went to the bath room, he found rice-bran and salt set out. He thought he was supposed to make little balls of the bran and put salts on them to eat.

He put some salt on the bran and dipped it into the water to make little dango and ate them. The maid brought him his supper in his room after he had finished. The man from the country said, "I ate rice-bran dango in the bath and I'm not hungry."

The maid said, "Then I'll take a piece of mochi to you when you wash your face tomorrow morning. You can eat it." She left him a piece of mochi in the morning.

The country jake decided to imitate folks correctly next time. He got up late and watched what men were doing. They had put the rice-bran into their towels and were rubbing their faces with it.

He concluded that was what he should do. He found his mochi and wrapped his towel around it and then rubbed his face with it. The mochi stuck all over his face when it got wet. He concluded that he had blundered again. He was sitting correctly when the maid brought his breakfast. She laughed and asked, "What happened to your face?"

*Too katchiri.*

Isogai Isamu
Hiroshima

## 259. "Turn the Long Head Around"

A feudal lord stopped at Saada and ordered a "furo" ["bath" or "the heel of a hoe"]. The villagers gathered together and decided that he meant he wanted the heel of a hoe. They pulled the handle out of the hoe and set up the heel. When the feudal lord saw it, he burst out laughing.

Then he asked for "chōzu mawase" ["a long head turned" or "basin of water for washing"]. The villagers gathered together again to discuss the order, but nobody understood. Then a man who knew things said that chōzu meant a long head and mawase meant to turn something around. He said, "Look for a man with a long head and turn it around."

So the villagers called out the man with the longest head in town and took him to the veranda of the inn where the feudal lord was stopping. Four or five men tried hard to turn his head around.

The feudal lord saw that and explained that the chōzu was water for him to wash his hands.

Miyako-gun, Fukuoka

## 260. **Pulling Screens and Tossing Dango**

When children are told they sound as though they came from Noma, they usually stop talking.

People at Noma call a screen a thing that does not sleep at night and falls down. Several men from Noma once went on a pilgrimage to the Grand Shrine of Ise. They went to Kyoto on their way home and put up at an inn. The screen that was set up where they were sleeping fell over. The men got up and talked over what to do about it. They decided that two of them at a time would take turns standing by the screen to hold it up.

After that they said that anyone going to Kyoto should be careful of anything that falls over easily at night without sleeping.

Yanagita Kunio
Fukuoka

## 261. **Hanging Noodles on the Ears**
[Putting Noodles around the Neck]

Some young fellows had some fun telling a foolish young man that the way to eat noodles was to put them around his neck first. They also told him the way to use a mosquito net was to jump into it from the top.

One time the foolish young man was invited to his bride's village for a feast. Noodles were served. He concluded these were what were to be put around the neck and he put the long noodles around his neck to eat them. He was supposed to spend the night there. Since it was summer, a mosquito net was hung for him in the parlor where he was to sleep. The young man decided that it was the bag to jump into and he jumped onto it to sleep.

Yamaguchi Asatarō
Ikinoshima, Nagasaki

## 262. Shaking Rice

A man who is about to die is allowed to hear rice being shaken. This is told at Inbi, Minamiamabe-gun, Ōita.

## 263. Not Celebrating New Year

A man went around trying to sell pines for New Year on the 29th Day of the last month of the lunar year. Everybody was through with celebrations and their decorations were down. He tossed his pine boughs into the sea. It happened that the pines were needed at the Dragon Palace and somebody came to meet the peddler.

Watara-mura, Iki-gun, Nagasaki

* * *

The man who could not sell pines at New Year tossed them into the sea. It happened that the pines were needed at the Dragon Palace. A maid came gladly to meet the man. She told him on the way to the Dragon Palace to ask for a mikankō cat when he was asked what he wanted for a gift. When he fed the cat rice steamed with red beans, it dropped gold. It was killed by the man's younger brother. After the man buried the cat, a mikan (tangerine) tree sprouted. He dug out lots of gold from its roots.

Yamaguchi Asatarō
Ikinoshima, Nagasaki

## 264. The Pheasant-Crow

A man from Saji went to buy some things at Mochigase. People made fun of him as he walked along. They said, "That fool from Saji has showed up." That made the man angry and he went home.

The man thought he would get even the next time he went. He went hunting the next morning and shot a pheasant and a lot of crows. He put the crows into a bag and loaded it onto his back. He hung the pheasant from a stick and set out for Mochigase. He called, "Crows for sale, crows for sale," as he walked along.

People said again, "That fool from Saji has showed up!"

As the man continued along, he met a gentleman. The man noticed the one from Saji and asked, "How much is a crow?"

The man from Saji replied, "I'm asking ten sen each."

The gentleman was pleased about that. He said, "Give me three crows." He handed over 30 sen.

The man from Saji reached into his bag and pulled out three crows and thanked the gentleman as he handed them to him. The astonished gentleman exclaimed, "Here, these are crows, aren't they?"

The man from Saji replied, "You asked for crows, didn't you, Sir?"

The gentleman was embarrassed and sneaked away.

Niikura Sato
Yazu-gun, Tottori

## 265. The Zatō's Eggs

A bosama went to Kogarumai and spent the night there. When he took out a small mosquito net from his bundle and hung it to sleep under, the villagers said, "Look, the zatō is building his nest." In the morning the blind man went off and forgot his two riceballs.

When the people at Kogarumai saw the riceballs, they said, "The zatō laid two eggs before he left." They talked about what to do because it would be terrible if they hatched into zatō.

Yanagita Kunio
Hachinohe, Aomori

## 266. Herring Roe

A man went from Zaibara Kenkuma-mura, Takashima-gun to the Grand Shrine of Ise on a pilgrimage. He was served herring roe along the way. He thought it made a fine sound when he chewed it and it tasted good.

The man bought some dried herring roe to take home. He tried to eat it without soaking it in water, but it didn't taste good. He threw it out because he thought it was some kind of stale food. He tossed it into a thicket behind the house. Snow covered it.

The man went to see it in the spring and it had become soft and looked bigger. He said, "This is something that should be thrown into the thicket to soak."

Even now, herring roe is called thicket roe in Zaibara.

Mitamura Kōji
Takashima, Shiga

## 267. The Mirror at Matsuyama

A farmer from the hills went on a pilgrimage to the Grand Shrine of Ise. He decided to look around. As he passed a certain shop, the farmer saw his father who he thought was dead. He bought him and took him home. It seemed too strange to tell his wife about and he laid his father on a shelf. He was a filial son and took out his father every morning and said, "Good morning, Father."

The farmer's wife wondered what he was doing everyday. She got the thing out and there a woman's face was reflected. She did not know it was a mirror. She thought, "My husband is keeping a woman hidden from me."

Then a quarrel started between the farmer and his wife. A neighbor who knew about the world came and stopped the quarrel. He explained what a mirror was.

Takeda Akira
Tokushima

# 16. *Tales about Birds, Beasts, Plants, and Trees*

## 268. The Sparrow's Filial Piety

The woodpecker serves Yama-no-kami and offers her worms every day. She and the sparrow were sisters long ago. They were both called to their mother when she was seriously ill and about to die. The sparrow was blackening her teeth at the time, but she stopped and flew hurriedly to her mother. The woodpecker was putting on rouge and powder, and by the time she went, she was not with her mother when she breathed her last.

The sparrow can live without trouble because of her filial piety, but the woodpecker must get up before daylight and hammer on trees, and get barely three worms. She cries at night, "Alas, my beak hurts!"

Ucihida Kunihiko
Tsugaru, Aomori

## 269. The Cuckoo Brothers

Once there was a mother and her two sons. Shortly after the older one was born, he became blind. His mother and younger brother would gather good things to eat and feed them to him. But the mother died. The younger brother was honest and ate only nut shells, stubs of grass, and such and he gave the good parts to his brother. The older brother was happy at first, but he gradually grew suspicious. Then one day he pecked his younger brother's throat and killed him. The brother who had been blind suddenly could see once more. He noticed that only stringy parts of mountain yams and grass roots, nothing good to eat, had come out of his younger brother's throat, and nothing like he had been eating everyday. He was filled with remorse. He clung to the lifeless body of his younger brother and cried, "Nodo tsukkita" [I tore his throat!] until blood came from his mouth. The deities disliked seeing that. They said to him. "If you tell your brother you are sorry 1008 times from morning to night, he may forgive you." The cuckoo has continued to pitifully call "nodo tsukkita" ever since until his throat is raw.

Hayami Kaichi
Chichibu, Saitama

## 270. The Shrike and the Cuckoo

A shrike carried off the younger brother of the cuckoo and ate him. That is why the cuckoo calls, "Otōto o kaese" [give me back my little brother]. And when the cuckoo comes, the shrike does not appear. The shrike is also called Jigoku no tori [the bird of Hell], and it does not like to be seen.

* * *

The little brother of the cuckoo was killed by the shrike. That is why the cuckoo calls, "otōto koishi" [I long for my little brother!]. The shrike catches worms and little birds and impales them on trees for the older brother cuckoo to make amends for its sin.

Suchi-gun, Shizuoka

## 271. The Cuckoo Who was a Shoemaker

Long ago the cuckoo made horseshoes and the shrike was a horse leader. The shrike always asked the cuckoo to shoe his horse, but he never paid his bill. The cuckoo would remind him and called, "Kutsu-no-dai wa dōshita ka" [What about the shoe bill]? The shrike was ashamed and hid somewhere when the cuckoo came out and called. He would fasten all sorts of little worms on twigs to keep the cuckoo in a good humor.

Itsuki Seiryū
Naka-gun, Wakayama

## 272. The Cuckoo and the Stepchild

There was a farmer at a certain place who had a wife and daughter. His second wife abused her stepchild. The father went to town one day, but he was late coming home. The woman sent the girl to meet him. She set out at sunset, but her father did not return. When the girl came back, her stepmother was angry and scolded her severely. The girl cried and cried until she turned into a cuckoo, calling "Matchi itta kedo" [but I went to town].

Matsuda Iwahei
Kesen-gun, Iwate

## 273. The Cuckoo and the Little Kettle

Once there was a stepmother who hated her stepchild beyond endurance. She told the girl to slice a long radish one time, but she hid the big knife. The girl could not find it and asked her stepmother, "Where is the big knife?"

The stepmother said angrily, "You lost it so you look for it." The girl looked for the knife until she died.

Her spirit became a hōchō bird and cried, "Hōchō totetaka" [did you take the big knife]?

Fujiwara Teijirō
Hienuki-gun, Iwate

## 274. A Legging on One Leg

Once upon a time there was a father whose son was named Kakkō. When the father came home tired from the hills one day, he did not see Kakkō anywhere. He was surprised and hurried off to look for him with one legging still unfastened on his leg. He called, "Kakkō, Kakkō!" and hurried from hill to valley, but he could not find the boy. He fell exhausted finally and turned into that kind of bird. This is the reason the kakkō has one black leg.

Seki Keigo
Tsukushi-gun, Fukuoka

## 275. Yoshi, Toku

Once upon a time there were two sisters named Oyoshi and Otoku. They were happy living with their mother, but a big flood come and the two girls were missing. Their mother went around here and there, trying to find her girls, but she didn't. She finally lost her mind and died. She became an owl. She calls on a summer night from dark till dawn, "Yoshi Toku!" People say that she is still looking for her two girls. On Shōdojima they call owls "yoshitoku."

Kawano Masao
Shōdojima, Kagawa

## 276. The Cuckoo and her Child

A mother asked her child who had just come home from playing to scratch her back, but he refused to do as she asked. The mother's back itched so much she could not stand it. Finally, she went to the cliff on the hill behind their house and rubbed her back on the rocks. She missed her footing for some reason and fell into the valley below and died.

When her boy saw that, he felt so bad that he began to cry, "Kakō, kakō" [I'll scratch it. I'll scratch it]!

The kami appeared to him and said, "You are crying and calling *kakō* so much that I will turn you into a bird so you can call *kakō* every day."

Then the boy became the bird who calls *kakō* 8008 times a day.

Kitaazumi-gun, Nagano

## 277. The Cuckoo and the Stepmother

Long ago a stepmother in a place called Kajima set out at the end of May to cut wheat at her garden patch on a very steep place in the foothills. She said to her little stepdaughter, "Bring my lunch to me on your back." When it was about noon, the child set out with her mother's lunch on her back. She called, "Where are you, Mother?"

The stepmother called from the highest place in the garden to torment the child, "Here I am! Here I am!" The girl struggled up with the lunch still on her back and sweating as she climbed. Then the stepmother flew down to the lowest place in the garden patch. "Here I am," she called. "Why are you fooling around?"

When the girl hurried back down carrying the lunch, the mother ran up to the highest place again and called, "Here I am. Why are you fooling around?"

The little girl struggled up again with the heavy lunch on her back. She was so hungry and tired from trying to catch up with her stepmother on the hot summer day that she fell dead. The stepmother was turned into a kakkō bird as punishment. She had to call "kakkō, kakkō" 8008 times a day until her mouth was torn and bloody and her voice gave out. If she did not cry that much, filthy maggots would come gushing out of her mouth. That is why every year when the grain ripens at Kajima this bird comes out and calls.

Dobashi Riki
Nishiyatsushiro-gun, Yamanashi

## 278. The Hunter and his Dogs

In early summer a bird called the ryōshi dori ["hunter bird"] comes out in the early evening and sings a lot at Yamakunidai in Shimoge-gun, Hizen [Ōita]. Nobody has ever seen its form. It has a sad voice. People say it calls "ryōshi koi, Kuro koi" ["come hunter, come Kuro"].

At the end of spring long ago a hunter set out with his dog named Kuro from a certain village in this valley. He found a large stag in the hills near Hikozan. It happened to be Hikozan Gongen [the sacred manifestation of the mountain]. The hunter followed it for seven days and seven nights, but he could not bring it down. Finally the hunter, his dog, and the stag were so exhausted that they fell near Iwaya at Hirata.

The hunter had a beautiful, gentle daughter. She worried because her father was so long about returning. She made riceballs and set out with them to look for him. She reached Iwaya after several days and learned that her father and Kuro had died. She was so grieved that she lost her mind. She kept going around until late spring. After that the bird could be heard every year in the evening of early summer.

Tradition says that the girl turned into this bird. There are rocks called even now Inuiwa [Dog Rock] and Nigirimeshiiwa [Riceball Rock] in the middle of the current of Yamakuni river near Iwaya in Hirata, and there is a clearly visible deep mark on a rock at the margin of the river which is said to be the print of the sacred deer's hoof.

Abe Sekiden
Shimoge-gun, Ōita

## 279. The Meadowlark and the Debt

Villagers around here say that the meadowlark calls "chew-chew peeyapeeya," but it is rather hard to pronounce. They tell the following story about it.

Long ago the Sun dwelt upon the earth. The meadowlark was a money lender in those days, and even the Sun borrowed from him. The Sun succeeded in life later and climbed to the sky without paying a single mon of its debt. The meadowlark was angry. He would fly up to the sky, urging the Sun to repay the money. He called, "I loaned money to the Sun. I loaned money to the Sun."

The Sun would reply, "I admit I borrowed money, but I am trying to send you lots of light and warmth. I promise to repay the loan, but excuse me from at least paying interest on it."

But the meadowlark wants high interest and continues to call, "Ri toru, ri toru [I'll get interest. I'll get interest]," as he climbs to the sky.

Mutō Tetsujō
Senhoku-gun, Akita

## 280. The Meadowlark Cowherd

Long ago when the meadowlark was a man, he used to tend a cow and a horse at a certain family. When his master would ask him if he had given the cow and horse water, he would say he had although he had not given any to them. He was reborn as a meadowlark for punishment. That is why the meadowlark was driven away from houses.

The meadowlark has children of its own, but when they ask for water and it flies down to look for some, all the water looks like fire. It can't drink. It can't perform anything artistic and only circles around in the sky calling "chew-chew."

Isogai Isamu
Aki, Hiroshima

## 281. The Bird Who Wants Water

A mother and son lived together long ago. She loved her child, but he never obeyed her. She worried so much that she became ill. Once when she was thirsty, she asked her boy to bring her a cup of water. He did not want to go for it and held a burning faggot from the hearth to her instead. When his mother saw it, she died suddenly.

The unfilial son was so shocked that he turned into a bird. A bright red bird was always seen in the tree by the mother's grave from that time. If the unfilial son who became that bird becomes thirsty and goes to drink water, the water looks as red as fire and he can't drink it. He can drink a little to keep alive when it rains.

He is always calling, "fure-fure" [rain, rain] to try to make it rain. This is a kingfisher.

Hayami Kaichi
Chichibu, Saitama

## 282. Ten or Eleven Persimmons

Long ago a stepmother put ten persimmons into her cupboard and went off somewhere on an errand. Her stepdaughter stayed at home to look after things while she was gone. The stepmother returned after attending to her errand. She opened the cupboard and said, "I left eleven persimmons here a while ago and they should still be here, but I find only ten. You must have eaten one." She accused the girl of doing it.

Her stepchild was surprised and said, "You certainly put only ten there. They are there. I don't remember touching them."

But the stepmother would not listen. She insisted, "There were eleven there for sure, and you must have eaten one." She continued to scold and abuse the girl. The stepchild, however, continued to say, "I don't remember it that way. I am sure there were only ten persimmons."

At last, the girl turned into a bird and flew around crying, "kaki-tō, kaki-tō" ["ten persimmons"].

The stepmother kept on saying, "There were eleven. There were eleven." At last, she turned into a bird, calling "jū-ichi, jū-ichi" ["eleven, eleven"].

Dobashi Riki
Nishiyatsushiro-gun, Yamanashi

## 283. The Unfilial Kite

Long ago there was a mother whose son would do the opposite of anything she would tell him to do. She thought she must do something to reform him. At last, when time came for the mother to die, she called her son to her and expressed her final wish. She said, "Please hold my funeral when it rains."

Her son grieved because he had always done the opposite of what his mother asked and decided at least to carry out her funeral as she asked. He held her funeral in the rain. That is why when the sky clouds over for rain, he recalls his mother and cries "piiyoro-yoro."

Katō Takashi
Yatsuka-gun, Shimane

## 284. The Unfilial Tree Frog

There was an unfilial son in a certain place, the sort that disobeyed his mother. If she asked him to fetch salt water [sea water was used in making bean curd], he would bring her fresh water, and if she asked him to fetch fresh water, he would bring her salt water. She was worried about what would happen to him in the end.

Then the mother suddenly became ill. Her life hung on for a few days and she worried if her unfilial son would do what had to be done after her death. She thought, "If I ask him to bury me in a good place, that rascal is the kind that will bury me in a poor place."

The woman called her son to her to express her last wish. She said, "Please bury me near the bank of a stream when I die." Then she died.

The unfilial son underwent a great change after his mother's death. He thought sincerely, "While my mother lived, I disobeyed her many times. I can not leave matters that way. I must at least do one thing as my mother asked."

The son buried his mother by the bank of a river according to his mother's last wish, doing the one thing after her death which she had asked for while still alive. Then the son turned into a tree frog. Now when it rains, the tree frog worries for fear a flood will wash away his mother's grave by the river bank. He cries, "Wa nyaya chasuga ya" ["What shall I do for my mother"].

Sakima Kōei
Okinawa

## 285. The Unfilial Pigeon

Long ago the pigeon was really a perverse fellow who never did anything his mother asked him to do. If his mother told him to go to the hills, he would go to the field. If she told him to go to the field, he would go to the garden to work.

His mother wanted to be buried on a quiet hillside when she died, but she thought that her son would do the opposite of whatever she asked, so before she died, she asked him to bury her in the sandbar of the river.

It happened that after the pigeon's mother died, he realized for the first time how wrong it had been for him not to have listened to what his mother said. This time he did just as she said and made her grave in the sandbar along the river. But when the river began to fill up in the rain, he became frantic for fear his mother's grave would be washed away.

Even now, when it looks like rain, the pigeon recalls this and grieves. He cries, "Totopoppo oya ga koishi" ["I want my mother!"].

It would have been better if he had obeyed his mother a little sooner.

Yanagita Kunio
Kashima-gun, Ishikawa

## 286. The Bird That Begs for Water

Long ago the bird who begs for water was the wife of a horse dealer. Several horses were kept in the stable and it was her duty to give them hay and water every morning and evening. She considered it too much of a bother to carry water to the horses from the river in front of the house and she always neglected them. She made it appear that she had watered them, but she really never did.

If her husband asked, "Did you water the horses?" the wife would answer, "Yes, I did."

The horses in the stable were always thirsty and longed for water. Their resentment was directed toward the housewife. The woman was reborn into a bird as punishment.

This bird was all bright red from its beak to its tail, even its breast, except for some rather blue feathers on its back. When it would fly down to a little stream to drink water, it would see its own red reflection that looked like fire. It would be too frightened to drink. It would fly to another river to see, but that would seem to be burning, too, and it could never drink. It would become so thirsty it could hardly endure it.

The bird would sip dew from tree leaves in the hills, but if there was no rain for a few days, the leaves would be dry and the bird would have nothing to drink. It was so eager for water that it became the bird that begs for water to make it rain.

That is why when people hear it call "hiyōroro-hiyōroro," they think rain will come soon. They comment to each other, "The bird that begs for water is calling a lot these days."

Dobashi Riki
Nishiyatsushiro-gun, Yamanashi

## 287. The Pigeon and his Parent

Long ago when a father went to dig mountain yams, he would give his son the soft parts and eat the stringy parts himself. The son was suspicious and thought his father was giving him the poor parts, so he split his father's stomach open to see. Only the stringy parts of the potatoes were there.

The son turned into a potato-digger bird as punishment. When that bird goes to water to drink, the water seems to be burning and it does not drink. It calls "waō-waō" when it wants to drink.

Nishitani Katsuya
Kinosaki-gun, Hyōgo

## 288. The Owl Dyer

The crow was a dyer long ago. The kite was a splendid looking, pure white bird in those days. He went to the crow to get his feathers dyed because he could be seen too easily by men. The kite was angry when the work was finished. He complained, "See what a dirty color you dyed my feathers!" He would not pay the bill.

Even now, if the crow and the kite meet, the crow demands that his bill be paid.

Yamaguchi Asatarō
Ikinoshima, Nagasaki

## 289. The Reed Thrush and the Straw Sandal

Long ago the reed thrush was the sandal porter at a temple called Dōgyōji. One day he lost one of his superior's high clogs. His master scolded him and told him to go and look for it. He would kill him if he did not find it. The sandal porter fell dead while he was going around looking for the clog.

The porter's soul became a reed thrush. It cries, "Dōgyōji, Dōgyōji, are you going to take my head for one high clog? If you're going to cut it off, cut away!"

Fujiwara Teijiro
Hienuki-gun, Iwate

## 290. The Wren, King of the Birds

Long ago a little wren went to where hawks of all kinds had gathered for a drinking bout. He said, "Please take me into your band." The hawks snubbed him and said, "If you want to join us as a comrade, catch a wild boar."

The wren promptly flew away and hopped into the ear of a wild boar that was asleep in a thicket. The startled boar ran off, but it was suffering so much from the little wren beating about in its ear that it accidentally struck its head on a rock and fell dead. Then the little wren went back with a great swagger to join the hawks in their drinking bout.

When that happened, a huge bear-hawk felt he could not be outclassed. He flew off to where two wild boar were running together. He decided to take them both at the same time. He grasped a boar with each of his right and left talons, but the boar started off in different directions, and they tore the body of the greedy hawk in half.

Yanagita Kunio
Harima (Hyōgo)

## 291. When the Earthworm and the Snake Traded Eyes

There is a story about how the earthworm and the frog traded eyes. The earthworm had eyes, but he had a poor voice. The frog had no eyes, but he had a good voice. One day the frog asked the earthworm to trade his eyes. When the earthworm asked how they could trade, the frog said, "I can ask the Moon."

Then the frog asked the Moon to make the trade. The Moon promptly allowed it, but to punish the frog for such an unreasonable request, he put the frog's eyes on his back and he changed his voice at the same time.

Sugiwara Takeo
Sakai-gun, Fukui

## 292. The Earthworm That Wears a Reel

Long ago two girls who were neighbors were both skillful weavers. They wove at their looms every day and competed with each other. When it was almost time for the village market day, they decided to wear dresses that they had woven to it. They raced to finish their weaving.

The girl who wanted to be judged on speed rather than style used coarse thread and she did rather loose weaving. At any rate, she finished her dress and it was ready to wear. The other girl thought she had plenty of time and wove as beautifully as she could. She used fine thread and wove smoothly, but the market day came before she had finished weaving.

The one who had finished her dress was happy as she put it on and went to market. The girl who had not finished could not do anything about it. She just hung the reel on her neck and climbed into a jar. She asked her husband to carry it on his shoulder. The two girls met in the midst of the crowd.

The one in the jar laughed and said, "There's Fat Thread over there. Look at her. Look at her!"

The other laughed back and said, "It's better to wear something, even if its thread is coarse. If the jar breaks, you will be naked."

They continued to make fun of each other. The husband became so ashamed that he threw the jar down onto the ground. The jar broke. The naked girl with only a reel around her neck was so ashamed to be seen by the crowd that she burrowed into the dirt.

She turned into an earthworm with a white ring around its neck.

Yamaguchi Asatarō
Ikinoshima, Nagasaki

### 293. The Kindness of the Bracken
[The Bracken and the Snake]

Once upon a time a snake was ill and fell onto the sprouts of some thatching reeds. It was too weak to move. The bracken that was still underground pitied the suffering snake. It lifted the viper with its soft hands and freed it from the tips of the thatching reeds. After that when people met a viper in the hills, they would ask, "Have you forgotten the kindness of the bracken, Viper Maid?" This is why the viper avoids hurting men.

Fujisawa Morihiko
Kazusa (Chiba)

### 294. The Wild Goose and the Tortoise

Once upon a time the tortoise turned to the wild goose and said, "I am tired of this place and I want to go somewhere else. Please take me with you." The wild goose agreed. It had the tortoise bite onto a stick and two geese held the ends as they flew up. When they flew over a certain village, the children were amused to see the tortoise biting the stick and the two geese carrying it. They began to shout.

The tortoise forgot his instructions and shouted back at the children. He fell from the stick at that moment. The shell of the tortoise had been divided since that time.

Iwasaki Toshio
Iwaki-gun, Fukushima

### 295. The Sparrow Wine-Dealer

The sparrow is the one who started wine making. Long ago sparrows used to pick up rice that was offered at graves and take it back to the bamboo thicket. They would drop it into bamboo stumps in which rain water had gathered and leave it there. It would eventually turn into wine.

Then the sparrows would gather there for a drinking bout and dance. It is said that sparrows would dance as many as one hundred numbers.

Takagi Toshio
Matsue, Izumo (Shimane)

## 296. The Lizard's Tail

The lizard borrowed man's tail and would not return it. That is why when a man comes near him, he thinks he has come for his tail. He leaves it and runs off.

## 297. The Louse and the Flea

Once upon a time a flea, a louse, and a mosquito were playing together. For some reason, the flea and the louse began to quarrel. Finally, the flea was so angry that he threw a big rock onto the louse's back. The rock bounced off and hit the mosquito.

The flea had put all his strength into throwing the rock, so he turned red like he is now. The louse has a black mark on its back where it was bruised by the rock. The reason the mosquito's hind legs are bent is that the rock hit them.

Seki Keigo
Nagasaki

## 298. The Origin of Fleas and Mosquitoes

When Shutendōji of Ōeyama was killed, he did not want to stop drinking human blood. His blood turned into fleas and the ashes left from burning him turned into lice.

Uchida Kunihiko
Tsugaru, Aomori

**A complete oral version:**

Long ago there was an unruly child who used to tease the children in his neighborhood. During a quarrel with a child in the neighborhood one day, he stabbed the child's throat with a dagger. He drank this child's blood, turned into a demon and flew off somewhere. His parents searched for him, but they could not find where he had gone. At that, he was such a bad boy that they gave up looking for him.

The demon-child then went off to Ōeyama in the Land of Ōmi and fought with a demon called Ibaraki-dōji. He struck him down and this demon surrendered. The boy then boasted that he had become the champion. He went to the streets of Kyoto and carried off people to eat. He could kidnap people anywhere until he would carry off a man from one place or another. Everyone was so frightened that they finally appealed to the Emperor. He had a guard placed at the big Rashōmon gate every night. The guard at Rashōmon was carried off every night after that.

A great champion called Raikō was then set to watch. He was ready to kill whatever demon appeared that night. He waited with sword in hand, but during the night he became drowsy. Although he tried to fight off sleep, he drifted off. Then a clammy wind came blowing and the demon appeared. He grabbed Raikō's helmet and tried to fly off with him. Raikō realized he was being carried away and he cut the strings of his helmet with his sword. He fell onto the roof of Rashōmon. The demon returned to try to take him again, but Raikō cut off one of the demon's arms.

The demon could not get along with only one arm, so he fled. Raikō took the demon's arm to his house and put it away. The demon came there the next day disguised as a friend. He said, "That was a great feat last night when you cut off the demon's arm. Please show it to me." Raikō gladly brought it out to show.

The demon who had appeared as a friend took the arm. He turned back into his true form and ran away with it. Raikō was thoroughly humiliated over having been fooled. He chased the demon, sword in hand, but he lost sight of him. There was nothing else to do but to give up the chase. He reported it to the Emperor. The Emperor then gave him the order, "Go forth and subjugate the demon."

Raikō made preparations immediately. He selected seven strong men such as Tsuna, Kintoku, and Suetake as his followers. Each of them dressed as a yamabushi, and carried a portable shrine containing a one *to* bottle of wine in it. They set out for Ōeyama. When they reached the mountain, they found it so steep and covered with briars and wisteria vines that they could go no further. They were troubled and talked over what to do. A tall green-faced man then came striding over the briars and vines. The men decided to ask him for advice. They called, "Hey, you!" But the man went on without answering. They tried calling, "Young man!"

The man stopped and asked, "Are you talking to me?" They said they were and that they had something to ask him. They wanted him to wait. He said, "I am in a hurry, so ask me quickly."

They asked, "What is a good way to Ōeyama?"

He replied, "If you walk fast after me, you will get there. Walk right along without looking back." The men followed him and passed over the briars lightly and without pain. Presently the men lost sight of the young man. They could only continue in the direction he had taken.

The group came at last to the cave where the demon lived. A big rock stood before the entrance and they could not open the way. They called, "Hey, you!"

One of the demon's servants came out and asked, "What do you want?"

Raikō said, "We are yamabushi who have lost our way. We have come here, so please let us spend the night with you."

The demon was glad to have them stay so he could have something at hand to eat. The men stayed there that night. Raikō took out the wine he carried in his portable shrine on his back. He said it was a gift for Shutendōji. The demon liked wine and was happy to accept it. He invited the men in and had heaps of flesh served, and had a lot of blood put into the cauldron. He invited Raikō to drink it. The demon sat down and began to drink the wine Raikō had given him. He enjoyed himself.

Raikō could not eat human flesh and blood, but he pretended to as he ate the riceballs and wine he had with him. He told the demon he had more wine. The demon asked the men to bring out all they had with them and he drank every bit of it. Shutendōji drank so much that he rolled over on his back. That pleased Raikō.

A demon servant then invited Raikō and his men to sleep in a little room. They got up in the night and put on their helmets and things they had in their altar boxes. When they were ready, they went out of the room to look around, but there wasn't a single demon in sight. They wondered where they had gone and hunted around. They were surely somewhere close, but they could not be sure.

While the men were trying to decide what to do, the young man who had guided them before appeared. He said, "I am Aotsurakonkō. I came here so you could overcome the demon. I have been acting as his servant. Come quickly. You wouldn't be able to find the place where the demon is hiding no matter how many days you searched."

He led the way and Raikō and his men were glad to follow. They came to a door of rock. The young man opened it, and beyond was a big room. Then the young man said, "I must leave you now." With that, he went off somewhere and could not be seen.

Ibarakidōji and Kanekusodōji were asleep on their backs. Tsuna and Kintoki passed the demons and went into the next room where Shutendōji lay sleeping on his back and snoring. He was drunk with wine. Kintoki straddled Shutendōji as though he had mounted a horse, but he decided it would be a pity to kill him then. He wanted to wake him up so he would know what was happening before killing him. He called "Shutendōji," but the demon only grunted and did not wake up. Kintoki kept on calling until the demon was conscious.

Then Raikō declared, "We have come to subjugate and destroy you at the command of the Emperor." The drunken Shutendōji remembered the wine and tried to get up.

At that moment, Raikō struck off the demon's head with all his strength. The head flew up and its teeth fastened onto Raikō's helmet. The other men finally put an end to him.

The demon's followers then appeared. They declared, "We are not demons. We were all carried off by the demon and were forced to serve him." They begged to be saved and they were rescued.

They burned the place, but they took Shutendōji's head to show the Emperor. They were praised highly and rewarded generously. The blood that came out when the demon's head was cut off turned into fleas. Horseflies and mosquitoes came from the ashes. The demon's joints did not burn. They turned into leaches and suck human blood.

*Dondo harai.*

Fujiwara Teijirō
Hienuki-gun, Iwate

## 299. The Origin of Tobacco

A mother who lost her only daughter spent her time weeping at the girl's grave. She saw a plant such as she had never seen before sprouting from the grave one day. The plant grew bigger and bigger as she watched and many leaves appeared. The mother took the leaves home. She tried steaming them and cooking them, but they were too bitter to eat.

The leaves dried in the meantime. The woman tried stuffing some of the dried leaves into the end of a bamboo tube and smoking them. The flavor was delicious beyond words. It comforted whatever sorrow she had. Then it gradually became popular and anyone could smoke it.

Iwakura Ichirō
Kikaijima, Kagoshima

## 300. Why the Jellyfish Has no Bones
[The Monkey's Liver]

Somebody said that the live liver of a monkey would cure the illness of the Princess of the Dragon Palace. When the tortoise deceived the monkey and brought him to the Dragon Palace, the jellyfish told the monkey about the scheme. The monkey deceived the tortoise and escaped cleverly.

It was discovered later that the jellyfish had told the monkey. His skin was peeled off and his bones were taken out. He became that formless thing he is today.

Takagi Toshio
Matsue, Shimane

## 301. The Mole and the Bullfrog

Long ago the Sun shone so brightly that the mole was angry about it. He said, "If the Sun is going to shine like this, I will shoot him." He took a bow and arrow and climbed onto a log.

The frog saw that and thought it was a terrible thing to do. He hurried to the Sun's place and said, "The mole is going to shoot you with an arrow. He has climbed onto a log, so please be careful."

The Sun declared that the mole was an outrageous fellow, who would no longer be able to walk above ground. He would have to move only underground as punishment. The Sun promised that he would warm the water when the frog was raising its young because he had been loyal and told the Sun in time.

That is why even now when there are little frogs in the mill pond or in the moat, the weather is warm. If the mole tries to face the Sun even a little, he dies.

*Koshiko.*

Noda Tarō
Tamana-gun, Kumamoto

## 302. The Charcoal, the Straw, and the Bean

Once upon a time an old woman put a kettle over her fire in the hearth to cook broad beans. She sat by the hearth breaking little sticks to feed the fire until it began to burn brightly. She began to feel drowsy in its warmth and dozed off. The beans in the kettle began to boil, and one of them puffed up with steam and popped out of the kettle onto the hearth.

A piece of straw and a piece of charcoal were already burning there. When they saw the bean that had fallen, the three of them began to talk. One said, "It is no fun to be in such a small place. Why not go on a journey to see the big, wide world?"

Another said, "Yes, that should be fine." And so the three set out.

The three went along until they came to a small stream that had no bridge over it. They talked about how to cross to the other side The straw said, "I'll lie across the stream to be a bridge." He lay on his side over the water, making a bridge from one bank to the other. The broad bean crossed the bridge first and reached the other side.

The charcoal started next, but unfortunately there was still a little place that was burning on it. When it got half way over the straw bridge, the straw caught on fire. That cut the straw and it fell with the charcoal into the stream. The bean began to cry when he saw the two carried away struggling in the water. He cried so hard his jaw came loose.

In the midst of his distress, a young girl came along on her way home from her sewing lesson. She asked the broad bean, "Why are you crying so hard?"

The broad bean told her everything that had happened and added, "And now my jaw has come loose and I don't know what to do about it."

The girl said, "I'm sorry. I'll sew it for you." She wanted to sew the bean up, but she didn't happen to have any white thread. There was no help for it, so she sewed him up with black thread. Even now there is a black line on the broad bean's head.

*Sore mo sorekkiri.*

Dobashi Riki
Nishiyatsushiro-gun, Yamanashi

## 303. The Long Radish, The Carrot, and the Burdock

A burdock, a carrot, and a long radish went on a pilgrimage to Ise. While they were stopping at an inn, the carrot and the radish talked about getting away from the burdock because it was too black. They slipped away while the burdock was still asleep. When he woke up, he noticed that the carrot and the long radish were not there. He asked the innkeeper about them.

The man said, "Mr. Carrot and Mr. Long Radish have already started *tō*" ["to go to seed" or "early"].

Ogasa-gun, Shizuoka

## 304. The Leak in an Old House

Long ago an old woman turned to her old man and asked, "What do you dislike the most?" He replied, "I dislike a wolf. And what do you dislike most?"

The old woman said, "I dislike a buru [a leak from rain]." It happened that a wolf was listening at the door. It began to rain presently and the old woman shouted, "Look, there's that buru! There's that buru!" The wolf fled in a hurry.

Now it happened that a cow thief was hiding in the rafters. He thought the fleeing wolf was a calf and he chased it. The thief fell into a hole along the way. The wolf thought it was a buru that had fallen into the hole. He went to the rabbit's house to report what had happened.

The rabbit went to the hole to find out what a buru looked like. As he started down into the hole to see, something below tried to catch hold of him. He shouted, "It's a buru. This won't do!"

He ran away.

Kawano Masao
Takamatsu, Kagawa

## 305. Help from Animals

Long ago in the land of Yashū [Shimotsuke or Tochigi] there was a man who made the strange boast that he could eat manjū by swallowing them whole. A bad man who knew of this man's streak of vanity put a needle into a manjū and laid it down. The vain man, unaware of that, swallowed the manjū in his usual way. He had such severe pain in his stomach that he went to bed.

The man opened the sliding door beside him and looked out as he lay there. A sparrow was in the leek patch behind the house eating the tops of leeks. For some reason or other, it would come there every day to eat leeks. Presently a piece of a needle with some leek around it came out from the sparrow's tail and dropped.

The man thought that a kami had surely taught the sparrow how to get rid of the needle. He tried it himself by eating a lot of leeks. Then the needle came out and his pain was gone. The man was so happy that he built a little shrine called Suzume-no-miya [Sparrow Shrine].

That is the name of the railroad station near it even now.

Yanagita Kunio
Kawachi-gun, Tochigi

## 306. Animals and People

Once upon a time a traveler rescued a man from drowning in the rough current of a tidal wave. The traveler said, "You were in danger. It was lucky that I came along." The man shed tears as he said, "You saved my life and I do not know how to repay you."

They walked along together and saw a snake that was struggling in the waves. The traveler rescued the snake and took it with him. A little further on, he saw a fox struggling in the current. He rescued it, too, so the group—the man, the snake, and the fox—went on together with the traveler.

The group came to a land where there was a fine, influential chōja, and they stayed overnight at his place. The traveler was a physician, really. Since there was no doctor in that land, people from all directions came for treatment. He became respected by everyone and received many gifts.

The man who had been rescued became jealous of this success. He said to the chōja one day, "That man is not really a doctor. He uses bad magic and there is no telling what evil he is doing." He aroused the suspicion of the chōja in that way.

The chōja was astonished. He had his staff of officials seize the doctor and put him into prison. The snake and the fox saw what happened, but they could not do anything about it. That man certainly was hateful.

The two animals talked all day and all night about how they might rescue their benefactor from prison. Then the snake hid under the step at the entrance of the chōja's house. When the chōja put one foot on the step to go out, the snake bit it. The chōja cried out in pain and fell over. His leg instantly swelled as big as a mallet. The poor man cried in pain night and day.

The fox then came disguised as a fortune teller. He laid out his fortune sticks and announced, "There is only one man in the world who can cure this sickness. He is being held in prison on the chōja's estate. He is a famous physician."

The chōja sent his men promptly to bring the doctor to him. The officers went to the doctor suffering in his cell and told him to come out immediately. The doctor was sure that was because they were going to execute him and he resigned himself, but they took him directly to their master, the chōja.

The sick man said, "Here, traveling doctor, I have fallen ill. Please cure me quickly." The doctor tended the foot and put medicine onto it. The wound that had been making the chōja cry with pain suddenly healed before their very eyes. The chōja was delighted. He gave the traveler a place of honor and thanked him warmly. The bad man was put into prison upon the advice of the fortune teller.

Mankind is the most ungrateful.

Sasaki Kizen
Kamihei-gun, Iwate

## 307. The Wolf and the Old Man

An old man went to plant beans in his garden patch. He would say as he planted each bean, "For every bean I plant, grow a thousand."

A wolf came out and sat on a flat rock. He looked on, intending to eat the old man when he took his noon nap. He taunted the old man by saying, "For every bean I plant, one bean." The old man noticed that and went home without taking a nap.

That night the old man and his old woman made mochi. They took it early next morning and spread it over the flat rock by the garden patch. Then the old man acted as though nothing out of the ordinary was going on as he planted beans. The wolf came again and sat on the rock, staring at the old man and repeating the mean formula.

When the old man finished planting beans, he set his hoe on the border of the garden and lay on his side with his head on it as a pillow and pretended to sleep. That delighted the wolf. He intended to take that opportunity to catch the old man and eat him, but his haunches were stuck to the rock and he could not get up.

The old man got to his feet nimbly and split the wolf's head with his hoe. That night he and his old woman made wolf soup to eat.

Sasaki Kizen
Shiwa-gun, Iwate

## 308. Animal Races

Long ago the badger went by to invite the mudsnail to go on a pilgrimage to Ise with him. The mudsnail said on the last day of their journey, "How about it, Master Badger? It's not much fun just to walk along like this. Why don't the two of us race from here to the Grand Shrine?"

The badger agreed. While he was getting ready to run, the mudsnail lifted its lid and fastened itself onto the badger's tail. In that way he could go flying along at the some rate as the badger without any effort. They reached the Great Gate of the shrine. The badger whisked his big fat tail in delight. It brushed the mudsnail off on the stone wall, and half of its shell broke off.

The mudsnail fell rolling onto the ground. He was a sly rascal and concealed his pain. He said, "Here, Master Badger, you're late, aren't you? I got here a while ago and I just slipped off a shoulder to rest."

Yanagita Kunio
Arita-gun, Wakayama

## 309. The Fox, the Lion, and the Tiger

Long ago there was an animal called a lion in India and foxes and wolves were in Japan. There were tigers in Korea. These animals were kings in their own countries.

The wolf said to the fox one day, "Since I am king in Japan, I cannot leave the land. Go to Korea and take the land there for me." The fox agreed and set out.

To begin with, he crossed over to Korea. When he met the tiger, he asked, "Who is the king of this land?" The tiger answered proudly, "I am. I can run so fast that it appears I leap over a thicket 1000 ri broad in a single jump."

The fox said, "Then will you race and show me?" They decided to run over a mountain road 1000 ri long. The fox caught onto the tiger's tail when it set out. The tiger thought running was strangely difficult that day, but he ran right along.

When he had nearly completed the 1000 ri course, he turned around to see how far the fox had come. The fox let go of his tail at that moment and broke into a run to finish the race. "How about it? I seem to be a little faster," said the fox boastfully.

The tiger of Korea then submitted to the wolf of Japan.

The fox asked what the neighboring country was called. He was told it was India. He decided to visit it and to take it, too. He set out promptly. When he arrived in India, he met a lion. He asked it, "Who is king of this land?" The lion replied, "It is settled that I am. I have a big voice. With a single roar I can send a kettle flying."

The fox said, "Please roar once to show me." The fox went into a cellar and held his ears. When the lion finished roaring, the fox came out of the cellar and said, "It really didn't amount to much, did it?"

The lion was chagrined. He said, "When I roar this time, it will kill little animals, but if you say so, I will roar once more." The fox went farther into the cellar than he had gone before and held his ears more firmly. When the lion finished roaring, the fox came out again and said casually, "It wasn't much, was it?"

The lion was angry that such a roar had not impressed the fox. He said, "The third time I will roar my head off. If you don't understand that, I don't care if my head drops off. I'll try it and show you."

The fox went into the cellar and held his ears as he had done before. The lion roared as loudly as he could. When he finished, the fox came out, and the lion's head was off. The fox picked it up and crossed over India back to Japan with the lion's head.

It is said that this is the lion head mask worn now in the lion dance.

Shita-gun, Shizuoka

## 310. Animal Feuds

An old wolf and a dog went around every day as friends. One day when the dog was lying down at his master's house, he heard somebody say, "The dog at our house is getting to be too old to be of any use. We must abandon him or kill him and skin him."

That surprised the dog. He ran right off to the wolf's den and said, "What shall I do? This is what they are saying at my house. Do you have a good idea for me? If you have, tell me about it."

The wolf laughed when he heard what had been said. He declared, "I may have to stay in the mountains, but I am never disturbed by such talk as that. There is no use to get excited. I have a good idea and will share it with you."

The dog was relieved, but he did not know what the wolf was thinking. He asked what to do. The wolf explained, "When the folks at your house go to work in the garden patch in the hills, they always take the baby with them and leave it in a basket beside the garden where they can watch it as they work. I will carry the baby off tomorrow. You must bark when I do that and chase me. I will leave the baby in the grass and run away. The folks at the house will decide to keep you because you rescued the baby." The dog thought that was a good idea and thanked the wolf.

When the people went to work as usual in their garden in the hills the next day, they put the baby in the basket at the edge of the garden. The wolf then came out and carried off the baby. The people were startled and made a big fuss, but they could not catch the wolf.

The old dog ran after the wolf and brought the baby back safely. The people had not thought the dog was worth that much, but since he was the rescuer of their child, they changed their minds and decided to keep him.

Two or three days later the wolf came to the dog's house and the dog thanked him for what he had done. The wolf said brazenly, "Since your life is pleasant now, give me the big rooster as thanks." The dog said, "That cock belongs to my house and I can't give it to you."

The wolf got angry. He said, "Come to my place tomorrow. I have my plans, too."

The dog thought the wolf was going to eat him, but there was no help for him. He said, "I'll be there." Then he parted from the wolf.

The cat that was kept at that house overheard what was said. She realized that the dog at her house was in danger and she wanted in some way to save him. She went to the dog who was sighing deeply. She said, "The color in your face is very bad. Are you worried about something? Is it about that bad wolf who came from the mountain just now? Did he make some demand on you?"

The dog then told her all that he was worried about. The cat comforted him and said, "I will go with you to the mountain and I will protect you."

When day came, the wolf called his comrades, the demons, together to eat the dog, and they talked in his cave in the mountains. The dog and the cat climbed up to it. The demon's ears stuck out of the hole a little and were moving. The cat thought they were rats.

She said, "I'll catch those rats and eat them to satisfy my hunger before I start to fight." She leaped onto the ears suddenly and bit them off completely.

The demons were astonished that their ears were bitten off. They cried, "We are no match for this!" And they ran off in a cloud of dust.

Sasaki Kizen
Kamihei-gun, Iwate

## 311. The Monkey and the Shellfish

Long ago the monkey went down to the seashore to play in the evening. Something seemed to be in the shadow of the rocks and he put his paw in to find out. Then it fastened onto his paw tightly. This was terrible for the monkey. He tried repeatedly to pull his paw away, but he could not get it free. The monkey grew pale and lifted his eyes towards the hills. He said repeatedly,

As I look to the hills, the sun is setting
Let me go, shellfish, let me go shellfish.

Finally he got his paw free and went home happy.

Kanno Norisuke
Momoo-gun, Miyagi

## 312. The Badger's Divination

Long ago a hunter lived with his daughter in the mountains. His daughter said one night, "Please do not go hunting tomorrow." Her father thought that strange. He asked, "Why not?"

She said, "I had a dream last night that makes me feel that way."

But hunting was how her father made his living, and he paid no attention to his girl's words. He set out the next morning as usual with his lunch and his dogs. He could not find any game for some reason that day. By the time the sun had set he had only caught a few birds. He started to go home, but one of his dogs caught onto his clothes and pulled him back. He thought there might be some good game, so he let the dog pull him along to a little shrine.

The man looked in and saw his daughter sitting there alone. He asked her what had happened. She said, "Right after you left for the hills, a lot of monkeys came and forced me to go with them. They dragged me here. They said they were going to make me the bride of the monkey leader. They have gone to get things to eat."

The father was frightened. He said, "I'll get ready for that." He placed one of his dogs under the floor and hid one behind his daughter. He loaded bullets into his gun and climbed into the rafters to wait for the monkeys to come back.

The monkeys returned in a short time. The hunter watched to see what they would do. There was one monkey leader and a number of younger ones. They all knelt. The leader said, "Somehow I feel out of sorts today. There is a strange smell, too, isn't there? Ask Uncle Badger to come and make a divination." He sent one of the young monkeys off on the errand.

The man watched the badger come. Its divination was, "A fire will flash from above and strike your leader, and if the rest of you are slow, the young monkeys will have the same fate. There is danger, danger. I can't stay long. I must leave."

The monkey leader said, "Please wait a little. I want to ask you more."

But it was no use. The hunter shot the monkeys.

Yamaguchi Asatarō
Ikinoshima, Nagasaki

## 313. Dividing Things That Were Picked Up

Long ago a badger, a monkey, and an otter set out on a pilgrimage to Mt. Yahiko. Along the way they picked up a piece of straw matting, a measure of salt, and one shō of beans. They began to argue about how to divide the things.

The clever badger stood up and said that the monkey could take the straw matting up a tree on the mountain and sit on it and enjoy the view. The otter could take the salt to a pond where it looked as though there would be a lot of fish. He could pour the salt in and float the fish up to catch them. The badger would eat the beans.

The monkey gladly took the straw matting up high in a tree. He spread out the matting and sat on it to enjoy the view, but it slipped and he fell from the tree, hurting his legs. The otter took the salt and poured it into a pond, but when he dived in, the salt made his eyes smart. They got red and hurt.

The two of them went to the badger's house to complain. But the badger fastened the husks of the boiled beans into his fur and cried that he and his wife had broken out with boils. The monkey and the otter went away, saying, "We are all in the same fix."

Toyama Rekirō
Minamikanbara-gun, Niigata

## 314. Three Mon for the Heron, Eight Mon for the Pigeon

Long ago a pigeon, a snipe, and a heron picked up a purse as they walked along a road together. When they quarreled over how to divide the money, an ant offered to be judge.

The ant said, "Three [san] mon for the heron [sagi], eight [hachi] mon for the pigeon [hato], four [shi] mon for the snipe [shigi], and the rest for the ant [ari mōke] fee."

The ant went off with what was left over.

Toyama Rekirō
Minamikanbara-gun, Niigata

## 315. The Straw Mat and the Soy Beans

The fox at Obana has no tail,
She was fooled by the badger of Babata.

The fox from Obana-mura and the badger from Babata once discussed how to divide a piece of straw matting and beans they picked up on the road at Kosatori.

The badger said, "Now, Fox, you take this straw mat up above the cliff and spread it out and sit on it as you look for people who are passing. That way, you can steal what you want. I will save the beans and wait for you."

The badger fooled the fox in this way with his seeming generosity, and the fox went off happy. She spread out the straw mat as the badger had told her to do and waited for people to come by.

But as the fox sat there the wind began to blow and it was not comfortable sitting on the straw mat. That is why she realized for the first time it was a poor plan. She went back to the badger's cave indignantly.

When the badger saw the fox coming back, he suddenly had a good idea. He fastened the husks of the beans into his fur and began to groan. He said, "I have broken out with small pox and the pain is more than I can stand." He had every appearance of being sick.

The fox wondered what had happened as she looked on. Then the badger said, "If you don't eat, you are going to starve, so I will tell you a plan. Go to the rice paddy at Hebita-mura where the water is standing on a night when it is going to freeze. Put your tail into the paddy and fish will be sure to come and fasten onto it. You will have a good catch in a short time."

The greedy fox followed the badger's advice. She went to the paddy at Hebita and put her tail into it. She lost her tail because it got frozen into the ice.

Shimoniigawa-gun, Toyama

## 316. The Cat and the Rat

The cat and the rat planned to have a feast together. They prepared the food for it and stored it in a cupboard in the interior of a temple. They agreed that they would enjoy it together when things were right.

One day the cat said, "There is going to be a funeral at the temple today. I'll go to see how things are." He went to the temple and ate what was on the top of their good food. When he came back, the rat asked, "How was the funeral?" The cat said, "It was a funeral of a man named Uwaname [lick the top]."

As the cat started out the next day, he said, "I'm going to the temple to see a funeral." He ate the middle of their feast and came home. The rat asked, "Whose funeral was it today?"

The cat answered, "It was for a man named Nakaname [lick the center]." On the next day the cat set out again, saying he was going to a funeral. This time he ate what was on the bottom of their feast. And he told the rat the funeral was for a man called Sokoname [lick the bottom]."

After seven days had passed, the rat said, "Now let's go to the temple to eat the feast we fixed the other day." The cat agreed and they set out together. They went into the interior of the temple, but when they looked, they discovered their feast was all gone.

The rat realized at last what had happened. He complained, "You have been going to the temple for funerals for Uwaname, Nakaname, and Sokoname, but you were eating our feast, weren't you?"

"Yes, that's it," replied the cat. "Since I am such a bad cat, I'll do this." And he caught his friend the rat and ate him.

That is why these two animals feel as they do about each other even to this day.

Sasaki Kizen
Shiwa-gun, Iwate

## 317. The Fox and the Kingfisher

Long ago the fox and the kingfisher met and decided to enjoy a feast together. They planned to fool a fish peddler to get fish to eat. It happened that a fish peddler came along just then. The kingfisher perched on the branch of a tree where it looked as though it would be easy to be caught. The fish peddler set his load down and tried to catch the bird, but it hopped over to another branch beyond.

The fox took the fish the peddler left and ate them all. When the kingfisher came back, there wasn't a single fish left. This made the kingfisher angry and he decided to get even with that tricky fox.

The kingfisher said, "Let's fool the fish peddler again. You turn into a post this time, Fox." The fox turned into a post and the kingfisher perched on it. The same fish peddler came along.

He said, "Here you are again, kingfisher," and he took his shoulder pole and swung it at the kingfisher with all his might. The kingfisher flew up at that moment and the fox that had turned into a post nearly died from the blow. He cried as he ran off.

Noda Tayoko
Sannohe-gun, Aomori

## 318. Tail Fishing

The fox and the otter decided to invite each other to a feast. The otter invited the fox to begin with. He prepared all sorts of good things and waited in the evening. His guest arrived smiling to himself in anticipation. The otter said, "Now, please eat a lot."

The fox declared, "This is a fine feast." He looked into the dishes and found that each had an unusual fish, whether it was a flat fish in a jar or on a plate. The fox admired everything and ate with relish.

Presently it was the fox's turn to invite the otter. He ran around from early morning to the borders of rice paddies and to the bank of the stream, trying to catch fish, but he could not catch a single one. The otter arrived in the evening. He said, "Good evening." He looked inside and saw the fox staring upward motionlessly.

The fox would not reply to anything the otter said. There was nothing for the otter to do but to go home. In the morning the fox went hustling over to apologize. He said, "I am sorry about last night, but my turn came to be Sky Watcher. Please come tonight by all means." The fox tried his hardest that day to catch fish, but it was of no use. He went home crestfallen.

The otter came again in the evening and said, "Good evening." The fox sat motionless staring at the ground, and there was nothing for the otter to do that night but to go home. The fox went over again in the morning to the otter and said, "Last night it was my turn to be Earth Watcher."

The otter said, "You must be saying that because you can't catch any fish, aren't you?"

"Yes, to tell the truth, that's how it is," admitted the fox.

The otter said, "Then I'll tell you how to catch fish. You have such a fine big tail. Put it down into the stream on a cold night. Lots of fish will fasten onto it."

The fox went home happy. He waited for the sun to go down and then went to the stream. He broke the ice and let his tail down just as the otter had told him to do. When he pulled it up presently, the ice rattled and made a pleasant sound, but no fish were hanging onto it. The result was the same no matter how often he tried it.

Then he resolved to leave his tail in, but it gradually began to hurt all the way up to his head. He endured it until morning. Then he heard children crossing the ice. That was dangerous for the fox and he tried to pull up his tail, but it was frozen fast. He cried, "I don't want any carp! Just let me have little ones for now!"

He pulled desperately and his tail broke off.

Fumino Shirakoma [Iwakura Ichirō]
Minamikanbara-gun, Niigata

## 319. The Otter and the Monkey

Long ago the monkey's tail was 33 fathoms long. He was fooled by the bear and went to fish for little fish one winter night. He stuck his long tail down into the river and waited patiently through the night. The water froze. When the monkey could endure the cold no longer, he tried to pull his tail up. It broke off at its base and his tail became short.

Takagi Toshio
Matsue, Shimane

## 320. The Monkey, the Crab, and the Persimmon

One day the crab set out to go somewhere in the hills and he took a riceball with him. As he was strolling along, a monkey came up with a persimmon seed in his hand. They talked it over and decided to trade the riceball for the persimmon seed.

The monkey ate the riceball immediately but the crab took the persimmon seed and planted it in front of his house. The crab would say every day, "Sprout, sprout, or I'll cut you with my scissors." That is why the seed sprouted right away.

Then the crab said, "Grow, grow, or I'll cut you with my scissors." That is why it grew big right away

Then the crab said, "Bear fruit, bear fruit, or I'll cut you with my scissors." And fruit grew on the persimmon tree right away.

Then the crab said, "Ripen, ripen, or I'll cut you with my scissors." In a short time the fruit was ripe.

The crab brought a sack and was going to climb the tree with it to pick the fruit, but he couldn't manage to climb. The monkey happened along while the crab was worrying about what to do.

The monkey asked, "What are you doing? If you want persimmons picked, I'll do it for you." He climbed the tree with the crab's sack quickly and began to eat the fruit. He threw green, puckery ones down onto the crab's head. The crab used his wits and called up, "Here, monkey, I have a good idea."

The monkey asked, "What is it?"

The crab said, "Try filling the sack with persimmons and hang it onto a dead branch and swing it up and down. That will be fun."

The monkey tried it right away, but the dead branch broke and the sack of persimmons fell to the ground. The crab rushed up and carried it off with him into his hole.

The monkey came down the tree. He demanded, "Give me that. If you don't, I'll leave a pile of turds in your hole." He stuck his bottom toward the crab's hole. The crab reached out and pinched the monkey's bottom and would not let go. It hurt the monkey so much that he offered to give the crab some of the hair on his tail.

The ancestor of the yamadachi crab got that hair, and that is why there are hairs on the crab's claws. And the monkey grows no hair on its bottom and it is red because of that.

Yame-gun, Fukuoka

## 321. The Mochi Race

It was New Year's when the bullfrog and the monkey met in the mountains. They could hear the pleasant sounds of people pounding mochi in the valley below. They both were hungry and talked about how to steal some mochi.

The bullfrog went to the well in the yard of the shōya in the village and jumped in. There was such a big splash that the people at the house thought their master's little boy had stumbled and fallen into the well. They ran over to it to see. When they left their work, the monkey stole the mochi, just as it was in the mortar, and ran back to the mountain with it. By the time the bullfrog came to see, the monkey had carried it off.

The bullfrog proposed, "Let's divide it equally."

The crafty monkey said, "Instead of that, let's roll the mortar down from the hill and the one who gets to it first wins it."

The bullfrog thought he would surely lose, but he gave in to the monkey. With the shout of "one, two, three!", the two of them rolled the mortar away. The quick-footed monkey fairly flew after the mortar while the slow-footed bullfrog followed down.

As luck would have it, the mochi rolled out of the mortar on the way down. It caught on the branch of a cryptomeria tree. The grateful bullfrog fastened onto it eagerly. The monkey came back up the hill all out of breath, his eyes bloodshot. He found the bullfrog with the delicious looking mochi held firmly in his mouth. The monkey suggested, "I say, Master Bullfrog, let's start eating it from here!"

The bullfrog replied, "It's my mochi. I'll eat it the way I like."

Toyama Rekirō
Minamikanbara-gun, Niigata

## 322. The Monkey, the Crab, and the Mochi

The monkey said to the crab one day, "It's such nice weather today, let's gather some mochi rice and make some mochi." The monkey went toward the east and the crab went toward the west and they gleaned a lot of rice. They brought it back, but when they were ready to pound it, they had no pestle.

The monkey said to the crab, "Won't you please go next door to borrow a pestle." The crab went to borrow it and the two of them started to pound the mochi. When they were finished, the crab was sent to return the pestle to the neighbor. The monkey put all the mochi into a bag while he was gone and climbed a persimmon tree growing in back.

The monkey began to eat it by himself. When the crab got back, the monkey was not around. He went this way and that asking about the monkey and finally found him in the persimmon tree growing in back. He went below the tree and said, "Please give me a piece, please give me a piece."

The monkey said, "Come up. Come up." He wouldn't give him a single piece. Then the dead branch the monkey was sitting on broke and he fell. The crab grabbed the bag of mochi and ran with it into his hole. The monkey said, "Please give me a piece. Please give me a piece." The crab said, "Come in. Come in." He would not give him a single piece.

The monkey grew angry and sent a pile of turds onto the crab. Then the crab pinched the monkey's bottom. That is why the monkey's bottom is red.

Noguchi Takashi
Ogi-gun, Saga

## 323. The Rice Field the Monkey and the Pheasant Cultivated

*Mukashi zatto mukashi.*

Long ago a monkey and a pheasant cultivated a rice field together. Presently the time came to transplant rice shoots. The pheasant stopped in at the monkey's house and said, "Master Monkey, let's transplant rice shoots in the field we are cultivating together." He found the monkey in bed.

The sly monkey replied, "I am sick with a stomach ache and I cannot get up. Please go and transplant the rice by yourself even though it is hard to do."

So the pheasant went to transplant the rice alone. When it came time to weed the rice field, the pheasant went to ask the monkey to help. The monkey said, "I have beri-beri and can't go. Please go on alone." There was no help for it, so the pheasant went to do the weeding alone.

Then came autumn and the time to harvest. The pheasant went again to the monkey's house, but the monkey said, "My back aches. It will be difficult, but please harvest the rice yourself."

The pheasant resigned himself again and went into the rice field in the hills and cut the rice himself. The rice had to be divided, so he set out promptly to the monkey's house.

The monkey divided the rice—one sheaf for the pheasant, two for the monkey—and he carried the greater part home for himself. The pheasant was not satisfied. He cried, "*Keen, keen*, that's not enough!"

A chestnut came rolling along in the wind from the mountain. He asked the pheasant, "Why are you crying?" The pheasant told him all that had happened. The chestnut comforted him, saying, "I'll take revenge for you."

Then the crab came crawling up from the river behind them and said, "I'll help, too!" And he joined them. Then the mortar came out of the shed and joined them. Finally some dung came out of the dung pit and became a helper.

The monkey came with his face red with wine to make fun of the pheasant. It was a cold, frosty night and the monkey complained he was cold as he poked the faggots burning in the hearth. The chestnut burst open and hit the monkey's paw, burning it. The monkey cried, "It's hot," and ran to the sink. When he put his paw into the water jar, the crab pinched it.

"It hurts," cried the monkey as he tried to run out the back entrance. But as he ran through the workroom, he slipped on the dung that was waiting for him there. He fell sprawled out. The mortar came falling onto the monkey from the rafters and crushed him. Then the chestnut, the crab, the dung, and all gathered around and told the monkey never to do anything bad again.

*Sore kitte no tompi parari.*

Terada Denichirō
Hiraga-gun, Akita

## 324. The Rice Field the Rat and the Weasel Cultivated

The rat and the weasel met on the sandbar of a river. The weasel said, "Let's dig up the grass here and plant millet seed together." The rat agreed, "That's a good plan." They dug up the grass together and sowed millet. It grew fine there.

The weasel went to the rat's house and said, "Let's go to weed." The rat said, "I have caught cold. Won't you please go and tend to it yourself." The good-natured weasel weeded the millet.

Several days later the weasel went to the rat again and said, "I think it is time to cultivate the soil in our millet patch." The rat declined to go. She said, "I don't feel like it today." The weasel went alone again to weed, fertilize and cultivate the patch. She worked all day before going home.

Presently the millet ripened with tops as bushy as a fox's tail. The weasel was happy watching it gradually ripen each day into a bright yellow. Then one night the rat went secretly and cut the tops off all the millet. She made mochi from the millet and she and her children ate it all up.

Not knowing anything about that, the weasel went to look over the millet and found the tops were all cut off and the plants dried up. The kite came along toward evening. The weasel asked, "Do you know who cut the tops off the millet?" The kite said, "I don't know anything about it." The weasel asked the crow and the sparrow, but they said they did not know.

The disappointed weasel went to the rat's house to tell what had happened. The rat pretended not to know and said, "That's too bad, isn't it!"

The rat's children came up and said, "Mother, that millet mochi last night . . ." Their mother was flustered and yelled, "Hush, keep still!" But the little rats kept on saying it. Then the weasel understood. She said angrily, "Then you are the one who cut the tops off the millet." She started to pull out all the rat's teeth, but she was a good-hearted weasel and soon relented.

She said, "You would have a hard time eating after this, so I will leave you two teeth in front." That is why it happens that the rat has two front teeth.

Iwakura Ichirō
Minamikanbara-gun, Niigata

## 325. The Battle between the Monkey and the Crab
[The Crab Story]

*Mukashi atta do shya.*

The monkey said to the crab, "Let's go and glean rice to make mochi." The crab agreed. The two set out together to glean the grain.

They steamed the rice and got a mortar from somewhere. The monkey said, "Let's go to a high place to pound it."

The crab agreed and they climbed a mountain. The crab said, "Isn't this a good place?" But the monkey said, "A little farther."

After they had climbed a little more, the crab said, "Isn't this a good place?" But the monkey said again to go a little farther. At last they came to the top of the mountain. Then the monkey said, "Let's pound now." They pitched in, calling "ensa-do attaraya" as they worked.

When the mochi was finished, the monkey thought of a trick that would let him eat the mochi alone. He rolled the mortar over and rolled it down to a level place. He went chasing after it, but the crab followed slowly and cried, "I can't keep up." The mochi fell into a thicket on the way down.

"This settles it," thought the crab, and he began to eat the mochi. The monkey came back, looking all around. He said, "Didn't the mochi fall out?"

The crab said calmly, "A little fell out."

The monkey said, "Won't you please give me some?"

The crab said, "Eat what was left in the mortar when it rolled away."

"But there isn't any in the mortar. Please give me some of the mochi where dirt is stuck to it," begged the monkey.

But the crab said, "Even if there is dirt or ashes on the mochi, it tastes good if it is knocked off."

The monkey got red with anger. He declared, "I'm going to the hills now and I will gather 1000 monkeys. We will knock off all the shells of crabs." He set out and left the crab wailing and crying.

A horse chestnut came along and asked, "Why are you crying?" The crab said, "The monkey has gone into the hills to get 1000 monkeys and he says they are going to knock my shell off."

The horse chestnut comforted him and said, "Don't cry. I will take revenge for you." The bee came along then and after him came cow dung and a mortar and pestle. They all decided to take revenge for the crab.

They went together to the monkey's house. The mortar and pestle hid in the rafters, the cow dung hid in the corner of the workroom, the bee hid in the window, and the crab hid in the water bucket, and the horse chestnut hid in the hearth.

Then the monkey came in and straddled the hearth. He stirred up the fire and said, "It's cold. It's cold." At that, the horse chestnut jumped up and burned the monkey's balls. "It's hot! It's hot!" he cried and went to the kitchen to cool himself in the water bucket. The crab pinched him. "Oh, it hurts! It hurts!" cried the monkey. Then the bee darted out and stung him on the cheek.

The monkey foamed at the mouth as he started to run out of the house, but he slipped on the cow dung and fell onto his back. The mortar and the pestle then came falling and crushed he monkey.

*Dotto harai.*

Uchida Takeshi
Kazuno-gun, Akita

## 326. The Revenge of the Crab

Long ago there was an old man and an old woman in a certain place. The old man went to the hills to cut wood and the old woman went to the river to wash clothes. A little box came floating downstream. The old woman said:

Little box with something in, come this way.
Little box with nothing in, go that way.

The little box came floating to the old woman. She picked it up and looked in. There was a persimmon inside. She took it home and put it into the cupboard to wait for her old man to come home.

He came home in the evening with a load of wood on his back. When he said, "I'm home now," the old woman responded, "Welcome home. When I went to the river to do the wash today, I picked up something good. Let's cut it and eat it together."

She took the persimmon out of the cupboard to show her old man. Then she got the big knife out for him to cut the persimmon. A big persimmon seed was in it.

The old man was surprised. He said, "A big persimmon seed like this is unusual. We had better plant it." He planted it in the garden in front of their house.

Every morning the old man got up and went where he had planted the seed and said:

If you don't sprout, I'll dig you up.
If you don't sprout, I'll dig you up.

He would bring his Enshū hoe and set it beside the place. The seed did not want to be dug up by an Enshū hoe, so it sprouted in a little while. Then every morning the old man put fertilizer and water onto the sprout and said:

If you don't grow big, I'll cut you with my shears.
If you don't grow big, I'll cut you with my shears.

He brought his shears out and left them by the persimmon sprout. It could not bear to be cut with the shears, so it grew well. Then the old man said:

If you don't bear fruit, I'll cut you down.
If you don't bear fruit, I'll cut you down.

He brought his hand ax every morning and left it by the tree. The persimmon tree could not stand the thought of being cut by a hand ax, and lots and lots of persimmons formed on it, like little bells.

Presently autumn came and the fruit on the tree ripened red. A monkey would come and climb the tree to eat the fruit while the old man and old woman were away in the hills. A crab crawled out of a place like, we might say, the stone wall of the guard house by the sandbar in the river.

He looked up at the monkey in the top of the tree and said, "You come every day to eat persimmons, but I can't climb the tree. Please pick one for me." The monkey said, "Here's one," and he picked a green persimmon and threw it down. The crab picked it up and tried to eat it, but it was too puckery.

He said, "This puckery kind won't do. Give me a sweet one." The monkey picked another green one and aimed it at the crab below. It hit the crab squarely on its shell and broke it, killing the crab.

The crab's child came along and saw his dead father. He felt so bad he began to cry. A bee flew over and asked, "Why are you crying?"

The little crab said, "I feel bad because the monkey threw a persimmon at my father and killed him. That's why I am crying."

The bee said, "Let's take revenge for your father. I'll help you." Thus it was decided that the little crab would take revenge for his father. He and the bee made preparations and started out. When they had gone as far as it would be to the shrine in our village, they met a five-shō mortar. It looked at the two and asked, "Where are you going?"

They explained the reason and added, "We are setting out to take revenge for the father."

The five-shō mortar said, "That is sad. I'll go with you." He set out on revenge, too. After the three had gone a little farther, about as far as to the village over there, they met a little needle. The needle looked at the three of them and asked, "Where are all of you going?" They said, "We are setting out to take revenge for the father."

The needle said, "I will help you," and it joined them as they went on. Then the four of them went about as far as the meadow at our village and met cow dung. When the cow dung saw the four of them, he asked, "Where are all of you going?" When he heard the reason, he said, "Then I'll go with you." He went with them, too. They met a little chestnut. He asked the same thing and decided to go with the rest.

Now there were six of them who went together farther and farther into the mountains till they came to a place like it is around Kayano in Yokozawa, where the monkey's house was. The monkey's old grandmother was there.

They said, "Please let us stay here tonight." The old monkey said, "This place is too small, so I can't let you stay." They asked, "Where is Master Monkey?" The old monkey said, "The monkey at my house has gone to the hills to get firewood."

They said, "Then please let us stay until he comes back. We will come in and sleep anywhere." They all went inside and talked things over. The crab went below the kitchen sink, the bee went into the tub of miso, the five-shō mortar climbed into the rafters, the needle went into the bedding, the cow dung went in front of the door to the workroom, and the chestnut went into the jar for live coals by the hearth and hid.

Presently it was evening and the monkey came home with a load of firewood on his back. "Oh, it's cold," he said as he stood on all fours over the hearth. The chestnut in the live coal jar popped out and hit the monkey's balls. The monkey cried, "It's hot! It's hot! Something has jumped out of the hearth and hit my balls and burned them."

His grandmother said, "The only thing to do is to put miso on!"

The monkey hurried to the miso tub and stuck his paw into it. The bee came flying out and stung the monkey's paw. The monkey cried, "There's something in the miso tub and it has bit me!" His grandmother said, "Put some water on it from the water jar under the sink."

The monkey rushed to the jar of water under the sink, and the crab pinched his arms hard. The monkey cried, "There's something here biting my arms!"

The monkey's grandmother said, "There's nothing else to do, so get under the quilts." The monkey climbed into the bedding and the needle pricked him. The monkey came flying out of the comforters crying, "There's something pricking me in bed!"

The grandmother began to be a little impatient. She said, "Well, there's something here and something there, and it's a bother. Go out to the river and wash yourself." The monkey started out in a flurry, but he stepped on the cow dung at the entrance to the workroom and slipped and fell.

Then the five-shō mortar came crashing down and crushed the monkey, and it died.

*Sore mo sorakkiri.*

Dobashi Riki
Nishiyatsushiro-gun, Yamanashi

## 327. The Sparrow
[The Sparrow's Revenge]

*Nanno mukashi atta ge na.*

Long ago the sparrow hatched her young in the hole that was for the handle of the stonemill. While she was away from her nest, a demon came and said, "Show me the sparrow's young ones."

He sniffed and said, "These are delicious." He ate all five of them. When the sparrow returned, all her children were gone. She asked everyone what happened, and they told her the demon had eaten them all.

The sparrow made millet dango and corn dango to take with her as she set out to take revenge on the demon. She met a cow as she went along. It said, "Give me a dango and I will go with you." She gave her a millet dango.

As the sparrow went on farther, a bee said, "Give me a dango and I'll go with you." The sparrow gave her one and she came along. When she went farther, she met a chestnut and a mortar and she gave each a dango.

They all went together to Hell and found the demon asleep by his hearth. The chestnut crawled into the ashes in the hearth, the cow dropped dung at the entrance to the back door, and the mortar hung itself above the back door. The bee hid in the back door.

When the chestnut in the hearth jumped up, the demon woke up with a start. He tried to run through the back door, but he slipped on the cow dung and fell. Then the bee stung him and the mortar fell onto him. Their revenge was accomplished at last.

*Mōshi mukashi ketchiri kō.*

Isogai Isamu
Yamagata-gun, Hiroshima

## 328. Kachi-Kachi Yama

*Tonto mukasatta kedo.*

An old man and an old woman went to their garden patch to plant beans. As they planted, the old woman would sing:

If I plant one bean, grow a thousand.
If I plant two beans, grow two thousand.

A badger came down the hill and sat on a rock and mocked her, singing:

If you plant one bean, a warped one.
If you plant two beans, rotten ones.

After the old woman chased the badger off, the old couple continued to sing as they worked. But the badger came back and mocked them again.

The old woman chased him away, and then the old man and old woman went home for lunch. They talked about how to get rid of the badger. The old woman said, "How about making some thick paste like mochi, Grandpa? We can spread it over the rock the badger sits on."

The old man said, "Yes, that's a good idea." After they ate lunch, they took the mochi and smeared it on the rock. Then they went on singing and planting beans as before. The badger came and sat on the rock and started to mock their song. This time the old man went for him and caught him. He tied the badger's four legs and hung him from the beams at home. He said, "Tonight we'll have badger soup and cooked wheat for supper."

He went back to the hills and the old woman stayed at home to pound the wheat. While the old woman worked, she sang, "Badger soup and cooked wheat tonight."

The badger started to talk. He said, "Please loosen the rope a little." He was able then to pull himself out. He said, "I'll pound the wheat while you turn it with the dipper." The old woman turned the wheat, but the badger swung the pestle down from above her and killed her with one blow. The badger stripped off her clothes quickly and put them on. He tied on her apron and fastened a towel over his head to look like the old woman.

He was cooking like the real old woman when the old man came home from the hills. As the old man ate the soup, he said, "This badger soup is delicious."

The badger replied, "Of course it is. It's made from your old woman." Then he leaped out of the window above the sink and ran away.

While the old man was weeping there, the rabbit came and said, "I'll take revenge for you."

To begin with, the rabbit went into the mountains and had a race cutting grass with the badger. The rabbit didn't cut any. Only the badger cut grass. The rabbit said, "Let's go home now."

The badger exclaimed, "Why, you haven't cut a bit of grass!" The rabbit said, "My stomach aches too much. Please carry me on your back."

The badger said, "So, that's why!" He put the rabbit on his back and started out.

The rabbit set fire to the grass on the badger's back. It began to crackle, *kachi-kachi*.

The badger asked, "What are you doing, Rabbit?" He answered, "I'm not doing anything," When the fire started to blaze up, the rabbit jumped down and ran away quickly. The badger went home badly burned.

While the badger was wondering if there was any medicine for his burns, the rabbit came by, calling, "Burn medicine! Burn medicine!" The badger bought some and put it on, but it smarted badly. It was red pepper, so it was extra strong. Then the rabbit came along selling bean paste, and put some on the badger, but that hurt, too.

After the badger recovered, the rabbit made a boat. The badger came along and said, "Please make me one, too." The rabbit agreed and made him a clay boat. When the boat was finished, the rabbit suggested that the badger should catch fish. The clay boat crumbled to pieces.

With that the rabbit completed his revenge.

Suzuki Tōzō
Kitamurayama-gun, Yamagata

## 329. The Raw Monkey Relish

An old man went to dig in his rice field in a place like Shirage Pond at the head of a little valley. When the old man started to dig, a big old monkey came out and sat on a rock at the edge of the field to mock the old man.

He said, "Swing the hoe to the right, swing it to the left, and swing it behind and hit your seat!" That made the old man angry and he chased the monkey, but it climbed a tall tree in the mountain and the old man could not catch it. He gave up and went back to his field to dig. The monkey came back and sat on the rock and made fun of the old man again. The old man chased it, but it climbed a tree and the old man could not catch it.

When the old man went home for lunch, he made sticky mochi and spread it over the rock the monkey had been sitting on. Then he started to dig again. The monkey came out and sat on the rock and started to make fun of the old man again. This time, the old man went after him. The monkey was stuck to the rock and could not get away.

The old man caught him and wound rope around him, tying him up. He took the monkey home. He said, "Granny, I brought the monkey. Fix raw monkey relish tonight." Then he went back to the field to work again.

After the old man left, the old woman decided to pound some rice to cook. The monkey said, "Granny, if you loosen the ropes a little, I'll help you pound rice." The old woman felt sorry for him, anyway, and loosened the rope just a little.

"Loosen it a little more," said the monkey, and she loosened the rope a little more. Then the monkey's hands and feet were free. He took the pestle and killed the old woman in the mortar and made raw relish of her. The old man came home in the evening. The monkey served him raw relish made from the old woman.

The old man ate it hungrily and declared it was delicious. The monkey's old woman disguise had fooled the old man. He said, "You ate Granny raw relish. Look for her bones under the porch."

Then he ran off.

*Shimyaa.*

Noda Tarō
Tamana-gun, Kumamoto

## 330. The Rabbit's Wiles

Long ago a deer, a rabbit, and a toad met in the mountains. They decided to do something pleasant together and they started to pound mochi.

The deer was clever. While he was pounding, he sent the pestle, the mortar, and all rolling down the hill. The three of them agreed that the one who picked up the mochi first could have it. They started to run.

The rabbit and the deer chased the mortar, but the toad followed slowly after them. He found that the mochi had fallen out of the mortar and he started to eat it. The toad said they had already made an agreement and he would not give the others any.

Since the toad would not give the rabbit and the deer any mochi, they decided to go and cut thatching reeds together. The two of them set out. The deer and the rabbit each cut three bundles of thatch. As they started back, the rabbit said, "Three bundles are too heavy to carry."

The deer said, "If they are heavy, give me one bundle."

After they had gone a little farther, the rabbit said, "Two bundles of thatch are too heavy."

The deer offered to carry one more. Presently the rabbit said, "One bundle of thatch is too heavy." The deer said, again, that he would carry it. After they walked on a little, the rabbit stopped and said, "I am too tired."

The deer said, "Then get onto my back." He let the rabbit get onto his back.

After the rabbit got up onto the deer's back, he started a fire. He said, "The hiuchi bird [fire lighter bird] is lively today." When the fire was burning well, the rabbit jumped down and ran away. The deer was burned to death.

The rabbit wanted to cook the deer meat and he said to the deer's children, "Lend me a kettle if I am going to cook deer meat for you." They brought him a kettle. He said, "I'll call you when it is ready. In the meantime, dance the lion dance at the shrine."

He tricked them and no matter how long the children danced, he did not call them. When they went back to see, they found he had eaten all the meat himself. He only left a little pile of turds in the kettle.

The home folks came back and heard from the children what had happened. They looked around for the rabbit and found him hiding behind the mortar in the workroom. Their grandfather caught the rabbit when he tried to get away through the opening the cats used. The old man said, "Bring me the spit."

The children were excited and brought him a hook. He said, "That's not what I said. I want the spit." This time the children made a mistake and brought him the rice ladle. The grandfather declared, "You don't know anything, I'll go myself to get it, so hold onto the rabbit."

He left one child holding the rabbit and went to get the spit. While the old man was gone, the rabbit asked the child, "How big are your old man's balls?"

The child let go with one hand to show him and said, "This big." The rabbit said, "You can only show half of it with one hand. Show me with both hands."

The child let go with both hands and said, "This big."

The rabbit took that instant to get away. Just then the old man came back with the spit. He caught hold of the rabbit's tail. It broke off, and the rabbit's tail has been short ever since.

*Shyami-shyakkiri.*

Suzuki Tōzō
Yoshiki-gun, Gifu

# *17. Miscellaneous Stories between Folk Tales and Legends*

## 331. Prince Yuriwaka

Prince Yuriwaka was born from a peach and he was called Momotarō when he was little. When he was old enough to marry his parents tried to get him to accept various brides, but he always declined. He would say the girl's face was as long as a horse's face or her hair was as long as a snake or her nose was as flat as a rice ladle. He heard that the king's daughter was beautiful and he went to the palace to become the bath heater.

When he asked the king for his daughter, the king replied, "If you conquer Onigashima, the demon stronghold, I will give you the princess."

Then Momotarō changed his name to Yuriwaka. He took 70 boats with him and arrived at Onigashima, now called Ikinoshima. They anchored below a place now called Tōjigami at Kurosaki. Demons lived there in those days and it was called Keimongoku. The demon leaders were called Tarō, Jirō and other such names. When the demons saw Yuriwaka come, they threw lots of rocks at him. Those stones remain even now and are called Oni-no-tsubute [Demon Rocks].

Yuriwaka raised his fan with the rising sun painted on it and fanned up a wind so the rocks could not hit him. He subdued the demons completely. He decided to bring one little demon back to Japan as a gift, but before he noticed the little demon blew up a wind that scattered all the boats of Yuriwaka's men and he could not leave. He made the little demon catch things in the sea for him to eat to survive. All the food he ate was boiled in the little demon's navel.

One day a wind that blew from the land drove a sardine boat to where Yuriwaka was. He asked the men to give him a ride back to land but they mistook him for a demon and refused. He finally got them to take him home in spite of that. He blew his little demon up to the sky with the fan decorated with the rising sun and told him not to come back until parched beans sprouted.

Yuriwaka tied himself to a beam of the boat and was finally able to return to his land. Nobody recognized him when he arrived at the king's palace. But there was a chestnut colored horse at the palace that never let anyone except Yuriwaka ride him. When Yuriwaka mounted him that unruly horse became remarkably gentle. Yuriwaka had him stand on his legs on a checker board. Everyone then recognized that he was Yuriwaka. He received the princess and became heir to the throne.

Origuchi Shinobu
Nagasaki

## 332. A Gift of Thanks from a Woman with a Newborn Babe

When a young man was passing a graveyard long ago, a woman with a newborn baby came out and asked him to hold it. It was very heavy when he held it. The baby was facing away from him. He had heard that if a child's bottom was not turned toward the ground something bad would happen to it, so he held it as it was for a while. The woman returned presently and told the young man she would grant him what he hoped for. He asked for strength.

When the young man was walking in the hills one day, a little snake came out and licked his big toe. The snake grew bigger and bigger until it finally took his big toe into its mouth. The man decided to step on the snake. He put his strength into pulling the snake back and finally killed it. The young man decided to find out how much strength the snake had when he reached home.

He put a rope around his toe and asked 30 men to pull on it, but they could not move it. He increased the number to 40 and then to 50, but still it did not move. When 75 men pulled on the rope there was the same pull as the snake had. That meant the young man had the strength of 75 men.

This power of his did not pass on to the sons in his family, but it was inherited by the daughters. When his daughter was 11 years old, two men were in the bath together outside when a shower came up. The girl picked up the tub with the men in it and carried it into the house.

Her father was angry when he saw that. He scolded his daughter. She sat on the porch while he was talking. She pulled a five-inch nail out of the board in the floor and began jabbing it into the wood until the floor was covered with nail holes.

Seki Keigo
Nagasaki

## 333. The Human Sacrifice at Nagara Bridge

Once four or five women were looking on while men wanted to build a bridge in the center of a village. One of them suggested that they take a woman with a knot in the tie on her hair and stuff her into the stones below the bridge as a human support. When they looked the women over they found that the one who had made the suggestion had a knot where her hair was tied. She was taken and placed under the stones.

The woman's daughter grew up and went to another island as a bride. Ten days and then twelve passed without her saying anything. Her husband said he did not want to keep a bride who wouldn't talk. He decided to take her home to her father. As they went along, they heard a pheasant cry. Then the girl sang:

The pheasant is killed because it cries.
My mother was sacrificed at Nagara because she spoke.

The husband understood for the first time why his wife had kept silent, and he took her back to his house.

Iwakura Ichirō
Kikaijima, Kagoshima

## 334. The Mandarin Ducks

There is a sad story that lingers about Shiraki Bridge in Harukimura.

Long ago when Tōdō, the lord of the castle at Tsu, crossed that bridge, a pair of mandarin ducks had alighted and were swimming. The lord drew his arrow and shot one of them for diversion on his journey. A beautiful girl appeared in his dream later and accused him of shooting her husband.

When the lord passed the bridge the next year he shot four or five ducks in the same way. He picked them up without anything in mind, but when he looked at them he noticed that the head of the duck he had shot the year before was there. He concluded that it was the girl who had appeared in his dream the year before and had accused him of killing her husband.

As might be expected, the lord felt sorry. He built Oshidoridera [Mandarin Duck Temple] at Shitayumi mountain to console the spirits of the pair of ducks. The bow of plain wood with which he had shot the pair of mandarin ducks was kept at the temple for a long time.

The temple later fell into decay, but the Shiraki Bridge remains.

Nishikasugai-gun, Aichi

## 335. The Silkworm God and the Horse

The feudal lord in a certain land had a beautiful only daughter. A war broke out one year and the feudal lord led a number of his men off to fight. However, no word came from them, no news at all, and his daughter and her mother were left behind, hoping each day for his success. Even though the girl was the daughter of the feudal lord, she had to feed the horse in the barn because it was war time.

Her father had taken horses with him, but there was one good one in the barn that her father had loved for a long time. The girl was worried about her father when she would go to feed it every day. One day she said half seriously as she fed the horse, "I don't know whether my father is dead or alive, but please go to the battlefield to see. If he is alive, bring him home on your back. If you do so, I will gladly submit to you."

The horse seemed to shake his head gladly and let out a shrill neigh. It started to stamp around as though eager to go outside. The girl noticed that and opened the barn. The horse leaped out briskly and ran off.

The girl wondered if it could be true when a week later the horse returned with her father on its back. She told the horse that he had done well and gave him a great feast. The family invited many friends to celebrate the occasion with a drinking party, but the horse did not seem to care for anything they gave him to eat. He only stamped around in the barn, shaking himself and refusing to be tied. Nobody could do anything with him.

This reminded the girl of things. She told of her promise to the horse and said there was a reason for it to be acting up. She explained it all to her mother and father and said she would go to see about it. The girl went to the barn to appease the horse with grass, but he watched his chance and fastened onto the hem of her dress and pulled her inside.

Then a great uproar broke out. The father rushed in and grew furious when he saw what had happened. He declared, "We are not fools enough to be classed with an animal." He thrust his lance through the horse and killed it. The horse was flayed and its hide was hung in the yard to dry. The flesh of the horse was served to the guests as the drinking party continued.

A week later the horse hide was still being dried in the yard. The sky, which had been clear, suddenly clouded over. Black clouds gathered and there was an evening downpour. A great wind blew, lightning flashed, thunder crashed, and all grew dark. It was all so terrifying that the people at the house wondered what was happening. They went out onto the porch to see.

The horse hide that been hanging in the yard flew up like a big bird. It came down while everyone was exclaiming in confusion. Before their very eyes, it wrapped itself around the daughter who was standing there and carried her up to the sky. It flew away with her. The weather cleared in the meantime.

The people wanted to somehow rescue the girl and there was

great ado, but they could not reach the sky from the earth below. The horse hide fell from the sky onto the mulberry patch near the feudal lord's palace a week later, and he went to look at it. His daughter was not in the horse hide, but there were many slender black silkworms eating mulberry leaves. The father concluded they were his transformed daughter and brought them home. He gave them tender mulberry leaves and took good care of them.

They gradually grew bigger and turned into white worms and formed pure white cocoons. These were boiled and lots of silk was taken from them. That is why there is the mark of a horse's hoof on the back of the silkworm even today.

Dobashi Riki
Nishiyatsuhiro-gun, Yamanashi

## 336. Failing to Eat the Mermaid

Long ago brothers invited neighbors to worship Nijūsanya Sama at their house. A beggar dressed in rags and carrying a torn bag on his back came there while they were celebrating. He said, "Well, well, are you all worshipping Kami Sama?" He sat on the porch, dangling his feet, and asked, "May I please worship with you?"

The host said, "Please join us." Two of the guests objected. They said, "It is not right to let this beggar worship with us."

The host replied, "No, a beggar is a man as we are. Please worship without saying such things." The guests could not say anything more, and the beggar was happy.

He washed his hands and feet and came in through the front door. He greeted everyone as he said, "Please let me join your worship." At last the moon rose. The host lifted down the wine and dango that had been offered to the kami and passed them around. After their worship had been concluded like this, the beggar spoke up and said to the host, "My house is in a certain place. I have been wanting to worship Nijūsanya myself once. I will use helpers at that time, so please come." Then he left.

When the time came the guests gathered. Two men from the village came with the former host and they were led to a high place on the mountain. They were surprised to find a house in such a place, but they were led to a splendid house there. It was built with clear paper doors throughout.

The former beggar came to greet the three as they entered. He said, "Please pass the time with some tea. I must go downstairs to tend to the cooking." He went to the kitchen. Two of the men said, "That beggar says he is going to do cooking, but we will see what is going on." They opened a little hole in the paper door to watch the kitchen.

It was a terrible sight. The beggar had an infant out on the chopping board and blood was flowing everywhere as he cooked. They were frightened. They said they had to piss and they ran off, leaving their leader behind. They ran so frantically that they missed their footing at the gate. They hit their heads on a stone and were killed.

What the beggar was cooking was actually a mermaid, a famous fish which ordinary men could not eat. He cooked it and served it himself. He was Nijūsanya-no-kami. The guest ate his fill of the feast. He was ready to start home after the moon rose.

The beggar brought out a sword and handed it to him. He said, "When you leave, there will be two men who have fallen dead at the gate, but do not look back. As you go ahead three shichi will be standing in a row. ["Shichi" is a kind of ghost like Ōenbashira that joins the earth and sky. It is said to be the soul of one who has met a violent death.] Turn windward and cut down the shichi in the center with this sword."

The man went out of the house and saw the two dead men fallen at the gate, but he did not look back. He went on and came to the black, the white and the yellow shichi standing there. The yellow one was in the center. The man turned windward and swung the sword and slashed at it. At the same moment, a shower of gold came falling and nearly covered the man.

He took the money home with him and became a wealthy man.

Iwakura Ichirō
Kikaijima, Kagoshima

## 337. The Day on Which Blood Flowed from the Eyes of the Stone Image

*Mukashi mukashi zatto mukashi.*

Long ago an old man heard about a jar of gold somewhere. He was asked by a grass-cutter one day, "What are you doing?"

The old man said, "There is a jar of gold somewhere around here and I am looking for it."

The grass-cutter asked, "Where are you looking for it?"

The old man said, "It's somewhere where no dew has fallen."

The grass-cutter was glad to hear that. He said, "I'll get up early tomorrow to look for it."

The old man thought, "This is going to be fun. I'll fool him." He set up a long pole in the night with a sedge hat on it so no dew would fall under it. He removed it early the next morning and pretended not to know anything about it.

The grass-cutter did not know what had happened, and he looked all over for a place where there was no dew. Then he came to that place. He was happy and began to dig.

The old man looked on and laughed. He said, "That man is a fool. I fixed that place up so no dew would fall on it last night. There he is, digging seriously."

The grass-cutter was unaware of the joke and dug away. Then he really found a jar of gold there. His family became very prosperous. That is why there are true things to be found in spite of lies.

Natori-gun, Miyagi

## 338. Fish That Talk

Long ago when Lord Tamura pursued the men far to the north, the region was still peaceful and there was a priest there. One day the priest decided to go into the mountains in the center of the Nanbu territory. He climbed up, following the Ai river at the border of Rikuchū, and came to a waterfall about ten feet high. A broad pool about as broad as 100 mats was at its base. The place is now called Masabō Falls.

The priest saw two big eels sporting around in the pool. He caught them and started to put them into a bag, but one of the eels got away. The priest started to leave with only one eel. A voice called from the pool, "Oh, Masabō, Masabō! When will you come back?"

The eel in the bag called back, "Masabō will come back, all right!"

The astonished priest took the eel out of the bag and set it free. The falls have been called Masabō Falls since that time.

Tome-gun, Miyagi

## 339. How the Little Snake Grew

One day when Nue went into the mountain he decided to spend the night there. He gathered dry wood and started a good fire, laid his gun down for a pillow and went to sleep. He woke up suddenly in the night. He looked around and saw a little snake crawling toward him. Nue picked it up and tossed it away, but it came right back. It was a little bigger than it was at first.

Nue picked it up again and threw it away, but it came back immediately. By that time the snake had become much larger than before. After this went on five or six times, the snake was so big Nue could not pick it up and throw it. He felt uneasy about that and decided to get up and stamp on the snake, but he couldn't crush it. On the contrary, it seemed to grow bigger each time he stamped on it.

It finally grew to be a monster more than six feet long. This was terrible and Nue was worried. He picked up his gun and shot the snake, but the bullet only glanced off and did not go through it. Nue was really frightened for the first time. He started to run home, but he missed his way and found himself running farther into the mountains.

There was nothing left to do but to follow a little stream down. The mountains finally seemed to close in. Nue tried to cross the stream, but the current was so swift that he could not walk in it. He wondered what to do as he forced himself along its bank. Luckily, he saw a big tree that had fallen across the stream and he crossed over on it. A white horse was standing there and seemed to be waiting for him. Nue mounted it and was able to reach home.

When he dismounted at his gate, the horse ran back immediately in the direction from which it had come. Nue was so humiliated over being frightened off by the monster snake that he went into the mountain again and again to shoot it, but he never could find a mountain that looked the same, nor could he find the river or the horse that had rescued him.

Sasaki Kizen
Kamihei-gun, Iwate

## 340. What Happens if a Shark's Bones Are Kicked

An official named Iwai Tomonoshin of the protectorate of Matsudaira under the Hamada shogunate was famed all over the land as a marksman. One year he crossed the sea to take his turn in attendance at the shogun's court.

A large shark appeared ahead of the boat struggling in the current of the Japan Sea. Tomonoshin promptly took an arrow and shot the shark from the bow he had at hand and he killed it.

When he landed at Osaka, he heard that an archery meet was to be held at Sanjūsangendō. This was a sport he liked and he joined the archers. He hit the target splendidly and Iwai Tomonoshin of the Iwashū Hamada clan became famous throughout the world.

When he returned to his inn, he was surprised to see shark's bones leaning against the railing. The innkeeper said he had bought them a few days before. Iwai recalled what had happened at sea and how the shark had annoyed everyone. He kicked the bones angrily. At that, the jaws of the shark snapped onto Tomonoshin's foot and bit him deeply. It did not seem to hurt much at first, but his foot swelled day by day, and the poison spread until it killed Tomonoshin.

That a shark's curse must be avoided is a proverb among villagers even now. A memorial is set up for Iwai Tomonoshin at Hachiman Shrine in Kiruko-machi today.

Chiyoen Shōju
Shimane

## 341. The Shadow Swallowed by a Shark

Once upon a time a samurai set out to a distant place on a boat. A fair wind filled the sails and the boat sped out to sea. Suddenly it stopped. The captain said, "A shark has surely swallowed the shadow of someone on board. Let everyone throw his towel into the sea. The towel that belongs to the person whose shadow has been swallowed will sink."

All the towels floated except the one belonging to the samurai. It sank. Everyone said, "Please jump into the sea and let the shark swallow you." There was no help for him, so the samurai agreed. He went to the prow of the boat and saw the big shark waiting there for him with its mouth open. The samurai aimed an arrow at the head of the shark.

It was strange how the shark let out a sound that nearly overturned the boat and fled. The boat then went ahead smoothly. Everyone disembarked when the boat reached port. Some time later, the samurai returned to that port on his way home. A great crowd was gathered around a shark that had been washed up onto the beach.

The samurai went over to look at it, too. He said, "This is surely the shark I shot with my arrow recently. Look, the arrow still stands on its head."

The samurai stuck his head into the shark's mouth to have a look. The pole that was propping its mouth open came loose for some reason and the shark's mouth snapped shut on the samurai's head, killing him. That shows that a shark will surely eat a man if it swallows his shadow.

Gotō Sadao
Kitaamabe-gun, Ōita

## 342. The Fish-Stone of Nagasaki

A man came to buy something called a spider's jewel. There are no spiders in good houses, but they can be found overhead in dirty houses. There was a dilapidated house far back in the hills, full of spider webs from the walls to the ceiling.

The man asked the owner of the house to sell it to him. The owner asked, "How can I sell a dirty house like this?" The buyer urged him to sell it and even offered 1000 ryō for it. The old man thought he was joking at first, but he agreed.

The buyer left, saying that he would bring the money the next day. The old man's spirit of greed was aroused. He thought that if the man would buy the house for 1000 ryō, there must be something special about it. He hired somebody to sweep it out thoroughly. When the buyer came the next day, the old man said, "I can't sell this house for only 1000 ryō."

The buyer had brought a big net to cover the house so that not a single spider could get away. He planned to give an extra 100 ryō because the owner was old, and he had 1100 ryō with him. But when he looked inside, the house had been swept clean and not a single spider was there. He left, saying, "At this rate, I would not take the house even if you gave it to me."

The old man lost the 1100 ryō because he was greedy.

Iwakura Ichirō
Kikaijima, Kagoshima

# 18. *The Fascination of Folk Tales*

## 343. Stories without an End

A man saw a snake on his way home from Haguro Shrine. He chased it, *shii*, and the snake glided, *zorot*. The man chase it, *shii*, and the snake glided, *zorot* . . . *shii* . . . *zorot* . . . *shii* . . . *zorot*, etc.

Seino Hisao
Higashimurayama-gun, Yamagata

## 344. Nonsense Stories

Stories with tricky words.

Long ago a certain man pointed his katana [sword] and put a little wheel on its tip. He went along rattling it. Somebody asked him what sword it was. He said it was a **mukashi** [old] **sword,** or **mukashi katana** ["old sword" or "don't tell a story"]. That is why the story must stop.

Sasaki Kizen
Kazuno-gun, Akita

### 345. The Story is Stripped Off

The story is stripped off, the chōja is bald.
The story is stripped off, the year has passed.
The story is stripped off, the mortar rests.

Nagasaki

### 346. A Story Like a Sanbasō

Well, there was an old man and an old woman. The old man went to the hills to cut wood. The old woman went to the river to do her washing. A kappa came out of the river and called, "Granny, give me a pull on your bottom!"

The old woman misunderstood his demand. She said, "I'm in the river and can't give you fire. It would go out in the river. Don't be silly." She got mad and went home.

She said to her old man, "The kappa in the river told me to give him fire, but I scolded him soundly." Her old man said, "If the kappa said that to you, I'll give him fire."

He lighted a piece of kindling wood and took it upstream. The old woman went downstream and called, "I'll give you fire, Kappa!" The kappa came out all dressed up with a hat on and called, "Really! Really!"

"I'll give you fire, Kappa!"

"Really! Really!"

Noguchi Tadayoshi
Hōtaku-gun, Kumamoto

### 347. Daytime Stories

If stories are told in the daytime, the rats will laugh.

Esashi-gun, Iwate

# Appended Material

# Notes to the Stories

1. "Momonokotarō," Shiwa-gun mukashibanashi 28. Narrated by Fujita Tamezō in Shiwa-gun, Iwate.
2. "Konbitarō," Mukashibanashi Kenkyū II 3 41. Narrated by Hirano Chūnosuke, aged 57, at Shinden Saraki-mura, Waga-gun, Iwate on August 10, 1935.
3. "Kibi," Nihon densetsu shū 268. Reported by Mizuo Hyōzō.
4. "Mukashibanashi no omoide," Mukashibanashi kenkyū II 2 8. Fujiwara recalled how his grandmother told the tale at Obonai, Senhoku-gun, Akita.
5. "Takenoko Dōji," Mukashibanashi kenkyū I 8 37. Recited by a maid, aged 26, Yamamoto Iseno, at a tile maker's in Hitoyoshi-mura, Tamana-gun, Kumamoto, on the evening of February 9, 1935.
6. "Kosodate yūrei," Shimabara hantō minwa shū 76. This is the outline of a story told by Seki's niece.
7. "Washi no sodatego," Shimabara hantō minwa shū 170. Recited by Tanaka Chōzō at Ohama-chō, Minamitakaku-gun, Nagasaki.
8. "Mamesuke no hanashi," Sado mukashibanashi shū 211. Collected by Amazawa Tairaka (pen name of Suzuki Tōzō).
9. "Kami sama no mōshigo," Shima I 5 72.
10. "Shidoko," Mukashibanashi kenkyū II 8 41. Recited by Nakamura Kiku, a 71-year-old woman, at Hisomi-mura, Kamoto-gun, Kumamoto on March 23, 1931.
11. "Tanishi Chōja," Tekkiri ane sama 112. Recited by Kimura Misao.
12. "Kaeru no muko," Shimabara hantō minwa shū 148. Recited by Shimogishi Masayoshi in Sugotani-mura, Minamitakaku-gun, Nagasaki.
13. "Tanishi musuko," Minzoku bunka II 7 8. Told at Hikimi Elementary School, Hikimi-mura, Mino-gun, Shimane.
14. "Kabuyaki Jinshirō," Mukashibanashi kenkyū II 2 31. This story was taken from Okunan shinpō, April 4, 1931.
15. "Yome no kago ni koushi," Kikaijima mukashibanashi shū 52. Told by Harumoto Ichikake of Kikaijima at Osaka in the summer of 1933.
16. "Shiratakihime," Kamuhara Yatan 152.
17. "Nazo no uta," Zoku Kai mukashibanashi shū 197. Told by Kobayashi Kōshirō on December 1, 1932.
18. "Tanabata San no hanashi," Mukashibanashi kenkyū II 12 38. Shishijima, Mitoyo-gun, Kagawa.
19. "Esugata nyōbō," Mukashibanashi kenkyū II 46, Gosen-mura, Nakakanbara-gun, Niigata.
20. "Tsuru no hōon," Kitaazumi-gun Kyōdo shikō, 2, Kōhi densetsu hen 155. Reported by Nakamura Koman in Miaso-mura, Kitaazumi-gun, Nagano.
21. "Kamo nyōbō," Mukashibanashi kenkyū I 1 13. Heard from a 72-year old man at Mikuni-machi, Sakai-gun, Fukui.

22. "Yamura no Yasuke," from "Nakafusayama oni taiji," **Minamiazumi-gun shi** 927.
23. "Konodori," **Ugo kakunodate chihō** ni **okeru chōchū sōmoku no minzokugakuteki shiryō** 44.
24. "Kikimimi sue," **Kōshō bungaku** 10 25. The first part, including the note, was told by Fumino Tsugi, a 75-year old woman on June 4, 1935; the last part was supplied by a lady named Fujiwara and by Maeda Kiyoshi on March 3.
25. "Hamaguri no uchi," **Minzokugaku** I 2 50.
26. "Uo nyōbō," **Kikimimi sōshi** 361. Reported by Mr. Tanaka.
27. "Ryūjin to hanauri," **Mukashibanashi kenkyū** I 5 40.
28. "Haha no medama," **Kikimimi sōshi** 182. This is a tale which Kikuchi Kazuo heard from his mother and reported in the winter of 1928 near Kouchi-aza, Yanagawa-mura, Esashi-gun, Iwate.
29. "Kaeru nyōbō," **Mukashibanashi kenkyū** II 7 29. Collected by Tazawa Tomee in Karikawa, Tachikawa-chō, Higashitagawa-gun, Yamagata.
30. "Hyōtan sen bon to hari sen bon no hanashi," **Dai-ni mukashibanashi gō** 17.
31. "Hachinohe chihō no mukashibanashi, Keshi no tane," **Mukashibanashi kenkyū** II 3 25. Reported by Kikuchi Hisao as told by his little girl, who heard it from friends.
32. "Hyōtan to kappa," **Shimabara hantō minwa shū** 41.
33. "Saru no mukoiri," **Mukashibanashi kenkyū** II 4 40.
34. "Komebukuro, Awabukuro," No. 2, **Tsugaru mugashiko shū** 73.
36. "Musume to tanishi," **Mukashibanashi kenkyū** I 12 34. Recited by a 55-year-old woman in Kitasaku-gun, Nagano.
37. "Babakkawa," **Kamuhara yatan** 117.
38. "Shika musume no kogae," **Rōō yatan** 152. A story told by Shōji at Furuyashiki.
39. "Furotaki Sanpachi," (Old) **Ikinoshima mukashibanashi shū** 94. Told by Uchiyama Hisayuki, a woman in Mushimizu-chō, Ikigun, Nagasaki.
40. "Mamako to honko," **Mukashibanashi** 51.
41. "Sokonashi bukuro," **Mukashibanashi kenkyū** I 5 33. Recited to Noda by his wet nurse in Yamato-gun, Fukuoka.
42. "Orinko, Korinko," **Mukashibanashi kenkyū** II 8 30. Recited by Terada's moher.
43. "Himasari gawa," **Chiisagata-gun mintan shū** 225. Told by the father of Koyama.
44. "Yokoana," **Shima** I 5 75.
45. "Senbakaya no hanashi," **Tōō ibun** 145.
46. "Utsubogusa no hana," **Yamato no densetsu** 298. Told by Takada Hisako in Tsukigase-mura, Soekami-gun, Nara.
47. **Shizuoka-ken densetsu mukashibanashi shū** 408 (no title). Reported by Arayama Tsuru from Shironishi-mura, Suchi-gun, Shizuoka.
48. "Uguisu ni natta Osono," **Tabi to densetsu** IX 5 75. Translator's note: In some versions a bamboo sprouts from the grave of the murdered girl and it is made into a flute. When it is blown, it sounds the voice of the child telling how she was killed.
49. "Kin no hasami ni kin no tebako," **Shimosuke Motegi mukashibanashi shū** 41.

50. "Teboko Oharuko," **Mukashibanashi kenkyū** I 8 40 [no title]. Dictated by Odajima Sada, a 63-year-old woman, at Kōgen, Yazawa-machi, Hienuki-gun, Iwate, on July 6, 1935. The original was clearly a **katarimono**.
51. "Akafuchi no shu," **Dai-ni gō** 27. Told by Satō Masashirō as heard from his father at Kawara-machi, Senhoku-gun, on May 13, 1933.
52. "Sannin kyōdai," **Kyōdo no denshō** 2 125. Reported by Sugawara Keikai at Motoyoshi Iridani School.
53. "Ane to otōto," first story: **Koshikijima mukashibanashi shū** 56; second story 57. Recited by Soki Shugeta, 66 years old, at Tenichiroku Shimokoshiki-mura, April 24, 1937.
54. "Wakagi no hōgi," **Shiwa-gun mukashibanashi shū** 16.
55. "Nusubito wanko," **Dai-ichi gō** 36.
56. "Mameko banashi," No. 3, **Kikimimi sōshi** 231. Reported by Murata Kōnosuke, written by Ono Ken, a second year student at Kurosawajiri Middle School.
57. "Yūgao Chōja," **Shiwa-gun mukashibanashi** 58.
58. "Shōjiki na ojii san," **Kii Arita-gun dōwa shū** 11 omote. Reported by Nakata.
59. "Obasaru, obasaru," **Tsugaru mugashiko shū** 67.
60. "Kanebukuro to hebi," **Zoku Kai mukashibanashi shū** 354. Told by Hashida Yoshisaburō, aged 66, on February 21, 1931. He was a carpenter when he was young.
61. "Kogane no tsubo," **Kamihei-gun mukashibanashi shū** 33. Reported by Sasaki Midoriko at Tōno-machi in 1921.
62. "Jiji to kogane no tsubo," **Rōō yatan** 307.
63. "Kane ga hebi ni naru hanashi," **Tekkiri ane sama** 255.
64. "Takara no okibun," **Inpaku mintan** I 2 74. Reported from Seikimura, Iwami-gun, Tottori.
65. "Zeni to kaeru," **Kai mukashibanashi shū** 173.
66. "Yume to yume," **Zoku Hida saihō nisshi** 134. Reported by a priest who heard it from his mother.
67. "Yumemi chōja," **Koshikijima mukashibanashi shū** 12. Told by Ishiwara Jirō, aged 78, on April 11, 1937.
68. "Sado no shiroi tsubaki," **Minamikanbara-gun mukashibanashi shū** 94, taken from Fumino Shirakoma (pen name of Iwakura Ichirō), **Kamuhara yatan** 1.
69. "Warashibe Chōja," **Akinokuni mukashibanashi shū** 110. Reported by Iwata Tadao of Kure City. He heard it from his grandfather.
70. "Gokudōsha no hanashi," **Awa-no-Iyayama mukashibanashi shū** 10. Told by Nishimura Kuni, an old woman, at Nishiiyayama, Mima-gun. Translator's note: Yanagita offers a second form under this type which will be omitted. Refer to Iwakura Ichirō, "Dobutsu enjō, nandai muko," No. 7, **Koshiki-jima mukashibanashi shū** 27. Reported by Hirasaki Hikotarō, aged 77, on April 17, 1937, at Shimokoshiki-mura, Satsuma-gun, Kagoshima.
71. "Danburi Chōja," **Nihon mukashibanashi shū**, jō 93. This is based upon **Kazuno shi** 51, Akita (1877).
72. "Sumiyaki Chōja," **Kikimimi sōshi** 27. This story is found around Kurosakijiri-machi, Waga-gun, Iwate. It is part of a story Sasaki's wife knew.

73. "Kamoe Kannon," **Tsuchi no iro** XIII 1 1.
74. "Shogatsu San no okori," **Mukashibanashi kenkyū** II 9 37. Told by Nishimura Mokuzō, aged 76, a farmer at Takayama Onsen-machi, Mikata-gun, Hyōgo on January 2, 1937. He said he heard it from Tamura Hidekura, who was from Hatta-mura.
75. "Ōmisoka no kyaku," **Dai-ichi gō** 60.
76. "Kasa Chōja," **Iwaki mukashibanashi shū** 32. Recited by Hoshi Sue, aged 76, at Nishiki-machi.
77. "Kōbō bata," **Mukashibanashi kenkyū** II 6 47. Reported by Kikuchi Hisao.
78. "Takara tenugui," (Old) **Ikinoshima mukashibanashi shū** 116 The place where the tale was collected and the narrator's name were omitted from the record.
79. "Kodomo ni natta ojii san no hanashi," **Dai-ni gō** 32. Sakagawa-mura, Haga-gun, Tochigi.
80. "Kogane no chōna," **Kikimimi sōshi** 70. A story by Nozaki Kimiko near Iwaizumi-machi, Shimohei-gun, Iwate, collected on June 23, 1930.
81. "Hanatare kozō," **Tabi to densetsu** II 7 20.
82. "Mafuku chōja to aohebi," **Aichi-ken densetsu shū** 252.
83. "Shimoina-gun Yamato-mura mukashibanashi," Fukihara No. 3 49.
84. "Ryūjin no denju," **Kikimimi sōshi** 463. Recited by Ōhora Kenshō on January 20, 1923 in the village.
85. "Kome-kura, ko-mekura," **Dai-ichi gō** 77. A tale Hamada heard as a child in Matsukuma-mura, Yatsushiro-gun, Kumamoto.
86. "Kaichū no ishiusu," **Awa-no-Iyayama mukashibanashi shū** 87. Told by Nakao Kōzō in Higashiiyayama-mura, Mima-gun, Tokushima, in the autumn of 1941.
87. "Mamechokotarō," In "Aizu mintan to hōgen," **Hōgen** IV 105.
88. "Sannin kyōdai no nara nashi mogi," **Dai-ni gō** 30. From the Hanamaki area in Hienuki-gun, Iwate.
89. "Fukube Chōja," **Kamihei-gun mukashibanashi shū** 26. Suzuki Shigeo reported that this story is found around Isawa-mura, Kamihei-gun, Iwate.
90. "Uta no yurai," **Mukashibanashi kenkyū, Geibi sōsho** 119. Reported by Hashimoto Chiyoko, a girl in the second year of high school in Toyomatsu-mura, Shinseki-gun, Hiroshima.
91. "Oni o warawasu," **Dai-ichi gō** 52. This is a story told at the market on the 1st day of the month at Meisei-mura, Minami azumi-gun, Nagano.
92. "Ane no hakarai," **Kikimimi sōshi** 94.
93. "Futari kyōdai," **Kikaijima mukashibanashi shū** 70. Told by Tomi Mitei.
94. "Nanatsu no kama," **Kai mukashibanashi shū** 91.
95. "Sutego to oni," **Zoku Kai mukashibanashi shū** 155. Told by Kawano Tsume, an old woman, on the 28th. (Are the 1000-ri boots from a foreign country? There is exactly the same story in Pentamerone where a poor mother abandons her children in a mountain forest.)
96. "Jōge no kappa," **Kikimimi sōshi** 44. Reported by Tanaka Kitami, who heard it on May 6, 1926, at rice planting time from Tanaba Ryūzō. He is said to have been born in Gosho-mura.

97. "Shōhōji no furunezumi," **Mukashibanashi kenkyū** I 11 29. Heard from Fujiwara Seijirō at his home on July 23, 1935.
98. "Hito ga uma ni naru," **Zoku Kai mukashibanashi shū** 130. Recited by Grandmother Dobashi Ichi on July 25, 1930.
99. "Abura tori," **Kikaijima mukashibanashi shū** 108. Told by Motoi Take.
100. "Onibaba to kozō," **Kikimimi sōshi** 91. Reported by Mutō Tetsujō, an abstract by Shiba Shizuko. Material gathered at Kakunodate Elementary School in Akita.
101. "Sanmai no ofuda," **Hidabito** V 5 21. Recorded at Kurabashira on September 12. Told by Okida Tsuya, 35 years old.
102. "Nomi ni natta yamajii no hanshi," **Dai-ni gō** 38. A story told in Sakagawa-mura, Haga-gun, Tochigi.
103. "Onibaba ni mimi kara kuwareta hanashi," **Iwaki mukashibanashi shū** 54. Told by Tanno Tamotsu, aged 65, at Onahana-machi, Iwaki-gun, Fukushima.
104. "Oita-shi, Moto-machi no Yuriwaka Daijin no tsuka," **Bungo densetsu shū** 10. Told by Wakasugi Yubei. Reported on January 5, 1931.
105. "Tomorokoshi no ne wa naze akai," **Akinokuni mukashibanashi shū** 97. Told by Morishige Tadataka, who was born in Kitami-mura, Toyota-gun, Hiroshima.
106. "Onibaba to sakana uri," **Echigo Sanjo Nanagō dan** 119.
107. "Mono kuwanu ogata," **Shiwa-gun mukashibanashi shū** 94.
108. "Kuchi no nai yomego," **Kyōdo no denshō** 3 116. Told in the region of Momoo-gun, Iwaki.
109. "Oni no imoto," **Koshikijima mukashibanashi shū** 126. Narrated by an old man, Harazaki Hikotarō, on April 26.
110. "Magotarō baba," **Kai mukashibanashi shū** 296.
111. "Kaibyō no hanashi," **Kikimimi sōshi** 344. The tale is one Sasaki recalls his grandmother telling many times.
112. "Nekomata," **Dai-ni gō** 21. Collected from Miyakawa-mura, Kazuno-gun, Akita.
113. "Nekoyama no hanashi," **Dai-ni gō** 19.
114. "Takara bakemono," **Kikaijima mukashibanashi shū** 136. Told by Haruzato Ichitake.
115. "Yamanashi no bakemono," **Shiwa-gun mukashibanashi** 66.
116. "Kinoko no bakemono," **Rōō yatan** 27.
117. "Bakemono dera," **Shiwa-gun mukashibanashi shū** 14.
118. **Tōno monogatri** No. 101. Told in Toyomane-mura, Shimohei-gun.
119. "Kikimimi zukin," **Rōō yatan** 86.
120. "Gonemon no hana," **Kai mukashibanashi shū** 30.
121. "O-Hera Daimyōjin," **Kamihei-gun mukashibanashi shū** 51.
122. "Tanuki to chagama," **Mukashibanashi** 1.
123. "Kitsune no ongaeshi," **Mukashibanashi kenkyū** I 4 42.
124. "Ōkami no ongaeshi," **Mukashibanashi kenkyū** II 9 35. Collected at Kiyotaki-mura, Kinosaki-gun, Hyōgo on August 18, 1936. Recited by Okamoto Kenzō, 54 or 55 years old, the village head.
125. "Togan no jiji to seigan no jiji," **Mukashibanashi kenkyū** II 10 29. Collected on April 29 in Hinuki-mura, Ōchi-gun, Shimne. Recited by Takahashi Umekichi.

126. "Shitakiri suzume," **Mukashibanashi kenkyū** I 1 27. The version is one Sugiwara recalls hearing as a child in Natsume-mura.
127. "Kome no naru hisago," **Dai-ni gō** 58. The story is from Miyaoi, Usa-gun, Oita.
128. **Tabi to densetsu** XII 7 17, (no title). Nobechi, Kamikita-gun, Aomori.
129. "Tora neko to oshō" **Kamihei-gun mukashibanashi shū** 118.
130. "Neko no tenko taiji," **Mitsui-gun mukashibanashi shū** 77. Reported by Kanno Takei. This is a story which Imamura's wife's mother heard often as a child.
131. "Hokekyō," **Kamuhara yatan** 44.
132. "Saru Chōja," **Mukashibanashi no kenkyū, Geibi sōsho** 54. Told in Kita-mura, Takata-gun, Hiroshima.
133. "Jiina no hatakeuchi," **Shiwa-gun mukashibanashi shū** 107.
134. "Korogeta nigirimeshi," **Akinokuni mukashibanashi shū** 65. Reported by Chikurinji Tachinobe at Itsukaichi-machi, Sakae-gun, Hiroshima. He said he heard it from an old lady, a relative, who was about 60 years old.
135. "Dango Jōdo," **Mukashibanashi kenkyū** II 1 43. Told by Abe Shichi, 55 years old.
136. "Hai maki jiji no hanashi," **Esashi-gun mukashibanashi** 15.
137. "Takekiri jiji," **Dai-ni gō** 62. Told around Ōmizo-machi.
138. "Utautai jiji," **Mukashibanshi kenkyū** II 5 34.
139. "Jii sama to saru," **Dai-ni gō** 67. Reported from Miyagawa-mura, Kazuno-gun, Akita.
140. "Kobutori," **Mukashibanashi kenkyū** II 4 42. Mamurogawa-mura, Mogami-gun, Yamagata.
141. "Isha don no atama," **Kai mukashibanashi shū** 40.
142. "Bakemono mondō," **Kawagoe chihō mukashibanashi shū** 100. Reported by Osawa Chieko, a third year student at Miyashita-cho, Kawagoe City, Saitama.
143. "Uta to yūrei," **Naori-gun mukashibanashi shū** 74. Reported by Gotō Haruko. Recited by Satō Yazaburō, 80 years old, in Okamoto-mura, Naori-gun, Ōita.
144. "Daiku to Oniroku," **Kikimimi sōshi** 106. This was reported by Oda Hideo in the winter of 1928. He heard it from an old woman at Kanegasaki, Isawa-gun.
145. "Gakumon no okage," **Fukuoka mukashibanashi shū** 232.
146. "Yamadera no bōsama Zuiton no hanashi," **Mukashibanashi** 30.
147. "Kitsune o damashita hanashi," **Tabi to densetsu** III 5 77.
148. "Kitsune o damashita hanashi," **Mukashibanashi kenkyū** II 10 14. This is one of several outlines recorded in the reference.
149. "Hidari katame no jiji," **Rōō yatan** 188.
150. "Wakamono ga kitsune o damashita hanashi," **Kogane no uma** 45.
151. "Kitsune ga warau," **Nihon mukashibanashi shū, jō** 88.
152. "Kōkō naru kahi no hanashi," **Fukuoka mukashibanashi shū** 150.
153. "Enami no Osan Gitsune," **Akinokuni mukashibanashi shū** 158.
154. "Osami Gitsune," (Old) **Ikinoshima mukashibanashi shū** 204. Told by Shimojo Shōsaburō in Watara-mura, Ikinoshima, Nagasaki.
155. "Tengu no kakure mino gasa," **Dai-ichi gō** 54. Collected at Asahi-mura, Kamiina-gun, Nagano.

156. "Kakure mino gasa," **Dai-ichi gō** 49. A story from Honjōji-mura, Minamikanbara-gun, Niigata.
157. "Tengu san," **Mukashibanashi kenkyū** II 9 28. The story is one which Yūki's mother heard when she was a little girl from her mother in Enoura-mura, Kitatakaku-gun, Nagasaki.
158. "Baba to tengu," **Mukashibanashi kenkyū** I 9 26.
159. "Tanukiemon," **Zoku Kai mukashibanashi shū** 120. Reported by Kobayashi Chūzō as written by Okachi Keiko, first year student in the Higher Elementary School, Ōshuku-mura, Higashiyatsushiro-gun, Yamanashi in February, 1932.
160. "Mizugumo," **Nihon mukashibanashi shū**, jō 47.
161. "Tako no ashi no hachihomme," **Shimabara hantō minwa shū** 26. This is a story told at Mishitsu, Moriyama-mura, Minamitakaku-gun, Nagasaki.
162. "Kusunoki o kiru hanashi," **Kai mukashibanashi shū** 244.
163. "Tengu to sumiyaki," **Mukashibanashi kenkyū** II 9 37. Collected on August 17, 1936, in Shimomura, Sanshō-mura, Kinosaki-gun, Hyōgo. Told by Obara Morimitsu, aged 44, a farmer.
164. Translator's note: The first two types of this story will be omitted because of their similarity the following type. Refer to Iwakura Ichirō, "Rōjin o suteru hanashi," **Mukashibanashi kenkyū** I 9 25, a selection from Okinoshima, Shimane.
A selection of the second type: Chiisagata-gun, Nagano: Hakoyama Kitarō, "Baba sute no hanashi," **Mukashibanashi kenkyū** I 1 36. From Osa-mura, Chiisagata-gun, Nagano.
165. "Rōjin suteba," **Kamihei-gun mukashibanashi shū** 167. There is a tradition of abandoning old people at Deederano in various villages.
166. "Niwatori no kakezu," **Kamuhara yatan** 48.
167. "Hito da, hito da," **Shima** II 248.
168. "Senryōbako dorobō," **Shimabara hantō mukashibanashi shū** 116.
169. "Chieari dono," **Kamuhara yatan** 141.
170. "Oyafukō musuko no hanashi," **Dai-ni gō** 85. From Sakagawa-mura, Haga-gun, Tochigi.
171. "Kogane no ushi," **Dai-ichi gō** 65.
172. "Kin no nasu," **Shima** II 468. Told by Nakamura Makoto on June 21 in Ōshima-gun.
173. "Nichirin no kudashigo," **Shima** II 487.
174. "Hanashi senryō," **Dai-ichi gō** 70.
175. "Atago Sama," **Kikimimi sōshi** 479.
176. "Ōoka saiban jitsugo shirabe," **Rōō yatan** 243.
177. "Tanuki no su ka niwatori no su ka," (Old) **Ikinoshima mukashibanashi shū** 156. Told by Tonogawa Kunitarō in Isafushi-mura, Iki-gun, Nagasaki.
178. "Motonari hyōtan," **Kikimimi sōshi** 55.
179. "Akagome ni kansuru densetsu," **Kyōdo kenkyū** I 7 50. Reported from Nadasaki-mura Kataoka, Kojima-gun, Okayama.
180. "Engi uta," **Kai mukashibanashi shū** 127.
181. "Kamekasu Nurinosuke," **Kamuhara yatan** 37.
182. "Zatō to ushioi," **Mukashibanashi kenkyū** I 4 46. The reporter was a farmer-carpenter, Hirao Yasuji, 70 years old.

183. It is possible to classify these stories in detail, but there is no point in doing so. We must draw the line somewhere. They can be classified as tales about precocious children. They must have originated as such, but at present most of them have been changed into jokes and are known as stories about a priest and his novice. The priest is laughed at. There are stories about the stupid novice in the group of foolish village tales. [Translator's note: Although Yanagita did not consider these as important folk tales, a tale or episode will be translated for each of the eleven groups he listed.] a: "Ochita mono," **Chiisagata-gun mintan shū** 199. Told by Koyama's father. b: "Kwan-kwan kuta-kuta," **Chiisagata-gun mintan shū** 194. Told by Koyama's father. c: "Oshō to kozō," **Kamuhara yatan** 89. d: "Oshō to kozō," **Akinokuni mukashibanashi shū** 151. e: "Kono hen ni hashira ippon," **Chiisagata-gun mintan shū** 196. Told by Koyama's father. f: "Oshō to kozō," **Akinokuni mukashibanashi shū** 153. g: "Oshō to kozō," **Dai-ichi gō** 58. From Toyona-mura, Kitashidara-gun, Aichi. h: "Oshō benjo ni ochi," **Fukuoka-ken mukashibanashi shū** 135. i: "Oshō to kozō," **Kikaijima mukashibanashi shū** 141. Narrated by Hamahata Yukihide. j: "Amename kozō," **Chiisagta-gun mintan shū** 198. Told by Nozaki Mine. k: "Katawari tsuki," **Kaga Enuma-gun mukashibanashi shū** 98. A story told in Nishidani-mura, Enuma-gun, Ishikawa.

184. "Utai gaikotsu," **Koshikijima mukashibanashi shū** 120. Told by Hamazaki Hikotarō on April 17.

185. There are three types of stories. The first is about forecasting for a boy and a girl who are born on the same night. The girl has fortune. This is connected with the Charcoal-maker Chōja theme. The second is about a child whose life is destined to be taken by a Water Spirit is saved by **mochi** or some other natural means. The third, called "The horsefly and the ax," or some such name, tells a forecast that the child will be killed by a hand ax. When the horsefly is bothering the child, the father waves it off with his hand ax, but accidentally kills the child. [Translator's note: The first type will be omitted here because it is close to the "Charcoal-maker Chōja" and to "Miidera," which follows. Refer to Dobashi Riki, "Umaretsuki un," **Kai mukashibanashi shū** 182.]

Type II: "Hyaku kan no kata ni kasa ichimai," **Mukashibanashi kenkyū** II 7 39. Collected at Takayama, a hot springs town in Mikata-gun, on January 2, 1937. Told by Nishimura Mokuzō, a farmer 76 years old. He said he heard it from a woodcutter from Wakayama.

Type III: "Yama-no-kami no sōdan," **Kikimimi sōshi** 30. Reported in summary by Tanaka Kitami.

186. "Miidera," **Sanuki Sanagi Shishijima mukashibanashi shū** 102. Translator's note: The usual characters used to write the Mii in Miidera mean "three wells," but folk versions interpret it in terms of a winnowing basket, a familiar object.

187. "Chii-chii bakama," **Sadogashima mukashibanashi shū** 210. Collected by Hasegawa Tamae.

188. "Hihibaba," **Kai mukashibanashi shū** 254. Told by Kitsuta Kan'emon.
189. **Tōnō monogatari** No. 28, 25.
190. "Kitsune no mukashibanashi," **Echigo Sanjo Nangō dan** 37.
191. "Yamabushi," **Shiwa-gun mukashibanashi** 148.
192. "Tanuki to komamonoya," **Mukashibanashi** 86. Translator's note: The size of the badger's scrotum is said to be as big as a straw mat or even eight mats in folk tales. This badger had expected to tease the peddler by getting all his needles out and losing them.
193. "Meuma no shiri o nozokaserareta otoko," **Esashi-gun mukashibanashi** 125.
194. "Hoin sama to kitsune," **Iwaki mukashibanashi shū** 65.
195. "Namake Tasuke," **Inpaku dōwa** 49.
196. "Kowai kao," **Kai mukashibanashi shū** 280.
197. "Onna ni baketa mujina," **Esashi-gun mukashibanashi** 130.
198. "Neko no shūnen," **Tekkiri ane sama** 251.
199. "Niwatori no ongaeshi," **Mukashibanashi kenkyū** I 2 23. Told at Mitsuke.
200. "Uta o utau neko," **Dai-ichi gō** 43.
201. "Numa no nushi," **Kyōdo no denshō** 1 167. Collected in Shiroishi-machi, Karita-gun, Miyagi. Reported by Kitazato Kōichi.
202. "Atama no ki," **Kikaijima mukashibanashi shū** 154. Told by Taira Shōsuke.
203. Stories of exaggertions began with episodes in genuine oral tales and developed from there. One such belongs to the "Wife from the Sky World" group. "Tenjo kyūri," **Mukashibanashi kenkyū** II 10 20.
204. **Ugo Kakunodate chihō ni okeru chōchū sōmoku no minzokugakuteki shiryō** 154 (no title).
205. "Nezumi kyō," **Mukashibanashi kenkyū** I 12 44. Recited by Utsumiya Omatsu, aged 78, and recorded by Narishige Kesao. Collected on June 9 in Seguchi Higashihamaga-mura, Hayami-gun, Ōita.
206. "Hekkoki anesa," **Kamuhara yatan**, 138.
207. "Dare da," **Akinokuni mukashibanashi shū** 221. The tale is one Isogai used to hear as a child from Kumagaya Shō for a bedtime story.
208. "Hetare jiji," **Tekkiri ane sama** 242.
209. "Nise hakke," **Kikimimi sōshi** 135. Told by Konuma Hide at Ashiaraigawa Tsuchibuchi Tōno-machi, Kamihei-gun.
210. "Nise hakke," No. 2, **Koshikijima mukashibanashi shū** 178. Recited by Harasaki Hikitarō on April 11.
211. "Uekiyama Hachibei," **Fukuoka-ken mukashibanashi shū** 76.
212. "Suzume o takusan toru hanashi," **Shimbara hantō minwa shū** 300.
213. "Ryōshi to heko iwai," **Fukuoka-ken mukashibanashi shū** 212.
214. "Tenjo ni nobotte Raijin no muko to narō to shita musuko no hanashi," **Esashi-gun mukashibanashi** 33.
215. "Ise ebi no koshi wa naze magatta ka," **Mukashibanashi kenkyū** II 3 34. Told by Yamaguchi's mother.
216. "Jishin ni natta Dairikibō," **Shiwa-gun mukashibanashi** 42.
217. "Kichigo banashi," **Fukuoka-ken mukashibanashi shū** 124.

218. "Sannin dorobō," Kamuhara yatan 148.
219. "Dōmo to Kōmo no hanashi," Fukuoka-ken mukashibanashi shū 228.
220. "Tempo kurabe," Kaga Enuma-gun mukashibanashi shū 116. Collected in Nishitani-mura.
221. "Sannin no hora," Kikaijima mukashibanashi shū 138. Told by Tomi Jittei.
222. "Saru no kuri hiroi," Shimabara hantō minwa shū 28. Told by Seki's aunt.
223. This is exactly the same form as "Kōketsu Palace." This sort of imagination occurs only in Tōhoku, or northeastern Japan. "Abura tori," Kikimimi sōshi 110.
224. "Sekkoki otoko," Shiwa-gun mukashibanashi 70.
225. "Mochizuki fūfu," Nihon zenkoku kokumin dōwa 270.
226. "Kodakara," Shima II 424.
227. "Tada no kusuri," Hanashi no sekai II 4 97.
228. "Oshō to kozō," Kai mukashibanashi 266.
229. "Shigoto sezu baba," Kaga-Enuma-gun mukashibanashi shū 67. Collected from Higashitani-mura, Enuma-gun, Ishikawa.
230. "Sannin naki," Mitsu-gun mukashibanashi shū 7. The story was told by Imamura's grandmother, but his aunt, Yamamoto Miho, retold it for him.
231. "Tōmaru kago," Kai mukashibanashi shū 278.
232. "Mekusari, Shirakumo, to Shiramitagari," Kikimimi sōshi 490. A story Sasaki's children were telling. They heard it from their aunt in the winter of 1928.
233. "Kubi no torikae," Bungo no kijin Kitchyomu san monogatari 123.
234. "Nagai na no ko," Kamuhara yatan 103.
235. "Moguramochi no yome san," Mukashibanashi kenkyū II 1 37.
236. "Kuwa o wasureta Kahei no hanashi," Mukashibanashi 21.
237. "Kinikake jii san," Shimotsuke Motegi mukashibanashi shū 8. Translator's note: Words having a cheerful meaning should be used when planting seeds.
238. "Kaki no ki e jōkyō," Chiisagata-gun mintan shū 184. Told by Koyama's father.
239. "Awate mono," Kai mukashibanashi shū 74.
240. "Yokufuka onna," Nansō no rizoku 99.
241. "Chōbei fūfu," Kaga Enuma-gun mukashibanashi shū 90. Collected in Nishitani-mura.
242. "Rōsoku no hanashi," Tabi to densetsu I 3 10.
243. "Chakurikaki," Tabi to densetsu III 2 81.
244. "Ochauri to furuiya to furuganeya," Zoku Kai mukashibanashi shū 444. Dobashi recalls this as having been told by his grandmother.
245. "Butsu no hanashi," Mukashibanashi kenkyū II 1 29.
246. "Baka musuko," Shiwa-gun mukashibanashi shū 144.
247. "Hashira kakushi," Shiwa-gun mukashibanashi 206.
248. "Baka muko," No. 3, Kunohe-gun shi 471.
249. "Baka muko," No. 2, Kunohe-gun shi 470.
250. "Baka muko," No. 1, Kunohe-gun shi 169.
251. "Okai monko," Shiwa-gun mukashibanashi 101.
252. "Kouta," Kikimimi sōshi 507. Translator's note: The stork and tortoise are felicitous symbols at a wedding. The son-in-law was

not aware of that and thought his father-in-law was going to tell their secret.

253. "Atama o makura ni musubitsuketa hanashi," **Iwaki mukashibanashi shū** 177.
254. "Sannin muko," **Kyōdo no denshō** 1 182. Collected in Kita-mura.
255. "Yosoiki kotoba," **Shimabara hantō minwa shū** 275.
256. "Yome ni ikitai hanashi," **Kikimimi sōshi** 571.
257. "Oya no Yokoo banashi," **Dai-ichi gō** 68.
258. "Inaka mono no shippai," **Akinokuni mukashibanashi shū** 239. Told by Aki Tachia in Kado-mura, Takata-gun, Hiroshima.
259. "Sashida banashi," No.2. **Fukuoka-ken mukashibanashi shū** 220.
260. "Chikuzen Noma banashi," **Dai-ichi gō** 76.
261. "Tobikomi bukuro to kubikake sōmen," (Old) **Ikinoshima mukashibanashi shū** 20. Told by Yoneda Yasuo of Watara-mura.
262. Translator's note: No source is given for this item. It may be remnant of a tale now lost.
263. (Old) **Ikinoshima mukashibanashi shū** 9. Told in Isafushi-mura, Iki-gun, Nagasaki.
264. "Karasu to kiji," **Inpaku mintan** I 4 194. Collected in Saji-mura by Nakatani Chōka.
265. "Oroka mura," **Mukashibanashi kenkyū** II 11 30.
266. "Yabu no ko," **Mukashibanashi kenkyū** I 10 47. from Kenkuma-mura, Takashima-gun, Shiga.
267. "Matsuyama kagami," **Awa-no-Iyayama mukashibanashi shū** 110. Told by Tsuchi Mizo.
268. **Tsugaru kōhi shū** 9 (no title).
269. "Hototogisu no hanashi," **Mukashibanashi kenkyū** II 3 33.
270. "Hototogisu," **Shizuoka-ken densetsu mukashibanashi shū** 359, 360. The first was reported by Itō Koto and the second by Arayama Teru.
271. "Hototogisu no densetsu," **Kyōdo kenkyū** IV 7 27.
272. "Hototogisu," No. 2., **Hōgen to dozoku** I No. 8 26.
273. "Hōchō dori," **Kōshō bungaku** 11 4. Reported by Fujiwara Seijirō, aged 53, on June 20, 1935.
274. "Kataashi kyahan," **Mukshibanshi kenkyū** I 9 22.
275. "Fukuro to shimai," **Dai-ichi-gō** 69.
276. "Hototogisu," **Kitazumi-gun Kyōdo shikō, Kōhi densetsu hen** II 2 159.
277. "Kakkō dori," **Kai mukashibanashi shū** 57. Dobashi's grandmother said that Kajima is a place in Suruga.
278. "Yabakei no ryōshi dori," **Kyōdo kenkyū** III 6 48.
279. **Ugo Kakunodate chihō ni okeru chōchū sōmoku minzokugakuteki shiryō** (no title) 78.
280. "Hibari no zenshin," **Akinokuni mukashibanashi shū** 142. Reported by Mukaigawa Yoshio in Kamikamakarishima-mura, Aki-gun, Hiroshima. Mr. Mukaigawa can not recall from whom he heard this tale, but he is sure that it is a tale about previous existence.
281. "Fure-fure," **Mukashibanashi kenkyū** II 3 33.
282. "Kaki tō to jūichi," **Zoku Kai mukashibanashi shū** 3.
283. "Tobi fukō," **Mukashibanashi kenkyū** II 1 33.
284. "Amagaku no hanashi," **Nantō setsuwa** 21.

285. "Hato no kōkō," **Nihon mukashibanashi shū**, jō 8.
286. "Mizukoi dori," **Zoku Kai mukashibanashi shū** 5. Recited by Hashita Toshiji, the aunt of Dobashi, on August 12, 1932.
287. "Imohori dori," **Mukashibanashi kenkyū** II 9 36. Recited by Iida Katsu, aged 65, a farmer at Mihara Sanshō-mura, Kinosaki-gun, on August 18, 1936.
288. "Somedai o harawanu tobi," (New) **Ikinoshima mukashibanashi shū** 115.
289. "Yoshikiri (gaigaizu) garagarazai," **Kōshō bungaku** 11 3. Reported by Fujiwara Toku, aged 45, on June 20, 1935.
290. "Misosazai mo taka no nakama," **Nihon mukashibanashi shū**, jō 14.
291. "Mimizu no me," **Mukashibanashi kenkyū** I 1 32. Recalled by Sugiwara.
292. "Kubi ni kase o kaketa mimizu," (Old) **Ikinoshima mukashibanashi shū** 128. Collected in Ishida-mura.
293. "Mamushi to sawarabi," **Nihon densetsu sōsho, Kazusa no maki** 197. Collected in Harada-ku, Ninomiyahongō-mura, Chiba.
294. "Gan to kame," **Iwaki mukashibanashi shū** 89. Recited by Bame Iso, aged 89, at Yumoto-machi.
295. "Suzume odori," **Nihon densetsu shū** 257. Reported by Shimizu Hyōzō.
296. Translator's note: This item has not been availble to the translator. The notation is from **Nihon mukashibanashi meii**, p. 203. **Bungo minwa shū**.
297. "Nomi to shirami to ka," **Shimabara hantō minwa shū** 22.
298. **Tsugaru kōhi shū** 10 (no title). Collected in Goshokawara-mura, Kitatsugaru-gun, Aomori.
Complete version: "Shutendōji," **Kōshō bungaku** 11 6. Fujiwara has recorded the version his father used to tell him.
299. "Tabako no okori," **Kikaijima mukashibanashi shū** 157.
300. "Kurage," **Nihon densetsu shū** 261. Reported by Shimizu Hyōzō.
301. "Nichirin San to mogura to donko," **Mukashibanashi kenkyū** I 1 44. Recited by an old man living in the neighborhood of the writer.
302. "Soramame to wara to sumi," **Zoku Kai mukashibanashi shū** 14. The story is one Dabashi's wife knew.
303. **Shizuoka-ken densetsu mukashibanashi shū** 492 (no title). Reported by Saino Nagako.
304. "Furuya no mori," **Dai-ni gō** 86.
305. "Suzume-no-miya," **Nihon mukashibanashi shū**, jō 170. Told about the village called Suzume-no-miya in Kawachi-gun.
306. "Ningen to hebi to kitsune," **Kikimimi sōshi** 460.
307. "Jiina to ōkami," **Shiwa-gun mukashibanashi** 40.
308. "Tanuki to tanishi," **Nihon mukashibanashi shū**, jō 14.
309. "Kitsune wa zurui," **Shizuoka-ken densetsu mukashibanashi shū** 445. Reported by Kano Suzu and Kishimoto Katsuyo from Yaitsu-machi.
310. "Ōkami to inu," **Rōō yatan** 257. Told by Shōji at Furuyashiki.
311. "Saru to shiohorigari," **Kyōdo no denshō** 3 110. Reported by Sugawara Keikai.

312. "Tanuki no onchō," (Old) **Ikinoshima mukashibanashi shū** 177. Recited by Shimojo Shōzō at Watara-mura.
313. "Mujina to saru to kawauso," **Echigo Sanjo Nanagō dan** 41.
314. "Ari no chūsai," **Dai-ichi gō** 48. Honshō-machi.
315. "Obana gitsune wa o no nai hanashi," **Etchū kyōdo kenkyū** III 10 1. From Hebita Nishifuse-mura, Shimoniikawa-gun.
316. "Neko to nezumi," **Shiwa-gun mukashibanashi** 35.
317. "Kitsune to kawasemi," **Tabi to densetsu** XI 12 57.
318. "Kitsune to kawauso," **Kamuhara yatan** 95.
319. "Saru no o," **Nihon densetsu shū** 255. Reported by Shimizu Hyōzō.
320. "Saru to kani," **Fukuoka-ken mukashibanashi shū** 188.
321. "Saru to gama," **Echigo Sanjo Nangō dan** 114.
322. "Saru no shiri wa naze akai," **Mukashibanashi kenkyū** II 6 18. Collected by a first year student, Noguchi Toshi, at Saga Girl's High School. Narrated by Tomioka Isamu, aged 64, of Ushizu-machi, Ogi-gun.
323. "Saru to kiji," **Mukashibanashi kenkyū** II 3 30. Collected at Asamai-machi, Hiraga-gun. Recited by Terada's grandmother.
324. "Nezumi to itachi," **Minamikanbara-gun mukashibanashi shū** 19. Taken from **Kamuhara yatan** 91.
325. "Saru to kani," **Dai-ichi gō** 38. Recited by Abe Tei, aged 49, at Nagamine Miyakawa-mura, Kazuno-gun.
326. "Kani no adauchi," No. 2, **Zoku Kai mukashibanashi shū** 224. Recalled from Dobashi's grandmother, Hashita Toshiji, on November 3, 1931.
327. "Suzume banashi," **Akinokuni mukashibanashi shū** 11. Collected at the Yomogi Inn in Hachiman-mura, Yamagata-gun, Hiroshima, in January, 1934.
328. "Kachi-kachi Yama," **Mukashibanashi kenkyū** II 9 40. Recalled by Suzuki from his grandmother.
329. "Sarun namasu," **Mukashibanashi kenkyū** I 1 43. The story was told by an old farmer in Noda's neighborhood.
330. "Saru to hiki, Kachi-kachi Yama," **Hidabito** IV 11 18. Recited at Kamidakara-mura on the 13th by Azuma Fuyo, aged 59, who came as a bride from Hitoegane.
331. "Yuriwaka Daijin," **Minzokugaku** I 2 71.
332. "Onna no dairiki," **Shimabra hantō mukashibanashi shū** 74. Told by Oba Kikaji in Yasunaka-mura.
333. "Kiji mo nakazuba," **Kikaijima mukashibanashi shū** 164. Told by Iwakura Sue, Iwakura's mother.
334. "Oshidoridera no yurai," **Aichi-ken densetsu shū** 318.
335. "Kaiko no hajime," **Kai mukashibanashi shū** 161. Dobashi's grandmother heard the story from her mother-in-law.
336. "Nijūsanya Sama," **Kikaijima mukashibanashi shū** 166. Told by Tomi Jittei.
337. "Zeni no tanto haetta tsubo," **Kyōdo no denshō** 1 173. Reported by Miura Shōgo.
338. "Masabō-no-taki," **Kyōdo no denshō** 1 177. Reported from Nishikiori Elementary School.
339. "Hataya no Nue," No. 2, **Kikimimi sōshi** 151.

340. "Fuka no tatari," **Tabi to densetsu** IX 3 30. Reported from Hamada-machi, Naka-gun, Shimane.
341. "Fuka ni kage o nomareta hanashi," **Mukashibanashi kenkyū** I 3 42. A story told on December 30, 1934, by Gotō's father, aged 70, who heard it from his grandfather.
342. "Kumo no tama," **Kikaijima mukashibanashi shū** 175. Told by Harusato Ichitake.
343. "Nemutai hanashi," **Mukashibanashi kenkyū** II 7 31. Collected on December 8, 1935 in Karikawa-mura, Higashimurayama-gun.
344. "Mukashi katana," **Kikimimi sōshi** 578.
345. "Mukashiya muketa," **Zen Nagasaki-ken kayōshū** 202. Translator's note: The rendition of this children's song may be open to question, but a song is no longer a song when it is explained clearly. The intention of this jingle is to show the story teller has no story to tell.
346. Translator's note: The **sanbasō** is a brief performance like a curtain raiser performed by an apprentice to put the audience into the mood to enjoy one by a master performer. It is usually a short, humorous dance, skit, or story. "Hanashi no sanbasō," **Mukashibanashi kenkyū** II 6 22. Told by Noguchi's mother in the summer of 1936.
347. "Rigen," **Esashi-gun shi** 253.

# Glossary

**afuri:** A word among others in the tale that are not explained.
**Ama Otome:** Said to be the deity of Nijūsanya; see **Nijūsanya.**
**amanojaku** or **amanjaku:** A demon with feminine attributes.
**ame:** Sweet gluten.
**an:** Sweet bean paste.
**anmochi:** mochi covered with sweet bean paste; see **mochi.**
**Aomori Gongen:** See Gongen.
**asanarō** or **asunarō:** A magic plant.
**Atago:** A deity associated with ancestral worship.
**azuki:** A small red bean.
**Azuki rice:** Red beans steamed with glutenous rice for a festive occasion (also called **sekihan**).

**Bashū-no-shū:** Worship related to the head of a horse.
**Benjo-no-kami:** See **kami.**
**Biwa:** A lute.
**bonboko:** See **bunbuku.**
**bosama:** See **zatō.**
**botamochi:** See **ohagi.**
**bu:** One percent or a coin of low denomination.
**Buddha:** A great Buddhist deity, often referred to as Hotoke or Shaka.
**bumbuku:** Am onomatopoeic term for boiling water written with the character for good fortune.

**Chinju:** The deity of the locality or the village.
**chō:** a measurement of 119 yards or 2.45 acres.
**chōja:** One upon whom unexpected good fortune is bestowed—a man, a woman, a couple, or a family.

**Daigongen:** A Great Temporary Manifestation of a deity, usually with a place name Fukayama Daigongen, the Great Temporary Manifestation at Fukayama.
**Daikoku:** A deity of good fortune; also the principal supporting pillar of the roof.
**daimyō:** A feudal lord.
**Daimyōjin:** A Great Manifestation.
 **Inari Daimyōjin:** The Great Manifestation of Inari.
 **Nekoza Daimyōjin:** The Great Manifestation of a Cat.
 **Ohera Daimyōjin:** The Great Manifestation in the Ladle.
**dango:** A small ball made into a cake from glutenous rice flour or other material.
**dengaku:** Fried tofu with miso on it; see **tōfu** and **miso.**
**dote:** A spectral bird.

**Ebisu:** A deity of good fortune.
**ekisha:** A diviner.

**Festival of the 5th Day of the Fifth Month:** Often called the **Iris** Festival.
**Festival of the 7th Day of the Seventh Month:** Often called **Tanabata.**
**Fukayama Daigongen:** See **Daigongen.**
**Fuku-no-kami:** See **Kami.**
**fukude mochi:** See **mochi.**
**furoshiki:** A cloth used for wrapping things that are carried.

**gajimaru:** A tropical tree.
**gamarijaku:** See **amanojaku.**
**gami:** See **Kami.**
**ge:** The last part of a two or three volume work.
**geta:** Wooden clogs.
**gidayu:** A dramatic recital accompanied by music.
**gō:** A unit of capacity, one tenth of a **shō**
**Gongen:** A temporary Manifestation of a deity or a sacred place.
  **Aomori Gongen**
  **Hakusan Gongen**
  **Hiko-san Gongen**
**goyō:** A highly esteemed variety of pine.
**goze:** A blind female ballad singer.
**gun:** An administrative district within a prefecture.

**Haguro:** The name of a sacred mountain.
**Hakama:** A loose divided skirt.
**Hakusan Gongen:** See Gongen.
**Hana-no-kami:** See **Kami.**
**Hannya:** God of wisdom.
**Hata-no-kami:** See **Kami.**
**Hatsu mizu:** First Water drawn at New Year.
**Hatsu yume:** First Dream of New Year (on the 2nd Night).
**hayamonogatari:** A brief humorous tale recited rapidly.
**hei:** A shinto symbol used in purification rites.
**Hi-no-kami:** See **Kami.**
**Higan:** The observance during Equinox.
**Hiko-san Gongen:** See **Gongen.**
**hōin:** See **yamabushi.**
**hōji:** A Budldhist memorial service.
**hokekyō:** A play on words: the cry of the nightingale and the name of a sutra.
**Hōki-gami:** The broom deity usually present at parturition.
**hongure:** Acorns or testes.
**hōsha:** A priest like a **yamabushi.**
**hōshi:** A general name for a Buddhist priest.
  **mekura hōshi:** See **zatō.**
**Hotoke:** A name used for Buddha or an ancestral spirit.
  **Ki-botoke:** A piece of a tree worshiped as the image of Buddha.
**Hyottoko:** A god of luck.

**Inari:** The field deity.
  **Inari Daimyōjin:** See **Daimyōjin.**
**Ise:** The Grand Shrine of Shinto faith.

**Jizō**: A Buddhist Bodhisattva that has become identified as a **kami**. He may be a single Jizō or a group of six or twelve figures.
  **Koyasu Jizō**: Protector of children.
**Jō**: The first volume of a two or three volume work.
**Jōdo**: Paradise.
**joruri**: A recital about heroes rendered with musical accompaniment.

**kachi-kachi**: An onomatopoeic term written various ways to refer to the sound of striking flint or burning brush.
**kaimochi**: See **ohagi**.
**Kami** or **gami**: A deity.
  **Benjo-no-kami**: Deity of the Privy.
  **Fuku-no-kami**: Deity of Good Fortune.
  **Hana-no-kami**: Deity of the Nose.
  **Hata-no-kami**: Deity of the Loom.
  **Hi-no-kami**: Deity of the Fire (in the kitchen).
  **Hōki-gami**: Deity of the Broom.
  **Kane-no-kami**: Deity of Gold.
  **Ki-no-kami**: Deity of a Tree.
  **Mizu-no-kami**: Deity of Water.
  **Neko-no-kami**: A Cat Deity.
  **Sai-no-kami**: Deity of the Border or to the approch to a village.
  **Sai-no-kami**: Deity of Dice.
  **Ujigami**: The clan deity or tutelary deity.
  **Yama-no-kami**: Mountain Deity.
**kan**: A unit of weight; also called **kanme**.
**Kane-no-kami**: See **Kami**.
**Kannon**: A Buddhist deity usually given feminine attributes; usually enshrined, but one that appears in revelations and dreams.
  **Kamoe Kannon**: Kannon at Kamoe
  **Senju Kannon**: Kannon with 1000 hands.
  **Kōshin Kannon**: Kannon associated with the Kōshin observance; see **Kōshin**.
**kappa**: A creature associated with streams.
**kasha**: A kind of ghost.
**katarimono**: A story recited to musical accompaniment.
**kaya**: Thatch (*torrera nucifera*).
**ken**: A prefecture.
**Ki-no-kami**: See **Kami**.
**Kō-jin**: See **Shin (Jin)**.
**koku**: A measurement of capacity, about two bushels.
**komekura**: A word play on rice storehouse and little blind men.
**Kōshin**: An observance on the night the two calendar signs of **Kanoe** (8th calendar sign) and Saru (monkey) coincide. See **Nijūsanya**
**kotatsu**: A frame covered with a quilt set over live coals as a warmer.
**Koyase Jizō**: See **Jizō**.
**Koyasu son**: A deity to protect the birth of a child.
**kunotsu**: A magic bird.
**kyōgen**: A comic interlude.

**mandara**: A picture of Buddhist paradise.
**manjū**: A steamed bun filled with sweet bean paste.

**medetashi:** An exclamation to the happy ending of a story.
**mihagusa:** A kind of plant.
**mikankō:** A magic cat.
**miko:** A woman with a special role in folk faith, a shamaness.
**miso:** fermented bean paste.
**Mizu-no-kami:** See **Kami.**
**mochi:** rice cake which is made by pounding steamed glutenous rice. This rice is used only on festive occasions. Besides steamed and pounded, the glutenous rice is ground into flour to make various cakes.
**mon:** A coin of low monetary value.
**muri:** dialect for **mori**, meaning leak.

**namu amida butsu:** Words in a Buddhist prayer.
**namu toraya:** "Hail, Tiger Cat."
**nara pears:** A wild fruit.
**Neko-gami:** See **Kami.**
**Nekoza Daimyōjin:** See Daimyōjin.
**Nijūsanya San:** See **San.**
**nishiki ki:** *uconymus alta.*
**nushi:** A guardian spirit in a tree, rock, pond, or the like.
  **Mizu-no-nushi:** Water Spirit.
  **Kumo-no-nushi:** Spider Spirit.

**o (omote):** The upper side of a folded page.
**obi:** A sash.
**ohagi:** A dango covered with sweet bean paste served at festivals.
**oni-baba:** An old she-demon.
**Onigashima:** A fictitious demon stronghold.
**ōnyūdō:** A kind of ghost.
**oshō:** A Buddhist priest.
**osōshi:** The same as **ekisha**, a diviner.

**Raijin:** See **Shin (Jin).**
**rakugo:** A comical story usually ending in a word play.
**renga:** A poem chain.
**ri:** A measure of distance, about two and a half miles.
**rokubu:** A mendicant pilgrim.
**ryō:** A coin of high monetary value.
**Ryūgu:** Dragon Palace, approached from the sea, a stream, a cave, or a tree.
**Ryūjin:** See **Shin (Jin).**
**ryūsengan:** A magic object.

**Sai-no-kami:** See **Kami.**
**sake:** Rice wine.
**samurai:** A warrior usually attached to a feudal lord.
**san, sama, son:** An honorific attached to the name of a shrine or festival to refer the deity at the place or a festival or an object.
  **Atago Sama:** A deity associated with ancestral worship.
  **Nichirin San:** The Sun.
  **Nijūsanya San:** The deity on the 23rd Night or **Kōshin.**

Ryūgu San: The deity at the Dragon Palace.
Shōgatsu San: The New Year Deity.
Tanabata San: The deity of the festival of the 7th Day of the Seventh Month.
Tentō San: The Sun.

**satori:** The name of a ghost.
**sembei:** A wafer made of rice flour.
**Shaka:** See **Buddha.**
**shamisen:** A three-stringed musical instrument.
**Shichi Fukujin:** See Shin (Jin).
**Shin or Jin:** Another reading for the character for **kami.**

Kōjin: Deity of the kitchen hearth.
Raijin: Thunder deity.
Ryūjin: Dragon Deity, sometimes given feminine attributes.
Shichi Fukujin: A group of seven deities popular at New Year.
Toshitokujin: A New Year Deity.
Yakujin or Yakubō: Deity of Pestilence.

**shingaku:** A teaching of ethical practices.
**shō:** A measure of capacity, about one and a half quarts.
**Shōgatsu San:** See **san.**
**shōgun:** Highest ranking civilian official. Official ranks in tales are vague.
**shōji:** An official representative of the feudal lord.
**shōya:** The village official answering to the feudal lord.
**son:** Title of veneration.
**sun:** A measure of length, about one inch.
**Suzume-no-miya:** Sparrow Shrine.

**tabi:** Footwear sewn from cloth.
**tabi sō:** An itinerant priest.
**Tanabata:** Vega, the Weaver Star.
**tara:** A kind of tree.
**tengu:** A demon that flies.
**tenko:** A ghost animal.
**Tentō San:** See San.
**to:** A measure of capacity ten times greater than a **shō.**
**tōfu:** Bean curd.
**toragame:** A kind of jar.
**toranomaki:** A magic object.
**torii:** The gate at the approach to a shrine.
**tororo:** Grated yam.
**Toshitokujin:** See Shin (Jin).
**tsukigusa:** A kind of plant.

**u (ura):** The underside of a folded page.
**Ujigami:** See **Kami.**
**Untoko:** A little lucky deity.

**Yahiko:** A sacred mountain.
**Yakujin:** See Shin (Jin).
**Yakushi:** A Buddhist deity, a god of healing.
**Yama-no-kami:** See **Kami.**

**Yamabushi:** A priest living in mountains and serving rural areas.
**Yamachichi:** A malevolent male encountered in mountains; also, **yamajii** or **yamaotoko.**
**Yamauba:** A female, usually malevolent, encountered in mountains; also, **yamanba, yamaonna,** or **yamababa.**
**yatsumetō:** A sword.
**yuta:** See **miko.**

**zatō:** A blind itinerant musician traveling a fixed route and often belonging to a group housed in a temple. Zatō told stories and entertained hosts where they were put up.

# Cross Reference Table

| Story | Meii | F.R. | H.H. | R.A. | M-1 | M-2 | NMS | H.I | Jiten |
|---|---|---|---|---|---|---|---|---|---|
| 1 | Ex. | 78 | 4 | 17 | — | — | 143 | 302 | 962 |
| 2 | Ex. | 79 | 78 | 18 | — | — | *140 | 301.B | †579 |
| 3 | Ex. | 70 | 21 | — | 56 | 48 | 114 | 408.B | 123 |
| 4 | — | — | — | — | — | — | 144 | 408.B | †123 |
| 5 | Ex. | 20 | 3 | — | 55 | 49 | *145 | 502.D | 540 |
| 6 | Ex. | — | — | — | — | — | 147.A | 768.B | 343 |
| 7 | — | — | — | — | — | — | 148 | 768.C | 1037 |
| 8 | Ex. | — | — | 28 | — | — | 136.A | 425.B | 62 |
| 9 | — | — | — | — | — | — | 138 | — | †593 |
| 10 | Ex. | — | — | — | — | 23 | 142.A | 433.B | 832 |
| 11 | Ex. | 61 | 28 | 27 | — | — | 134 | 245.A | 548 |
| 12 | — | — | — | — | — | — | 135 | 425.A | 185 |
| 13 | — | — | — | — | — | — | 134 | 425.A | †548 |
| 14 | Ex. | — | 13 | 54 | — | 42 | 121 | 545 | 219 |
| 15 | Ex. | — | — | — | — | — | 122 | 896 | 100 |
| 16 | Ex. | — | — | — | — | — | 133 | 1925 | 976 |
| 17 | Ex. | — | — | — | — | — | 129 | 516.A | 681 |
| 18 | Ex. | 39 | — | 23 | — | — | 118 | 400 | 621 |
| 19 | Ex. | 36 | 24 | 48 | — | 53 | *120.A | 516 | †126 |
| 20 | Ex. | — | — | 25 | — | — | 115 | 413.A | 605 |
| 21 | Ex. | — | — | — | — | — | 115 | 413.A | †661 |
| 22 | — | — | — | — | 60 | 56 | 115 | 413.A | †661 |
| 23 | — | — | — | — | — | — | 115 | 413.A | 661 |
| 24 | — | — | 31 | — | 61 | 57 | 116.A | 413.D | 252 |
| 25 | Ex. | — | — | — | — | — | 112 | 413.B | 756 |
| 26 | — | — | 27 | — | — | — | 112 | 413.B | 92 |
| 27 | Ex. | — | — | — | — | — | *114 | 470.B | 1014 |
| 28 | Ex. | 60 | 30 | — | 62 | 59 | 110 | 413.C | 830 |
| 29 | Ex. | — | — | — | — | 58 | 111 | 412.E | 184 |
| 30 | Ex. | 57/58 | 29 | — | 16 | 18 | 101.B | 312.B | 831 |
| 31 | — | — | — | — | — | — | 102.B | 312.B | 167 |
| 32 | — | — | — | — | — | — | 101.C | 312.B | 211 |
| 33 | Ex. | — | — | 47 | 14 | 33 | 103 | 312.A | 396 |
| 34 | Ex. | 71/73 | — | — | 57 | 50 | 205.A | 510.A | 700 |
| 35 | — | — | — | 38 | — | — | 205.A | — | †700 |
| 36 | Ex. | — | — | — | — | — | *206 | 875 | 387 |
| 37 | Ex. | 59/63 | 22 | — | 58 | 51 | *209 | 510.B | 109 |
| 38 | — | — | — | — | — | — | 209 | 1696.B | †109 |
| 39 | Ex. | — | 23 | 24 | — | — | 211 | 314 | 726 |
| 40 | Ex. | 72 | — | — | — | — | 212 | 480.A | 876 |
| 41 | — | — | — | — | — | — | 212 | 480.A | †876 |
| 42 | Ex. | 75 | 76 | — | — | — | 207 | 327.A | †151 |
| 43 | Ex. | — | — | — | — | — | 207 | 327.A | — |
| 44 | — | — | — | — | — | — | 220.A | — | 876 |
| 45 | — | — | — | — | — | — | — | — | 508 |
| 46 | — | — | — | — | — | — | — | — | 878 |

See p. 346 for a full explanation of codes and entries.

| Story | Meii | F.R. | H.H. | R.A. | M-1 | M-2 | NMS | H.I | Jiten |
|---|---|---|---|---|---|---|---|---|---|
| 47 | — | — | — | — | — | — | — | — | 880 |
| 48 | Ex. | — | — | — | — | — | 217 | 720 | †876 |
| 49 | — | 74 | — | — | — | — | 216 | 720 | †876 |
| 50 | Ex. | 76 | 100 | 30 | — | — | 205 | 706 | 610 |
| 51 | Ex. | — | — | — | 27 | — | 181 | 832 | 266 |
| 52 | — | — | — | — | — | 81 | *123 | — | †403 |
| 53 | Ex. | — | — | — | — | 82 | 180 | — | — |
| 54 | Ex. | — | — | — | — | — | 174 | 563 | 728 |
| 55 | Ex. | 62 | 74 | — | — | — | 173 | 1525 | 362 |
| 56 | — | — | 69 | — | — | 22 | 223 | 470.A | †362 |
| 57 | Ex. | — | — | — | 70 | — | 461 | 1200 | 743 |
| 58 | Ex. | 48 | — | — | 63 | 60 | 163.B | 550.B | 648 |
| 59 | — | — | — | — | — | — | 163.C | 550.A | 111 |
| 60 | Ex. | — | — | 44 | — | — | 161 | 834.A | 623 |
| 61 | — | 47 | 40 | — | — | — | *161 | 834.A | †372 |
| 62 | — | — | — | — | — | — | 163.B | — | 372 |
| 63 | — | — | — | — | — | — | 161 | 834.A | †372 |
| 64 | — | — | — | — | — | — | — | — | — |
| 65 | Ex. | — | — | — | — | — | 162.A | 834.B | 774 |
| 66 | Ex. | — | 39 | — | — | 40 | *160 | 1645 | 890 |
| 67 | Ex. | — | 5 | — | — | 41 | *156 | 725 | 991 |
| 68 | Ex. | — | — | 45 | 44/45 | — | *158 | 165.A | 991 |
| 69 | Ex. | 44 | — | 50 | 47 | 44 | *155 | 842.A | 1040 |
| 70 | Ex. | 40 | 63 | — | — | — | 127 | 554 | 743 |
| 71 | — | — | — | — | 46 | 43 | 159 | 1615.AA | †743 |
| 72 | Ex. | 38 | 25 | 43 | 48 | 45 | 149.B | 930.C | 490 |
| 73 | — | — | — | — | — | — | 149.A | — | 79 |
| 74 | Ex. | — | — | — | — | 64 | 202 | 751.B | 146 |
| 75 | Ex. | — | — | — | — | 61 | 199.B | 750.B | 145 |
| 76 | Ex. | — | — | — | 65 | 63 | 203 | 503.H | 192 |
| 77 | Ex. | — | — | — | — | — | *198.B | 751.A | 324 |
| 78 | Ex. | — | — | — | — | — | *198.A | 752 | 537 |
| 79 | Ex. | — | 72 | — | 72 | — | 661 | 734 | 1032 |
| 80 | Ex. | — | — | — | — | 20 | 226.A | 729 | 330 |
| 81 | Ex. | 82 | 32 | — | 21 | 22 | 223 | 470.A | 1013 |
| 82 | — | — | — | — | — | — | 223 | 470.A | 328 |
| 83 | — | — | — | — | — | — | 164.A | 671 | †241 |
| 84 | — | 50 | 70 | — | — | — | 224 | — | †1015 |
| 85 | Ex. | — | — | — | — | — | 223 | 470.A | †1015 |
| 86 | Ex. | 81 | 35 | 39 | 69 | 83 | 167 | 565 | 411 |
| 87 | — | — | — | — | — | — | *136.C | 425.B | †165 |
| 88 | Ex. | — | 34 | — | — | 30 | 176 | 551 | 679 |
| 89 | — | — | — | — | — | — | 177 | — | †538 |
| 90 | — | — | — | — | — | 28 | 247.B | 312.C | †165 |
| 91 | Ex. | — | 7 | 16 | — | — | 247.A | 312.C | 167 |
| 92 | — | — | — | — | — | — | *248 | 312.C | †164 |
| 93 | — | — | — | — | — | — | *178.A | 303 | †164 |
| 94 | — | — | — | — | — | — | — | — | — |

| Story | Meii | F.R. | H.H. | R.A. | M-1 | M-2 | NMS | H.I | Jiten |
|---|---|---|---|---|---|---|---|---|---|
| 95 | — | — | — | 20 | — | — | 247.B | 327 | †164 |
| 96 | Ex. | — | 33 | 22 | 20 | 21 | 225 | 428 | 888 |
| 97 | Ex. | — | — | — | — | — | 256 | 1300 | 389 |
| 98 | Ex. | — | — | — | — | — | 250 | 567 | 556 |
| 99 | — | — | — | — | — | — | *251 | 956.A | 314 |
| 100 | Ex. | — | 73 | 19 | — | 31 | 240 | 334 | 407 |
| 101 | — | — | — | — | — | — | 240 | 334 | †407 |
| 102 | — | — | — | — | — | — | 240 | 334 | †407 |
| 103 | — | — | — | — | — | — | *242 | 334 | — |
| 104 | — | — | — | — | — | — | 651 | 974 | 897 |
| 105 | Ex. | 69 | 30 | 21 | 33 | 29 | 245 | 333.A | 620 |
| 106 | Ex. | 64 | 19 | — | 32 | 27 | 243 | 333.B | 97 |
| 107 | Ex. | 65/66 | 18 | — | 31 | 26 | 244 | 1373.A | 302 |
| 108 | Ex. | — | — | — | — | — | 244 | 1373.A | 284 |
| 109 | Ex. | — | 62 | — | — | — | 249 | 315.A | 78 |
| 110 | Ex. | — | — | — | — | — | 252 | 121 | 508 |
| 111 | Ex. | — | 60 | — | — | 38 | 253.A | 121.X | 708 |
| 112 | Ex. | — | — | — | — | — | 231 | — | 711 |
| 113 | Ex. | — | — | — | — | — | *231 | — | †711 |
| 114 | Ex. | — | — | — | — | 64 | *258 | 326.A | 537 |
| 115 | — | — | — | — | — | — | *268 | 326.G | 980 |
| 116 | — | — | — | — | — | — | 471 | — | 775 |
| 117 | Ex. | — | — | — | — | — | 259 | 1152 | 734 |
| 118 | Ex. | — | — | — | — | — | 276 | — | 778 |
| 119 | Ex. | 51 | — | 40 | 73 | 78 | 164.A | 171 | 241 |
| 120 | Ex. | — | — | — | 107 | 105 | 469 | 1002.B | 277 |
| 121 | Ex. | — | — | — | — | — | *470 | 1002.C | 466 |
| 122 | Ex. | — | — | 31 | 72 | 76 | *237.B | 325 | 823 |
| 123 | — | — | — | — | — | — | 239 | 325 | 255 |
| 124 | — | — | — | 7 | — | — | 228 | 156 | 637 |
| 125 | Ex. | 34 | 47 | — | — | — | 165 | 560 | 69 |
| 126 | Ex. | — | 17 | 33 | — | — | 191 | 480.D | 424 |
| 127 | Ex. | — | 16 | — | — | — | 192 | 480.F | 334 |
| 128 | Ex. | — | — | — | — | — | 193 | 408.C | 331 |
| 129 | Ex. | — | — | — | — | — | *230 | 215.C | 704 |
| 130 | Ex. | — | — | — | — | — | 232.A | 178.E | 707 |
| 131 | Ex. | — | — | — | — | 65 | 192.B | 480.E | 902 |
| 132 | — | 34 | 47 | — | 12 | 14 | 165 | 560 | †637 |
| 133 | Ex. | — | — | — | — | 66 | 185 | 480.C | 713 |
| 134 | Ex. | — | 9 | — | — | — | 184 | 480.B | 421 |
| 135 | — | 53/54 | — | — | 66 | 68 | 184 | 480.B | †421 |
| 136 | Ex. | 29/35 | 14 | 35 | 68 | 71 | 187 | 503.E,F | 749 |
| 137 | Ex. | — | 15 | 34 | — | — | 189 | 530.D | 540 |
| 138 | — | 55 | — | — | — | 72 | *188 | 503.C | 663 |
| 139 | Ex. | — | 10 | 37 | — | 74 | 195 | 179.B | 390 |
| 140 | Ex. | — | 68 | 36 | 67 | 70 | 194 | 503.A | 354 |
| 141 | Ex. | — | — | — | — | — | 260 | — | 734 |
| 142 | Ex. | — | — | — | — | — | 241 | 326.E | 216 |

See p. 346 for a full explanation of codes and entries.

| Story | Meii | F.R. | H.H. | R.A. | M-1 | M-2 | NMS | H.I | Jiten |
|---|---|---|---|---|---|---|---|---|---|
| 143 | Ex. | — | — | — | — | — | *400 | 326.H | 726 |
| 144 | Ex. | 30 | 8 | — | — | — | *263 | 812 | 523 |
| 145 | — | — | — | — | — | — | 264 | 327.B | 360 |
| 146 | — | — | — | — | 37 | 34 | 262 | 66.D | 478 |
| 147 | — | — | — | — | — | — | 280 | — | †222 |
| 148 | — | — | — | — | — | — | 280 | 66.B | 222 |
| 149 | — | — | — | — | 38 | 35 | 281 | 66.C | 203 |
| 150 | Ex. | — | — | — | 37 | 34 | 282 | 66.B | 687 |
| 151 | — | — | — | — | 43 | — | — | — | 727 |
| 152 | — | — | — | — | — | — | 474 | 751.C | 314 |
| 153 | Ex. | — | — | — | 40 | 37 | 287 | 148 | 733 |
| 154 | Ex. | — | 57 | — | — | — | 283 | 1002.F | 968 |
| 155 | Ex. | — | — | — | — | — | 468 | 1002.A | 538 |
| 156 | — | — | — | — | — | — | 468 | 1002.A | 189 |
| 157 | — | — | — | — | — | — | 468 | 1002.A | †189 |
| 158 | — | — | — | — | — | — | 471 | 1002.D | 677 |
| 159 | — | — | 58 | — | — | 36 | *473 | 1002.E | 553 |
| 160 | Ex. | — | — | — | 23 | 24 | 659 | 731 | 290 |
| 161 | Ex. | — | — | — | — | — | *403 | 185 | 543 |
| 162 | Ex. | — | 37 | — | — | — | *656 | 577 | 530 |
| 163 | Ex. | 68 | 59 | — | 30 | 25 | *265 | 180 | — |
| 164 | — | 42 | — | — | — | — | 523.A | 981 | 110 |
| 165 | — | — | — | — | — | — | 523.A | 981 | †110 |
| 166 | Ex. | — | — | — | — | — | — | — | †41 |
| 167 | Ex. | — | — | — | — | — | 623 | 1537.B | 703 |
| 168 | — | — | — | — | — | — | 173 | 1525 | — |
| 169 | Ex. | 84/88 | 45 | 56 | 92 | 85 | *624 | 1537.A | 576 |
| 170 | Ex. | — | — | — | — | — | *618 | 1535 | 565 |
| 171 | Ex. | 89 | — | — | 91 | 84 | 621 | 1539 | 504 |
| 172 | Ex. | 83 | — | 49 | — | 46 | 522 | 707 | 278 |
| 173 | — | — | — | — | — | — | — | — | — |
| 174 | Ex. | 45/40 | 82 | 46 | — | — | 515 | 910.B | 752 |
| 175 | Ex. | — | — | — | 93 | 86 | 485 | 1861 | 687 |
| 176 | — | — | — | — | — | — | — | — | 580 |
| 177 | Ex. | — | 93 | — | — | — | 507 | — | 551 |
| 178 | Ex. | — | — | — | — | — | — | — | 947 |
| 179 | Ex. | — | — | — | — | — | 667 | 994 | — |
| 180 | Ex. | — | — | — | — | — | 427 | — | 84 |
| 181 | — | — | — | — | — | — | 439 | 1775 | †763 |
| 182 | — | — | — | — | — | — | — | — | 763 |
| 183a | — | — | — | 62 | — | — | 539 | 1562 | 154 |
| 183b | — | — | — | — | — | — | 535 | 1572.A | 154 |
| 183c | — | — | — | — | — | — | 543 | 1360.A | 154 |
| 183d | — | — | — | — | — | — | 534 | 1541 | 154 |
| 183e | — | — | — | — | — | — | 533 | 1567.A | 154 |
| 183f | — | — | — | — | — | — | — | — | 154 |
| 183g | — | — | — | — | — | — | 524 | 465.B | 154 |
| 183h | — | — | — | — | — | — | 530 | 1567.B | 154 |

| Story | Meii | F.R. | H.H. | R.A. | M-1 | M-2 | NMS | H.I | Jiten |
|---|---|---|---|---|---|---|---|---|---|
| 183i | — | — | — | 62 | — | — | 644 | 1360 | 154 |
| 183j | — | — | — | — | — | — | 532 | 1313 | 154 |
| 183k | — | — | — | — | — | — | — | — | 154 |
| 184 | Ex. | — | — | 42 | 19 | — | *218 | 780 | 102 |
| 185 | Ex. | — | — | — | — | — | 151.C | 934.B | 124 |
| 186 | — | — | — | — | — | — | 151.A | 930.C | †124 |
| 187 | Ex. | — | — | — | — | — | 259 | 326.B | 576 |
| 188 | Ex. | — | — | — | — | — | — | 121.Y | †537 |
| 189 | — | — | — | — | — | — | 267 | 1131.A | 955 |
| 190 | — | — | — | — | — | — | *278 | 812.A | — |
| 191 | Ex. | — | — | — | — | — | 269 | 326.D | — |
| 192 | — | — | — | — | — | — | 266 | 326.F | †551 |
| 193 | — | — | — | — | 35 | 33 | 270 | 145.A | †254 |
| 194 | — | — | — | — | 35 | — | 275.A | 145.B | 982 |
| 195 | — | — | — | — | — | — | — | — | 249 |
| 196 | Ex. | — | — | — | — | — | 411 | 1705 | 688 |
| 197 | — | — | — | — | — | — | — | — | 457 |
| 198 | — | — | — | — | — | — | 254 | 216.B | 708 |
| 199 | Ex. | — | — | — | — | — | 229 | 216.A | 710 |
| 200 | — | — | — | — | — | — | 255 | 215.A | 710 |
| 201 | Ex. | — | — | — | — | — | *258 | 255 | 960 |
| 202 | Ex. | — | — | — | — | — | 456 | 1886 | †101 |
| 203 | — | — | — | — | — | — | — | — | †101 |
| 204 | — | — | — | — | — | — | 388 | 1933 | 880 |
| 205 | Ex. | 94 | 79 | — | — | 89 | 382 | 1530.A | 712 |
| 206 | Ex. | — | — | — | — | — | 377 | 1520 | 833 |
| 207 | Ex. | — | — | — | — | — | 384 | 1530.B | 564 |
| 208 | Ex. | 55/56 | — | — | — | — | *386 | — | †564 |
| 209 | Ex. | — | — | — | — | — | 626.A | 1641 | 894 |
| 210 | Ex. | 85 | 44 | — | — | — | 626.C | 1641 | †894 |
| 211 | Ex. | — | — | — | — | — | 466 | 1640 | 124 |
| 212 | Ex. | — | — | — | — | — | *465.A | — | 485 |
| 213 | Ex. | 103 | 61 | — | 108 | 106 | 464 | 1890 | 868 |
| 214 | Ex. | 92 | — | — | — | — | *463.A | 800 | 310 |
| 215 | Ex. | — | — | — | — | — | 482 | 1960.A | 130 |
| 216 | Ex. | — | — | — | 88/89 | 87 | 480 | 1962.A | 579 |
| 217 | — | — | — | — | — | — | — | — | 558 |
| 218 | Ex. | — | — | — | — | — | *625 | 325.B | 1037 |
| 219 | Ex. | — | — | — | — | — | 481 | 660.B | 641 |
| 220 | — | — | 66/67 | 51/52 | — | — | 489 | 921 | 624 |
| 221 | — | 86/87 | 65 | — | — | — | 492 | 1960.E | 149 |
| 222 | — | — | — | — | — | — | *506 | 1928 | 594 |
| 223 | — | — | — | — | — | — | 251 | 956.A | 124 |
| 224 | — | — | 98 | — | — | — | 430 | 1950 | 808 |
| 225 | — | 45 | 37 | — | 94 | 88 | 497 | 1351.B | 943 |
| 226 | — | — | — | — | 50 | — | 484 | 1645.C | 589 |
| 227 | — | 105 | — | 58 | 103 | 101 | — | 1704 | 309 |
| 228 | — | 96/101 | 89 | — | — | — | 520 | 924 | 368 |

See p. 346 for a full explanation of codes and entries.

| Story | Meii | F.R. | H.H. | R.A. | M-1 | M-2 | NMS | H.I | Jiten |
|---|---|---|---|---|---|---|---|---|---|
| 229 | — | — | — | — | — | — | 393 | 2076 | 402 |
| 230 | — | 91 | — | — | — | — | *395 | — | 405 |
| 231 | — | — | — | — | — | — | *447 | — | — |
| 232 | Ex. | 99 | 81 | — | — | — | 431.B | 1565.A | 405 |
| 233 | — | — | — | — | — | — | *494 | 852.A | 283 |
| 234 | — | 97 | 75 | — | — | — | 638 | 2080 | 667 |
| 235 | — | — | 89 | 13 | — | — | *380 | 2031 | 953 |
| 236 | Ex. | — | — | — | — | — | *420 | 1211 | 219 |
| 237 | — | — | — | — | — | — | — | — | 256 |
| 238 | — | — | — | — | — | — | 318 | 1570.A | 555 |
| 239 | Ex. | — | — | — | — | — | 405.A | 2043 | 516 |
| 240 | — | — | — | — | — | — | 392 | 1550 | 41 |
| 241 | — | 104 | 83 | — | 99 | 96 | 332 | 1565 | 378 |
| 242 | — | — | — | — | — | — | — | — | 103 |
| 243 | — | — | — | — | — | — | 331 | — | 583 |
| 244 | — | — | — | — | — | — | *435 | 1376.C | 817 |
| 245 | — | — | — | — | — | — | 333.B | 1264 | 284 |
| 246 | — | 90 | 80 | — | — | — | 330.B | 1696.A | 571 |
| 247 | — | — | — | — | — | — | 339 | 1698.I | 175 |
| 248 | — | — | — | — | 105 | 103 | 336.A | 1698.J | 285 |
| 249 | — | — | — | — | — | — | 345 | — | 65 |
| 250 | — | — | — | — | — | — | 362.A | 1262/1265 | 567 |
| 251 | — | — | — | — | — | — | 361 | 1339 | 956 |
| 252 | Ex. | — | — | — | — | — | 359 | 1691.C | 227 |
| 253 | — | — | — | 60 | — | — | 348.A | 1269 | 984 |
| 254 | — | — | — | — | — | — | 476 | 1890.F | 406 |
| 255 | — | — | — | — | — | — | *367 | — | 179 |
| 256 | — | — | — | — | — | — | — | — | 1003 |
| 257 | — | 106/107 | 92 | — | 97/8/100 | 94/5/6 | 314 | — | 175 |
| 258 | — | — | — | — | — | — | 310 | — | 822 |
| 259 | — | — | — | — | — | — | 303 | — | 591 |
| 260 | — | — | — | — | — | — | 313 | — | 774 |
| 261 | — | — | — | — | — | — | 312 | 1852.D | 897 |
| 262 | — | — | — | — | — | — | — | — | 817 |
| 263 | — | — | — | — | — | — | — | — | 456 |
| 264 | — | — | — | — | — | — | 550 | — | 244 |
| 265 | — | — | — | — | — | — | *329 | — | 384 |
| 266 | — | — | — | — | — | — | 327 | — | 195 |
| 267 | — | 98 | 71 | 55 | — | — | 319 | 1336.A | †186 |
| 268 | — | 4 | 49 | — | 3 | 3 | 47.A | 249.A | 484 |
| 269 | — | — | — | — | 5 | 5 | 46 | 249.F | 851 |
| 270 | — | 5 | — | — | — | — | 46 | 249.F | 953 |
| 271 | Ex. | — | — | — | 6 | 6 | *71 | — | 850 |
| 272 | — | — | — | — | — | — | 54 | — | 852 |
| 273 | — | — | — | — | — | — | 55 | — | 852 |
| 274 | Ex. | — | — | — | — | 7 | 58 | 249.E | 201 |
| 275 | — | — | — | — | — | — | 59 | — | 999 |
| 276 | — | — | — | — | — | — | *49 | — | 208 |

| Story | Meii | F.R. | H.H. | R.A. | M-1 | M-2 | NMS | H.I | Jiten |
|---|---|---|---|---|---|---|---|---|---|
| 277 | — | — | 56 | — | — | — | 54 | — | 208 |
| 278 | — | — | — | — | — | — | 61 | — | 1019 |
| 279 | Ex. | — | — | — | — | 8 | 68 | 249.K | 782 |
| 280 | — | — | — | — | — | — | 50.B | — | 781 |
| 281 | Ex. | — | — | — | — | — | 50.A | 249.G | 886 |
| 282 | Ex. | — | — | — | — | — | *57 | — | 188 |
| 283 | Ex. | — | — | — | — | — | 48 | 249.B | 655 |
| 284 | — | 3 | — | — | — | — | 48 | 249.B | 23 |
| 285 | — | 2 | — | — | 4 | 4 | 48 | 249.C | †747 |
| 286 | — | — | — | — | — | — | 50.B | 249.G | 886 |
| 287 | — | 2 | — | — | — | — | 50.A | 249.G | 747 |
| 288 | Ex. | 6 | 50 | — | 7 | 10 | 67 | 249.J | 805 |
| 289 | Ex. | — | — | — | — | — | 53 | 249.H | 998 |
| 290 | Ex. | 1 | — | 8 | 9 | 11 | 19.B | 228 | 891 |
| 291 | — | — | — | — | — | — | 74 | 234 | 898 |
| 292 | — | — | — | — | — | 9 | 76 | 902.B | 195 |
| 293 | — | — | — | — | — | — | 81 | — | 1041 |
| 294 | Ex. | — | — | — | — | — | 64 | 225.A | 237 |
| 295 | — | — | — | — | — | — | — | — | 475 |
| 296 | — | — | — | — | — | — | *77 | — | 643 |
| 297 | — | — | — | — | — | — | *79 | 282 | 965 |
| 298 | — | — | — | — | — | — | 78 | 282.X | 721 |
| 299 | Ex. | — | — | — | — | — | *82 | — | 554 |
| 300 | — | — | — | 11 | 2 | 2 | 35 | 91 | 293 |
| 301 | — | — | — | — | — | — | 73 | 296 | 952 |
| 302 | Ex. | — | — | — | — | 91 | 43 | 295 | 489 |
| 303 | — | — | — | — | — | — | — | — | 525 |
| 304 | Ex. | 33 | 46 | 12 | 95 | 16 | 33.B | 177 | 817 |
| 305 | — | — | — | — | 74 | — | — | — | — |
| 306 | — | — | — | — | — | — | *234.A | 160 | — |
| 307 | — | — | — | — | — | — | 32.A | — | — |
| 308 | Ex. | 4/12 | 52 | 9/10 | 10 | 12 | 11 | 275 | 632 |
| 309 | — | — | — | — | — | — | *17 | 275.B | 251 |
| 310 | — | — | — | — | — | — | *31 | 101 | 631 |
| 311 | — | — | — | — | — | — | — | — | 392 |
| 312 | — | — | — | — | — | — | 256 | 66.A | 551 |
| 313 | Ex. | — | — | 2 | 11 | 13 | *70 | 3 | 791 |
| 314 | — | — | — | — | — | — | 9 | 277.C | 377 |
| 315 | — | — | — | — | — | — | 24 | 3 | †791 |
| 316 | — | — | — | — | — | — | *6 | 15 | 709 |
| 317 | Ex. | — | — | — | — | — | *4 | 1 | 251 |
| 318 | Ex. | 10 | 54 | 1 | — | — | 3 | 2.K | 429 |
| 319 | — | 11 | — | — | 1 | 1 | 3 | 2.K | †233 |
| 320 | — | — | — | 5 | — | — | 24 | 9.Y | 393 |
| 321 | Ex. | 31 | 48 | — | 13 | 15 | 21 | 90 | 954 |
| 322 | Ex. | — | — | 5 | — | — | 20 | 9.X | †394 |
| 323 | — | — | — | 6 | — | — | 26 | 9.M | 394 |
| 324 | Ex. | — | — | — | — | — | *34 | 2048 | 714 |

See p. 346 for a full explanation of codes and entries.

| Story | Meii | F.R. | H.H. | R.A. | M-1 | M-2 | NMS | H.I | Jiten |
|---|---|---|---|---|---|---|---|---|---|
| 325 | Ex. | 30 | — | — | — | — | 26 | 210 | †388 |
| 326 | — | — | — | — | — | — | *27.A | 9.F | 214 |
| 327 | Ex. | — | — | — | — | — | 29 | 333.C | 486 |
| 328 | Ex. | — | — | 3a-b | — | — | 32.C | 176 | 206 |
| 329 | — | — | — | — | — | — | 32.C | 176 | †206 |
| 330 | — | — | — | — | — | — | 320 | 176 | †206 |
| 331 | Ex. | 77 | 6 | — | — | — | 621 | 974 | 992 |
| 332 | — | — | — | — | 84 | — | *670 | 768.A | 112 |
| 333 | — | — | — | — | — | — | 662 | 948 | 671 |
| 334 | — | — | — | — | — | — | 663 | 756.X | — |
| 335 | — | — | — | — | — | — | 108.A | 411.E | 181 |
| 336 | — | — | — | — | — | — | — | — | 698 |
| 337 | — | — | — | — | — | — | 166 | 912 | 496 |
| 338 | — | — | — | — | 24 | — | 657 | 256 | 958 |
| 339 | — | — | — | — | — | — | — | — | 355 |
| 340 | — | — | — | — | — | — | — | — | 801 |
| 341 | — | — | — | — | — | — | *671 | 973 | †801 |
| 342 | — | — | — | — | 77 | — | 660 | 623 | 669 |
| 343 | — | — | 99 | 14 | — | — | 642 | 2300 | 746 |
| 344 | — | — | — | — | — | — | 636.B | 2271 | 101 |
| 345 | — | — | — | — | — | — | — | — | †101 |
| 346 | — | — | — | — | — | — | — | — | †210 |
| 347 | — | — | — | — | — | — | — | — | 790 |

Explanation of codes:

- * indicates that Seki found the same tale to be "normative" as Yanagita.
- † indicates that the story in question appears in *Nihon mukashibanashi jiten*, but not as the main item in an entry.
- Ex. indicates that the story translated in this book is the same tale that Yanagita chose to summarize as an example in *Mukashibanashi meii.*

Entries:

- Meii Yanagita Kunio, *Nihon mukashibanashi meii*
- F.R. Fritz Rumpf, *Japanische Volksmärchen*
- H.H. Horst Hammitzsch, *Japanische Volksmärchen*
- R.A. Robert Adams, transl., *Folktales of Japan* (edited by Seki Keigo)
- M-1 Fanny Hagin Mayer, transl., *Japanese Folk Tales* (edited by Yanagita Kunio), 1954
- M-2 Fanny Hagin Mayer, transl., *Japanese Folk Tales, A Revised Selection* (edited by Yanagita Kunio), 1966
- NMS Seki Keigo, *Nihon mukashibanashi shūsei*
- H.I. Hiroko Ikeda, *A Type and Motif Index of Japanese Folk-Literature*
- Jiten Inada Kōji, et al., eds., *Nihon mukashibanashi jiten*

# Bibliography of Sources

Numbers in brackets refer to the story numbers in this book. Place of publication has been omitted for Tokyo publishers.


*Aichi-ken, densetsu shū.* Aichi-ken Kyōiku-kai, ed. Kyōdo Kenkyūsha, 1937. [82, 183, 334]

*Akinokuni mukashibanashi shū.* ISOGAI Isamu. Oka Shoin, 1934. [69, 105, 134, 153, 183, 183, 207, 258, 280, 327]

*Awa-no-Iyayama*, TAKEDA Akira. Sanseidō, 1943. [70, 86, 267]

*Bungo densetsu shū.* ICHIBA Naojirō. Ōita: Kyōdo Shiseki Densetsu Kenkyūkai, 1931. [104]

*Bungo no kijin Kitchyomu san monogatari.* MIYAMOTO Kiyoshi. Ōita: Ōita Minyū Shinbun, 1927. [233]

*Chiisagata-gun mintan shū*, KOYAMA Masao. Kyōdo Kenkyūsha, 1933. [43, 183, 183, 183, 238]

*Dai-ichi mukashibanashi gō* (*Tabi to densetsu* IV 4) 1, 1931. [55, 75, 91, 137, 155, 156, 171, 174, 183, 200, 257, 260, 275, 314, 325]

*Dai-ni mukashibanashi gō* (*Tabi to densetsu* VII 12), 1934 [30, 51, 79, 85, 88, 102, 112, 113, 127, 139, 170, 200, 304]

*Echigo Sanjo Nanagō dan*, TOYAMA Rekirō. Kyōdo Kenkyūshal, 1926. [106, 190, 313, 321]

*Esashi-gun mukashibanashi*, SASAKI Kizen. Kyōdo Kenkyūsha, 1922. [136, 193, 197, 214]

*Esashi-gun shi*, Iwate-ken Kyōiku Kai, Esashi-gun Bukai, ed. Published by Eds., 1925. [347]

*Fukihara*, No. 3. Ina Tomi Shōgakkō Kyōdo Kenkyūkai, ed. Kamiina-gun, Nagano: Published by Eds., 1932. [83]

(*Mukashibanashi no kenkyū*) *Geibi sōsho.* Hiroshima Shihan Gakkō Kyōdo Kenkyūshitsu. Hiroshima: Published by Eds., 1939. [90, 132]

*Fukuoka-ken mukashibanashi shū.* Fukuoka-ken Kyōikukai. Iwasaki Bijitsusha, 1975. [145, 152, 183, 211, 213, 217, 219, 259, 320] Selections made from manuscript version prior to publication of book.

*Hanashi no sekai* II, 1920. [227]

*Hidabito.* Hida Kōkō Minzoku Gakkai. Takayama: Published by WADA Toshihiko. IV (1936) [330]; V (1937) [101]

*Hōgen* IV. Shunyūdō, 1934. [87]

*Hōgen to dozoku.* TACHIBANA Shōichi. Morioka: Hōgensha, No. 8, 1937. [272]

(Old) *Ikinoshima mukashibanashi shū.* YAMAGUCHI Asatarō. Kyōdo Kenkyūsha, 1935. [39, 78, 154, 177, 261, 263, 292, 312]

(New) *Ikinoshima mukashibanashi shū.* YAMAGUCHI Asatarō. Sanseidō, 1943. [288]

*Inpaku dōwa.* Inpaku Shiwakai. Tottori: Yokoyama Shoten, 1925. [195]

*Inpaku mintan.* Tottori Kyōdo Kenkyūkai. Tottori: Published by the group, I 1936. [64, 246, 264]

*Iwaki mukashibanashi shū.* IWASAKI Toshio. Sanseidō, 1942. [76, 103, 194, 253, 254, 294]

*Kaga Enuma-gun mukashibanashi shū.* YAMASHITA Hisao. Ogawa Shoten, 1935. [183, 220, 229, 241]

*Kai mukashibanashi shū.* DOBASHI Riki. Kyōdo Kenkyūsha, 1930. [65,

94, 110, 120, 141, 162, 180, 185, 188, 196, 228, 231, 239, 277 335]
*Kamihei-gun mukashibanashi shū.* SASAKI Kizen. Sanseidō, 1943. [61, 89, 121, 129, 165]
*Kamuhara yatan.* FUMINO Shirakoma (IWAKURA Ichiro). Genkyūsha, 1932. [16, 37, 131, 166, 169, 181, 183, 183, 206, 218, 234, 318]
*Kawagoe chihō mukashibanashi shū.* SUZUKI Tōzō. Minkan Denshō no Kai, 1937. [35, 142]
*Kii Arita-gun dōwa shū.* MORIGUCHI Seiichi. Mimeographed by the author, 1916. [58]
*Kikaijima mukashibanashi shū.* IWAKURA Ichirō. Sanseidō, 1943. [15, 93, 99, 114, 183, 202, 221, 299, 333, 336, 342]
*Kikimimi sōshi.* SASAKI Kizen. Sangensha, 1931. [26, 28, 56, 72, 80, 84, 92, 96, 100, 111, 144, 175, 178, 185, 209, 223, 232, 306, 339, 344]
*Kitaazumi-gun kyōdo shikō. Kōhi densetsu hen* II 2; Shinano Kyōikukai Kitaazumi-gun Bukai. Kyōdo Kenkyūsha, 1930. [20, 276]
*Kogane no uma.* MORIGUCHI Tari. Jitsugyō no Nihonsha, 1926. New edition, Mikuni Shobō, 1942. This edition was used. [150]
*Koshikijima mukashibanashi shū.* IWAKURA Ichirō. Sanseidō, 1944. [53, 67, 70, 109, 184, 210]
*Kōshō bungaku, Kōshō Bungaku no Kai.* Sakai: Mimeographed, 1936. [24, 273, 289, 298]
*Kunohe-gun shi.* Iwate-ken Kyōikukai Kunohe-gun Bukai. Morioka: Published by Eds., 1936. [248, 249, 250]
*Kyōdo kenkyū.* YANAGITA Kunio and TAKAGI Toshio, eds. I (1913-1914) [179]; II (1914-1915) [135]; III (1915-1916) [278]; IV (1916-1917) [271].
*Kyōdo no denshō.* YAMAMOTO Kinjirō, ed. Sendai: No. 1 (1931) [201, 254, 337, 338]; No. 3 (1935) [108-311].
*Minamiazumi-gun shi.* Nagano-ken Minamiazumi-gun, Hensen, ed. Toshima-machi, Minamiazumi-gun, Nagano: Minamiazumi Kyōikukai, 1913. [22]
*Minamikanbara-gun mukashibanashi shū.* IWAKURA Ichirō. Sanseidō, 1943. [68, 324]
*Minzoku bunka.* YAMAOKA Yoshimitsu, ed. Vol. II (1941). [13]
*Minzokugaku.* OKAMURA Chiaki and KOIZUMI Magane, eds. I (1929). [25, 331]
*Mitsu-gun mukashibanashi shū.* IMAMURA Katsuomi. Sanseidō, 1943. [130, 230]
*Mukashibanashi.* Ina Minzoku Kenkyūkai. Iida: Shinano Kyōdo Shuppansha, 1934. [40, 122, 146, 192, 236]
*Mukashibanashi kenkyū.* HAGIWARA Masanori, ed. Vol. I (1935-1936). [5, 21, 27, 36, 41, 50, 97, 123, 126, 158, 164, 164, 182, 199, 205, 266, 274, 291, 301, 329, 341]
*Mukashibanashi kenkyū.* SEKI Keigo, ed. Vol. II (1936-1937). [2, 4, 10, 14, 18, 19, 29, 31, 33, 42, 74, 77, 124, 125, 135, 138, 140, 148, 157, 163, 164, 185, 203, 215, 235, 245, 265, 267, 281, 283, 287, 322, 323, 328, 343, 346]
*Nansō no rizoku.* UCHIDA Kunihiko. Ōsetsu shooku, 1915. [240]
*Nantō setsuwa.* SAKIMA Kōei. Kyōdo Kenkyūsha, 1922. [284]
*Naori-gun mukashibanashi shū.* SUZUKI Kiyomi. Sanseidō, 1943. [143]
*Nihon densetsu sōsho, Kazusa no maki.* FUJISAWA Morihiko. Nihon

Densetsu Kankōkai, 1917. [293]

*Nihon densetsu shū*. TAKAGI Toshio. Musashino Shoin, 1913. [3, 295, 300, 319]

*Nihon mukashibanashi shū, jō*. YANAGITA Kunio. Ars. 1930. [15, 160, 285, 290, 305, 308]

*Nihon zenkoku kokumin dōwa*. ISHII Kendō. Dōbunkan, 1911. [225]

*Rōō yatan*. SASAKI Kizen. Kyōdo Kenkyūsha, 1927. [38, 62, 116, 119, 149, 176, 310]

*Sado mukashibanashi shū*. SUZUKI Tōzō. Minkan Denshō no Kai, 1939. [8]

*Sadogashima mukashibanashi shū*. SUZUKI Tōzō. Sanseidō, 1942. [187]

*Sanuki Sanagi Shishijima mukashibanashi shū*. TAKEDA Akira. Sanseidō, 1944. [186]

*Shima*. YANAGITA Kunio and HIKA Shunchō, eds. I (1933) [9, 44]; II (1934) [167, 172, 173, 226]

*Shimabara hantō minwa shū*. SEKI Keigo. Kensetsusha, 1935. [6, 7, 12, 32, 161, 212, 222, 255, 297]

*Shimabara hantō mukashibanashi shū*. SEKI Keigo. Sanseidō, 1942. [116, 168, 274, 332]

*Shimotsuke Motegi mukashibanashi shū*. KATŌ Kaichi. Sangensha, 1935. [49, 237]

*Shintasu mintan shū*. KONDO Kiichi (YANAGITA Kunio). Kyōdo Kenkyūsha, 1928. [160]

*Shiwa-gun mukashibanashi*. SASAKI Kizen. Kyōdo Kenkyūsha, 1926. [1, 57, 115, 191, 216, 224, 247, 251, 307, 316]

*Shiwa-gun mukashibanashi shū*. OGASAWARA Kenkichi. Sanseidō, 1942. [107, 117, 133, 246]

*Shizuoka-ken densetsu mukashibanashi shū*. Shizuoka Shihan Gakkō Kyōdo Kenkyūkai, ed. Shizuoka: Yajima Shoten, 1934. [47, 270, 303, 309]

*Tabi to densetsu*. HAGIWARA Masanori, ed. I (1928) [242]; II (1929) [81]; III (1930) [71, 147, 243]; IX (1936) [48, 340]; X (1938) [317]; XI (1939) [128]

*Tekkiri ane sama*. NODA Tayoko (manuscript of Gonohe mukashibanashi until 1958). Miraisha, 1958. [198, 208]

*Tōno monogatari*. YANAGITA Kunio. Shūseidō, 1910. [118]

*Tōō ibun*. SASAKI Kizen. Sakamoto Shoten, 1926. [45]

*Tsuchi no iro*. ITŌ Tetsuji, ed. Hamamatsu: Hamamatsu Kodomo Kyōkai. XIII (1934). [73]

*Tsugaru kōki shū*. UCHIDA Kunihiko. Kyōdo Kenkyūsha, 1937. [268, 298]

*Tsugaru mugashiko shū*. KAWAI Yūtarō. Aomori: Tōō Nippōsha, 1930. [34, 59, 67]

*Ugo Kakunodate chihō ni okeru chōchū sōmoku no minzokugakuteki shiryō*. MUTŌ Tetsujō. Attic Museum, 1935. [23, 204, 279]

*Yamato no densetsu*. TAKADA Jūrō. Nara: Yamato Shiseki Kenkyūkai, 1933. [46]

*Zen Nagasaki kayō shū*. MURATA Yoichi, ed. Koransha, 1931. [345]

*Zoku Hida saihō nisshi*. SAWADA Shirōsaku. Osaka: Published by author, 1939. [66]

*Zoku Kai mukashibanashi shū*. DOBASHI Riki. Kyōdo Kenkyūsha, 1936. [17, 60, 95, 98, 159, 244, 282, 286, 302, 326]

# Alphabetical List of Titles

[Note: Titles printed in **bold face** are those indicated by Yanagita Kunio in *Mukashibanashi meii* as being of particular importance.]

# General Index

www.ingramcontent.com/pod-product-compliance
Lightning Source LLC
Chambersburg PA
CBHW020946310726
48980CB00001B/67